Thrilling romance, spicy adventure in these Violet Winspear stories from Harlequin's Romance Library...

The Cazalet Bride ... On an adventurous holiday in Spain, Ricki met the formidable Don Arturo de Cazalet, and impulsively accepted a job caring for his nephew, Jaime. The boy soon grew to love her. Ricki only wished the Don could feel the same way. (#1434)

Beloved Castaway ... Morvenna fiercely resisted her growing attraction to Roque de Braz Ferro. He was a man with a heart as hard as his name, whose arrogance was overpowering. But on this savage, beautiful island that was his domain, falling in love was inevitable! (#1472)

The Castle of the Seven Lilacs ... Baron Breck von Linden had offered Siran a job and asked her to come to his castle in the mountains. But it was his brother, Kurt, who was making it difficult for Siran to stay—Kurt who wouldn't let himself be loved. (#1514)

The third collection of
3 Great Novels by

Violet Winspear

Harlequin Books

TORONTO • LONDON • NEW YORK • AMSTERDAM
SYDNEY • HAMBURG • PARIS

Harlequin Omnibus 27

These books by Violet Winspear were originally published
as follows:

THE CAZALET BRIDE
Copyright © 1970 by Violet Winspear
First published in 1970 by Mills & Boon Limited
Harlequin edition (#1434) published October 1970

BELOVED CASTAWAY
Copyright © 1968 by Violet Winspear
First published in 1968 by Mills & Boon Limited
Harlequin edition (#1472) published February 1971

THE CASTLE OF THE SEVEN LILACS
Copyright © 1971 by Violet Winspear
First published in 1971 by Mills & Boon Limited
Harlequin edition (#1514) published August 1971

ISBN 373-70326-0

First **Harlequin Omnibus** edition published April 1976

Second printing April 1976
Third printing November 1976
Fourth printing May 1977
Fifth printing November 1978
Sixth printing August 1979

Contents

The Cazalet Bride

Ricki had lost her temper at her employer once too often. Now, braced for instant dismissal, she was surprised when Don Arturo asked her to marry him.

"You need not fear that I would expect love of you," he said coldly. "Ours would be merely a marriage of convenience."

But how could she face an empty marriage, knowing that he would never return her love?

CHAPTER ONE

RICKI O'NEILL had felt the grip of Toledo's fascination from the moment the tour bus from Madrid entered the city and serpentined through its narrow streets, which were shaded by medieval-roofed buildings.

Toledo, somehow lost in time, a tiered city built on rock, lapped by the waters of the Tagus and facing toward the somber plains of Castile on its fourth side. Most of the tall granite houses, Ricki noticed, were enclosed within walled courtyards; worn flights of steps led up to decaying palaces and down into dim cellars where music of a strange, haunting tone seeped out of iron-grilled windows. The cobbled alleyways seemed to hold the echoes of spurred and booted feet, while to Ricki's mind any sudden burst of laughter could be that of maskers setting out on their revels, cloaks billowing, dark eyes glinting through face masks of velvet. The old *España* of steel at the hip and a gleam of *el diablo* in the eye still haunted the atmosphere of Toledo, and Ricki's sense of adventure was aroused by it.

A tour of this old, historical city ended her holiday in Spain. Fourteen days she had thoroughly enjoyed despite warnings from well-meaning friends in England that she was inviting trouble traveling around a foreign country on her own. "You must be kidding about going abroad on your own," they said. "That won't be much fun—and think of those Latin wolves!" Well, once spirited Ricki had made up her mind to do something there was no stopping her—and it had been fun.

Right now she was enjoying a coffee at a sidewalk café, and as she sipped at it, her forehead was puckered in thought. She was pondering her decision to quit the hospital before taking her holiday. She had done so not in a mood of defiance but out of the knowledge that she would never settle down to a routine existence. She had grown tired, as well, of tangling with her superior in the physiotherapy department.

Ricki was convinced that a chat and a laugh were beneficial to her patients while they were being treated, but Miss Hardcastle thought otherwise and she would tartly snap at Ricki that she wasn't treating these people in their homes or in her own time. "We have to keep to a routine here or everything goes to pot," she was fond of saying. "Now do hustle that old Mrs. Brown of yours out of the end cubicle—the woman seems to think she's sunbathing on the Costa Brava instead of having the infrared lamp on her back."

Fond of elderly people, Ricki had staunchly defended her patients' right to dream, but she had known once and for all that afternoon that she didn't want to be hemmed in by routine any longer, her every thought and action regulated by a disk ticking on a wall. She had given her notice quickly, giving herself no time to think about the matter. Thinking put the lid on things, according to her Irish father; it made you timid when often you'd be better off adventurous.

Ricki took a bite out of a sugary bun and absently noticed that here and there on the plaza evening lamps were popping alight. Dad was right, and now that she was a fully fledged physio she could work free-lance if she so wished. It would be fun, and a relief not to have old Hard-as-Stone bawling her out for allowing mothers to have their kiddies in the cubicles with them. Well, they got so restless in that drab old waiting room....

Aunt Meg and Uncle Jack had been dubious about

this break she had made from the hospital, but they had never really grown used to how different she was from her cousin, Helen. Dear, unimaginative Helen, who had never understood how Ricki had become involved in mad pranks at school. How she came to fall through the ice on the canal that hoary winter—and how on earth she could go on that ban-the-bomb march with all those rowdy students!

"If everyone sat on the fence and blinked at events like lazy cats, nothing would get done," Ricki had rejoined. "Anyway, it was fun. We sang protest songs as we marched along, and our leaders, don't forget, were churchmen. It wasn't a rowdy sort of parade."

"The trouble with you, Ricki," Helen said primly, "is that you take after that crazy Irish father of yours."

Ricki flicked sugar crumbs from the side of her mouth and grinned to herself as she thought of her father. He was an actor: gay, improvident Tynan O'Neill, the eternal dreamer of grandiloquent dreams and spinner of whimsical tales, a charmer who would never settle down. Ten years ago, when his wife had died suddenly, he had brought Ricki across from Dublin to England to live with her mother's sister. Twelve-year-old Ricki had kicked up the dust at the idea of being parted from him, but for once he had been adamant.

"Actors' digs are no place for a girl to be brought up in," he had soothed, while her tears made a damp patch on the shoulder of his suit. "Now be sensible, darlin', and ease off the waterworks. You'll be fine with your English auntie, much better off than you'd be with a carousing rebel like meself."

"No, I won't!" Ricki had stormed. "She's all bread-and-butter and go-and-wash-your-hands! Pops, you can't leave me here with people I hardly know—you can't!"

Tynan had sighed and clasped her close, for there was

a bond of the spirit between them. "You'll grow up a little lady with her, not a hoyden," he groaned. "Ricki, me heart, it's what my Beth would wish me to do, to put you in the care of her sister."

Children are adaptable and the Graysons had been kind to her, if somewhat bewildered at times by a personality so different from their daughter's. With the passing of the years Ricki had grown to regard her father as one does an untameable child. Now and again they met in London for lunch and a show, but there was never any talk of them setting up house together. Tynan liked his freedom too much, and Ricki wasn't the sort to impose herself, even on her own father. She worried about him, of course, but knew him to be happy in his drifting way. He should, she often thought, have lived in the days of the colorful, strolling players.

Now she noticed that the strollers along the Plaza de Zocodover had grown more numerous. The evening *paseo* was in full swing, and a glance at her wristwatch revealed that it was almost half-past seven. Golly, was it that late! She had promised herself a look inside the cathedral that reared its Gothic pinnacles above the crowding roofs of the city, for she would be on her way back to Madrid in the morning and wouldn't get another chance to explore the place.

She settled her bill, but as she rose from the table and gathered up her handbag and gloves, she was suddenly aware of feeling rather blue.

Her holiday was all but over, and as she made her way across the plaza and along the cobbled turnings that led to the cathedral, she was acutely aware that she would be very sorry to leave Spain. She liked the people, their grave way of smiling at you and their open affection toward their children. There were wolves about, of course, but when approached by one of the pack it was generally effective to start walking determinedly toward a *guardia civil*, unmistakable in his green uniform and Napoleonic hat.

It was more than an hour later when Ricki came out of the cathedral, bemused by its rich offerings of carvings and tilework and the Madonnas arrayed in real brocades and somber jewelry. Darkness had now settled down over the narrow streets, which were lit by flickering lamps in wall brackets. The doors and walls of the houses were inscrutable, offering no cheerful glimpses into lighted parlors, and in a while it began to dawn on Ricki that instead of nearing the peopled gaiety of the main square she seemed, in her overconfidence, to have wandered off course into a web of murky lanes.

This realization brought her up short and she glanced around. Cats spat at each other down a nearby cul-de-sac, and Ricki jumped like a cat herself as a trash-can lid clattered to the cobbles. She turned to retrace her footsteps—and felt the lurch of her heart as a lean figure shifted out of a wall lamp. Alarm jangled through her. She knew instinctively that the man was either a pest or a petty thief who had been silently following her for some time.

He moved, his shadow lancing along the wall, and Ricki wildly debated banging on one of the nail-headed doors for admittance. No, there was little hope of anyone hearing her puny fists hammering on the stout wood, and it was obvious that a scream would receive scant attention in this neighborhood!

Ricki wheeled about, feeling trapped and scared, and raced for all she was worth from the lean satyr who menaced her in this murky alleyway. She was built for speed and wearing flat shoes, and she might have eluded the man if in her panic she had not darted down the cul-de-sac where those cats were snarling over the fish heads they had unearthed. As Ricki blundered into their lair, they streaked past her legs into the night and she gave a cry as she almost stumbled over the fallen trash-can lid—and felt at the same time the clutch of hands on her suede jacket!

Nothing had ever been so frightening, but it soon became evident that the thief was after her handbag and a fierce little scuffle ensued as she fought to hold on to it. She kicked at his shins in fear and temper, a veritable vixen who wasn't going to be robbed of what was hers without a struggle. She called him quite a few names, which petered out into a cry as she felt the strap of her bag wrenched out of her grasp. In a flash the thief was scurrying away into the shadows with her handbag, leaving her shaken and roughed up.

"You fool girl!" she muttered shakily. "You silly little boob!" For gone with her bag was the last of her British money and roughly three pounds in pesetas, though thank goodness she had had the sense to leave her passport and steamer ticket locked in her suitcase at the inn where she was staying here in Toledo. To have lost those would have been a real catastrophe; as it was, it was going to be awkward being without money. The police weren't likely to recover her handbag overnight.

Her breath recovered, she hastened past the place where the thief had lurked, not the type of girl to go right to pieces, though her heart was still hammering against her ribs from that frightening encounter. Her holiday had gone so well up to now...it was infuriating to have proved right those skeptics who had said that girls traveling alone were asking for trouble of one sort or another. The only answer was judo, Ricki told herself wryly, remembering with a shudder the bony strength of that alley rat.

A few minutes later she rounded a corner and found with relief that she was facing a main road. She was standing at the curb, glancing around for someone who could direct her to the Plaza de Zocodover, when the lights of an oncoming car illuminated her slim young figure. The car stopped right beside her and the driver thrust a dark head out of the window. Ricki met eyes of an unbelievable darkness and she stared right into them until, gripped by a shyness that suddenly gave way to panic, she darted around the long hood of the car and sped across the road toward a small shop.

Green, amber and ruby red pharmacy bottles glowed in the window. She made a grab for the door handle, but it turned impotently in her grasp—the shop was shut. And behind her someone was gripping her shoulders and spinning her around as easily as though she were a doll!

Etched and shadowed by the thrusts of colored light from the shop window, the man's face was both striking and forbidding. His cheekbones and the shaping of temple and jaw were pure El Greco, his mouth was a stern line, his hair and eyebrows black as night. Ricki's heart skipped such a beat that she almost lost her breath—the face she was looking at belonged to a devil or a saint, and with her nerves already in a tumult she was ready to believe the worst!

"It is most indiscreet in certain parts of Spain for a women to be walking alone after dusk," he said crisply, in a deep-toned, accented voice. "You are a *turista,* and presumably lost, eh?"

Stock-still in his grasp but with her heart racing, Ricki realized both from his educated use of English and the cut of his suit that this particular Spaniard was way above the class who ogled you in the street or snatched your handbag in a gloomy alleyway, and in a voice that shook slightly she admitted that she was a tourist and hopelessly lost.

The *señor's* very dark eyes flicked over her, taking in her ruffled appearance and the fright that still lingered in her eyes. "You appear very shaken up," he said.

Then his voice sharpened "What has happened—have you been pestered in some way?"

"M-my handbag's been snatched," she told him. "It was rather an awful experience—it happened back in one of those dark lanes."

"You were wandering alone in those *callejons*?" His nostrils dilated with disapproval as he gazed down at her. "I presume that you are British and accustomed to doing just what you please, without heed for the consequences."

In an instant this lean autocrat had Ricki bridling. "I—I lost my way after coming out of the cathedral," she hotly defended herself. "Anyway, I wasn't expecting to be stalked in the dark and robbed!"

"*Por mi vida!* A woman who walks alone at night is tempting the devil's eye—why is it that you did not keep with the rest of your party?"

"I happen to be here on my own," Ricki said, with dignity. "I've been here two days and tonight's encounter was unexpected by me because, *señor*, I've found your country and *most* of your people wholly charming."

"Added to which the British are far from chicken hearted, eh?" The severity of his mouth suddenly relaxed into a smile—well, it wasn't actually a smile, just a movement of his lips that showed a white glimmer of teeth. "Now if you will tell me where you are staying, which inn or hotel, I will drive you there. Then it will be necessary to report the theft of your handbag to the police—did the bag contain much of value?"

"My British money and about three pounds in pesetas." She shrugged. "Luckily my passport and travel documents are in my suitcase at the inn, which is situated in the Calle de Torres."

"*Vaya?* I stay with friends quite close to Tower Street, so it will not take me out of my way to drive you

there. Come, *señorita!*'' His hand on her shoulder propelled her across the road to his car, a long station
wagon with wood trim and the interior ease of soft beige
upholstery. He switched on the roof light, then with an
elbow on the wheel he studied Ricki in the seat beside
him. It was so cool an appraisal that she was able to
meet it without embarrassment, for this man wasn't
"picking her up." He wasn't interested in her as a
woman, only as a tourist who had suffered a misfortune
she could have avoided—his eyes plainly said—had she
behaved with the sense and discretion of a *señorita*.
How very dark his eyes were! Her fingers crept unknow-
ingly to the traveler's charm that hung on a thin chain
about her neck. Her hair clung close to her head and
was the rust shade of beech leaves in autumn. Her eyes
were the color of Irish moss, well set in a face that was
thin and elfish. There was a feminine boyishness about
her, a hint of truculent shyness where men were concerned, and she wore a brown suede jacket lined with
silk as green as peridots, a brown skirt linked to a cream
shirt by a green belt, and flats of pigskin suede.

A wild goose never laid a tame egg, and Tynan
O'Neill and his English wife had hatched a rare mixture
in Ricki—her mouth, half-sensitive, half-tempestuous,
was the clue to her disposition.

"You seem to me very young to be traveling through
Spain on your own," commented the Spaniard. "Your
parents must put much more faith in your common
sense than they should—as you have demonstrated
tonight."

"I happen to be old enough to vote." Ricki's tone
was as stiff as her spine against the comfortable
passenger seat of his car. "My father—I have no
mother—knows that he has no need to worry about me.
I admit that it might have been wiser to do my sight-
seeing before it grew dark, but I'm leaving Toledo in the

morning and I wanted very much to see the interior of the cathedral.''

"And its many attractions stole time away before you realized, eh?'' The Spaniard's fine eyes held a momentary flash of amusement. "Tell me, are you now quite without funds?''

"I shall be by the time I've ransacked the toe of a stocking in order to settle my bill at the inn,'' she admitted ruefully. "My bus fare back to Madrid is already paid, but I shall have to ask the British consul for a loan—there's my fare to London from the steamer I'm going home on.''

"You speak like a young woman who deplores the idea of dependence upon the goodwill of a man.'' A hint of mockery edged that accented voice which did certain things to English words that gave them a new, startling flavor. "It is not a favorable asset, I think, for a woman to be too independent.''

"Oh, I've noticed that here in Spain the rooster still crows the tune, *señor.*'' A twinkle darted into Ricki's eye. "I'll admit it is the natural way of things, but when a girl's doing a job that not many years ago was mainly done by men, she's apt to get into the habit of thinking and acting for herself—and rather liking it!''

"Ah, now you intrigue me.'' A quick interest gleamed in his eyes. "And where do you do this work?''

"In a hospital, *señor.*''

"Most interesting.'' His glance dwelt on her slim, well-kept, ringless hands. "A job once reserved for men, eh? Are you by any chance a masseuse?''

"That's part of my work.'' She looked impressed by his shrewdness. "I'm a physiotherapist.''

He drew an audible breath, then he started the car and a startled sort of silence hung between them for several minutes. Ricki's side glance dwelt on the man's haughty Latin nose and thoughtfully jutting lower lip, then he abruptly spoke. "I must introduce myself! My name is Arturo de Cazalet, and various other appellations you would no doubt find confusing. Now please to tell me how you are called?"

Ricki's startled eyes raced up and down his profile, while her mind was suddenly full of the things her hospital friends had said about Latins. Here she was in the car of one of them and for all his distinguished appearance and impressive name he could be one devil of a wolf!

"I—I hardly see why it's necessary for you to know my name," she said coldly. "Look, we're nearing the Plaza de Zocodover. If you will let me out—"

"You will again lose yourself, no doubt." His tone was droll. "Please do dismiss those foolish thoughts you have just been having! I ask your name, *señorita*, because I am going to suggest that we dine together for the purpose of discussing the problem which confronts me."

"Really, *señor....*" Ricki didn't know what to make of the man.

"Yes, really, *señorita!*" He gave her a quick flash of a glance, half-mocking, half-serious. "My problem involves a child, so on that count, perhaps, you will relax your guard and not fence with me. I have to be in the right mood and atmosphere to enjoy a fencing match with a woman, and right now my mind is occupied by the problem I speak of. Your name, please!"

Ricki gave it, responding to the "crack of the whip" as spontaneously as in her training days. He repeated her name after her, making it sound like Rickee Oneeill, and his glance flicked her slim, boyish figure as the car turned into the parking place beside the inn where she was booked for the night. "You have the name of a boy," he said, bringing the car to a halt.

"Well, it's really Veronica," she admitted. "But I've

always been called Ricki. I was a bit of a tomboy as a child, you see.''

''I can see.'' The corners of his stern, thinly cut mouth again relaxed into a faint smile. ''Veronica is an interesting name. It is, you know, a pass with the cape in bullfighting, very intricate and daring. I wonder if your name is significant? It could well be, as you came alone to Spain and saw no harm in wandering the *callejons* of Toledo.''

''Señor Cazalet—'' Ricki faced him with a flush in her cheeks ''—who exactly are you and what is it you are going to ask of me?''

''I am the owner of sheep and olive *estancias* in Andalusia,'' he told her, ''but my car is not the correct place for us to remain in discussion. Come, we will go into the inn, where I shall order dinner and contact the police for you while you go to your room and wash your face and hands.''

Just as though I'm a child, Ricki thought, preceding him into the inn and watching with wide eyes as the innkeeper bowed and beamed, quickly provided a telephone and clapped loud hands that brought his waiters running to take the orders of this lordly-looking don from Andalusia, who accepted all this attention with the suave matter of factness of someone who was used to it.

When Ricki came down from her room half an hour later, having changed into a white pleated dress with mini sleeves and a peridot green belt that matched her shoes, a table had been neatly laid and set in an alcove that was rather like an inglenook, and Don Arturo was waiting to tell her that he had informed the local police of the theft of her bag. It would be several days before the thief was caught, no doubt, and in that time he would have spent her pesetas and found a crony to change the British pounds for him. The don added that he hoped she had nothing of real value in her bag.

"There is a compact and lipstick holder decorated with jade shamrocks," she said regretfully. "But wouldn't they be traceable?"

"There is certainly a chance of that, Miss O'Neill." He had mastered her name as he seemed to be mastering her. "The inspector of police is calling in to see you later on and you can then describe these baubles to him; in the meantime, *señorita*, please to be seated." He gestured to their table with his lean, strong, El Greco hands, and Ricki slipped into one of the wall seats with the impish reflection that her friends back in England were going to be really impressed when she told them she had dined with a real don and actually given him advice regarding a child of his.

While he spoke to one of the waiters, Ricki studied him in his impeccable stone-gray suit with a wine clove in the buttonhole and thought it strange that he should need the advice of a stranger. He had seemed impressed when she had told him she was a physiotherapist—could it be that his child was making a slow recovery from an illness or accident and he wished to discuss the child's symptoms with her in order to get a European opinion? Possible, but a bit farfetched in view of the cleverness of Spanish doctors and the fact that this man seemed wealthy enough to afford the best opinion available. However, contact with parents at the hospital had taught Ricki that where children were concerned a hundred and one opinions were often not enough to satisfy really devoted parents.

Arturo de Cazalet had said he owned *estancias*, therefore, his child—doubtless a son—would mean all that much more to him. Perhaps in his concern he needed tonight someone to talk to about the boy, for there was in his proud, dark face a look of sadness...or was it a brooding bitterness?

As she pondered his brooding look, he suddenly met

her eyes across the table and she at once dropped her gaze to his hands, noticing his signet ring stamped with an *escudo* and his cuff links of chased gold on steel. The *escudo* was obvious proof that he belonged to an old, proud family, and Ricki's bewilderment was intensified as she again asked herself what this sophisticated *hidalgo* could want with a gauche young tourist like herself.

"You are looking puzzled, Miss O'Neill." There was a teasing note in his voice. "You ask yourself why I should invite you to dine with me, and the most obvious answer fails to occur to you—ah, here comes our wine! It should help you to relax."

The Alella Marfil was in a sea green bottle meshed in silvery threads and Ricki's smile held a quick enchantment that put lights in her eyes and deepened the fey hollows beneath her cheekbones. "My father would say of such a bottle that it held the dews of dawn," she said. "He's an Irishman and a bit of a poet."

"I had thought you had a look I have seen in Jerez." Don Arturo took up his wine glass as he spoke. "There have been Spanish-Irish families there for many years and the moss green eyes and hair with fire sparks in it crops up in the children of these people. Strange, indeed fascinating, how we carry like wine the tones and flavors of past vintages—do you not think, *señorita*?"

She nodded and smiled rather shyly, comparing the rare vintage of this table talk to that of her usual companions: brash young housemen, occasionally a male member of her own profession, several times a gangling, likeable footballer who lived near her relatives at Hendon.

"*Salud, señorita de los ojos grandes!*" The Don raised his wineglass with an unselfconscious flourish, and they drank together. "*Es bueno?*" he asked.

"*Muy fino, señor,*" she said, a faint flush in her

cheeks because, having taught herself a kind of mongrel Spanish with language records during the months she had saved up for this holiday, she more or less understood that he had just called her the young lady of the large eyes. Oh lord, what did he want of her?

"Ah, so you learn a little Spanish," he said, as their first course was brought to the table, stuffed filets of sole, rolled, poached and garnished with muscat grapes. Vegetables were served on separate plates, small potatoes, green peas and buttered carrots. From childhood Ricki had loved carrots. These were small and sweet, orange as marigolds, and Ricki broke into a laugh as she and her companion reached together for a pepperpot. "Please, after you," he smiled, holding it in his fingers so that she could take it.

"Not so likely, Don Arturo!" She shook her head, her mouth crinkling into the first natural smile she had yet managed in his company. "Help me to pepper, help me to temper!"

"Are not green eyes already a danger signal of temper?" His eyes held that disconcerting flash of very adult amusement, but he obligingly peppered his own vegetables before standing the pot in front of her own plate. "A peppercorn is very small, yet how it seasons every dinner—a saying we have in Spain, *señorita*," he added, but she caught the quirk to his lips and wondered if he was implying that she seasoned this meal for him.

It was much more appetizing than her lunch had been, so it did seem likely that the innkeeper had urged his cook to extra effort on behalf of the important *señor* who dined here tonight.

"These bus tours, they are an *olla podrida*, eh?" the don remarked, as she enjoyed a fresh fruit salad while he ate wedges of a strong-looking cheese. "A mixture of sights, scents and sounds that must be very confusing at times. Tell me, did you visit the Prado while you were in Madrid?''

He pronounced it Madreeth and Ricki couldn't help thinking how attractive Spanish words sounded when a Spaniard spoke them. "I wouldn't have missed all those wonderful paintings for the world," she replied. "I especially like the works of Murillo and Goya."

"Murillo was of Andalusia, which is why he painted with so much extra warmth. El Greco no doubt troubled you, you could not look at his paintings with ease, eh?" The don's dark eyes searched her face. "You like the things that are warm, gay, of the world of fairy tales—it is *manifestado* that life has not yet really touc..ed you, though you are trained in an occupation and—" a glint of *el diablo* came into his eyes, "—old enough to vote."

"I could appreciate the depth to the El Greco paintings even if their torment worried me," she said defensively. "I'm not that much of a child."

"Do not be on the defensive about being young," he chided her. "It is the best time of life to be young, and I am sure that you enjoyed every moment of the marionette theatre in El Retiro Park."

Ricki caught her breath. Was she that transparent to this man? But then it was fairly obvious that he knew the world and what made women laugh and cry. "Don Arturo—" she sugared her coffee, her boyish head bent over the task "—why did you ask me to dine with you?"

She felt his dark glance upon her, and his fierce, fine bone structure was imprinted on her mind along with that lurking expression of bitter sadness. He had stepped straight out of an El Greco canvas and all that was needed to complete the picture were black and silver doublet and hose, and the shimmer of Toledo steel to match a temper that was no doubt swift and cutting. She gave a little shiver and heard a tall old clock ticking nearby, filling in with the mutter of conversation from other tables the small void of silence before he replied to her.

"*Con su permiso*?" He had taken a cigar case from his pocket.

"I—I like the aroma," she said nervously. "Please light up."

He clipped and lighted the slim Havana very deliberately, then with his very straight shoulders at rest against the paneling of their alcove, smoke weaving about his dark head, he said quietly, "We of the Latin countries believe a great deal in the machinations of chance. Do you, Miss O'Neill?"

"I—I am inclined to be superstitious," she admitted.

"Then you will agree with me that it is fortuitous that I, who am in need of a physio-attendant, should be here in Toledo at the same time as yourself. More than that, you appear out of the deep blue of Toledo's *callejons*." He inspected the tip of his cigar, then added, "It seems to me that chance arranged our meeting, there can be no other explanation."

Again there was silence between them, stunned on Ricki's part, then her voice returned and seemed overloud. "You need a physio-attendant?" she exclaimed. "Me?"

"You, for several reasons, Miss O'Neill." And his eyes looking into hers were suddenly damascened steel; he had made up his mind about what he wanted, but Ricki tensed in her seat as though about to leap up and run. At once his hand closed over hers as it gripped the table edge; his lean fingers locked around her wrist and she was held captive.

"You said of Spain that you found the place and the people wholly charming," he reminded her. "You have not a close tie with your father, otherwise he would not be persuaded to let you travel abroad without companionship. You are spirited but sensitive, with much imagination—the child also has these qualities and I think he would find you *simpatica*. Tell me, have you dealt much with children in the course of your work?''

"Yes, I've had children as patients," she admitted. "But, Don Arturo, what you're asking is impossible—I couldn't stay here and treat the child of a complete stranger."

"Permit me to tell you about the boy." The lean fingers tightened around her wrist, compelling as the dark eyes that gazed straight into hers. She wasn't going to be allowed to do other than listen! "When you have heard the story of Jaime, I think you might find it in your heart to accept a post which would not be uncongenial. My *estancia* offers much of interest, and it is true of Andalusia that it is a place where no bitter herb takes root."

"Do you speak of the soil—or of the heart, Señor Cazalet?" The question was out almost before Ricki realized that she was asking for a snubbing, or a flash of steel-edged temper, but with a slight shrug of his gray-clad shoulders he sat back against the dark paneling of the alcove seat. His eyelids were narrowed from her question and he looked faintly dangerous, like a man whose armor had felt the tip of a shaft through a chink that would not mend. The base of his chin had an obdurate squareness to it and it was plain to Ricki that she was dealing with a man who allowed few people to cross him. The arguments of women—if there were any women, apart from herself, who gave him an argument—were feathers to be blown out of his way.

"Jaime is my nephew," he said curtly. "Right away that should be a point in his favor, for you thought him my son, eh? He is seven years old, and for the past two years he has been confined to a wheelchair owing to a car accident which killed his parents. The parents were my brother, Leandro, and his wife, Conquesta. It was a *milagro*—a miracle, you say—that the boy ever lived, for his spine was very badly hurt. The doctors say that he may walk one day, but so far there has been no sign of this, though God grant that a second miracle should occur and he will be as other children." The don spread the fingers of his left hand, then closed them together as though to hold tightly to his wish.

" 'They can conquer who believe they can.' " The don's eyes brooded through the smoke of his cigar. "Somehow we of his family have failed to provide the incentive which might help him to throw off the shackles of his invalid chair. If there had been other children, a sister preferably, the boy would not be so alone in his child's world which is also an adult world of suffering. There are children on the *estancia* of course, but they are tough little *peons* who like to play their rough boyish games. It is impossible for Jaime to be other than—" the don shrugged regretfully "—a baby in a pushcart. He used to ask for his *mamaita*—his mother—but that phase has passed and he now spends much of his time drawing in a sketchbook and coloring the pictures."

A sigh stole from the lips that looked so hard; it reached Ricki and touched her. "These are not happy pictures, *señorita*. Always they are of cars that have crashed and of people lying broken and dead. I tell him to make pictures of the livestock about the farm; I take him to the fruit groves when the trees are in blossom in the hope that their beauty will banish the horror which haunts his mind, but still his pencils make these tormented pictures. Had his injuries healed, his mind also would have healed, but as things are he lives in a world of his own peopled by his dead loves. My brother, the boy's father, was a young man of considerable *sal*, a Spanish expression for extreme charm and fascination. Conquesta—" the don looked at the tip of his cigar

"—to say she was beautiful is not nearly enough. *Bellissima* was my brother's name for her, and you will concur that it conveys much more than that rather film-starish, overused word which men today apply to every bleached blonde who saunters in a bikini along the beaches of the Costa Brava and the Costa del Sol."

Don Arturo ground out his half-smoked cigar as though it had gone bitter on him. "That world is full of cosmetics-covered beauties whom I should not care to face first thing in the morning, but that is beside the point. My nephew, you understand, requires certain treatments and exercises which must be given only by a trained person. Several physio-attendants have been employed by me in the eight months during which Jaime has been home from the hospital, but they have grown bored with life on a farm which is many miles from a city. Jaime's most recent attendant left a fortnight ago, and here in Toledo I was to pick up his new one. On my arrival at his hotel, I found he had left a message canceling the arrangement, having gone instead to Barcelona to attend someone else. I was most annoyed. I took a drive in order to cool my anger, and it was on my way back that my headlights showed me suddenly a young *turista* who looked as though she had found some trouble for herself."

He stroked the high bridge of his nose. "Women are as attracted to hidden danger as mice to cheese," he added sardonically.

"That's unfair, *señor*," she protested. "I got lost."

"And I found you." His unsparing gaze took in each detail of her young face, the humor that curved her mouth, the hint of distress that lingered in her wide eyes after his story of Jaime, the little boy who was unable to walk since the accident which had killed his charming parents.

"In you, Miss O'Neill, my nephew might find what

he needs. You are trained to help him physically, and you possess certain youthful qualities which might help him to emerge from his world of shadows. Please—" the don spoke like a man who was unused to pleading, the proud flare to his nostrils making of his plea a demand "—will you come to the *estancia* to be the *compañera* of my nephew?"

Ricki sustained the compelling intensity of his gaze, but she did so with an effort. How did one refuse such a man? And how deny the nurse and the woman in her, especially when she had just been told that a child needed her in both capacities? When she knew also that she was free to accept private employment now she had quit the hospital? But even as her heart went out to the child, Ricki felt herself shrinking from the man.

There was an imperiousness about him that she had never met with before. He was part of a feudal system that made the rich landowner in Spain a power to be reckoned with, a man whose attitude toward his employees would be one of absolute authority.

"I sympathize with your problem, Don Arturo, and I am touched by your story," she said, "but I'm leaving Spain tomorrow and I regret that I just haven't the time to think over your proposition—"

His fingers snapped impatiently. "I find evasiveness irritating. Come, you feel the lure of Spain, the individuality which is unique to this country of mine, and the salary I shall offer will be more than adequate. Why do you hesitate? Have you a *novio* back in England whom you cannot be parted from?"

"It isn't that," she protested. "But it would be rather rash of a girl to accept employment from a man she has known only a few hours—"

"It can be readily established that I am Arturo de Cazalet y Aguinarda and not Don Pluto who plans to carry you off to the dark regions." His eyes held shifting glimmers of amusement. "The inspector of police will vouch for me, and I have friends living not far from here who have known me for many years."

"Please—" Ricki was blushing "I don't doubt your identity or your sincerity—"

"Then what do you doubt, *señorita*? That you would not find me amiable to work for? But is it not a fact that people in authority in hospitals are martinets of discipline? I should not be that bad. Jaime would be entirely in your charge and I would not interfere with whatever regime you set up for him. It seems to me, in fact, that you would have much more freedom at the Granja de la Valle than you can ever have had tied to the routine of hospital work."

A shrewd thrust and it got to Ricki, but this man... well, he looked like one of those in whose blood ran the forces which said, "Take what you want, and pay for it!" His courtesy was unassailable, and there was even a lurking magic in that dark smile of his, but Ricki couldn't quite believe that he would leave the entire management of his nephew to a woman. And what of his wife? Were not the women of important Spanish households on the domineering side?

"Still the green eyes are hazed by questions." The don leaned forward and filled the liqueur glass which now stood alone in front of her, the other things having been quietly whipped away by the quick-moving waiters who had obviously enjoyed waiting on a man so *distinguido*. "Please to drink this," he said, "but carefully. It is a brandy of my country, distilled not for its bouquet or its flavor, but to put fire in the blood." His smile was faintly mocking. "What question would you like to ask me—but first drink your *cognac*."

She sipped at it, and then found herself saying, "You must be very devoted to your nephew, *señor*. I gather you have no children of your own?"

"It would be a trifle inconvenient for a man to go in for children before he has acquired a wife," the don said dryly. "You were wondering, eh, what my wife might be like and whether you would get along with her?"

Ricki blushed vividly and half blamed it on the fiery brandy. He chuckled as he took note of her scarlet cheeks. "It is strange," he drawled, "that the British woman who is self-confident enough to travel alone to a foreign country is yet able to blush. Spanish women have an interior self-assurance which makes blushing a near impossibility for them, but I doubt their ability to cope with customs officials, foreign currency, booking in at hotels and sight-seeing without someone to chatter and cling to. I admire your initiative, Miss O'Neill, but do you really enjoy being all alone and dependent upon no one but yourself?"

"A working girl has to be independent," she replied. "It wouldn't do to be a clinging vine in a hospital—good lord, you wouldn't last a week, let alone a year."

"And is it your intention to continue to work in a hospital?"

"Well...." she hesitated. "You do acquire a lot of valuable experience, but I must admit that I do intend to branch out. I—I suppose as a Spaniard it strikes you as a bit unnatural that girls should have careers? But it's handy to have a career. It's something you can always fall back on—I mean, marriage doesn't always give you everything you want."

"You speak of material things?" He tossed back his brandy.

She shook her head and stared into the tawny pool at the bottom of her glass. "I meant that marriage ought to be all-satisfying, but it seems to fall short of that these days. In my country, at least. I don't know about Spain."

"Here in Spain also—" his tone was edged with irony "—if marriage is not established on a sound basis of mutual understanding and tolerance, the edifice is tottery. Spanish people, however, rarely hasten into marriage, which is probably the main cause of swift erosion. They find time to get to know each other, without doubt the best way to start any association—including the one we were discussing. Miss O'Neill, would you consider coming to Andalusia for a month, to establish whether our ways and our climate will suit you? If you found the lack of city distractions too much to bear—"

"Those would be the last things I'd miss." She laughed at the idea. "Living in the country wouldn't worry me—why, I used to love tramping the Irish heaths with my father when I was a child. We used to fly a big box kite and gather armfuls of russet and lilac heather to take home to my mother." A sigh escaped her. "I lost the wilds when my mother died and my father took me to live with my aunt and uncle in England."

"It is a heritage beyond price to carry always the memory of talking and playing with someone young at heart," murmured Don Arturo. "You can understand why I wish the same for Jaime."

Ricki nodded and felt moved by his words, for it was as important to a child to have companionship as it was to have adult care, and Don Arturo was probably too busy about the *estancia* to be able to give his nephew more than an hour or two of his company. Poor little boy! The emotional stress of his loneliness could be hindering his progress toward complete recovery, and there must be a chance of that if the doctors had said so.

She gazed across at the boy's uncle, half fascinated by the idea of working for him, half fearful of it. He was a masterful man. He challenged what was boyishly independent in her, and she knew they would have clashes if she agreed to work for him.

"But how would I manage, *señor*?" she asked. "My Spanish is not a quarter as good as your English."

"Do you find it puzzling that a Spaniard should speak your language with fluency?" he asked, a faint smile in his eyes.

She nodded and thought him a man who would intrigue anyone.

"It has long been a custom in my family that its members be brought up bilingual," he explained. "For years we have conducted business with those of English-speaking countries, and then again there is English blood in myself and in Jaime. My grandmother came from your country, Miss O'Neill, and when the child was born he had an English nanny."

"The child speaks English also?" Ricki exclaimed.

"But of course." The don quirked a night-black eyebrow. "When he grows up he will be in business with me and it will be necessary now and again for him to travel abroad.... "Ah—" the don threw out an expressive hand "—see how I speak of him as being able to take an active part in the business when he is older? I forget that at present there is small indication that he will be able to do this. The ability to walk again is there, but the will lies dormant—the right person, Miss O'Neill, could arouse it."

"You think I might be that person, *señor*?" Ricki spoke very seriously, her gaze intent upon his proud, stern-featured face.

"I *hope* you might be that person," he conceded.

Ricki held her breath a moment. She could try the job. This man wasn't likely to keep her a prisoner in his valley if she found the place and the people uncongenial. "Very well, *señor*," she plunged. "I'll try out the job for a month just to see how we get along."

He studied her for a long moment, then inclined his dark head in a slightly ironic way. "We will agree to part without regrets if you cannot settle down at the Granja de la Valle," he said, "and now I see the inspector of police approaching our table to talk about the theft of your handbag. Be lavish with your Irish smile, *señorita*, for the good inspector can be of much help with the formalities pertaining to your employment here in Spain."

Her employment here in Spain! Fingers of excitement and apprehension clutched at Ricki's heart and were still clinging when she at last retired to her room, the don's strangely formal, "Good night and good repose," echoing in her ears. What was she letting herself in for? The child sounded a most unhappy little scrap, and she couldn't help thinking that the shadows that hung about Jaime were also clouding the heart of his uncle.

Was she doing a wise thing in agreeing to go to this farm in an Andalusian valley, with a man who carried lines of bitterness beside his night-dark eyes and his mouth that smiled so gravely?

CHAPTER TWO

IT SEEMED that when you dealt with someone of the Cazalet standing, formalities were overcome with the minimum of time and trouble. Ricki's permit to reside and work in Spain was hurried through by the obliging inspector of police, and soon the morning had come when she was to set out with her new employer to his home in Andalusia.

She had enjoyed the extra days in Toledo, during which she had written a long letter to her father and met the friends of Don Arturo who lived in the city. They had asked him to bring her to *merienda* in the large walled patio of their house, and though the beautiful Castilian they spoke was beyond her, she had liked their dignity and hospitality. They were of the old aristocracy of Spain and their close friendship with Don Arturo was further proof that she was employed by a man of important standing.

Ricki was excited, apprehensive and yet determined to make a go of the job. In a way it was what she had been longing for, the chance to take care of someone who really needed her, in surroundings that were new to her. "The Granja is quite large," Don Arturo had told her, "and I have several other farms that are run by tenant farmers. From son to son, these people have always worked the Cazalet land—no doubt in England you have similar systems?"

She had nodded, recalling her father's tales of the ancient untitled families of Kerry and Mayo, whose roots were buried deep in the turbulent history of Ireland. So here in Spain the old cultures lingered on, and Arturo de Cazalet was without a doubt the *patrono* of the isolated community to which he was taking her.

The night before they left Toledo, Ricki had a strange dream. She was at the wheel of a car and she was driving very fast—suddenly the brakes seemed not to be working properly and she awoke in a sweat as the car was hurtling down a hill to unavoidable destruction.

She still had the dream in mind while she washed and dressed. It could be associated with the fact that her patient-to-be had received his injury in a car crash. On the other hand, Ricki wondered if the dream was some kind of warning—she stood in front of the cheval glass with her comb poised in the air—a warning that she should put a brake on an action that could be leading her into some sort of danger?

Then, catching her wide-eyed reflection in the glass, she pulled a mocking face at herself. The strange, rather mysterious atmosphere of Toledo was working on her imagination, but once out of its environs she would no longer imagine Arturo de Cazalet in the dark raiment of medieval days, steel at his hip, his lean figure wrapped in the folds of a cloak. A devil or a saint! His face still as forbidding to her as on the night he had swung her to face him and she had looked into eyes so dark that many secrets could be hiding in them.

She finished combing her hair and firmly told herself that he was just a man, the anxious uncle of a small sick boy, and after locking her pajamas and toilet bag in her suitcase, she went and looked out of the small-paned window. Women were on their way to morning Mass with their heads mantled in black shawls. A milkman stood ladling milk into a customer's jug from one of his Ali Baba cans, and the air was rich with the smell of warm bread from a baker's shop and musical with the tolling of Toledo's many deep-toned bells.

Ricki took a deep breath of the morning air and felt anticipation quiver along her spine. Arturo de Cazalet did unnerve her a little, but if they had not met she would by now have been back in England. Instead she was going deeper into the heart of Spain, across the plains of Andalusia to the Granja de la Valle—the farm of the valley.

"Spanish hospitality is next to none," someone had said when she had talked about taking a holiday in Spain, "providing you tread to the tune they play."

Words which could prove to be significant when applied to the household of a man like Arturo de Cazalet, but there was comfort in the thought that she was free to leave if her trial month didn't work out. At that point the brass chamber clock gave a whir and began to sound the hour. Lord, she had better be getting downstairs— she was having breakfast with her employer before they set out on their long drive. She buttoned the jacket of her olive green suit, worn with a white blouse in waffle piqué, took a final peep at her reflection to insure that all was neat, then, carrying her suitcase, she went downstairs to the dining room of the inn.

"*Buen' dia*, Miss O'Neill." The don, lean and aloof in conservative pinstripe with a charcoal gray tie knotted to perfection at the crisp collar of a light gray shirt, escorted her to their table. "I regret that the police have not yet recovered your handbag and its contents," he said as he liberally sugared a half of pink melon. "My good friend the condesa informed me at dinner last night that a woman is lost without a capacious handbag in which to carry her odds and ends and, there beside you on your seat, you will find a gift from her. You can write to thank her from the Granja, for we have no time to call in upon her this morning."

Ricki, melon-filled spoon halfway to her mouth, lowered it again and turned to look at the fairly large package that lay beside her on the banquette. She unwrapped the brown paper and gave a gasp of delight and surprise. The Condesa Quintalar, whom she had met the other afternoon, had given her a handsome bag of Moroccan leather; it hung on a shoulder strap and was firmly latched at the front. "But I couldn't possibly accept anything like this!" she gasped.

"I think you had better." The don gave her his brief, grave-eyed smile. "The condesa would be most offended if you refuse to accept her gift. As she remarked, she is no longer young and active and it would please her to know that the bag was being used by a useful young woman."

"How kind of her to say that!" Ricki flushed and ran her slim fingers over the intriguing raised figures on the bag. "I—I shouldn't want her to think me ungrateful, and I'll look after the bag for all I'm worth."

"From the sturdy look of it, you have a most effective weapon if you find yourself at the mercy of another desperado." The quirk of Don Arturo's left brow gave him a look of saturnine humour. "Whenever you get the urge to explore, it might be wise to carry it with you. Much of Andalusia is still untamed, you know. There are caves in the hills where *gitanos* live, and the tough *vaqueros* who tend the bull herds might not understand that perfectly respectable British girls wander about on their own. The girls of Andalusia do not—unless they are of a certain class. We of the south, you see, cling to many of the old traditions."

"I'll try to behave as much like a *señorita* as possible." Ricki's eyes were dancing as she bent over her melon. "Please tell me some more about Andalusia, *señor*. It's a fascinating place."

"It is as barbaric in many ways and as exciting as in

the days when the Moors ruled it and built alcazars as full of color and intrigue as the courts of Baghdad. It was then called Betica, and it is still the seat of superstition, where everything has a meaning, an omen and a portent." The don glanced up from his plate of ham and eggs *flamenco*, his face as dark and fine-boned as a Saracen's. "We growers of the olive and the *morales*—mulberries, you say—have many beliefs which would no doubt seem pagan to the outside world."

"You're forgetting that my paternal roots are Irish," Ricki said, breaking a twist of crisp bread and buttering it. "In remote parts of Ireland there are superstitions galore, and beliefs run rife that the spirits of the old chiefs haunt the moorlands. Any country which is really old must have the past clinging to it—whispers in the wind, you know, and shapes in the early morning mists."

Her words were followed by a small silence and when she glanced up, a piece of ham spread on her fork, she found Don Arturo looking at her very intently. The disturbing quality about his eyes wasn't due entirely to the fact that they were so striking; he seemed to pull down a shutter on his own private thoughts while having the ability to read other people's. *He knows he frightens me a little*, Ricki thought, *and he thinks me a bit of a child. Funny for two people like us to have come together like this—we're so different, yet in a way we think alike.*

"There are very few visitors to my country, Miss O'Neill, of whom it can be said that they have that certain something that makes for affinity with the Spain of the Spaniards, but," his lean fingers turned the lid of the honey jar, "I think you may have it."

"Why—thank you, *señor*." She gave him a smile, but he didn't return it.

"I am not paying you a compliment." The honey gleamed as he spread a piece of bread with it. "The *piropo*, as we call it, is coined lightly and not meant to be taken seriously, something it might be wise to remember when you meet the young and volatile men of the south. They invented the *piropo*, the flirtatious compliment, and are masters of the game.''

"You are a man of the south, *señor*," she dared say.

"My mother was of Castile and I take after her. My brother was more the son of my father, and yet Jaime shows the reserve of our Castilian blood and in several ways he could be a son of mine.''

Don Arturo spoke with his usual coolness, but Ricki wondered how deep went his shaft of pain that the boy wasn't really his. Somehow she knew that this could have been so if Conquesta had not become beguiled by the brother who had been gayer, more a part of the warm languorous south than the rocks and shadows and fierce pride of Castile.

"Who is taking care of Jaime while you are away, *señor*?" she asked, curious about his household, which seemed to be an all-male one with none of the usual female cousins and aunts bustling about and bossing the men in the matriarchal way which seemed necessary to the Spaniard's temperament.

"The boy is in the care of my head guard and his wife. Sophina is a good sort, with a large family of *picaros* who are to her, she asserts, even as she boxes their ears, as precious as the oil of the olive.'' He dabbed honey from his lips and Ricki glimpsed the fleeting smile that lit up the jet of his eyes. "The peasant without olive oil is poor indeed and in Andalusia we place more value on the olive tree than on the grape vine.''

"You cultivate mainly the olive, *señor*?" She accepted a tangerine from the dish he held out and began to peel it, the scent of it wafting her to Hendon at Christmastide, the only time when they had tangerines.

How far away Hendon seemed right now: the red brick school, being a physio student in London and living in lodgings, working at the hospital and suddenly facing up to the fact that she was restless, chained, longing for wider horizons in which to try her wings.

"The Cazalet olive is quite famous, not for eating, you understand, but for the oil," the don told her. "Something in our soil seems to enrich the trees and make them dark, and the darker the tree, the more fruitfully it yields. I will tell you of one of our superstitions which I think you will find rather charming." He smiled that brief, rather haunting smile of his. "Over the door of the big warehouse in which the barrels of oil are stored, and I have no objection to the practice, my workers always nail a juniper bush in order to keep evil spirits from entering the oil and turning it rancid."

"Yes, I do like that," she smiled, "it's like corn in the house to ensure bread on the table, and it would seem to work as the Cazalet oil is so renowned. Do you know," her eyes glistened, "Andalusia sounds just my kind of place."

"We will hope so." He inclined his head in his serious way, and she had a sudden mad and impossible impulse to ruffle his smooth black hair, to see him shaken out of his cool containment into the abandonment of emotion. What would he be like then, this proud autocrat who was shot through with the superstition of his land, courteous as the Castilian knights of long ago, reserved and aloof as the cool peaks of the Sierras that frowned down upon the sun-ambered plains of Andalusia?

He rose from their table and she lingered a moment to apply a dash of lipstick—war paint, she amusedly told herself, for wasn't she about to take on a job that had some very challenging aspects to it? Ten minutes later she and the don were being bowed out of the inn by the proprietor and she was slipping into the long station wagon and settling back against the soft upholstery for the long drive across country. Her employer slid in beside her, lithe and lean and darkly masculine. As he switched on the ignition her eyes dwelt on his hand with its well-shaped, deeply indented fingernails, dark hair curling at his wrist where the requisite amount of starched cuff showed just below his sleeve. The strange intimacy of the moment struck through Ricki and she tightened her hold on the leather handbag which his friend the condesa had given her. There was no going back now, she thought, as the car rolled out of the shadows of the Calle de Torres into the sunshine of the main plaza. Her journey to Cazalet's farm in the valley had begun.

Spanish mornings are gold washed, free of the trying heat of the sun's zenith which sends people indoors to the shuttered coolness of their houses for the siesta, and soon the car was out in the country and the don had stepped up their speed. The station wagon was a hardy vehicle that took little heed of the potholes of Spanish roads, and because of the ease of its shock absorbers Ricki bounced quite comfortably as they sped along.

The don, a hint of a twinkle in his eyes, did the honors of a tour guide and whenever they passed places of interest he told her something about them. The camaraderie you could assume with an Englishman was not entirely possible with this autocratic Spaniard, but he had the Latin gift for description and Ricki suspected that he again thought of her as a child who needed entertaining on a long journey. She didn't mind. She rather liked the sound of his deep bass voice, and when the ruins of an old Castilian castle were outlined on a hill and she wanted to take a look at them, he stopped the car with a shrug of his shoulders and indulged her whim. He talked about the battles between the knights and the Moors, lounging against a broken battlement with a cheroot in his hand, the warm breeze ruffling his hair out of its usual smoothness. Ricki didn't have to close her eyes to imagine him in dark gleaming armor, mounted on a *destrier*, the face pieces of his helmet hiding all but the devilish gleam of his eyes. Arturo de Cazalet belonged to those times.

A sword of Spain, the icebrook's temper flashed into her mind.

They returned to the car and drove on for another hour or so, until the heat grew really trying and he stopped in the courtyard of a vine-covered *tasca* and said they would have lunch there. Ricki was thirsty, and she didn't have to tell him so; as soon as one of the waitresses came to their table he ordered a couple of iced *horchatas*. Ricki clasped her glass in both hands, reveling in the coolness.

"I hope you are going to be able to stand the heat of the south." The don frowned across at her, his glance taking in the red brown tendrils that clung to her temples and somehow intensified the paleness of her skin. "The Granja is much protected from the sun owing to its situation in the valley, but Andalusia is very hot country and now and again we are subjected to a sultry blow called the *solano*. The peasants say it is like the breath of a dragon and, the air at those times does seem full of a fire that plays on the emotions and shreds the temper."

"I'm mopping up all this warmth like a sponge," she assured him. "It's lovely after the chilliness of Ireland and England."

"But you are rather pale. I thought..." he gestured with a hint of male impatience toward the heat haze that lay over everything beyond their vine-sheltered table.

"Oh this?" She flicked a finger at her own cheek. "Don't take any notice of my lack of color, *señor*. I have what is called Irish skin. Very fashionable in the poke-bonnet-and-veil era, but a bit of a bind these days when a girl likes to get a nice nutty tan.''

''I see.'' He laughed and she widened her moss green eyes at the sound. So he *could* laugh, though it was a bit like a subterranean rumble, as though mirth had lain unused and undisturbed in him for a long time—a couple of years or longer! Ricki turned her eyes carefully away from him and took a look at the other people lunching here. Sun-darkened farmers mostly, smocked and breeched, long canes resting against the edges of their tables, their penetrating country eyes shaded by the brims of ancient felt hats. Some of them were eyeing her European looks and clothing with frank curiosity; she supposed they were comparing her grayhound lines with the more buxom contours of the Spanish girls who waited on the tables. She had heard that the more old-fashioned type of Spaniard liked his women well rounded.

She and her employer lingered here in the coolness over a lunch of cold, spiced *gaspacho*, then omelettes rolled around meat and vegetables, and finally fresh fruit salad, which was so artistically arranged and delectable here in Spain. Especially delicious were these little sugared grapes, Ricki thought, tucking into them with youthful appreciation.

''You are now ready for some coffee?'' the don inquired, having watched her enjoyment of the grapes with a hint of sardonic amusement.

''Yes, please!'' She nodded, tendrils of her tawny hair dancing at her temples. ''The food and the sun are making me sleepy, and I don't want to fall asleep in the car and miss our entrance into Andalusia.''

He ordered coffee, then regarded her with faintly quizzical eye. ''I am trying to remember what it felt like to be as young as yourself,'' he remarked at last, ''and on the threshold of a new experience.''

"I don't see much silver in your hair, Don Arturo," she scoffed, adding daringly, "Nor did your joints creak as you were climbing in and out of the car."

"One can be old in more than years," he rejoined, somewhat moodily. "even so, most Spaniards of the middle thirties are well married and the fathers of growing children."

"Well, what's stopping you from getting married?" The words were out before she could stop them and, too late, she put a hand to her lips, horrified by a remark which would have been accepted as a mere piece of backchat had she been in the company of a young houseman back home. Coffee was brought and she took hold of her glass in a fever of embarrassment. "Oh!" She put down the hot glass as quickly as she had picked it up and gave her fingers a shake.

"You are overimpulsive," drawled the don, "but having played with fire and burned your fingers, perhaps you will be more careful in the future."

The tingle in her fingertips spread all over her at that remark, and she resolved to keep a check on her tongue in future. He was too quick at cutting you down to size for forgetting he was the *patrono*.

They continued their journey about half an hour later and now he drove so swiftly that all passing scenery was turned to an uninteresting blur. Ricki sat staring out of the window, disliking the dark, withdrawn man at her side. She wished fiercely that she had never met him and agreed to work for him. It was obvious a woman had injured his pride, and now all other women must suffer for it. There was no doubt in Ricki's mind. He couldn't bear the thought of marriage because the beautiful Conquesta had chosen to love his brother instead of him. Well, the poor girl had not enjoyed the gaiety and *sal* of Leandro de Cazalet for so very long. . . it was as though a curse had been put upon the romance!

Shadows were lancing across the land when they passed under the towering Sierras. The lean brown hands on the wheel of the car no longer showed white lines of knuckles and their speed had slowed. In a while he said to her, "Welcome to Andalusia, Miss O'Neill."

Ricki gritted her teeth, uncertain whether to laugh or cry at such arrogant courtesy after hours of a silence so chilly that she had barely felt the heat. She wanted to retort that he didn't have to be polite. The hint had been taken that she was only the physio-attendant and she wouldn't step out of line again in a hurry.

"Are those mountains the Sierras?" she asked in a stiff voice, knowing full well they could be nothing else—dark jagged teeth that seemed to snap shut on her freedom as the car skimmed beneath them.

She gave a little shiver of apprehension, noticing here and there the strange shapes of cacti pointing gray green fingers in patches of desert; the palm trees were stubby and frondy, and there were many limestone rocks with a bare pallor.

"Soon the countryside will grow more pastoral." The don seemed to feel her disappointment and her silent criticism. "There!" He suddenly gestured to their left, where a hillside was covered with woolly sheep and brown goats whose neck bells clanged under their tufted chins as they gave sudden skittish leaps.

"The lad with them is a *serrano*, a hill shepherd who guards the flock during their summer pastorage," the don told her.

"The sheep are all colors!" she exclaimed.

"That is from the varying colors of the soil," he explained. "It dyes their wool."

Ricki glanced back out of the car window and saw as in a frame the spaciousness of the plains, the shepherd lad standing motionless as his flock milled about him, and the ice blue crests of the wild mountains turning pewter under the westering sun. Then the car stirred a cloud of obscuring dust and she sank back, knowing she had glimpsed something of the nature of the Spanish in that mixture of the pastoral and the untamed.

Now, indeed, were they entering a more fertile region and Ricki saw men and women in large straw hats busily at work in terraced fields. Herds of red ocher cows munched placidly at the clover, with here and there rice birds standing on their strong haunches like sculptures. Mules and donkeys wended past the car, small moving hillocks of wood, cork or vegetables, and Ricki saw closely her first Andalusians. Lithe, middle-sized men with sun-seamed faces and lively dark eyes. They wore the country smock and leggings and the shabby felts that were respectfully touched but not raised; these men of the soil were *caballeros* at heart who knew themselves equal to all men and subservient to none. Ricki liked the look of them; they had, she thought, something of a Gaelic toughness and charm about them. They would be quick to anger, but also quick to laugh, and there would be poetry in their songs and legends.

The car passed an old ruin of a watermill and all along the banks of the stream frogs could be heard croaking. It was an evening sound and shadows were deepening to a grape tinge when at last they came into the region where the Cazalet land was planted richly with oats, barley and rye; tobacco, maize and clover. Also there were the mulberry groves, and the olive trees! Ranks of them growing black against the rusty earth and looking bible-old. Strange gnarled little trees, yielding the life oil of this land of plains and valleys.

A village and a church were suddenly etched on a craggy hillside ahead of them, and when they drew near Ricki saw whitewashed houses suspended on the rim of a huge, widening valley of sheer rock with a dense bottomland of shrubs and trees. To live in one of those houses would be like living in midair she thought. You would feel like Miranda of the Balcony!

She grinned at her own whimsy in the gloom of the car and knew, with a quickening of her heartbeats, that they were nearing the end of their journey. The village fell away behind them and the headlights speared a path on the ravine ledge along which they were now driving. Ricki heard, in a while, the turmoil of rushing waters beneath them and she gave herself up to the strange almost fatalistic sensation of being whirled through the night to an uncertain destiny by the dark, grim-profiled man beside her.

"Soon now we will be at the Granja," he said. "You must be feeling tired."

She agreed that the long drive had tired her, chilled by a harshness in his voice which told her that her tiredness was of no real interest to him. She gazed out at the darkness and saw her face dimly reflected in the glass of the window. Her eyes were huge, like those of a child who needed her bed and someone comforting to tuck in the covers and press lips that cared to her temple. Oh, long gone were those days, childhood days. . . and then, like the touch of a ghost, it came to Ricki that it was on this precarious ravine road that Conquesta and her husband had been killed!

The don shifted gears and Ricki felt her stomach go over as the car began to travel downhill. He was unaware of her eyes upon him, but the pain and tension in him were reaching out to touch her and she gave a sudden uncontrollable little gasp.

"This is a bad road in the dark, but I am used to it," he said, curtly. "See, we now turn on to the track that leads to the Granja."

Ricki relaxed her grip on her bag, but the thuds of her heart were still shaking her. He turned briefly to look at her and the gleam from the dashboard showed his strong, almost savage cheekbones and the hollows beneath them. Lines were etched beside the extreme darkness of his eyes—never had eyes been so dark, without a ray of another color to catch and hold the light. "You have guessed that my brother and his wife were killed on that road back there, eh?" His nostrils flared at the edges with the emotion of the moment. "What you cannot know is that Leandro had decided to take his wife and his child for a drive in a car of mine. There was something amiss with the brakes, which I had noticed the day before, but he did not know this and I was calling at one of the other farms. Had I been at home. . . ." His expressive shrug finished the rest of the sentence.

"You blame yourself, in part, for the accident?" Ricki gasped.

"Can I do otherwise?" The car bumped over a rut and Ricki gritted her teeth. "I should have remembered that Leandro was in the habit of regarding my possessions as his own."

Bitter, significant words, Ricki thought, shaken by relief as the headlights shone suddenly on the high, outer walls of the Granja. They drove under an immense archway into the *plazuela*, a large patio of stone, with wrought-iron lanterns that showed, in a ghostly way, the shapes of the buildings inside the patio and the outline of the old Iberian farmhouse itself. The place looked at once fascinating and forbidding to the girl who had come to live and work there.

Dogs barked and a man came running out of a stone house at the side of the entrance way. He was pulling on a jacket which had big gilt buttons gleaming on it. "*Patrono*," Ricki heard him exclaim, "we were not expecting your arrival until the morning. Did my Benedito misunderstand your telegraph message?"

"I decided after all not to break our drive but to come straight home. How have things been, Marco?" The don had swung out of the car and was extending a helping hand to Ricki. She stepped out onto cobbles, and when his hand released hers she still felt its lingering strength. Marco was the *guardo jurado*, the sworn guard of an important family who wears a brown uniform, leather leggings and a broad-brimmed hat. With a curious eye on Ricki, he assured Don Arturo that *el niño* had been quite content during the absence of his uncle.

"Thank the good *Dios* for that." The don spoke rather dryly, then he took Ricki lightly under the elbow and drew her into the ray of light from one of the wall-bracketed lanterns. "This is Miss O'Neill," he told Marco, "and she will be in charge of the boy from now on."

"Welcome to the Granja, *señorita*." Marco's English was rough but understandable. Ricki had been told by her employer that during his father's lifetime he had spent a couple of years in England learning business methods, and Marco and his wife had gone with him to look after his apartment and cook for him.

"*Señor*, you are home already?" A big, swarthy woman hastened across from the guard's house, her starched apron making a rustling sound at each step, the lantern light on her gleaming black hair. Ricki was unsurprised when the woman ducked in a *reverencia*. Her entire appearance against this background called for a curtsy to the master with his look of lean, dark, inborn authority. This was another world, almost another century, Ricki realized. The feudal past was still very much a part of the lives of these people.

The woman was Marco's wife, Sophina, and she was full of talk as they crossed the patio and entered the Granja through an arched doorway. Ricki noticed that there were several stories to the farmhouse, each one with its own outside gallery reached by wrought-iron staircases. The eaves of the immense roof overhung the galleries, no doubt to provide shade during the sun-filled days.

Ricki felt lost and small in the great hall of the house, which had a vaulted ceiling networked by beams from which hung chandeliers of wrought brass. These were unlit, but in wall sconces there were lamps that smoked faintly and threw shadows. A great central table stood on massive carved legs, set around with high-backed chairs, in front of a carved cavern of a fireplace with side niches in which kitchen lads had crouched to turn the spits on which pig and calf had been roasted in the old days.

The hall was forbidding and yet fascinating to Ricki, with its floor of close-set cobbles and the tall reading desk on which stood a big leather-bound Bible in which were recorded, no doubt, the births, marriages and deaths of the long line of Cazalets.

So absorbed was Ricki in looking around the hall that she gave quite a jump when Don Arturo spoke to her. "Sophina will show you to your room, Miss O'Neill," he said, a faint smile in his eyes at the way she was staring at crossed pikes and poignards on the stone walls. "A meal will be sent up to you, and you can eat it in bed. I am sure you must be almost asleep on your feet— you must forgive me for subjecting you to such a long and tiring drive."

"I quite understand that you were anxious to get home to your nephew, *señor*, and supper in bed sounds super," she added smilingly.

"Super?" He raised an inquiring eyebrow.

"Inviting—just the thing," she explained. "Haven't you a word like that in Spanish?"

"I suppose we might say *muy bien*, which means very nice." He spoke with a seriousness that faintly amused

her, then as they crossed to the stairs she glanced down
and saw beneath their feet, picked out in the cobbles,
the same *escudo* which was carved on his signet ring.
"Oh, look!" she exclaimed, as though the pair of them
were tourists and she was pointing out something he had
never seen.

"You are interested in such ancient things?" he
asked. "That has been in my family for many years.
You see, it is a hawk on a field of iris, and the small
cygne represents the women who have married the
Cazalet hawks. This family stems way back to a Marius
Cazalet, a sea rover from the shores of England who
finally grew tired of roving and settled here in Andalusia
to be an olive grower—much in the same way as other
colonials settled here to found large sherry *bodegas*."

"How fascinating," Ricki breathed. She gazed up at
him in awe, startled deep inside herself to learn that an
Englishman had founded this house of hawks. She saw
something flicker in the don's eyes, a smile perhaps, and
she said shyly, "It must be an immense responsibility,
Don Arturo, to be the head of a family which has gone
on and on for hundreds of years. Why, you're living a
link with the past!"

"And very often I feel the weight of it all." He spoke
in a dry tone of voice. "Now I will wish you *buena
noche*, Miss O'Neill. I hope you sleep well and find
yourself undisturbed by the countryside quiet. The
other physio-attendants were city dwellers who found
our quiet and the low hooting of the owls very hard to
get used to."

The other physios were men, weren't they?" she said.

"That is so." The don's eyes grew thoughtful as he
regarded her upraised face with its elfin contours. "This
is the first time I have put Jaime in the care of a female
physiotherapist and no doubt he will be most surprised
at the innovation."

"I hope his surprise will be a pleasant one." Ricki crossed her fingers, then with a murmur of good night she went upstairs with Sophina. The *guardesa* was never lost for conversation and she was full of the time she and her husband had spent in England with the don. "The English so amused me at times," she chuckled. "They are so shy. Not at all like us Spanish."

"I think some of you are very reserved," Ricki remarked, thinking of her employer.

"Ah, but we do not hide behind newspapers when we travel on a bus or a train—we talk together, *señorita*. We are interested in what goes on in each other's lives." Sophina cast a side look over Ricki's slim figure. "You will be able to manage the *niño*?" she asked dubiously. "There is not much of you."

"I am trained to handle the handicapped," Ricki said stiffly, not quite sure that she liked this woman with her gypsy looks. Her name alone painted a picture of caravans and brown feet stamping out a pagan rhythm.

The rooms of the *estancia* were all on different levels, steps going up and then down, so that Ricki felt hopelessly lost when Sophina at last opened a door and told her that here she would sleep. "A servant will fetch you up a *brasero*," she said. "It grows cold in the night—the Sierras are crowned with ice, you know—and now I will show you the *salon de aguas* and perhaps you would like to take a peep at the *niño*?"

"May I?" Ricki was full of curiosity about the boy she was to take care of. "I don't want to wake him up."

"He sleeps deeply, for he has been given a sedative— the poor little one became restless when he learned that the *patrono* was returning." Sophina led Ricki farther along the corridor.

"Excited, I expect," Ricki smiled. "Don Arturo must be like a father to the boy."

"*Señorita*," Sophina looked at her with eyes which

seemed to visualize grave things in a witchball, "I wish I could tell you this was so, but Jaimito does not like his uncle. They are not *simpatico*, which is much of a pity." She threw open a door as she spoke and Ricki took in vaguely an old-fashioned bathroom whose tub was surrounded by mulberry and blue tiles....

The Don and his young nephew were not in sympathy—the boy disliked the man who blamed himself in part for that tragic crash. He should have remembered, he had said, that Leandro had never been able to resist *his* possessions—*whether they were cars or girls,* Ricki added to herself.

"This is where the *niño* sleeps." Sophina beckoned Ricki into a room that was lit softly by a small pewter lamp on the bedside table. "He has dreams, bad ones, and it would not be good for him to awake in the darkness." Sophina's shadow was huge on the white wall as she stood at the bedside of the sleeping child. "He has a fine young face, eh? From his parents he gets those good looks."

Jaime de Cazalet was certainly a good-looking child, with fine-boned features and brows that were like dark wings above his closed eyes. His dark hair was tousled from his restless tossing about and showed a small edition of the peak that saved his uncle's hairline from severity. But the face was not that of a fit child. Shadows lurked at the corners of the pale little mouth and his fingers were clenched upon the sheet...as though in sleep he clung to a hand. His mother's? As he lived again the moment when the brakes of his uncle's car had failed to function and the vehicle hurtled to disaster down that ravine road!

"Hasn't he a soft toy of some sort which he could have in bed with him?" Ricki whispered.

"He is too old for such toy, *señorita*." Sophina

looked scornful. "This is a child with already the mind of an adult."

"But look how he clenches the covers." Ricki was distressed by this sign of mental tension in the child. "A cuddly toy might help him to sleep with more relaxation."

"I noticed when in England that the children had these toys of wool which they took into their beds at night," Sophina shrugged, tolerantly, but without real understanding. "It is a custom of you people, but Spanish children do not care for such things."

Ricki opened her mouth to retort that they might if they were given them, then she swallowed her words. She didn't wish to antagonize Sophina, and once she had sole charge of Jaime she could provide him with a cuddly toy and leave him to accept or reject the comfort of it at night.

As they left his room, she thought it a pity that Don Arturo had failed to win his nephew's trust and affection.

"Were Jaime's parents happy together?" She just had to ask.

"*Ay Dios mio*, happiness is a big word with many shades of meaning," Sophina peered hard at her. "You have not yet loved a man, eh?"

Ricki shook her head and felt herself flushing.

"Into the love pot goes as much bitter as sweet, this you will learn when you take a man." Sophina paused midway between a flickering wall lamp and a niche in which hung a portrait of a man in a sombre purple doublet and starched ruff. The eyes were almost alive— dark Cazalet eyes, unrelieved by a ray of light.

"Doña Conquesta and her husband took their happiness and it stopped the heart of the old *patrono* and turned to stone the heart of his older son—there was a curse on such happiness from the very beginning!"

With her second and small finger Sophina made the sign of the devil's horns, then she touched wood and muttered something in Spanish. "Doña Conquesta was to have married Don Arturo. It was arranged when she was sixteen and he twenty-one. The old *patrono* and the father of Doña Conquesta wished very much for an alliance between their two houses and it was, of course, for the eldest son to provide this. The courtship lasted five years. We call it eating the iron, which means on the one hand that a young man is barred from his girl by the grille of her window, and also that he must content himself in patience—which often takes a will of iron—until the time comes for their marriage." Sophina paused, her voice sinking down.

"Only a few weeks before the wedding was to take place, Doña Conquesta ran off with Don Arturo's own brother, leaving a note to say they were going to be married. Leandro was very handsome, with honey on his tongue, and the shock of the elopement struck down the old *patrono*. The honor of Spanish houses is not lightly used and though Don Arturo could have been harsh toward that reckless pair, he forgave them when it became known that Conquesta was to have a child. *Madre mia*, that was much for him to bear! But she was one of those who could not help the devils she roused in the hearts of men. So it is in Spain sometimes, *señorita*." Sophina spread her hands. "Here the emotions are closer to the surface."

"It's a tragic story all around," Ricki murmured. "I feel sorry for Don Arturo, but surely he will marry some day? He's still a young man...."

"Many men lose their trust in women, but among them there are those who lose all desire to love again. Don Arturo does not have to marry in order to provide an heir for the property. There is Jaime. It is true the boy cannot walk, but you have come to help remedy that, eh?'' Sophina beamed and left Ricki at the door at her bedroom. ''Supper will be sent up to you, Miss Oneeill. *Buena noche.*''

''Good night, Sophina. Thank you for taking me to see the boy.''

Ricki entered her room and quietly closed the door behind her. The *brasero* had been brought and placed on the hearth, and she stood with the warmth of it at her feet as she took stock of her surroundings. There was a big mahogany bedstead with gilded inlay and carvings of imps, satyrs and fauns running up its posts, a cavernous wardrobe with fretwork around the top of it, several chairs cushioned with old gold brocade to match the curtains, and a dressing table with a nest of drawers, a mirror shaped like a shield and a cheval set of old cream lace on which stood a pair of china bowls painted with flamenco dancers, matching candlesticks and a round brass box on little feet which could be used for trinkets or hairpins.

It was a large room, lamplit, with pools of shadow between the dark-as-beer furniture. The curtains moved and though she guessed a window was open behind them, that slight movement held her gaze and quickened her heart. This farm in the valley was a house of memories. Here a boy and a man were caught in a dark web which ghosts had spun.

One broken dream is not the end of dreaming, stole into her mind. *Still build your castles though your castles fall.*

A brass jug of hot water had been placed on the washstand, and in a china dish there was a fresh bar of olive-oil soap. Ricki washed, then she unlocked her suitcase, took out her pajamas and slipped into them. She put her underwear in a drawer and hung her few dresses and skirts in the cavernous wardrobe—where they looked as forlorn as she in this immense bedroom.

She was in bed when there was a tap on the door and a slim, middle-aged man carried in a tray on which stood her supper. He approached the bed, his eyes dark and inscrutable, and arranged the legged tray over her lap.

"*Gracias*," she said shyly.

He inclined his head, said good night in Spanish and doubtless took away with him the impression that the *patrono* was *loco* to bring such a child of a woman here to take care of the *niño*. Ricki gave a wry grin as she tucked into a tasty rabbit stew redolent of herbs. She was fully aware that she looked about sixteen in her pierrot pajamas, but her look of youth might prove an advantage in dealing with Jaime. He would not look upon her as an adult and that might give him the confidence to make her a friend.

Ricki ate her supper slowly, enjoying every mouthful of the stew, then she wiped her lips on the napkin and placed the tray on the bed table. That had been good, like the country food she had liked as a child, when she and her parents had lived in Ireland.

She turned out the lamp and slid down under crisp sheets that smelled of rosemary. *Rosemary for remembrance*. She remembered how in Don Arturo's car she had flared into dislike of the man; how compassion for his nephew Jaime had taken the place of resentment in her heart.

She was longing to begin her new job, and was resolving as her eyes drooped and closed to do all she could to take away the shadows from that small face. Owls hooted down in the valley as Ricki drifted off to sleep.

It must have been about an hour later when she suddenly awoke, feeling a strange coldness feathering her cheek and her left arm that was outside the covers. She sat up, staring into the darkness that was loud with the ticking of the clock and the beating of her heart. She fumbled with the matches in a box on the bed table and lit the lamp, the dark surfaces of the furniture picking up glimmers, though the shadows lurking in the dim recesses of the room were not driven away.

What was it that had touched her subconscious and roused her? Her glance stole round the room and fixed on the long folds of brocade that concealed the windows. The folds billowed, then flattened, and she told herself bracingly that it was only the night air moving the curtains into that long body-shape....

All the same, someone could have come up from the patio! There was a stairway and the gallery out there.... It was no good, she wouldn't rest until she had satisfied herself there was no one out there. She slid out of bed and forced herself to go across and look behind those folds of old gold brocade. There was a pair of long carved shutters behind them, reaching to the floor and opening on to the gallery—and one of them was standing ajar!

Ricki stood there, a hand clenching the curtain, her skin goosey from the ice-tinged air that stole through the opening. Then telling herself not to be an overimaginative idiot, she quickly closed the shutters and dived back into bed. But now she was reluctant to put out the lamp, though she knew full well that the house was guarded against intruders—and there was no such thing as a ghost. "Oh!" She shied back as a gray cat leaped on her bed, its fur bristling and its emerald eyes fixed on her startled face. "Oh, you gray devil!" she gasped. "It was you all the time!"

The cat made a noise in its throat and began to knead her quilt with its paws, and Ricki had to laugh, realizing he was an intruder from the patio outbuildings who had found her shutters open and wandered in...like a veritable gray ghost. "I'm sorry, fluff," Ricki got out of bed again and lifted the animal off her quilt, "but I'm afraid I don't fancy what might be hiding in that long fur of yours." She carried him to the door and let him out into the corridor. He turned as if to dart back in again, but she shooed him off and watched him wander away into the shadows.

A wall lamp still burned low in the corridor opposite her room, where Jaime's nursery suite was situated, and Ricki stood in her doorway thinking of the things Sophina had said about the child's mother. Too beautiful for her own good, the kind who had roused devils in the hearts of men...now she and her husband were dead, and her young son was an invalid...the threefold tragedy having occurred in the car of the man she should have married!

Then, quite distinctly, Ricki heard footsteps. Her head turned quickly and when she saw who was rounding the corridor bend to her left, the inevitable thought flashed through her mind, *Think of the devil and he'll appear!*

She withdrew hastily into her room, hoping Don Arturo had not spotted her, but when he reached her door she heard him pause, then he deliberately pushed open the door, forcing her to retreat backward from him. "You are finding difficulty in getting to sleep, Miss O'Neill?" he inquired.

"A—a cat got into my room," she faltered. "I've just let him out."

"A cat?" He arched a black eyebrow, his glance ran round her room and came back to her pajama-clad figure. "You are nervous of them?"

"I don't much care for them on my bed," she rejoined, knowing full well that if she looked scared at this moment, the gray Persian was not the culprit. It was that she hadn't known, until a couple of hours ago, that she was in the house of a man who had every cause to feel bitter towards women.

His eyes flicked her face, then he shot his cuff and

glanced at his wristwatch. "You had better return to your bed," he said. "It is now past midnight."

"The witching hour." She gave a nervous laugh. "Cats, witches—your house has an odd effect on the imagination, *señor*."

"That may well be, but do not let your imagination run away with you." He inclined his dark head and withdrew into the corridor. "Once again, *buena noche, señorita*."

"*Buena noche, señor*." She closed her door and stood with her back to it for many seconds. Her heart was hammering. Had that remark of his held the tinge of warning?

CHAPTER THREE

RICKI AWOKE to the sound of her bedroom door closing. She turned a drowsy head and saw that last night's supper tray had been replaced by a glass in an attractive holder with a handle to it. She sat up and reached for the glass, which held hot chocolate flavored with cinnamon and topped by a swirl of cream. Ricki quite liked the bittersweetness of Spanish chocolate, but she much preferred to start her day with a cup of tea.

"This is your morning drink, my girl," she told herself, gazing round the big room from which last night's phantoms had been chased by the morning sunlight. She could hear farmyard noises down in the patio and as soon as she finished her chocolate she shrugged into her dressing gown and stepped into the velvet *torero* shoes she had bought to wear as slippers. She crossed to a window and stared out at the lacy ironwork in which it was caged. Vines and tendrils clambered along the iron with creamy bells among the greenery, but still she had an odd sensation of being imprisoned—held captive by Don Arturo de Cazalet!

It was an absurdity she could smile at in the light of day, and she opened the carved shutters onto the gallery and watched the men and boys bustling about down in the patio, harnessing sturdy horses to farm carts, shooing the hens, slapping the haunches of cows wending out to pasture, and making altogether a colorful, rustic picture in their Andalusian work clothes.

Back in her room after a bath, for which the water

had been lovely and hot this morning, Ricki put on an apricot-colored blouse and a checkered skirt. She was wondering what to do about breakfast when there was a brisk tap on the door and Sophina came in with a tray on which there were fresh hot bread from the *panaderia*, two boiled eggs for the *señorita* from the black Spanish hens and honey from their own beehives.

"What lovely brown eggs," Ricki smiled, sitting down at the small table by one of the windows. "You are making a fuss of me."

"It is at the orders of the *patrono* that we make the *señorita* feel at home." Sophina poured out Ricki's coffee and set down the pot. "Now I go to see to the *niño*."

"Does he know I'm here?" Ricki sugared her coffee, not at all keen on the don giving orders that she be made to feel at home. She was one of the hired help and wasn't expecting special treatment.

"Jaimito knows he has a new attendant, but when the *patrono* telegraphed he said not to tell his nephew that he was bringing an English miss to the *estancia*. He wished for Jaime to have a surprise." Sophina bustled to the door, where she turned to survey Ricki with a faint maliciousness in her gypsy eyes. "Me, I think he will take you for another child like himself. He will suppose you are here to play with him rather than to be his attendant."

"Perhaps that's what he needs," Ricki gave a brown egg a smart tap with a spoon, "someone to play with."

"We will see." Sophina seemed almost to be taunting her.

"Everyone else seems to have failed with him, from what I can gather," Ricki said, but when she saw the jetty narrowing of the *guardesa*'s eyes, she realized that her retort had been rather unwise. You didn't say a thing like that to a Spanish matron with a brood of sons, not unless you were out to make an enemy of her! Ricki could have bitten her reckless tongue.

"I will awake the *niño* and serve him his breakfast—I am at least capable of doing that!" There was a sharp rustle of starched apron as Sophina withdrew from the room and closed the door.

Ricki sat frowning a moment at the coffee pot, then with a shrug she continued with her breakfast. The sun was bright and promising, and it wasn't in her nature to remain pessimistic for long. But before going along to Jaime's room she touched for luck the charm on a chain which her father had given her the day they had crossed the Irish Channel to England and she left behind her the land she had loved from infancy and the people she had known and was used to.

"It's a traveler's charm," her father said, when he had fastened it around her neck. "Life's a long journey, you're going to find, and every now and again we come to crossroads where we have to take one road or the other. There's nothing and no one to tell us which turn we should take, and it's good luck or bad that beguiles us down one or the other. We're true Gaels, you and I, Ricki. We'll always plunge without taking heed of the consequences, so I'm giving you the charm to make sure you'll always have a bit of luck about you. It'll give you heart when you're needing it."

The charm was a silver shamrock and Ricki wore it day and night. She had a habit of touching it for luck, true Gael indeed that she was despite her mother's English blood. And it seemed right now to bring her father a little closer—what would he say, dear Tynan, when he read her letter and learned that she was working in Spain, employed as physio-attendant to the nephew of an Andalusian landowner?

She paused outside Jaime's room, took a deep breath and opened the door and walked in. . . .

"Glory be!" she exclaimed. There was half a melon in a puddle of chocolate on the rug beside the bed, also several iced sweet rolls and a spoon. The tray and a glass in a holder had been picked up and placed on the bedside table. At the other side of the boy's bed stood Don Arturo, his eyes snapping darkly in a face that might have been carved from tawny stone. "Good morning, Miss O'Neill." He gestured curtly at the mess on the floor. "I hoped Jaime would be in a good mood to greet you, but as you can see he has deposited his breakfast all over the floor and he now refuses to be washed and dressed."

There wasn't any fear or defiance in the childish eyes gazing at Ricki—they were empty, uninterested. Then he turned away, his profile an olive carving against the white pillow. He neither listened to the angry man nor cared much, that was evident, for his "surprise" in the form of Ricki.

The don bent over his nephew and Ricki saw a nerve twitching beside the firm mouth as he spoke to the boy. "Come now," he said, "it is not *cortesia* to behave in this way toward your new attendant. Miss O'Neill will think you a sulky baby instead of the *señorito* of a Spanish house. *Chico*, I will now sit you up and you will say *buenos dias* to the *señorita*. Come—*aprisa*!"

The lean hands were about to take hold of the child when Ricki caught at the don's sleeve. "It might be best if you left me alone with Jaime," she suggested tentatively. "We will make friends in our own way."

Don Arturo straightened up, then he turned to face her, his brows drawn together in a frown. "You think it is my presence which causes him to behave in this way?" he asked.

She bit her lip and had difficulty in sustaining his dark gaze. A twist of a smile distorted the don's lips as he took in her look of discomfiture. "You are quite right, Miss O'Neill, in your assumption that I am unwanted in this room. Very well, I will leave it. I am sure *you* will manage to make friends with Jaime."

He turned on his heel and walked to the door, where he treated her to a faintly sardonic bow before closing it behind him. Ricki drew a sigh, then she sat down on the bed beside the small, rigid figure of her patient. "Well, I must say I'm a bit disappointed in my reception, Jaime," she said. "Don't you care to have a girl here to talk to? I bet I know far more stories than all your male nurses." She gently touched his shoulder. "Do you like stories?"

He gave a little quiver at her touch, but she knew it was not one of active recoil and she carefully turned him to face her. "My name is Ricki," she smiled. "How about having a go at saying it?"

But the child merely batted his long eyelashes and kept his mouth tightly shut. Ricki didn't press him to speak but got to her feet and walked to a shelved recess which held a number of books. She inspected their titles and noticed with interest that quite a few of them were in English—*Tales of the Crusades, The Amber Witch, House of Asgard, Conquest of Peru*. Books in the large print such as children prefer and could best follow. She took down a volume of *Don Quixote* and was delighted to find that it was illustrated by Doré—a scuffled, much handled copy of the adventures of gaunt, romantic Don Quixote and his rotund squire, Sancho Panza. There was an illustration of the quixotic knight tilting at the windmills and she broke into a laugh.

"Have you read this story, Jaime?" She returned to his bedside and showed him the book.

He scowled a little and shook his head.

"I bet you can read, a big boy like you," she said. "But as this copy is in English I daresay you'd have a bit of bother with the words. I shall have to read it to you, it's so comical in parts."

"It is a book of my uncle's," he muttered. "They are the books he had when he was a boy."

"Oh, don't tell me that's why you don't read them? He enjoyed them and now he wants you to do the same," she spoke in a tone much lighter than her thoughts. The antagonism which Jaime felt toward his uncle was tinged with something more serious than a childish dislike, and it was plain that she was going to have to deal with more than the physical hurts of this handsome, moody child. She felt almost unnerved for a moment, then she took a grip on herself.

"I've a theory about books," she said. "I always think them extra enjoyable when they've been handled and enjoyed by somebody else. A brand-new book seems so stiff and starchy, so that all the time you're worrying about creasing its pages and getting cookie crumbs in its seams."

Jaime stared at her, solemn as a small owl, then the corners of his mouth slowly, grudgingly relaxed. "You say funny things," he remarked.

"I'm a funny person," she admitted obligingly.

"And your hair is like curled-up leaves when they fall from the trees," he added.

"And there was I thinkin' the Spanish were all very gallant," she said, imitating her father's brogue. "Hair like leaves, you say, and no doubt a face like a lemon."

Jaime's face crinkled and then, as though not for a long time had his throat been exercised in this way, he laughed. "You are, I think, a g-nome," he said. "They live in the woods and cast spells."

"A g-nome, eh?" She smiled at the way he pronounced it. "Well, as they say in Ireland, the best friendships start with a blow on the nose. Now how about coming to my room for a fresh breakfast while I have this mess on the rug cleared up?"

"I—cannot walk, *señorita*." His face grew moody again.

"We'll take a taxi," she said, putting on a smile as

she brought his wheelchair to the side of the bed and expertly helped him into it. He glanced up at her with wide, intrigued eyes, as though never before had anyone thought to play such games with him.

"What is a taxee?" he asked.

"It's a shiny black coach that takes you for spins all over the place. To balls and banquets and ballets...." And so, talking the nonsense that had such a purpose behind it, Ricki wheeled him to her room, where she pressed the service bell and had a manservant bring her charge a boiled egg, bread and butter and some fruit. "There was an *accidente*," she attempted to explain, when the man brought the tray. "Jaimito jogged his elbow and upset his other tray."

But the manservant, Alvarez, looked mystified until the grinning boy told him in Spanish what he had done with his breakfast.

"By the pigs of St. Antony!" The usual dignified Alvarez was waving his hands about as he went out of the room. "*Qué demonio!*"

"He calls me a demon," Jaime informed Ricki.

"I can't say I blame him, my lad. Don't you know that there are thousands of children who never know what it is to have rolls and chocolate?" She shook open the linen napkin that had been brought with his tray, then as she tucked it into the front of his dressing gown she noticed a rather strange object hanging on a cord about his neck. "What's this, Jaime?" she asked, fingering it.

"My amulet to drive away sickness," he told her. "It has been blessed by a gypsy *bruja* who lives in a cave in the hills."

"There are no such things as witches—who gave you this?" She was superstitious herself, but there were limits!

"Sophina. Sh—she said it would help to make me

walk.'' He watched with his enormous dark eyes as Ricki set about buttering bread and slicing it into slim fingers. "There are *brujas*, Rickee. They fly among the clouds when there are storms. I—I do not care much for storms.''

"Storms bring the rain, and rain means good crops. Why don't you dip your 'soldiers' in your egg, Jaime? I always do when no one's watching me.''

"It is good like this,'' he nodded as he sampled her suggestion. "It is the Engleesh way?''

"Yes, the English way,'' Ricki agreed absently. She was thinking about the pagan charm Sophina had hung about the boy's neck. His recovery was not dependent upon a miracle or the black powers of magic, but if Jaime was being encouraged to believe it was, then he wouldn't work physically or mentally to help himself get out of the wheelchair onto his own two feet. She wouldn't go so far as to remove the charm, but he would have to be won away from the idea that the magic of a witch was going to help him get better. Maybe she could dream up some magic of her own connected with his treatments—the hidden healing eye of the infrared lamp, for instance, might be turned to good account.

"These are warriors storming a castle,'' he was muttering away to himself, "now they raze it to the ground, so!'' He whacked at the empty eggshell with his spoon until it was a mess of fragments. "*Olé*, the House of Cazalet is no more!''

Ricki went strangely cold when this child said that, and her fingers were clumsy as she peeled him an orange and separated it into segments. "Here are the spoils of war,'' she said. "They must be made short work of . . . and by the way, shouldn't a Cazalet knight be knocking down the castles of his—enemies?''

Jaime chewed his orange and looked at her with an unchildlike expression in his dark eyes. "It was the

señor tio's castle I was knocking down," he said. "I do
not care for him, or this place."

"Jaime!" She was profoundly shocked by the almost
calm way he said it, as though a reason dictated his dislike rather than a childish prejudice. "That's a very rude
and ungrateful thing to say. Your uncle thinks a lot of
you—you're all he has, you know—and you should try
to be friends with him. Why won't you try? What silly
thing do you think you have against him?"

"I just do not like him," the child retorted, "and
when I can walk I am going to leave this place and be a
vaquero like my father was."

"You father was not a *vaquero*," she protested. "He
was a gentleman like your uncle—a *caballero*."

"My father was a rider with the bulls at the ranch of
my grandfather," the boy said, his eyes flashing and his
resemblance to his hated uncle at its most acute. "I
should live there, also, but Don Arturo keeps me here
because he knows I *hate* it here!"

"I—don't think that's quite true, Jaime," Ricki said,
distressed by the hornets' nest she had poked and disturbed with her remark about knights, castles and
enemies. *The tongue of a Gael can cast spells and stir
cauldrons,* her father often said. *Beware of yours, my
girl!*

"Does your grandfather live far from the *estancia*?"
she asked, for the hornets were out now, and she had to
know everything if she was going to be of any real help
to this small troubled soul with the eyes too big for his
face.

It turned out that the boy's grandfather had a ranch
of fighting bulls on land above the valley. His *devisa*
was famous, Ricki was proudly informed, and his *vaqueros* the very toughest. She encouraged this conversation all through the next hour, while she put her young
patient through a series of light exercises in order to test

his general musculature. The accident had caused severe damage to several discs in his spine and these, she noticed quickly, had undergone bone-grafting operations. The spine was weakened and he might never be the *vaquero* he longed to be, but there certainly seemed no real physical reason why he shouldn't walk again. He *would* walk again, Ricki resolved, surprising him with a light kiss on his olive-skinned shoulder.

"You kissed me!" His eyes grew larger than ever.

"Do you mind?" she laughed, getting him into his small striped shirt and short trousers. "Don't tell me you're one of those cold chaps who doesn't care to be kissed."

"It is all right," he said thoughtfully. "Quite pleasant."

Her heart gave a little kick when she stole a look at his face, for it looked suddenly pinched and she knew he was remembering his mother's kisses.

"Well, my *vaquero*," she said, "I'm going downstairs to have a look round. Are you coming with me? We'll get Alvarez to carry your ch—mount to the foot of the stairs."

"No, I stay here!" He shook an emphatic head and began to beat his hands like a troubled adult on the arms of his chair, not fooled, coaxed or ready to fall in with the idea that it was his mount. He began to speak rapidly in Spanish, his words finally merging into English. "I will stay up here and draw pictures, Rickee. I like it better up here."

Because up here, she knew, he wouldn't be so likely to run into his uncle. She couldn't suppress a sigh, wondering again what on earth she had let herself in for by coming to this house of past regrets and present hates. "Do you want to do your drawing here in my room, up at that little table by the window?" she asked.

"That would be most nice, Rickee." He gave her arm

a stroke as she wheeled him to the table, and glanced up sideways into her eyes. "I thought only cats had green eyes," he said.

"Ooh, but I am a cat," she whispered. "A Manx cat without a tail." She heard him laughing as she left him by her window and went to his nursery suite to get his drawing book and his pencils. She flipped through the book on her way back and saw some of those drawings his uncle had told her about. Grim, unchildlike, the results of a mind that couldn't forget.

"How about drawing something like this, Jaime?" She sat down at the table beside him and sketched for several minutes, the result being a somewhat erratic horned sheep clambering up some rocks.

"He is a demon sheep," Jaime chuckled. "You draw very funny things, Rickee."

"I thought we'd agreed that I'm a bit of a funny one." Ricki gave his chin a tweak. "Draw some animals and *vaqueros* for me, eh?"

"Perhaps I had better," he agreed. "Then you will know a *vaquero* when you see one—and also a sheep," he added, giggling to himself.

Good, she thought. *Learn to laugh, my lamb.*

"Ah, while I think of it!" She hurried to her handbag on the dressing table and opened it. "I bought you some candies in Toledo and I almost forgot all about them."

"When Sophina forgets, she says she has a head with more holes in it than a sieve," Jaime said, his eyes fixed on the paper bags Ricki was taking out of her handbag. "What kind of candies?"

"Here you are, pink and white sugar pigs and hard candies like gooseberries." She gave them to him. "Now don't go swallowing one of those. You suck them."

"You can have one of those," he pointed to the hard candies, and bit the curly tail off a sugar pig. "These are nice, and funny. *Mil gracias, mi tata.*"

"Which means?" She cocked a green eye at him, one cheek bulging with a hard gooseberry.

"My nurse." He bent quickly, shyly over his sketch-book, and Ricki's throat was hurting as she said goodbye for now and went off on an exploration of the immense and rambling patio downstairs. It extended around the back of the farmhouse, and what she intended to look for was an attractive, secluded nook where Jaime could do some basking in the sunshine. It wasn't good for him to spend so much time indoors, and the mornings with him were exclusively hers, a couple of hours after his siesta being given over to lessons he took with a Señor Andres.

An artist, the don had told her, who was earning his living as tutor to various children of local landowners. He was of Andalusia...and he had been, the don had added, a friend of Jaime's father.

Ricki was very curious about this friend of Leandro's and inclined to wonder if it was he who was insidiously turning Jaime against his uncle.

Down in the patio there was a strong smell of hay from the stables and the grunt, stamp and crow of farm animals. Ricki noticed with interest the wall niche that held a time-weathered statue of the Madonna, and the stone slot nearby, where the adventurous sons of this house had sharpened their swords in the days when cloaked lookouts had walked the battlements of the old watchtower, still standing guard over the various buildings of the Granja.

There was, despite its tinge of tragedy, a certain enchantment about this farm in the valley. A variety of birds nested in the jutting eaves of the outhouses, while pigeons strutted and cooed on the rim of the stone drinking trough near the big cowsheds. Camphors, jacarandas and flowering vines softened the rather severe structure of the Granja, while the colonnade of archways that led into the house gave it a cloistered, almost Moorish appearance.

Ricki couldn't resist taking a look inside the watchtower, which was now used as a storehouse for sacks of grain and seed, blocks of fodder and heaps of dried heather for fuel. A large dog raised his head from his paws when Ricki poked her head around the door, and he looked so fierce and wolfish that she had to force herself to stand still when he came across to investigate her. "Hullo, boy," she said, and to her relief he cocked his ears, wagged his tail and was, after all, a veritable sheep in wolfskin.

He was trotting beside her when she came upon a low, arching door set in a rough stone wall. The latch was stiff, unused, then the door gave with a groan to her push and she was gazing into a sort of orchard with a very neglected air. The fruit trees which had once borne oranges, medlars and lemons had gone to seed, the paths among them were overgrown with weeds and shrubs, and lichen had set like rust in the carvings of stone seats and pergolas.

"Well, what have we here, Sancho?" Ricki queried of her companion, then compelled by curiosity she walked into the orchard, forgetting to close the door behind her. She felt at once like the girl who had ventured into the hidden garden of the dragon everyone feared—only to find he had a gentle heart, after all. She plucked a sprig of wild vervain—the magical plant—and came at last through a tangle of thickets to a small, tiled pool at the bottom of the garden.

The neglected pool of a nymph, surely, with clusters of snails just showing their shells under about a foot of leaf-spattered water and lilies floating idly on heart-shaped leaves.

The pool was large enough to swim in—yet it had been allowed to get into this state! It was bordered by stone flags that would catch quite a bit of sunshine if the trees were cut back—what was *that* among the trees? Glimpsing a roof, Ricki pushed through some more tangled shrubs and discovered a small garden house, a delightful place, covered from its roof to its foundations by large seashells which had been cemented together and arranged into patterns. There was an arched doorway, its edges decorated with hundreds of smaller shells, and a dimness beyond the arch that reminded Ricki of a sea cave. She was rather doubtful about venturing inside, then Sancho, as she had christened the dog, took the initiative and she cautiously followed him.

There was a wrought-iron table inside the little house of shells, chairs to match and a couple of windows that let in very little light because of the trees that had encroached upon the place. A bracketed shelf held several earthenware planters, but the plants had long since withered from lack of water. The cushions on the chairs had run to mildew, and the rush matting was probably crawling with ants and beetles.

Ricki withdrew into the open, away from faint scamperings and stirrings of bat wings, feeling as though she had disturbed a couple of ghosts as well.

She was standing there, looking at the house of shells and wondering why, along with the pool, it had been abandoned to decay, when the sudden prick of the dog's ears warned her that someone was coming. She tensed, her mind still on the mystery of the place, then she swung round and saw Don Arturo striding toward her.

His black polo sweater and the black line of his brows, she noticed, added to his look of Dantesque fury. She gave a shiver as he came up and towered over her. . . or seemed to at the moment.

"What are you doing in here?" he demanded. "Your place is with my nephew—you are employed to take care of him, not to wander these premises like a *turista*!"

"I'm well aware of that, Don Arturo." She flushed to her ear tips at being caught here and reprimanded like a—a ninny of a nursemaid. His temper sparked her own and she added, with spirit, "You need not worry that I shall neglect the duties you're paying for, *señor*, but as it happens I'm looking for a quiet spot where Jaime can soak up some sunshine and also do light exercises. He doesn't get out of his room enough to suit him or me, and you did say I could set up a regime you would not interfere with."

"That is perfectly correct," he allowed, the fire still shimmering in the black flint of his eyes. "I agree that the child should have more fresh air and sunshine, but that does not answer my question. Why are you roaming about in here? This is not a place for a child."

"The door was not locked," she replied, feeling the slow, hard thumps of her heart and the burning in her cheeks because he made her feel such an intruder. "I'm sorry if I'm trespassing, but if this is a sort of Bluebeard's garden, then you had better keep the door bolted."

"You are very impertinent." His nostrils were drawn in tautly, then he rammed his hands into his pockets as though he didn't trust himself and the use to which he might put them. "You possess the audacity of your race, Miss O'Neill, and on that count I suppose I must make allowances for finding you here. There is little to interest you, as you can see. The place is a ruin and I plan to have the door bricked in."

"But there's a swimming pool and a quaint little garden house," Ricki protested. "They could be cleaned out and put to use—"

"Quite out of the question!" He spoke harshly, the bones showing tautly under the tawny skin of his face. "The Caseta Conchilla, as the garden house was once called, is now the abode of bats and beetles, while the pool always took more water than can be spared. This is hot, dry country, Miss O'Neill. Unlike in England, when the rain falls here, it often evaporates before even touching the ground.''

"Would you spare the water, *señor*, if I assured you that it would be of immense benefit to Jaime to learn how to swim?" When Ricki was eager or determined, her eyes became green as jewels in her elfin face that was neither pretty nor plain. Her flash of anger, even of fear, was forgotten now as she gave voice to the idea that had come into her mind the moment she had come upon that neglected swimming pool.

"The buoyancy of water," she explained, "provides a sense of support for anyone who has lost the use of his legs. It gives a real surge of confidence when such a person actually finds himself moving along in the water, and swimming is also good for the general muscle tone. Believe me, *señor*, a pool to swim in would be of invaluable help to Jaime."

"It was not suggested by any of the physio-attendants that a pool to swim in would be so beneficial," the don said, with no softening in his tone or his expression.

"Perhaps they didn't care enough to—tackle you about it?" she rejoined.

"Or perhaps they lacked the audacity, eh?" The don gazed down quizzically into Ricki's eager eyes, searching them for a long moment. "You demand a lot, Miss O'Neill, when you ask that I reopen this place," he said at last.

"Bricking in memories is making permanent lumber of them," she dared to say, feeling certain, now, that the ghosts she had disturbed had been those of Conquesta and Leandro. "Throw them out with the rubbish that has accumulated in the *caseta*, let the place come back to life to the sound of Jaime's laughter. I promise it will, *señor*."

"You have a very persuasive tongue," he said grimly. "And you know—witch that you are—that I am vulnerable where the boy is concerned." He fell silent and took a long look around him, then his eyes came back to Ricki's face. "I do not give in to your request very willingly, let me warn you of that, but I will comply for the child's sake."

"Thank you, *señor*," she said gratefully. "I'm sure you won't regret your decision when you see how much progress Jaime will make."

"If the pool will make him happier or help him to walk, then so be it." There was no emotion in the don's crisp voice, but as though afraid his eyes might reveal something, he looked away from Ricki toward the house of shells, just showing through the trees. "My servants will not bless you, you realize, when I give orders that the *caseta* and the pool be cleared out and cleaned. To them this place is *mala suerte*."

"A place of bad luck!" Ricki caught her breath on the words. "But I'm sure they'll feel differently when the trees have been trimmed and everything is looking sunny and fresh. Right now it's a garden of ghosts— enough to frighten anyone."

"The ghosts, I notice, did not stop you from venturing into the garden." He spoke in a droll tone of voice, his black-clad shoulders now at rest against the massive trunk of an encina tree. "But if I remember rightly there is a superstition, is there not, that the pure in heart are able to pass even through fire without being scorched?"

"I shouldn't like to try it," she laughed.

"Your heart is not pure enough?" he mocked. "You feel that your quick temper and inclination toward self-will put you on a lower plane than the angels?"

"Exactly, *señor*." She spoke lightly, but wasn't sure she was amused by his remark. He had plenty of temper and self-will himself, along with the pride of Lucifer!

She studied him through the density of her Irish lashes and saw his gaze brooding upon the quaint garden house—the Caseta Conchilla, as *they* had called it. A line of Keats thrust sharp through Ricki's mind, with its Gaelic capacity for storing up pieces of lore, legend and poetry: *Everything that reminds me of her goes through me like a spear.*

In that moment, as though sensing in the atmosphere something that disturbed him, the dog thrust his wolf's head against Ricki and gave a little whine. She bent to pat him, and her employer said curtly, "We do not as a rule make pets of the dogs about the *estancia*. Their main function is to guard the sheep and the house, and that animal might well have bitten you as you are a stranger." Ricki glanced up and caught the flicker of curiosity in Don Arturo's dark eyes. "Does nothing shake that audacious British heart of yours?" he asked.

"The days are over when women went into flutters at the sight of mice and men," she rejoined flippantly.

"Mice and men might not disturb you, but fluttering above your head right now is a stinging fly which has no doubt flown out of the pool behind you. It will give you Spanish hellfire if it should get its fangs into that white neck of yours, so I advise you to stand very still." The don's gaze was fixed like a gimlet upon the thing hovering above her head, then she gave a little cry as swift as a lash he suddenly reached out and swung her clear of the *bicho.* He then set her down on the overgrown path in front of him and crisply suggested that she lead the way out of "this jungle."

Still feeling the hard pressure of his arms, Ricki hurried ahead of him to the arch of a door through which he would have to stoop. Her white neck, as he had called it, was now pink and she felt rather than heard him behind her, walking as lithely and silently as a panther. She reached the door and hurriedly opened it, finding herself out on the patio with a sharp sense of relief.

"I must go and tell Jaime about the swimming pool," she said, knocking from her skirt the fluff of the wild puffballs she had brushed against in her hurry, just now, to get out of that garden. "Th—thank you for saving me from being stung, *señor*, and for agreeing to the clearance of the pool."

"You are welcome, Miss O'Neill, if swimming exercises will aid my nephew." He gave a curt inclination of his dark head. "It will be a week or more before the pool is ready for use, and I take it you will require new furniture for the *caseta*? You intend to make use of the place as a garden house?"

"If I may, *señor*?" She felt a bit heartless, and yet was certain that it was for the best to let the sunshine and a child's laughter dispel the ghosts of the *caseta*. They had lingered there too long, haunting this man, keeping him locked in memories that were best forgotten. She excused herself from him, then hastened indoors and up the stairs into the maze of corridors where her room was situated.

They were rather dim and mysterious even in daylight, with stained glass windows throwing zephyrs of amber, ruby and royal blue onto portraits of proud-looking Cazalet women wearing gowns of encrusted brocade and tightly pleated collars. The men wore more somber attire, always a Spanish characteristic even in the days when gallants of other lands had dressed like peacocks.

Ricki adventured into several rooms before finding her own. One of them contained a huge *cama de matrimonio*, so formidable that it must have frightened the wits out of every bride brought into this house. She grinned as she withdrew and closed the door on that canopied bridal bed, hemmed in by big dark presses and watched over by the imps, satyrs and dragons carved all over the woodwork. *Goodness*, she thought, *you would have to be in love to spend the first night of your marriage in that chamber of horrors!*

JAIME WAS STILL BENT industriously over his sketchbook, but he glanced up with the same grave smile that characterized his uncle when Ricki lightly encircled his shoulders with her arm. She never made the mistake of ruffling a child's hair, not even when tempted by the young silkiness of it and the innocence of the nape which it revealed. Boys in particular didn't like such a caress, and they carried this dislike into manhood. Funny creatures! *It didn't do to ruffle their dignity*, Ricki reflected, treating Jaime to her impish grin.

"Do you like surprises?" she whispered.

He nodded, and listened with slowly widening eyes as Ricki told him that in about a week or so they would have a swimming pool to play in and a summerhouse where he could have his books and his drawing pencils and even his lunch if he felt like it.

"Your Uncle Arturo is having the pool and the *caseta* made ready for us. Don't you think that's extremely kind of him, Jaime?" She casually picked up his sketchbook. "It proves how fond he is of you."

Jaime hunched a shoulder, plainly uninterested in his uncle's fondness for him.

"Well, aren't you looking forward to the fun and games we shall have when the pool's ready?" she asked, trying not to show she was disappointed in his reaction to her news.

"How will it be possible for *me* to go into the water? I shall sink, Rickee!" He blinked those incredible lashes at her and she only just managed not to grab him and hug him. She was filled with compassion, but it would be wrong to pet him right now and perhaps give him the idea she approved of this dislike he harbored for Don Arturo.

"Of course you won't sink," she assured him. "At first you'll float about in an inflated rubber ring, and then very gradually you will gain confidence and begin to swim on your own."

"I will be able to swim even though I—I cannot walk?"

"Of course you will." She imitated his awestruck voice.

"It is like magic," he said.

"Nothing of the sort, my lad. It isn't going to take magic to get you running and riding, it's going to take willpower and the belief that you can do those things. Do you trust me, Jaime, and believe me?" She held his gaze, compelling a response from him, an eagerness to believe, but he gave a sigh and glanced away from her, and telling herself not to feel defeated at this stage in the game she began to flip through the pages of his sketch-book. Too many of the drawings depicted overturned cars, with puffs of flame billowing from them, and people thrown like broken dolls to the roadside—yet they were clever, they showed a budding talent, and Ricki guessed that he was having some sort of lessons in sketching from Señor Andres. But why did the man encourage this kind of thing?

"Why do you draw pictures like these, my poppet?" she asked.

He didn't answer right away, and then he said, "What is pop-pet?"

"Well now, in Spanish you might say *guapo*, or *mi amigo*. It's a term of affection, Jaime."

"It means you—you like me?" he queried.

"It means exactly that, my poppet. And now we'll put away these books and pencils and clean ourselves up for lunch. Do you fancy having it downstairs?" she added casually.

"No, up here!" He shook his head emphatically. "Always I have it up here, and then after siesta Señor Andres comes."

"Ah yes, Señor Andres!" Ricki's green eyes flashed with curiosity and a hint of temper. "I'm looking forward to meeting him."

Ricki wasn't certain whether the man was fairly young or getting on in years. A child's definition could not be relied on, for the early thirties was a pensionable age in the eyes of the young. She was tempted to question Jaime about him, and then she decided to judge for herself whether her employer had let a fox into the coop by allowing this Señor Andres to come here and have Jaime to himself for several hours each day. The boy had to have some schooling, but it seemed to Ricki that it might have been wiser to employ a stranger rather than a man who had been a friend of Leandro's.

"Are you fond of Señor Andres?" she asked Jaime, as they sat at their lunch.

The boy nodded. "He is quite a pop-pet, you will see. He draws *muy fíno* and he teaches me."

What, to draw all those car-crash pictures? she wondered, barely tasting her rice pudding flavored with cinnamon and thick slices of lemon.

They finished lunch and Ricki was about to settle Jaime for his siesta when Sophina appeared. Ricki guessed that the *guardesa's* family had kept her occupied all morning, now she came bustling in, bent on preparing Jaime for his nap. "You must take your own siesta, *señorita*." She hustled Ricki to the door. "Go now, and leave me to see to the *niño*."

Remembering her brush with Sophina at breakfast time, Ricki didn't argue. "Sleep tight, *guapo*." She gave Jaime a wave from the door. "I'll see you later."

The *estancia* slumbered in the grip of the afternoon heat, but Ricki was feeling too restless to take to her bed for a couple of hours, and she made her way downstairs. No doubt she was breaking a rule of Spanish etiquette by wandering about during siesta, but a girl, she argued with herself, couldn't act like a señorita if she wasn't one.

Mmmm, was this the living room? How long and cool it was, with oval-shaped openings framing the patio, and colored rugs scattered like islands about the polished floor. The walls were ivory pale, their surfaces broken here and there by some bold, very Spanish-looking paintings. Long cane seats invited relaxation, while more formal chairs had the Cazalet *escudo* carved into their high backs, its irises, hawks and swans picked out in color. A brilliant fringed shawl lay over a black grand piano, and a screen of royal blue leather concealed a stone fireplace. Ricki slowly turned to take in everything, and when she suddenly met her own reflection in a large mirror set in wrought-iron, she saw the question her eyes were large with.

Who was it who played that magnificent piano? Was it her employer, and could she hope that there would be evenings when he would invite her to listen to him?

Then she shrugged her shoulders, dismissing the idea that he would ever show her such friendliness, and curled down into one of the cushioned cane chairs. Her eyes brooded on the patio beyond the archways, where the brilliant tiles and tubbed geraniums shimmered in the hot sun. In a while she dozed off to sleep.

She awoke suddenly about an hour and a half later, drowsily stretched herself and rubbed a crick out of her neck.

"Such a pity that Sleeping Beauty should awake just as I was about to give her the traditional kiss!" The voice was gay and audacious, the accent Spanish, and Ricki jumped confusedly to her feet as she noticed a man lounging in the archway facing her. His jacket hung from his shoulders like a cloak, and he had a rather self-indulgent mouth and a lurking devilry in his brown eyes.

"Permit me to introduce myself," he came toward her, not tall but with a faint swagger that suggested a mixture of bandit and Don Juan. "My name is Alvedo Andres. I am both an artist and tutor to the young Jaime. You, I venture, are the English miss?"

"The name is O'Neill," she said, irritated that he should have come upon her while she slept. It put her at a disadvantage, robbed her of the dignity she meant to assume when they met. "Jaime has talked about you, Señor Andres. You're—quite a favorite with him, aren't you?"

"Ah, does that not quite meet with your approval— Miss O'Neill?" As he mockingly emphasized her name, his eyes were taking her in from her tousled hair to her ankles. "So Don Arturo does not bring here a miss who I thought would be muscular and manly. He brings one who has the green eyes of a witch."

"Let's get something straight, Señor Andres." Ricki drew herself up very straight. "Don't run away with the idea that I'm green all through. I'm good at my job and I'm not easily bossed about—or particularly keen on being flirted with."

"You think I would flirt with you?" His grin was wicked.

"You'll probably try—as I'm not overburdened with muscle and young enough to be thought fairly innocent."

Ricki, not really acquainted as yet with the temperament of the Andalusian male, aroused a sudden sharp interest in those brown eyes. "Life at the Granja looks like it's becoming more interesting,'' he smiled. ''I had heard that British girls were spirited yet cool, a combination that intrigues me. Fire under ice is very likely to cause a sudden warm melting.''

''For a man who has only heard about the British, you speak very fluent English,'' Ricki said in a cool tone of voice.

''That is easily explained.'' He strolled to a small table and flipped open the lid of a cigarette box, extracting one with his rather blunt fingers and holding it to the flame of a lighter shaped like a swan. He studied the swan before replacing it on the table, his eyes narrowing through the smoke of his cigarette as they came to Ricki's face. ''I have known the Cazalets since I was a child—my father was a tenant farmer of one of their ranches—and they were brought up bilingual because of their grandmother, who was from England.''

''Yes, I've been told that Don Arturo had an English grandmother.'' Ricki sat down in one of the S-shaped chairs. Its upholstery of amber velvet made quite a setting for her youthfulness, and she was unaware that it was a *dos-à-dos*—a loveseat.

Alvedo Andres came over with a casual air and sat in the other rounded seat, so they were facing each other. ''She was teaching music in Madrid when the grandfather of Don Arturo met her. He was there on business and when he returned to the Granja one week later, she came, too, as his wife.'' A hint of the devilry gleamed in the tutor's eyes as they studied Ricki's face. ''Much is said about the deliberateness of Spanish courtship, but let a man of Andalusia fall madly in love and he will waste scant time taking legal possession of the girl.''

''It hardly shows that Don Arturo has English blood in his veins,'' Ricki said thoughtfully.

''Who can tell anything about such a man?'' The tutor flicked ash carelessly to the polished floor. ''His mother was a Castilian and they carry their pride like a banner and are cold in comparison to us gay-hearted Andalusians."

Yet, Ricki reflected, the don had once loved very deeply...still loved, from all the signs, the memory of Conquesta!

"You can respect him," Alvedo went on, "but can you love him? Leandro, his brother, was the son of the father's right eye. He was the golden boy, the charmer. One of those who would have stayed carefree and youthful all his days—had his days not been numbered," Alvedo added darkly.

"It was indeed a tragedy the way he and his wife died," Ricki agreed, something in the tutor's manner making her think of what she had read in a book about the Spaniards of the south, that they were more vivacious than those of other regions—and also more vindictive.

"How much have you been told about Leandro and his wife?" Alvedo regarded her through narrowed lids. "The don would not be very communicative on the subject, but Sophina likes to gossip and with her gypsy blood she makes a drama out of most things."

"I know that Conquesta was to have married Don Arturo," Ricki replied, feeling the race of her heart, aware in this moment that she might be close to a man who was hiding hate behind a façade of respect for his employer. "You and Jaime's father were friends, I've been told, *señor*."

"That is so! Our ages were the same, you see. Our interests and diversions the same...." The tutor was gazing beyond Ricki, and there was a hot, dark look in his eyes. "There were few to match Leandro. He had the *bizarro en el talle*, the gallant shape as we say. Few women could resist him."

The Spanish tutor sucked in his breath, then he thrust

an elbow upon the back of the loveseat and said, deliberately, "One does not take anything from a Cazalet without paying for it. Leandro paid, did he not?"

"But the crash was an accident," Ricki exclaimed. "An accident pure and simple, n-not some sort of fateful retribution for what he had done."

"Who implies that fate took a hand?" Alvedo spoke in a lowered voice now, and what he said seemed even more effective. "A man of intense pride had been robbed of a very lovely bride. So lovely, in fact, that until she moved or spoke and otherwise betrayed herself as a human being, she might have been a creation of Goya, or Renoir. She was a picture and the Granja was to be her frame... the darkly paneled hall, this *cuarto de estar* with its velvet loveseats and Moorish archways, the *caseta* of shells where she would sit among the wild roses and laugh when we tried to beguile her into the pool. Like a beautiful cat she hated the water but adored the sun, and I can see her still, a golden-skinned creature with dark hair that had streaks of gold in it...."

He rose abruptly to his feet and went to toss the stub of his cigarette into the fireplace behind the Cordoban screen; when he turned around, the royal blue leather framed him. He was a good-looking man, but not in a way that would make him outstanding in a crowd. He had none of the high pride of Cazalet, nor that air of physical and mental power which made Don Arturo a man out of the ordinary... a man to fear, perhaps, if you crossed him!

"It was whispered around at the time, and still the whispers linger among the people of these parts, that it was very strange Arturo's brother and sister-in-law should have crashed and died in a car owned by him. Almost too much of a coincidence to be believable as an accident—pure and simple."

The young Spaniard's gaze locked with Ricki's and

her eyes, which in gaiety were green as the Irish hills, were now gray and troubled. She could feel her inward rebellion against the thing Señor Andres was implying, yet hadn't she seen for herself that first night in Toledo that Arturo de Cazalet was either a devil or a saint?

"You shouldn't be sayin' such things," she said, and the brogue of her childhood was back in her voice, as it always was in moments of stress. "Don Arturo never stopped loving Conquesta and he forgave her and his brother for the way they treated him. . . ."

"Poor little English miss," Alvedo took in, with taunting eyes, the distress of Ricki's face, "you will learn before long that we of Spain are still medieval in our hearts. The feuds and vendettas have not been completely subdued." Then he swung away from her as a lean shadow fell through one of the archways.

"*Buenas tardes, señor*," he said smoothly. "I go now to give Jaimito his lessons."

The young tutor departed and Ricki was left gazing at her employer with eyes that held small clouds of doubt. *Grind our hatred sharp on his offspring and all his race to come*! That line from Virgil flashed through her mind as Don Arturo confronted her in his dark detachment. Then, because to look into those dense, handsome eyes was too disquieting, Ricki got nervously to her feet.

"What have you and that young man been discussing—the arts?" he queried, in a faintly caustic tone of voice.

"Yes, *señor*," she said, because how could she admit the truth?

"How interesting." His mouth curled into a smile, the sort that told Ricki he had guessed she and the Spanish tutor had been discussing him and the things that were still whispered about him.

CHAPTER FOUR

"I've TOLD YOU BEFORE, Sophina," Ricki said with patience much tried, "fried, spicy foods are not good for Jaime. Yes, I know your own children thrive on them, but they are able to take active exercises while my patient, as yet, is still confined to his wheelchair."

"It seems to me a shame to deprive the *chico* of my crisp *churros*, which he likes to eat so much. Being a cripple he is denied so many other enjoyments," Sophina returned, looking most affronted by the way the English miss had near enough ordered her, and her golden, delicious *churros*, out of the boy's room.

Ricki couldn't abide the word which Sophina had just applied to Jaime, and she caught angrily at her arm and forcibly pulled her away from the boy's half-open door. "I won't have you saying such things within earshot of Jaime," she said, her eyes tiger green. "I'm absolutely confident that he's going to walk again, but he needs to be sure in mind as well as strong in body before he'll make the effort, and hearing himself called a cripple—and being hung round with magic charms—isn't going to help one scrap. He is not a cripple, do you hear? And it isn't going to take the blessed charms of a cave-dwelling witch to get him up on his feet and walking."

Ricki took a deep breath and felt better at having got all that off her mind. Sophina stood clutching her dish of *churros* to her, an angry flush mounting under the swarthy skin of her face. "*You* are not averse to using your green-eyed charms on the *patrono*," she hit back.

"It is all around the valley that only a witch could have talked him into having the pool and the *caseta* put back into repair."

"Swimming exercises will help Jaime," Ricki said, a sudden heat in her cheeks, "and that is the only reason Don Arturo has capitulated over the matter. I might also add that it's silly of you and the other people working here to refer to the *caseta* as a place of gremlins. You'll only frighten the boy with such talk."

"You were not here when the old *patrono* died." Sophina gave Ricki a baleful look. "It was in that *casa del duende* where he found the elopement note from Doña Conquesta, and the shock of it so hurt him in the heart that he suffered a stroke. Don Arturo had a lot of feeling for his father, though Leandro was known to be the favored son.

"But that is the way of people, to misplace their love more often than not, and it was plain afterward that Doña Conquesta regretted what she had done. There is no divorce in Spain," Sophina added with finalty. "Marriage here is dissolved only by death."

"You are saying that Doña Conquesta regretted her runaway marriage?" Ricki exclaimed.

"The regret showed in her eyes whenever she came to the Granja," Sophina said emphatically. "Leandro was a handsome one, but good looks are not the whole story of a man, are they?"

"And that poor girl was so young," Ricki murmured. "She felt herself to be a sacrifice to a dynastic marriage, then realized too late that it was the idea she had fled away from and not the man involved—"

But Ricki was speaking to herself, for Sophina, still ruffled, had turned and marched off with her cloth-covered *churros*. Ricki gave a sigh. She hadn't meant to have a tiff with Sophina, but fried foods weren't good for Jaime, and the very atmosphere of this house seemed to involve her in a dramatic situation over the simplest matter. Then she gave a shrug. She had enough on her plate already without adding Sophina's *churros* to the mixture, and wearing a faintly wry grin she returned to Jaimie's room, where he was copying the bulls out of a book she had recently bought him.

So absorbed was he in his sketching that he hadn't heard her come in, but suddenly he sensed her presence and glanced up with a grave, dark-eyed smile that caught quite painfully at her heart. Each day with this child increased her longing to see him straight, sturdy and fearless as the young *peons* about the *estancia*, and so far her care and her skill had made him a lot more limber than he had been and far less inclined to be moody.

Mi tata, he would often call her, and when she ran her slim, trained hands over his back and his legs and then gave his toes a tickle, he would sometimes kick out his feet as he giggled and hardly realize that she was proving to him that he could move his limbs.

A parcel was brought up to the nursery suite that morning. It was quite large and when unwrapped proved to be two separate boxes from a large department store in Seville, one containing half a dozen tailored smocks for Ricki, the other a selection of model toys for Jaime—airplanes, boats, rocket ships and a submarine.

"We'll have a lot of fun putting these together, my lamb," Ricki smiled.

"Yes." Jaime said, and when she looked at him she saw that his lower lip was jutting. His resemblance to his uncle when he did that was rather disconcerting, she thought.

"You'll have to thank your uncle for his present," she added.

"It is a pity these are not tubes of paint and brushes,"

the child responded off-handedly. "I need some of those."

"That's a very ungrateful remark, Jaime!" Ricki rarely spoke so severely to him. "It's kind of your uncle to give you the toys, and you'll thank him for them."

"It would be *cortesia* to do so. The *señor tio* will expect that," he agreed coolly, pushing aside the box of toys and giving her smocks his attention. They were not white as she had expected them to be, but a cool green in crisp nylon. Her measurements had been sent with the order and the one she tried on fitted perfectly and looked less severe than medical white.

"Well, do you like your *tata*, you naughty boy?" Ricki stolled up and down in imitation of a mannequin.

He watched her with a smile and looked quite unrepentant about his remark concerning his uncle's gift. "You are like a *fotografia en colores*," he informed her. "I like very much my green *tata*."

Ricki had to smile, and at the same time she wondered if the don's choice of green for her smocks had been motivated by irony. Did he think the color expressed her, the green kid he had found in Toledo and brought to his house—this mysterious Granja with its stalking sense of a drama not yet fully played out!

WORK ON THE SWIMMING POOL was almost completed and now and again Ricki persuaded her patient to go with her for a look at the transformation that was taking place around the pool and inside the *caseta*. Don Arturo had ordered teak furniture for the little house of shells, and it had been made by one of the estate carpenters, a brown, bowlegged Andalusian with a real gift for carving in his hands. Ricki had taken cuttings from various plants, including the exquisite maranta, the prayer plant, and a fresh collection of pots stood along the shelf where Conquesta's plants had withered and died. Bright, new matting had been laid over the floor, and she had cleaned and polished the shells all around the doorway. She didn't know whether Don Arturo ever visited the place, and she tried not to remember that it was here his dreams had died.

Alvarez would carry Jaime's wheelchair downstairs, while Ricki took the boy piggyback.

It wasn't often that they encountered the master of the house, his supervision of the olive groves and the pressing mills kept him busy, but one morning they met him on the stairs as they were going down them. He halted abruptly under the stained glass window at the gallery bend, the lancets of sun-hot color playing over his dark face as he stood frowning at Ricki with the boy straddling her shoulders. He gestured at Alvarez to continue on his way with the chair, then carefully but firmly he lifted his nephew off Ricki's shoulders. In future, he told her curtly, Alvarez would first carry down the chair and then the boy.

"You overestimate your strength, Miss O'Neill," he added. "These stairs are very steep, and of stone."

Ricki could feel her emotional temperature rising, and his autocratic manner didn't make her feel like shaking down the mercury. "Jaime's weight is extremely light compared to that of the people I used to handle at the hospital," she pointed out.

"Let me remind you that you are no longer employed at the hospital." His eyes and his tone of voice remained coldly detached. "You are now in my house—"

"And obliged to take your orders, of course!" she flashed. "Very well, *señor*, when we return from our walk, Alvarez shall carry Jaime upstairs."

His eyes flicked her face, took in her green smock; then he swung about and carried Jaime down the stairs to the hall. Ricki followed, her eyes meeting Jaime's over his uncle's shoulder. The boy pulled a face, but her own facial muscles remained rigid, and strangely it angered her that the child should show his dislike of his uncle in that rude way. She scolded him about it as she wheeled him around one of the side patios—somehow she had lost all desire to visit the pool and the *caseta*—and he at once turned his head and gave her a wondering look. "You do not like him, so why should I?" Jaime demanded sulkily.

"Don Arturo is your uncle and your guardian," she replied stiffly. "You owe him respect, Jaimito. He cares for you as—well, he would for a son."

"I am the son of Leandro de Cazalet," Jaime said, haughtily. "My father and mother died because of Don Arturo—and I *hate* him!"

"*Jaime*—that's a very terrible thing to say!" Distress and shock mingled in her exclamation. "Whoever told you such a thing?"

"It is a secret who told me," he muttered.

"That person was telling you a very wicked lie," Ricki said, for though it could never be denied that Leandro and his wife had died in his brother's car, it was not to be faced that Arturo de Cazalet had resorted to the cruel vendetta in order to satisfy his honor. It was something to be pushed to the back of the mind, there to lie hidden beneath everyday thoughts and feelings.

"Jaime." She took the boy's chin in her fingers and lifted his face to hers; his cheek was smooth against hers and she could feel the fluttering of his long lashes. "It's wrong to hate people unless you're very sure that they deserve it. Your uncle loved your mother and I don't think he would ever have knowingly hurt her, so don't be turned against him by the whispers of a mischief-maker."

The boy drew his cheek away from hers and looked directly into her eyes. His lips moved, then his lashes faltered and made shadows on his cheeks. "He makes me shiver when he comes near me," he muttered. "Why does he do that?"

"Because he's as proud as a Saracen prince and unbending as a piece of Toledan steel," she laughed, straightening up and pushing the boy's wheelchair toward a bush of wild white roses. There was a tiled bench nearby and she sat down and told him one of the tales her Gaelic imagination could spin out of the air as a spider on the rose bush spun a silver web. A rose token and a dark armored knight drifted into her tale, and Jaime listened with a finger in his mouth, solemn-eyed as a little owl. Ricki's eyes dwelt on his fine Cazalet bones, for how like his uncle he was! A likeness that must often have jabbed at his mother's heart, if it was indeed true that she regretted running off with Leandro and realized too late that it was Arturo she loved!

"What is a trysting tree?" Jaime's voice broke in on her tale.

"Oh—" she gave a start, for she had continued to weave her tale even as her thoughts wandered in another direction. "It's a special tree, *guapo*, where lovers meet to discuss their future together."

"And to kiss," he nodded wisely. "People always kiss when they love each other. And they quarrel."

She glanced at him sharply and wondered if his parents had quarreled in front of him. Then, with a sigh, he said "Rickee, I wish I could run after that butterfly—that one there!"

She saw it, just like a piece of gold brocade blowing about among the flowers of the patio, and though the woman in her longed to take the child against her heart, the nurse in her had to say, bracingly, "Mere wishes are silly fishes, Jaime. The exercises we're doing together are strengthening your back and leg muscles, and when your mind accepts the fact that you *can* walk, then you will do so."

"Will I really, Rickee?" He clutched at her hand. "I hate being a baby who has to be pushed around in a chair. I want to be like Paco, who rides the ponies and climbs the hills."

"If you want those things with all your heart and mind, then there isn't anything to stop you from having them," she assured him.

"Truly?" His great dark eyes dwelt on hers, and this time she drew him against her and hugged his thin young body. "It's about time for us to go in and have lunch," she said. "There's blackbird pudding for dessert."

This was her name for rice pudding stuffed with prunes, and as she felt the boy laughing against her, she thanked heaven for the Gaelic gift of nonsense which had always enabled her to make contact with children. Jaime needed that contact more than any other child she had known.

AFTER LUNCH, with the boy settled down for his siesta, Ricki went to her room to change into a cotton shift of striped cinnamon and cedar against white. She stepped into hemp-soled walking shoes and took a shady hat out of the wardrobe, for she had decided to take a leisurely walk into the village. The shops opened again around four o'clock and she had a few things to buy and a letter to her father to mail.

A wanderer himself, he had not been too surprised by her decision to work in Spain. "But watch out for those romantic-looking dons," he had written back. "One of them might want to make you his *señorita*, and I don't think my Gael of a girl would care to be locked up in oriental seclusion!"

Ricki had gaily assured him in her answering letter that she had no intention of getting involved with a romantic-looking don. She knew only a couple, anyway. One was her employer, who was decidedly not interested in making her his *señorita*, and the other was her patient's grandfather—a local breeder of fighting bulls whom she had not yet had the pleasure of meeting.

That letter was tucked in Ricki's shoulder bag as she ran downstairs and made her way out of the house, which was wrapped in the lazy, sun-hot meshes of siesta. All the olive workers went home to rest for a couple of hours, but Ricki was never entirely sure what her employer did with himself in the afternoons. She suspected that he pored over the estate accounts in his study, but the door was always firmly closed and she never glimpsed him at his big desk. In fact, it was enormous and of dark carved wood that matched the wall paneling of the dragon's lair, as Ricki thought of the room. The chairs were of leather, the hard sort that didn't look very comfortable. There were hundreds of books behind glass, and on the desk a lifelike bronze hand that he used as a letter weight, an inkstand of hammered silver, and always a white rose in a small vase.

The room was very austere apart from that single rose, and it seemed to Ricki of special significance that Don Arturo should have one placed in front of him each day. . .as if to remind him of a certain woman's loveliness, and the stab of the thorn that had left a wound that would not heal.

Ricki crossed the main patio, where a couple of dogs slumbered in the shade of carts and earthy smells from the cowsheds and stables hung on the hot air. She passed by the guard's house and out under the bold archway where several lizards clung motionless, jade green against the lichened stone. She saw to her left the cluster of sheds where the olives for eating were sorted and bottled, and the pressing mills where the bulk of the fruit was crushed and the golden oil drawn off into immense butts. Beyond, in the many acres of grooves, the olive trees grew thick as black bees against the brick red soil, but even more fascinating to Ricki was the mulberry tree plantation, where silk was produced, and she passed through its cool gloom and out on the dusty road that wound in a corniche around the wide, dramatic bowl that was the valley.

Her head and eyes well shaded by the hat she was wearing, Ricki wasn't unbearably conscious of the heat of the full sun. Her eyes feasted on the valley, which seemed to belong entirely to her on this golden afternoon, and she recognized some of the flowers that dappled its slopes with color. Flax, pennyroyal and salvias, the flowers of Our Lady which often decorated the wayside shrines. Wild irises were drained of their blue by the fiery fingers of the sun, and cactuses, the cruel flowers, grew in isolation in their strangeness.

Above the land the Sierras etched a craggy fringe against the sky, their peaks mantled even in summer by layers of icy snow that blew its breath down upon the valley when the sun had burned itself out for the day. The extremes of the Andalusian climate made its people gay and harsh by turns, Ricki reflected, as she wandered on, her objective a ledge of rock that beetled above the valley and was crowned dramatically by the ruins of a Moorish castle. Somewhere hidden in the tall, seedy grass of the slopes she could hear the tinkle of goat and sheep bells, a rustic music that had no doubt lulled off to sleep the shepherd who tended the flock. The seesaw of grasshoppers was tireless, and water rushed from a mountain stream past the rocks where Ricki climbed, her shoulder bag swinging against her lightly clad body and a prickle of sweat breaking out on her skin. She paused to gaze out over the valley, and her eyes dwelt for a long moment on the rambling shape of the house where she worked. All looked very still there; a transient peace seemed to enfold the place, while turned to golden limpets were the whitewashed houses that clung to the craggy hillsides.

The valley seemed held in a spell, and Ricki had a feeling she was at one of those crossroads her father had once spoken about. Perhaps the letter she carried in her bag, which would be in his hands several days from now, sent her thoughts winging to the day when her roots had been torn out of Irish soil and replanted in England's. She had been but a child, yet old enough to feel with pain her transition from the known and loved to the unknown. She had settled down as time went by, but always there had been that inner restlessness, that longing for the scents and sounds of the land of her heart.

Here in Spain she felt she had come home again, and with a slightly perplexed smile she finished her climb and entered what had been the courtyard of the castle. The remains of a stairway led to the battlements, and she made for an embrasure where juniper bushes grew up the stone and offered cool green shelter from the sun.

This was a quiet spot she had discovered on a previous walk, and she sat watching the swoop of dark hawks through the sky, not questioning any longer her wisdom in choosing to work in this valley in the wilds. It held affection in the form of Jaime, challenge in her duels with his guardian, and an untamed beauty for which her spirit had clamored through the years. Right this moment she wouldn't have changed places with anyone...she was comfortably perched above the world, held in the sun-woven meshes of a transient peace herself.

She heard no footstep, but a piece of stone shifted, broke loose and went clattering down the side of the ruined ramparts. Ricki turned startled green eyes in that direction. "Oh!" she exclaimed. "It's you!"

Alvedo Andres lifted his arms and then let them fall despairingly. "What a way for a romantic Andalusian to be greeted by a pretty woman," he said.

"I'm sorry, Alvedo." She grinned impishly. "My thoughts were on the wing with those hawks, and you startled me. Do you come here often, *caballero*?"

This was a gibe at the Cordoban hat he wore tilted over a gray, dark eye. He swept it off and gave her a faintly mocking bow. "I suspected that you came here, and somehow we find little time to speak together at the Granja. Always there is my pupil upstairs, and when I come downstairs there is Don Arturo standing like a dark shadow between us. He chills my ardor, *chiquita*, but since that first day I have been wanting to say that I find you charming."

"You call it the *piropo*, don't you?" she chaffed. "The Andalusian compliment which women collect like beads, but which they don't take too seriously."

He came and leaned against the wall where she sat, a lean bandit in tight dark trousers, a white shirt open at his throat, his Cordoban hat held in fingers on which a couple of gold rings glinted, his narrow feet encased in highly polished shoes. His bold Andalusian eyes took Ricki in from her slender ankles to her shaded green eyes, but Ricki's clear skin didn't go pink under his scrutiny as it was inclined to when a pair of darker, much cooler eyes appraised her.

"But most Spanish women would inform you, little English miss, that the *piropo* adds to life the dash of spice that the peppercorns, the sesame seeds and the chillies add to a dish. But then," his mouth curled in a rather unkind smile, "I am forgetting how prosaic is English cooking."

"Andalusians aren't the only men around who can coin a compliment," Ricki said, a glint in her eye. "I've known several British medical students and I speak from experience.''

A gleam of speculation came into his eyes at that last word she used, then she felt his hand move along the wall embrasure until his fingers brushed her arm. She at once withdrew her arm from his touch and heard him laugh below his breath.

"I knew I was right about you," he chuckled. "It is the bold ones who are cold, and the sensitive who have to protect their warm hearts under a prickly shell."

"It's evident, Señor Andres, that you consider yourself quite an authority on women," she rejoined, rather more shaken by that perceptive remark of his than she cared to admit.

"Please continue to call me Alvedo." His eyes were laughing at her. "I like very much the way you say it— every woman should have a voice that caresses the ear, and even great beauty is spoiled if that quality is missing."

"Bead number two," Ricki said, miming the act of stringing them. "At this rate I shan't leave Andalusia without taking some booty home with me."

"You are leaving Andalusia?" Alvedo went taut as a blade beside her.

"Not immediately," she shrugged. "But once Jaime starts to get around I shall be redundant."

"You feel confident, then, that the child will walk again?"

"Extremely confident, *señor*." Ricki turned her head in order to meet his eyes and the look in them. They were frank and interested, certainly not the eyes of a man who encouraged the boy to hate his uncle. "His spine wasn't permanently damaged and there is no physical reason why he shouldn't walk again. His trouble is mainly centered in his mind. He suffers from a feeling of insecurity which stems from the twofold loss of his parents, and which, if he could truly believe that he is loved by his uncle, he would lose.''

"Someone," she added meaningfully, "is encouraging him to believe that his uncle was responsible for the accident which killed his parents and injured him."

"The child was bound to hear rumors," Alvedo said, deliberately. "And let us not blind our eyes to fact, *chiquita*. The car was Arturo's; the brakes were faulty, and Leandro had been in the habit for years of making use of his brother's possessions. How was he to resist that shiny sports model Arturo had unexpectedly bought himself...which Arturo rarely used himself, being always a man who prefers the horse for locomotion rather than the modern convenience of the car?"

"A chain of coincidences can't be linked to—to hang a man," Ricki said, with force. "Don Arturo is only human and as likely to be attracted by a shiny sports car as the next man. Maybe he meant to use if more often, and then his interest in his new toy fizzed out."

"You leap swiftly to defend the man," Alvedo's eyes were raking her face in sudden curiosity. "It is possible that you find him attractive?"

"Yes, I'm head over heels in love with him," Ricki returned, with irony. "Be sensible, Alvedo! I'm merely pointing out that there is no conclusive evidence that Don Arturo meant to harm his brother, his sister-in-law and his small, defenseless nephew!"

"A clever man would ensure that the evidence would not be conclusive," Alvedo drawled. "The presence in the car of Conquesta and the child was probably unforeseen by him...it was Leandro he wanted out of the way...."

Because in Spain a marriage was dissolved only by death! The words echoed through Ricki's mind like a knell, then she jumped to her feet and said she had errands in the village.

"We will go together in my car," Alvedo said. "It is Saturday and I am not due at the Granja."

Ricki did not protest, for all at once her earlier burst of energy seemed switched off and the thought of walking to the village in this heat was unbearable. "Thank you for the offer," she said, and they went down the rather precarious stairway and crossed the masonry-strewn courtyard to the broken arch that framed the roadway. Alvedo stepped out first, then extended a hand to help Ricki over a sill of broken rock. She stumbled, and at once he caught her to him and their eyes locked as her head tilted back and her lips parted in alarm.

"You have a mouth of innocence and the eyes of eternal woman," Alvedo murmured. "What would you do if I kissed you?"

"I might slap your face," she said coldly.

"But this is not the Victorian age," he mocked. "What is a kiss between a man and a woman?"

"What indeed—when they mean nothing to each other?" She shook free of him and adjusted her hat, then she walked over to his parked car, which was low slung, not very up-to-date in style, but powerful-looking under a layer of road dust. He had parked under some overhanging trees, but their shade had not prevented the leather from getting hot, and Ricki sat stiffly beside Alvedo as they drove into the village.

"The silence of resentment is worse than an outburst of temper," Alvedo exclaimed. "Come, is it so terrible that I wanted to kiss you? Must I pretend that I do not find you attractive?"

"Your Andalusian girls are much lovelier than I," she rejoined.

"Yes, between the ages of fifteen and twenty, then unfortunately they grow broad in the beam."

"And in the mind, if all I hear about you Spaniards is true."

"You think we retain the roving eye even after marriage?" He shot her an amused side-glance. "Tell me, do you not desire to marry and have a large family to adore and dominate? *Los niños* appear to mean a lot to you."

"I do love children," she admitted. "I suppose the day will come when I shall want a few of my own, but at present I'm enjoying my career too much to want to settle down to marriage."

"You are really enjoying your employment at the Granja?" He halted the car in the village square and turned to face her, his eyes narrowed against the sun as it struck down through the boughs of bitter-orange trees. "The other physio-attendants grew quickly tired of its isolation, its air of feudalism and the shadows and sounds that haunt its corridors of a night. What attraction can a place like that hold for a girl like you?"

"I'm a romantic, Alvedo," she said lightly. "I like ancient houses steeped in history—and I have grown fond of Jaime. Now I have some shopping to do—" she reached for the door handle beside her, and at once he leaned over and his fingers rested on hers.

"Meet me afterward at the café next to the post office for a cool drink," he murmured, his warm breath against her ear. "I will then drive you home, for it is not wise for a woman to walk alone across the fields when dusk begins to fall."

"Do you think I'd be tempting the devil's eye?" she quipped.

"Who knows?" His voice dropped a note lower. "People hereabouts say strange things about the valley, and few of them venture there after dark. You will meet me a little later, eh?"

"A long cool drink would be welcome." She slanted him a smile. "I don't happen to be scared of ghosts."

"Even the ghost of Conquesta de Cazalet?" he murmured.

He let Ricki out of the car and as she walked away from him, she gave a queer little shiver. Was Alvedo Andres merely an attractive young man who liked to flirt, or did he wear a smiling mask behind which he made mischief? Leandro de Cazalet had been Alvedo's friend from boyhood...and Alvedo had said himself that the vendetta was not yet dead in Spain!

Then Ricki shook off such thoughts, reminding herself that there was something in the atmosphere of the valley that dramatized all situations, etched them in black as the shadows of trees and rocks were etched against whitewashed walls by the sun. Here the past lingered on in the twisting lanes set with rows of quaint little houses. Geraniums and creepers tumbled from the window grilles, and dark-clad women sat at their lace making in doorways. Tiny stores were hidden away in the lanes, with windows like so many pebble lenses behind which one glimpsed strange goods and foods.

There was one like a medieval spicery which sold the kind of confectionery Ricki couldn't resist. Candied greengages, honeynut balls, cherries dipped in chocolate—Byzantine sweets that had once delighted the harem favorites of the Moorish courts.

While Ricki waited to be served, she felt herself under observation by a trio of women standing near the counter. She gave them a smile and though they smiled briefly in return they didn't speak, and feeling somewhat out of place she half turned from them—aware that they were whispering together—to study half-abstractedly the quaint foodstuffs on display. The jars of spices, olives in wine, sacks of pistachio nuts, sticks of cinnamon and bundles of rosemary. There were also a garlic press, a stack of green watermelons, knobbly eggplants and honey in blue china jars. And as she stood there, a stranger in a strange place, she couldn't help remembering what Alvedo had said to her when they had first met: that the people of the valley still whispered about the man she worked for.

After the three women had left the shop, the proprietress gave her attention to Ricki. She was a rather sibylline old lady, but friendly enough, her jetty eyes fixed upon Ricki as she handed across the counter a net of foil-wrapped chocolate fish for Jaime. "*Mil gracias, señora.*" Ricki was touched. "May the oil in your house burn sweetly."

"*Mi agrado.*" The brown old face creased in a network of pleased wrinkles that Ricki should reply to her in Spanish, and she at once voiced her regret at the *chico's accidente grave.* It was *fatalista* that he had not died. "God's will!" she added, crossing herself. Then she suddenly leaned forward across the counter and caught at Ricki's wrist with a hand like a brown claw. "Have you heard the Devil's Tears?" she whispered.

Ricki stared at her. "I—I don't understand you," she faltered. "What do you mean?"

"The Devil's Tears—they run down over the rocks where the auto fell over the ravine," the old lady drew in her breath with a hiss. "A bad place to die—a bad place!"

Ricki joined Alvedo in a mood of faint melancholy, and a sleepy-eyed waiter brought Granizada to their table under an awning. The drink was made of shaved ice and lemon juice; the ice was like snow in the tall glasses, and Ricki, who had grown hot walking around, was grateful for it.

While waiting for Ricki to join him, Alvedo had been making sketches of the people passing back and forth across the square, a peddler on a burro hung with baskets and tiny bells, women yarning at the fountain with pitchers on hips and shoulders, a cowled monk looking dark under a colorful *taurine* poster.

Ricki felt a slight jolt of surprise as she studied the

sketches, for although she could see that Alvedo's technical ability was quite good, his people and animals
somehow lacked the fluid movement she had noticed in
several of young Jaime's drawings. But perhaps
Alvedo's real talent lay in painting on canvas, and she
glanced up to pay him a polite compliment only to find
eyes fixed hard and glittering upon her. He *knew*, she
thought wildly, that already the child exceeded him in
talent. . . and he didn't like the knowledge!

"H-how medieval these people look," she said, a
shade too heartily. "There must be scenes for putting on
canvas all over Spain?"

He nodded, then took the sketches rather roughly out
of her hand and tore them into pieces.

"Oh, why did you do that?" she exclaimed.

"You know why!" He shrugged, and dropped the
pieces into the ashtray between them. They left the café
in a short while, and he drove the car at such a rate
along the valley road that Ricki clung by her fingertips
to the edge of her seat. She caught at one point his side-
long glance, and she wanted to cry out to him to slow
down. . . for it was here, to the sound of water rushing
below in the increasing darkness, that another car had
hurtled over the edge of the ravine. . . .

Then, abruptly, he braked and everything was still
but for the sound of the Devil's Tears and the beating of
Ricki's heart. She gazed, appalled, at the few inches of
roadway that divided them from the ravine that in the
gloom was bottomless as human folly. She shivered and
turned to look at Alvedo as he caught at her hands.
"The devil got into me just then," he said contritely.
"But when I drive along this road I always feel compelled to go fast when I reach this particular spot—" He
broke off and stared into the twilight that deepened over
the valley and turned trees to strange shapes whose
foliage rustled and moved. . . .

Had he also loved Conquesta, Ricki wondered. *Had she captured his heart as well, only to break it?*

"Does the past haunt you as well, Alvedo?" Ricki asked.

"So it must be, for anyone who knew Conquesta," he replied. "She was lovely and laughing...except when Arturo was one of our group. You felt at once the change in Conquesta when he appeared. As a rose folds in its petals when the darkness and the coldness touch them, so it was with her in his company. Her laughter would lose its gaiety, her eyes their sparkle. They would follow him and seem to beg of him...to let her go!"

"He loved her," Ricki whispered. "In his place—"

"Would I have let her go?" Alvedo demanded. "Perhaps not."

"Then why condemn *him* so harshly? He's only a man and, being also a Spaniard, hardly likely to see anything wrong in an arranged marriage. I've been told," Ricki added, "that Conquesta regretted her runaway marriage when it was too late—"

"Some called it regret, but it could have been fear." Alvedo's gold rings were digging into Ricki's fingers. "Leandro should have taken Conquesta away from the valley, but he accepted a position at her father's ranch and, gay-hearted Andaluz that he was, he saw no harm in reestablishing contact with his brother.... Ah, but you shiver, *pequeña*! I forget that you sit here in the evening air in so light a dress."

Before Ricki realized his intention and could ward it off, he put his arms around her, and the further surprise of hearing the galloping of a horse held her motionless as a large gray and its rider loomed out of the dusk. She stared, wide-eyed, as the rider reined in beside the car and took in swiftly her lightly clad figure in Alvedo's arms. "So this is where you are!" The words seemed to flick against Ricki's skin. "You have been absent from the Granja for several hours, Miss O'Neill.''

Don Arturo sat looking down at her as though at a cheap little sensation-seeker, his nostrils dilated in a scornful way that both angered Ricki and made her pull sharply out of the tutor's arms. "I'm surely entitled to a little recreation while my patient takes his siesta," she flared. "It's no more than you allow your other hirelings."

"My other hirelings, as you put it, do not take their recreation in parked cars on public highways." His face against the starlight was chiseled and utterly cold. "I came in search of you, Miss O'Neill, because Jaime has had a fall—not a serious one, but it frightened him and he will not be consoled—"

"A fall, *señor*?" Ricki's anger was lost in a rush of concern. "Oh, what was he doing—how did it happen?"

"I imagine he was trying to walk." Don Arturo wheeled his mount so he was facing toward the Granja. He added sardonically, "I will ride ahead to tell the boy that his beloved *tata* is on her way home to him— *pronto!*"

The big gray broke into a gallop at the prod of a spur, and Alvedo swore under his breath as he grabbed at the starter. The engine raked the quiet with a grating sound, the car started forward, then stalled, and Alvedo wished the Cazalets in a place deeper, hotter than the valley.

"Hurry up and get her going," Ricki urged.

"The gas tank is low," he muttered. "She will warm up in a few seconds."

Again he produced the raking sounds that seemed to grate against Ricki's ragged nerves, and she caught at the door handle. "I can make it faster on foot," she said, and the next instant she was out of the car and running down the road with Alvedo calling her name in exasperated tones.

When she reached the Granja she was out of breath and had a stitch in her side. She hastened across the hall and up the stairs, the flames of the wall lamps dipping in the breeze she created as she hurried along the gallery and rounded the bends that led to the nursery suite. The bedroom door was standing ajar and when she pushed it open the first thing she saw was a man's shadow etched by the lamplight against the white wall; standing below it beside his nephew's bed was Don Arturo and he was urging the child to cease crying before he made himself sick. "What is a small bump on the head of a growing boy of seven years?" he asked. "Come now, let me dry those silly tears for you."

The man drew a handkerchief from a hip pocket of his riding breeches, but the boy would not be persuaded to lift his face from the pillow in which it was buried. "Go away—you!" he said, muffledly. "I don't w-want you—I w-want Rickee!"

"I'm here, Jaimie." She crossed the room, not looking at Don Arturo, set aside her handbag and sat down on the side of the bed. She took hold of Jaime's thin, shaking shoulders and, realizing this was indeed his beloved *tata*, the boy huddled into her arms like a forlorn puppy and as she stroked back the dark hair from his feverish forehead she saw the slight, shiny bump he had sustained.

"What were you doing, *guapo*?" she murmured. "I've told you not to try any tricks when you're alone, now haven't I?"

"I w-wanted to see if I could s-stand up," he hicupped.

"On the bed, my silly pigeon?" she asked.

He nodded against her, and this time she did look at his uncle, a half smile on her lips. Don Arturo did not return her smile but stood lean, dark and withdrawn at the foot of the bed, his hands deep in the pockets of his

breeches. The look of him always faintly startled Ricki
when she saw him in riding attire; somehow his tweed
jacket, khaki cords and knee-length boots fastened by
straps brought out the Andalusian in him. She was less
conscious of his crisp haughtiness, more aware of a lithe
strength overlaid by sun-darkened skin. His brother,
Leandro, must have resembled him as he looked standing there, the lamplight shadowing the lines beside his
mouth and the hint of gray at his temples.

"The confusion does not strike you as too serious,
Miss O'Neill?" he asked formally.

Somewhat chilled, she took another look at the
bump. "Does your head hurt at all, Jaime?" she wanted
to know.

"It aches." The child wrapped his arms about her
neck and pressed his forehead against her. He sniffed,
and she accepted with a murmur of thanks the handkerchief Don Arturo held out to her. "Come on, have a
good blow," she said to the boy. He obeyed her, lying
passive while she wiped the last of his tears from his
face. "All this crying has given you a worse headache
than you would have had," she scolded. Then she added
casually, "Did you manage to stand up?"

His eyes wavered to his uncle, then back to her face.
"A bit," he said. "But it hurt me, and that was when I
fell off the bed."

"You are a bungler, aren't you?" She smiled and felt
the collar of his pajamas. "Oh dear, you're quite damp
from all that crying, Jaime. I'd better get you out of
these into a warm bath, then we'll have some supper,
eh?"

"Just you and me?" he urged. "No one else, all right,
Rickee!"

Ricki didn't dare look at the breeched figure of his
uncle, and curiously enough she felt rather sorry for
him. His concern for the boy had sent him out searching

for her, yet here was Jaime letting him know openly that he wasn't wanted. Not that she could imagine her autocratic employer sitting down to nursery supper and drinking hot chocolate out of mugs with Don Quixote pictures on them!

He was looking quite impassive as he said to his nephew, "If you continue to feel so active, *picaro*, you will soon need a pony of your own. One of the mares is soon to foal; she is a spirited creature and her foal is sure to be a fine one. You would like him when he is born?"

"My *abuelito* promised to let me pick out a pony when I am able to go to his ranch," Jaime replied, referring to his grandfather, Don Enrique Salvadori, whose daughter had been Jaime's mother. "Thank you all the same, *señor tio*."

With a sigh that was just audible, *señor tio* swung toward the door. "Please to come and take coffee with me later on, Miss O'Neill," he said as he strode past her. "When you and the *niño* have had your nursery party together."

The door closed on his lean, upright figure, and Ricki gave her young patient a very serious look. Just now she had glimpsed pain in the don's eyes, though he had spoken in a droll tone of voice, and she knew that it hurt him to be excluded from Jaime's trust and affection. "Why won't you make an effort to be friends with your uncle?" she asked the boy. "He keeps trying to establish a bridge, and you keep knocking it down. Now how would you like it if you offered me a candy and I turned up my nose and refused it?"

The boy gazed at her with solemn eyes for several moments, then he said, "Your nose is already turned up, Rickee," and he touched the slight tilt that made her look—she often thought—more than ever like something that belonged in the woods where the toadstools grew.

"I bet," Jaime added, his glance shifting to the large brown shape of her handbag, "that if I wanted a candy you would give me one."

"You can want one until you've had your supper, you little limb of the devil!" She had to laugh, if below there lurked a sigh, as she went into the adjoining bathroom and turned on the hot water tap. She took a jar of bath crystals from a glass shelf and scattered them into the water, where they dissolved as her days here would start dissolving now Jaime had started to show signs of active progress. He would, she reflected, be out of her care within a matter of weeks, and Don Arturo would be dismissing her from his employ.

Her eyes met her reflection in the bathroom mirror, and she saw her own look of distress. There would, inevitably, be trouble with Jaime when his uncle sent his green *tata*, his playmate and storyteller, away from the Granja. She pushed tiredly at her hair. She could only hope, in the short time she had left here, to bring about a change of heart in Jaime with regard to his guardian. Things could not be left as they were between them. The trouble was that the heart within each person was an island, with love a castaway accepted or rejected upon the bounds or limits of that island!

Jaime was tubbed and put into a pair of pajamas, then, sitting among the fresh sheets of his bed, he tackled with Ricki the supper which Alvarez brought up to them. A light soup, then veal kidneys with baby vegetables cooked in butter, followed by ice cream. Jaime loved ice cream and Ricki wondered if it had been made and sent up at the specific orders of his uncle. . . a little fuss making after his fright.

His fright was now forgotten, and he was looking very proud of his bump because it was the outward sign of his first victory over his helplessness. It shone like his eyes as he came up from a deep submersion in his chocolate mug, a brown mustache decorating his upper lip.

"I am full," he announced, as Ricki took the mug and set it down on the tray with the other depleted dishes. She wiped his mouth and decided to give him his net of chocolate fish in the morning; she didn't want his sleep disturbed by a bilious attack.

"Sing to me, Rickee," he coaxed, snuggling down against the pillows. "Sing about the little nut tree."

She smiled and stroked the dark hair out of his eyes, feeling the grip of tenderness about her throat as she gazed down at his small, fine-boned face in the lamplight, his long lashes trembling with the threat of sleep, his nose a proud miniature of his uncle's. This child was indeed a Cazalet, and it was the Castilian blood in him that made his hates and his loves equally strong.

"All right, my squirrel, I'll sing about the nut tree," she murmured and watched him drift off to sleep to the fey little tune. She bent over him and brushed a light kiss across his bruised forehead. "Sleep tight, *guapo*," she said softly. "Dream about the pony your *abuelito* is going to give you, and which you will soon be riding."

She lowered the lamp, carefully picked up the supper tray and let herself out of the nursery suite. Her face had grown pensive; she was remembering the don's invitation to coffee downstairs, and the cold, curt look of him as he had gazed down at her in Alvedo's arms. He had plainly taken that interlude for a romantic one, and she wondered if he was going to haul her over the coals, suggest that she behave with the discretion more becoming to a physio-attendant. It seemed likely, for he didn't usually invite her to take coffee with him.

He wasn't always at home in the evenings, and when people came to dine they were usually neighboring landowners. To her relief Ricki had never received a summons to be the only female among a group of stern-faced Spaniards, who smoked cigars so strong that their aroma lingered in the air the morning after one of those business gatherings. She quite enjoyed her own company after she had settled Jaime for the night, the *brasero* in her room glowing with crushed olive stones, a fuel both warming and pleasant smelling, a good book on hand to read, and always a small glass of wine to round off her dinner. That sophisticated glass of wine on her dinner tray always made her feel less like a Jane Eyre figure in a Victorian romance!

While Ricki was washing and changing her dress for her interview with the don, she heard a couple of ominous storm growls in the distance, and she was on her way downstairs when lightning lit up the stained glass windows and thunder boomed out over the valley. Ricki wasn't exactly nervous about storms, but the electricity in the air always had an odd effect on the emotions—suddenly she was running the rest of the way down the stairs, arriving like someone pursued outside the half-open doorway of her employer's study.

She paused on the threshold of the "dragon's lair," slim and hesitant in a dress the color of young olive leaves, then from a far corner of the hall a door creaked open and she swung around to see emerging out of the door—it gave access to the cellars—a tall figure clad in shadows.

He closed the door and came striding into the lamplight where Ricki stood, her shoulders pressing the jamb of the study doorway, her hands at either side of her gripping the wood, her green eyes gone to jade in her elfin face.

"Thunder on the left, a warning, eh?" The don's eyes flicked her slim, tensed figure. "Are you afraid of the elements, Miss O'Neill? You surprise me, I thought you emancipated in every way."

"Oh, I am," she assured him airily, but as she preceded him into his "lair," she knew she was feeling far more sure of herself.

In the study the ruby red curtains were drawn, logs burned cheerily in the fireplace, and lamplight muted the room's severity almost to coziness. In the air, mingling with the resinous smell of the logs, hung the aroma of the coffee that was brewing on a portable stove.

Ricki took a startled breath, for the atmosphere was curiously intimate. The very fact that the don was brewing their coffee was proof that he didn't wish their tête-à-tête to be disturbed.

CHAPTER FIVE

DON ARTURO DREW FORWARDS a small side chair with bandy legs and scarlet cushions, and Ricki sat down with a murmur of thanks. She felt him looking at her and her glance settled on every article in the room that saved her from a direct meeting with his disturbing eyes. A carved card table of mahogany, with pools for counters and card trays let into the inlaid wood. A porcelain figurine on the mantelshelf which, significantly enough, was that of a girl with a dragon crouching at her feet. The cigarette box of hammered silver that opened and closed under the touch of long fingers, and the slim volume of Castilian verse that lay open on the reading arm of the chair the don sat down in, facing hers.

She gave him a nervous smile and watched through her lashes as he lit his cigarette. He wore a smoking jacket of dark corduroy, and there was about him a rather deliberate air as he crossed his long legs and took a pull at his cigarette. "Perhaps you will pour out our coffee, Miss O'Neill?" he suggested. "I know how nervous it makes a woman to see a man handling fine china with his clumsy hands."

"What experts you Spaniards are about women," she said lightly, glad to have something with which to occupy her hands and her attention. "Will you take sugar, *señor*, or wild honey in your coffee?"

"Wild honey, *señorita*. Like most Spaniards I have a sweet tooth. Tell me," he was looking sardonic as he accepted his cup of coffee from her hand, "was the young

Alvedo providing you with an example of our expertise when I am interrupted him?''

"I am sure you drew your own conclusions," she fenced.

"Perhaps so." He took a sip at his coffee. "But beware of starting a casual flirtation, perhaps out of boredom, which a fiery Andaluz might mistake for something more serious."

"I am sure Alvedo is far too sophisticated to be in any danger from a girl like me," Ricki said sweetly. "There is no straw in his hair as far as I can see."

"Others of this region are still a trifle old-fashioned," the don said crisply, "and I would advise a little more discretion about the places you choose for your demonstrations of affection."

Ricki almost choked on a mouthful of coffee at that one, and because he was looking so very much the Castilian overlord tonight—and looking down that hawk nose of his—she felt she had to defend what had not occurred for the sake of defending romance. The spontaneous embrace between a young couple really in love, the joyful warmth that had obviously played so small a part in his own courtship. . . .

"When two people are in love," she said, "they are quite lost to their surroundings when alone together—as if marooned on a tropical island."

"Then it must have come as quite a shock when I galloped onto your island and broke the spell," he drawled. "No wonder you looked at me with daggers in your eyes."

"Yes, no wonder," she agreed airily. "Will you have another cup of coffee, *señor*?"

"Thank you, no." He turned aside to place his cup and saucer on a side table, and Ricki took in swiftly the hard, fine definition of his profile, its severity and its hint of suffering. She tensed in her chair and knew suddenly that he was not enjoying this teasing game. Suddenly it had jabbed home to her that he had found her with Alvedo where the Devil's Tears ran down over the rocks where the lovely Conquesta had died. What a place to choose for a kiss! That was what he must be thinking!

She was gazing at him rather helplessly, wondering how to put right the false impression she had foolishly created in his mind, when he said, "I am expecting company tomorrow evening, Miss O'Neill, and I wish you to dine with us."

His tone commanded rather than invited, and Ricki's immediate thoughts were dominated by a sudden picture of herself among a group of his dark, cigar-smoking business associates. "There is no need for apprehension," he gave a rather unkind laugh. "Don Enrique Salvadori comes to dine and he will be bringing his sisters with him."

"Jaime's grandfather?" Relief and interest shone in her eyes.

"Exactly so, the *abuelito* of young Jaime." Don Arturo quirked a quizzical eyebrow. "The *señor grandero* wishes to meet the nurse of his grandson, and I am sure you will find him a most diverting man to converse with. The little aunts are also very charming. They are unmarried twins, you know, and alike to look at as a pair of seashells, one with the demure ways, the other with the sharp wit, of ladies in a Jane Austen novel."

His teeth glimmered in a smile, and his eyes for a moment were almost boyish. "I have never known them wear anything but black silk to their ankles, with lace jabots at their throats. Can you imagine them?"

Ricki returned his smile. "Who introduced you to the novels of Jane Austen, *señor*—your English grandmother?"

"Was it much of a surprise," he looked directly into

her eyes, "to learn that I have all this English blood running in my veins?"

"You're so entirely Spanish in looks and outlook that it was bound to surprise me," she admitted. Then her glance ran from his, circling the walls of his study, dark but for the bright splash here and there of a painting. "I try to visualize your grandmother in this rambling Spanish house, *señor*, and I wonder if she ever rebelled against the almost oriental seclusion of those days."

"She and my grandfather were very happy together." said the don, looking amused. "She came willingly to her oriental seclusion, as you put it, and the match was—as we put it—*buen amor*."

Heaven made, Ricki translated to herself. A real love match for the English girl who came to live in this house in the valley . . . the Cazalet house that in those days had not had a shadow hanging over it.

"Tell me something, Miss O'Neill," the don had disposed of his cigarette and was sitting forward with his long hands clasped around his knees. "Several times I have passed Jaime's room of an evening and I have heard you singing to him. I have tried to fathom the words. They had an attractive strangeness to them."

"Oh—" Ricki flushed slightly, for she didn't have much of a voice and from Sophina she had learned that her employer was fond of good music and singers. A Portuguese opera singer came to stay at the Granja now and again, Sophina had said. She had a lovely name, Irena Marcos, and Ricki had wondered if the singer was as beautiful as her name.

"I sometimes sing to Jaime in Gaelic," she explained. "My father's people lived in the wilds of Ireland and I picked up the Gaelic from them."

"Children have remarkably quick ears, have they not?" He smiled slightly. "I, as a child, picked up a love of music from my grandmother and she taught me how to play the piano.''

"I wondered who it was who played the piano in the *cuarto de estar*." Ricki smiled back shyly at him and thought how different he looked right now, talking about his grandmother and touching on his childhood. A fleeting gentleness had stolen the stern look from his face, and she guessed that tonight he had needed someone to talk to after the worry of Jaime's fall.

"Do *you* find this house an intimidating one?" he asked. "There are many corridors, many old portraits and tapestries and furniture that creaks a little in the night."

"Don't forget the owls, *señor*," she half laughed. "It is an old house, but I find it fascinating."

"I am glad to hear you say that." His gaze held hers. "We agreed, did we not, to part company if you found this house too isolated, too far from the diversions you are used to. It is fortunate that you find Alvedo Andres such a good companion—"

"Alvedo and I are just friends," she broke in.

"Of course," he inclined his head and seemed not to be particularly interested in the relationship. "This Granja, you know, has its foundations in the Roman occupation, and no doubt you have seen the Latin inscriptions carved on some of the walls and on the stone well in the main patio?"

"There's a strong Moorish atmosphere which I like best of all," she said. "The tiled bases of the fountains and the seats of the patio benches are beautiful."

"The colors and patterns of the *azulejos* are definitely oriental," he agreed. "*El suspiro de Moro* is still heard in Andalusia, echoing in the music of the fountains they designed. Some of the country people talk of seeing them riding through the morning mists."

"The trails of mist do look rather like white cloaks,"

she smiled. "Andalusians remind me of the Irish, they are so poetical in their superstitions."

"Some of those books tell fascinating stories of the Moorish occupation," he gestured at the ceiling-high book cabinets. "The intrigues at the Byzantine courts, the battles between the knights of Castile and the sheikhs, the badinage between the harem beauties and their masters. It is a colorful world you would enjoy, *niña*, if you could read Castilian."

"I must teach myself," she laughed.

"I daresay the young Alvedo would enjoy that task," he suggested.

"Perhaps." She shivered suddenly and leaned forward to feel the warmth of the fire against her hands; somehow she did not think she would be here long enough to learn how to read the Castilian language. She could hear the thunder booming above the Sierras and dying to a low echo over the valley; the logs hissed as big drops of rain came down the chimney. You became part of a household pattern without fully realizing it, and she knew that when the time came for her to leave the Granja, the break would hurt, although it had hardly hurt at all to leave the hospital.

From a corner of her eye she saw her employer rise to his feet. "We will have a glass of the wine which I brought up from the cellar this evening," he said, and while he busied himself pouring it out, Ricki rose also and took a look at the paintings on the wall of the study. They were medieval Spanish scenes that made her think of Alvedo's sketches and the way he had torn them to pieces in front of her. He didn't like it, she thought again, that young Jaime showed signs of natural artistic talent. It was his jealousy of the boy that had made him drive so furiously along that ravine road...and her wild fear of that moment was showing in her eyes as the don came across to her with the filled wine glasses.

She felt his sharp scrutiny as she took from his hand a flared bowl on a filigreed stem of silver. The wine was limpid, innocent-looking—until she tasted it. "My goodness!" Her eyes were misty from the sweet strength of the wine as they met the don's. "How strange a flavor, yet nice. It isn't sherry?"

He shook his dark head. "It is a pomegranate wine which we distill here at the Granja," he told her.

Wine of the gods! Fruit of regret for Persephone, who ate one of the pomegranate and was carried down into Hades by its dark overlord! Ricki couldn't resist a glance at her own dark host, and she guessed from the smile curling on his lips that he was sharing her thoughts.

"So fragile a vessel," he held up his goblet, "to hold so strong a wine. Drink up, Miss O'Neill."

And telling herself not to be so fanciful, she obeyed him as he strolled away from her to stand where the long ruby curtains were drawn across the windows. Ricki heard the thunder, then the curtains billowed behind Don Arturo like a tongue of flame...*Lucifer after his abdication from the heavens*, she thought wildly, and because he was so disturbingly quick at reading her mind she turned hurriedly to one of the wall paintings. "What an intriguing picture that is," she said. "Is the man with the ladder a lamplighter?"

"He is a La Manchan romantic carrying a wooing ladder on his back," the don explained. "A young man would place such a ladder against the iron *rejas* of a girl's window and woo her through the bars."

"Eating the iron," Ricki murmured.

"Exactly so." Eyes dark as night swept her young face. "You are interested in the old romantic customs of Spain, *señorita*?"

"All things romantic have an appeal for women," she replied, "and the boldness of your land, the hot sun, the hint of cruelty, all combine together to produce the right setting for—passion.''

"Not for love?" came his deep-throated question. "Spain is said to be the last stronghold of romantic love."

"I can believe that," she admitted, "if you are talking about the volcanic kind."

"Would it really be worth having if it were not a strong and turbulent emotion?" he asked. "It should be dangerous and exciting and, in a woman, spiced with fear, for that fear spices love in a man."

"You make it sound a cruel experience, Don Arturo." Ricki's fingers had clenched on the silver stem of her wine glass.

"They say there is truth in wine." He smiled as he studied the limpid gleam of the pomegranate wine. "Love is conquest and submission. It hangs colored lanterns in the poorest cottage, and when born of illusion it dies of disillusion. It is rooted in the soul of woman to love, we say here in Spain, and she can no more evade it than—"

"The moth who cannot resist a flame!" Ricki's eyes were drawn to his as those words were drawn out of her, and she was nettled by his male assumption that love was the main preoccupation of all women. "It's a bit turn-of-the-century, *señor*, to assume that all women are panting to be enslaved by a man and his demands," she took a breath. "When women discarded all those hampering petticoats, they discarded with them the male-encouraged notion that they were meant to be bound by restrictions. Women enjoy now a sense of being equal and free."

"To kick up their heels?" he drawled.

"Not at all." Her eyes flashed danger green. "To take our proper place in the scheme of things, and maybe do something about stopping you men from blowing the world sky high with your explosive tempers and bombs.''

"You advocate a United Nations of women, eh?'' He looked amused.

"It isn't such a bad idea.'' She tilted her chin. "I bet we'd make a better job of keeping the peace than you men seem able to. Wine, women and wars are all you think about!''

"*Ay Dios mio!*'' He arched a black brow at her outburst. "I bring here a nurse for my nephew and find I have a young Dido on my hands. It will all be the same one hundred years from now, you know, so just enjoy the things meant for a girl to think and dream about.''

"That's a typical male remark,'' she flashed. "You men just can't bear the thought of women having anything in their minds other than wedding bells and babies!''

"Well, do you not see, *chica*,'' amusement was slashing a line down his swarthy cheek, "we have to believe, more than ever in this technical age, that there is something simple and fundamental left in our lives. There is really nothing that is more fundamental than a woman, and if she should become enchanted by science and inflicted with political ambitions she would lose her earthy magic and we men our one abiding anchor. It has always been the one great strength of woman that through everything she has remained the eternal Eve, offering the consolation of her arms and her simplicity after man has bitten once again the apple of discord.''

'You put it very colorfully, *señor*.'' Ricki gazed into her wineglass, and there was a flush—perhaps from the wine—in her cheeks. How had they got around to discussing such disconcerting subjects as love, wedding bells, and the arms of Eve? She breathed a low sigh of relief when he switched to a more avuncular topic and asked for a rundown on Jaime's progress to date.

He listened to her with quite a serious air, but she caught the twinkle in his eye when he said, "You know, Miss O'Neill, the career-minded are usually very detached in their attitude toward human relationships, but you are as protective toward my nephew as a young tigress with a cub."

"*A tigress with a cub*! She felt the blush that ran up her neck into her cheeks at that remark. "Y-you rarely see us together," she faltered. "How can you know—"

"I see all that I wish to see here at the Granja." He spoke dryly. "Come, you look quite guilty. Do you not like to be caught out as a woman of warmth rather than a cool-hearted career woman?"

"Jaime is an easy child to grow fond of...." Then, meeting his eyes, she said, "I hope you don't mind the attachment that has formed between us?"

"He will feel it, when the time comes for it to be broken," Jaime's guardian said crisply.

Ricki winced as though a lash had flicked her skin, for she too would feel it when she parted from Jaime and lost his childish affection, his grave-eyed smile and the way he cuddled down at night with the amusing rag-rabbit she had made him. During the day she had to hide the rabbit in her room. Sophina would jeer at him, he said, for having such a toy. She would tell her sons that Jaime de Cazalet was a baby.

"It isn't easy for a woman to keep her distance with a child," Ricki said stiffly. "And it's often easier for a child who has suffered to give trust and affection to a stranger. Jaime is sensitive beyond his years, and past events and the people connected with them are still painful to him."

"You are really quite a philosopher yourself, Miss O'Neill," the don drawled.

"I am merely a person trained in the art of caring for hurt people," she rejoined. "Once Jaime is able to get about like a normal boy, he will forget the past—"

"And forgive the ogre, eh, for helping to kill his mother?"

The don's face was a mask of pain as he spoke, and his eyes were night dark, with lines biting deep at the sides of them. Ricki stared back at him wordlessly, and now there was no sound of thunder, no hiss of rain. The storm outside had abated, but here in the study the tension could be felt. Then Ricki's employer swung away from her and the click of his wineglass on wood was like a sharp tap against a nerve. She gave a shiver and realized that the whispers had crept into *her* mind and left doubts—doubts which her eyes had not been able to conceal from him!

"It grows late," he said, and, when he turned to face her, his expression was the one she was most used to, stern, a trifle grave, with faint shadows haunting the planes and hollows of temple and jaw. He took her wineglass and as he set it down on the table, the rims faintly clinked in an echo, it seemed to Ricki, of duelists touching foils before a fight. He followed her from the study, after extinguishing the lamps, and they walked side by side across the hall, across the *escudo* set in the cobbles, and she felt the light touch of his fingers under her elbow as they mounted the stairs.'

There is something curiously intimate about going upstairs with a man, and Ricki was conscious of this. The brush of dark corduroy against her bare arm, the warm, hard feel of a male hand under her elbow, the square shoulder several inches above her head. What was he thinking, she wondered. He was so withdrawn when he was silent, even though they touched as they reached the head of the stairs and the gallery lay ahead of them, pooled with shadows and niches.

"When my mother came to this house as a bride—" he spoke so abruptly that Ricki gave a start "—she wished to bring certain goods and chattels from her home in Castile. My father indulged her whim and that is why Aguinarda portraits hang on the walls of this Andalusian farmhouse, and why such suits of armor stand on guard in its corridors.'' He slanted down at Ricki his brief flicker of a smile and pointed out in a wall niche the black and visored armor she often hurried past on her way to her room. It was realistically shaped to the figure of a tall man, and there was a black plume on the helmet that moved in a sudden draft.

The don held open her door, and as she passed him, she looked up at him and wanted to ask if the whispers in the valley held truth or misconception. Her heart drove the question to her lips, but all that came out was a husky, ''*Buena noche, señor*. Thank you for the invitation, and the pomegranate wine.''

''Wine of the dark god, eh?'' His dark eyes scanned her upraised face. ''I hope you do not feel that it was Pluto, after all, who came by in his chariot and carried you off?''

She smiled as if at a jest, but after he had said goodnight and left her alone in the dimness of her room, she stood for several minutes leaning against the closed door, listening to her heartbeats and thinking of what he had left unsaid—Pluto, after carrying off the girl, had held her in bondage!

Ricki walked through the shadows of her room, plucking her warm dressing gown off the rail of her bed and throwing it around her shoulders as she went out onto the gallery above the main patio. The rain had ceased and left behind in the air a wonderful freshness in which mingled the smell of drenched creepers and trees. Ricki drank in the tangy air like wine...wine of Andalusia...combating just a little the curious mixture of fear and fascination which had befallen her in the don's company tonight.

Her eyes followed the flight of a moth that seemed to glimmer pale emerald in the darkness; she heard a grasshopper among the trees and caught the restless whinny of a horse down in the stables. Perhaps the spirited gray which the master of the valley liked to gallop about on!

Strange, unpredictable man, she thought, and now she knew why her nighttime encounter with him in Toledo had made her wary of him; she had sensed in him depths dangerous to a woman because they held loneliness and reserve, and pain.

"We of Spain have medieval hearts," Alvedo Andres had said.

And here at the Granja, Ricki had discovered this to be true. This old Iberian farmhouse held the past a prisoner, situated as it was in a valley where hawks nested among the rocks, where hidden streams caught the sun like broken glass, and thyme and spruce grew wild among the ancient olive trees. The Granja slumbered in the hot sun with the grace of a tiger. It brooded in the dusk with the hooded eyes of an eagle. . . .

"And you, my girl," Ricki laughed ruefully to herself, "have too much imagination by far! To your bed, you Gael, otherwise you'll be short on the beauty sleep you need for the don's dinner party tomorrow night!"

NEXT MORNING, Ricki could not keep from Jaime the fact that his grandfather was coming to the Granja that evening. This exciting piece of news kept him lively all day, and when his bedtime came around he was still chattering away like a cricket. His *abuelito* was coming upstairs to see him, wasn't he? Also Tia Rosina—and Tia Beatriz, though she was not quite so soft and nice as Tia Rosina?

Yes, Ricki assured him. Those three good people would be bound to come up and see him. Now would he be a good *muchacho* and go to sleep?

"I cannot go to sleep," he rejoined. "My stomach is full of bees."

"You funny one, you!" She laughed and thought it an apt description of excitement. "I promise on my honor to bring the little aunts and the grandfather up to see you later on. Now do settle down, poppet. I must have a bath, and then I have to dress up in my finery. I dare not be late downstairs."

"Are you afraid of the *patrono*?" Jaime asked in a whisper. "Shall I ask my *abuelito* to take both of us away from him?"

"Now don't be silly," she chided. "Don Arturo is not an ogre."

At last she got her charge off to sleep and went along to her room to get ready for the dinner party. She put on her best dress, the green of wood sorel, with a *bateau* neckline which bared her white young shoulders. The lamp on her dressing table cast a flattering glow over her reflection in the mirror, and not displeased she picked up a chiffon handkerchief, lowered the lamp and made her way toward the stairs.

Was it by chance or design that Don Arturo was standing at the foot of them as she negotiated their twists and turns to the hall? Anyway there he was, looking dark and distinguished in his evening clothes, the sophisticated glint of gold at his shirt cuffs.

"Spaniards are punctual only at the bullfight—Don Enrique especially so." He smiled down gravely at Ricki, then indicated that she precede him into the *cuarto de estar*. "Would you care for a glass of wine while we wait, Miss O'Neill? No doubt you are feeling somewhat nervous at the thought of meeting these relatives of Jaime?"

She agreed that a glass of wine would be welcome and went to stand by the fireplace. The fire had been lit and the Cordoban screen moved to one side; the vivid blue leather framed Ricki as she stood feeling slight and very feminine in her attractive dress.

"This is not pomegranate wine, Miss O'Neill." The don's glance flickered over her as he picked up a decanter. "It is a prosaic sherry which I am sure will not stir that vivid imagination of yours to thoughts I find rather disconcerting."

She blinked at the idea of disconcerting *him*.

"You do not appear to think me like other men," he said dryly.

"Well, you're my employer," she fenced.

"I am sure my status as your employer has little to do with the way you regard me." His eyes quizzed her disconcerted face as he handed her a glass of sherry. "Do I look so very different from other men?"

She could almost have laughed aloud at the question. His look of lordly hauteur was not seen every day, and who else had eyes so dense and compelling?

"You are a strange, elusive child," he then murmured.

"I'm not a child!" she protested, conscious of his gaze upon the neckline of her dress and the way it revealed more of her shoulders than would be thought decorous by a Spanish woman. "Do I look childish?" she asked defiantly.

"You look very charming," he said indulgently. "The green of your gown matches your eyes and contrasts with your hair—and now please excuse me! I hear the car of Don Enrique."

He strode from the room and Ricki was left gazing wide-eyed at her reflection in the baroque wall mirror. She ought to feel flattered by the don's remark but knew he had no more than told a "child" that she looked presentable for a party.

The room in which they dined was large and ornate, with Pastrana tapestries on the walls, Iberian figurines on pedestals, and furniture with a wine-toned gloss to it. Moorish chandeliers hung from the high, painted ceiling, and it seemed to Ricki as dinner proceeded that each minuscule tinkle of the jewel-toned crystals was like the echo of the long-lost laughter of the houris who had once lounged under the lamps in a Moorish palace. The crusading Aguinardas had probably taken the lamps as booty, now they lighted the dining *sala* of this Andalusian farmhouse.

"I notice you are fascinated by the Moorish ceiling, Miss O'Neill." Don Enrique Salvadori was a charming, still very vigorous man with a head of iron gray hair, cheekbones that thrust prominently from sun-seamed skin, and a black patch over his left eye that gave him the look of a Spanish buccaneer.

"I'm astonished," she smiled back at him, "by such a love of beauty in such a barbaric people."

"I had no idea such a thought was running through your mind." His smile revealed strong, still very excellent teeth. "But beauty and cruelty often go hand in hand, you know," he added, and she was aware at once of the sharp lift of Don Arturo's head.

Don Enrique helped himself to pepper. "The occupation by Moors of Andalusia influenced not only our architecture but our temperament. We Spaniards love beauty," here his lively right eye flashed from Ricki's green eyes to her white young shoulders, "but we are also addicted to the bullfight."

"Enrique," spoke up Tia Beatriz, the more dominant of the sixty-year-old twins, "I am sure Miss Oneeil is not interested in the bullfight. Very few English people are. They think it cruel, do they not, Miss Oneeil?"

"I'm afraid so," she admitted.

"Yet many of your tourists are to be seen attending the *corridas* in Barcelona and Seville," said Don Enrique.

"I expect they go mainly out of curiosity. I can't imagine many of them enjoying so barbaric and one-sided a sport," Ricki replied.

"Hardly one-sided, *niña*!" Back went the iron gray head of the *ganadero* and he roared with laughter. "Bulls are strong, fearless, agile and cunning. An *espada* is but a man, with only a piece of silk to cloak his frailty and his fear of those curving weapons of horn *el toro* carries upon his great head."

"The matador isn't alone as the animal is," Ricki argued. "He has his team of picadors and that poor bag of bones called a horse to distract the bull's attention."

"Ah, the horse." Don Enrique pulled a mouth. "It is the horse in the bullring who upsets the British, eh? They do not care to see the poor brute put through the agony of the *puntago*?"

"Who would?" she shuddered. "Their vocal chords are cut, aren't they, so they can't scream?"

"I regret so." A tinge of amusement flickered on the old man's mouth and he cast a glance across the table at Don Arturo. "You are right, *hombre*, she has the spirited heart, this one."

Ricki felt startled by the remark, but she wouldn't look at the man who had said it in the first place and so reveal that she had taken notice of it. What had he implied, anyway? That she was a female who could not be pushed around—a type he must find very irritating with his Latin ideas regarding women!

"How cruel men can be!" she exclaimed, half out of annoyance with that lean dark autocrat facing her.

"You think there is no cruelty in women?" The question came swiftly from across the table, cutting like a lash. "Do not flatter yourself, Miss O'Neill."

"Arturo," Tia Rosina gave his wrist a tap with her fan, "what an ungallant remark. Why, one look at

Jaime's nurse is enough to show how kind she is. Such beautiful eyes!"

"But green as a tigress's," he gibed.

Ricki looked at him, then, and couldn't keep a flash of animosity out of her green eyes. He saw it all right and mockingly raised his wineglass as if to say that he felt exactly the same way about her.

A manservant brought in a big platter of rich Spanish trifle and when it had been served they began eating it. Don Enrique—who had refused a helping of the dessert—talked to Ricki of the tapestry on one of the paneled walls. It depicted the battle of Lepanto, with Spanish galleons sailing into action against a scimitar of Turkish galleys, the long lines of oars dipping into the churning sea, the sun glinting on armor and steel, the gold and crimson emblems of Castile blowing in the wind.

Ricki wondered, as she listened to the man at her side, whether he spoke so kindly in order to soothe the sting left by her employer's remark about the cruelty of women. The old rancher must have flicked by it, as well, for it had been his daughter who had taught Don Arturo how cruel a woman could be!

The long, very Spanish meal came to an end, and the two little aunts went with Ricki to the *cuarto de estar*, the men remaining at table for a smoke and glasses of Manzanilla, the sea-matured wine so well liked by Spaniards.

"It was much of a surprise to us, when we learned that Arturo had brought here an English woman to care for Jaime." Tia Beatriz stirred her coffee and frankly studied Ricki, who had sat down in one of the old gold loveseats. "He is a man who is not easy to know, someone you might find a little difficult at times."

"I don't see him very much," Ricki said, keeping her voice light and friendly. "Jaime, of course, is no trouble at all and we're friends already."

"Is there any hope that he will eventually walk, Miss Oneeil?" Tia Rosina was looking at Ricki with gentle, inquiring eyes. "I am sure that Arturo's infelicity at times is brought on by worry about the *pequeño*. He grows impatient to see him as other boys, which is only natural. Jaime will be the next master of the Granja if Arturo does not marry—"

"Sister, you are too much the *romantica*," Tia Beatriz scoffed. "Arturo is a man—unlike yourself he will not marry himself to a memory."

Tia Rosina flushed and fingered the golden lyre-brooch that was pinned among the creamy frills of the lace jabot at the neck of her black dress. "You never liked Juan Leparos, did you, Beatriz? You helped, I know, to have him sent away from the ranch."

"He was a common bullherder," her sister said tartly. "You would not have been happy with such as he."

"Happier than one who has no children of her own," Tia Rosina returned, with a flash of spirit. "I should not now be married to a memory, as you put it."

"No, you would be a grass widow," Tia Beatriz rejoined. "When your *vaquero* grew weary of your refined ways, he would soon have sought gayer distractions in the cafés, and you know it, my sister."

Tia Rosina gazed down into her black silk lap, and Ricki couldn't help feeling compassion for the gentle twin whose romance with a *vaquero* had been thwarted by her dominant, less appealing sister. They were amazingly alike to look at, but the touch of hardness in Beatriz would always have made her less attractive than Rosina.

"What are your impressions of this part of Andalusia, Miss Oneeil?" Beatriz had a sharp way of springing a question and waiting like a jetty-eyed bird for a reply. "As you are from England, you cannot be used to the extremes of temperature which we have here?"

Or the extremes in temperament, Ricki thought.

"I love the sun," she smiled. "I don't know whether you've heard or not, but Don Arturo agreed to have the small swimming pool and the adjacent summerhouse cleaned out so Jaime and I can use them. Water exercises will be of immense benefit to him, you see."

"The pool and the *caseta* are to be restored to use?" Beatriz exchanged a significant glance with her sister, then sat forward and peered hard at Ricki. "How clever of you to have persuaded Arturo to do this thing—to let the son of Leandro have for a playground the place where so much unhappiness for this house had its beginning. It was there—and I presume you have heard by now the servants' version of the story—that the old Señor Cazalet found Conquesta's note of elopement and collapsed from a fatal stroke."

Ricki murmured an assent, and suddenly the full force of the Cazalet tragedy swept over her, plunging her into a vivid recollection of the furious way Don Arturo had come striding toward her through the twining shadows and brambles of that ghostly garden. He had looked as though he meant to strike her, but she had opened the slave door and entered the garden in all innocence. She hadn't known that she was invading a place which held such grim memories for him.

"W-when I suggested to Don Arturo that he reopen the place, I had no idea his father had been stricken down in the *caseta*," she faltered. "H-he didn't tell me—"

"Will there be danger in allowing Jaimito to go into water?" Tia Rosina asked nervously.

"Hardly any at all," Ricki assured her. "I shall be with him all the time, and then again he will have the added security of an inflated ring. He will love the water, so please don't worry."

"How can we help but worry, Miss Oneeil?" Tia

Beatriz had a brooding look as she spoke. "The child only just escaped death in his uncle's car, therefore it would not do for him to meet it in Arturo's pool—" and there she broke off, a finger swiftly at her lips as the door opened to admit the two dons.

"The man is an artist with the cape," Don Enrique was proclaiming. "His Veronica is the most daring thing I have seen in years—he lets the bull fairly scorch the silk of his cape!"

"I, too, have seen a Veronica equally daring." Don Arturo spoke deliberately and his eyes captured Ricki's as he crossed the room in his graceful yet autocratic way, holding her gaze as he passed the loveseat in which she sat and paused to lean his shoulders against the dark marble of the mantelshelf.

"Well, little aunts, do you approve of Jaime's nurse?" he asked, glancing with a hint of sardonic amusement from one twin to the other. "Is she as you expected her to be?"

Tia Beatriz shrugged her shoulders. "She is very young, Arturo, and you know that in my opinion a male attendant is better for the child." She gave him a sharp look. "Why did you suddenly decide to employ a mere girl?"

He arched an arrogant black brow at the question, while Don Enrique, now enthroned in a high-backed chair, gave a snort of impatience. "Beatriz, you grow acid on the vine, while Rosina goes to sugar," he growled. "The boy needs a young woman around him, someone to sing and cry with him, and to give him the cuddling he misses from his *mamaita*."

Ricki caught her breath at the remark, and she couldn't for the life of her stop her glance from leaping to the man who lounged beside the glowing cavern of the fireplace. He seemed quite unmoved, until the flames suddenly leaped and highlighted his profile and she saw how taut the muscle was beside his mouth.

"Enrique—" Tia Rosina fluttered her fan nervously, "I think it would be nice for Miss Oneeil and Jaimito to come and spend a few days at the ranch. We could take them into Seville in the carriage and I am sure they would both enjoy a look at the Alcazar."

"You would like to visit our ranch, Miss Oneeil?" Don Enrique asked. "You did not think the small *picaro* would find it tiring?"

Before replying to these questions, Ricki thought it tactful to turn to her employer for his opinion. He nodded gravely in answer to the query in her eyes. "If Jaime is fit enough to travel, then by all means accept the invitation," he said.

He spoke rather coldly, she thought, but she did like the idea of visiting the Salvadori ranch, and the change of environment was bound to do Jaime a lot of good. "I should like to come," she said to the Salvadoris. "Thank you for inviting me."

The old rancher stretched out benevolently in his chair, his iron gray head pillowed against the padding, a big dark-stoned ring gleaming on his hand as he gestured with his cigar. "We will show you the *tientas*, the testing of the young bulls. You will enjoy that, Miss Oneeil," his right eye twinkled, "for it does not involve any cruelty at all. Also, as I am soon to be seventy years young, we will have a party and you will learn to dance the Angelina."

"I've heard of the Angelina," Ricki smiled, liking this rugged, old-young man very much. "It's a ring dance, isn't it?"

"Yes, and gay as first love, *niña*," he told her enthusiastically, spilling cigar ash down his silk waistcoat and ignoring his sister Beatriz as she tut-tutted. "The rings when formed are made up of girls and men in alternate positions. The music strikes up and *olé*, we dance!

Arturo," he flashed an imperious glance at the younger man, "go to the piano and play the music of the Angelina for Miss Oneeil."

"You would like me to play?" Don Arturo looked directly at Ricki.

"Very much, *señor*," she replied. "I'm fond of good music."

"Then I will play." He shrugged, as if not really interested in her likes or dislikes, and as she watched him go to the piano and put back the lid she told herself yet again that he was coldest, most armored individual she had ever met in her life. What did the Salvadoris secretly think of him? Did it worry them that he had the legal guardianship of young Jaime? Possibly, judging from the way Tia Beatriz had spoken earlier!

He ran his fingers along the keyboard, as though he hadn't played for a long time and they needed flexing, but as soon as he began to play he brought the primitive rhythm of the dance right into the room, and Don Enrique began to beat time to it, nodding at her to do the same. But she was too shy of her employer's dark, sardonic eyes, and she wondered if the lovely silk shawl draping the piano had belonged to his grandmother.

A cameo of him as a small boy sprang into her mind, seated at that keyboard, raised to its level by a pile of sheet music, learning his scales and glancing up now and again for the smiling approval of his fair-skinned grandmother. So vivid was the impression that she gave a start when Tia Rosina leaned forward from her couch to say quietly, "Arturo plays now a song his grandmother was very fond of. She, also, came from England."

"I know the song," Ricki whispered back.

"Then will you not sing it for us?" asked Tia Rosina.

"Oh no!" Ricki shook her head and spoke louder than she intended, catching at once the mocking attention of Don Arturo.

"Come, are you shy?" He lifted his voice above the music. "I heard you singing earlier."

"That was different." She blushed as the dark eyes of the Salvadori family dwelt on her, simultaneously.

"Miss O'Neill is afraid that we will be more critical of her singing than Jaime," said the don mockingly. "The British are an amazing race, are they not? The men dare the devil himself on the battlefield, and the women are the most intelligent in the world, yet neither can bear to be caught out in a sentimental action. They would rather be thought cold than warm."

"Better to be reserved than truly cold!" Ricki was sparked to temper and she just had to get in a thrust at him.

He raised a black eyebrow and their eyes met across the room in a jet and emerald explosion. "Never challenge a Spaniard," he said, "unless you are prepared to accept the consequences."

And as she sat there in her loveseat, shaken by the implication of his words, he finished off what he was playing and rose from the piano bench. "There, I have done my party piece," he said, shutting down the lid.

"I have known you to play for hours when Irena Marcos has been here," Tia Beatriz reminded him. "Do you find her more inspiring than you find us, Arturo?"

"You are always stimulating company, little aunt," he rejoined dryly. "But I must admit that Irena is so superb a singer that it is a joy to accompany her."

"At the piano, and no doubt elsewhere," Tia Beatriz suggested tartly. "Does she plan to visit the Granja in the near future?"

"I should not be at all surprised to see her car come sweeping through our gates one of these days," he drawled. "And now shall we have some fresh hot coffee with *coñac*?"

"That would be welcome before we make a move,"

said Don Enrique, and his one shrewd eye was fixed on Ricki as her employer went over to press the service bell.

"It always makes me feel a little sad when a party is almost over," mourned Tia Rosina, and her sister remarked at once that it was childish to want to hang on to used-up pleasures. Ricki, however, gave her favorite twin a sympathetic smile, knowing exactly how she felt.

"Before very long we will be having *my* party at the ranch," Don Enrique reminded Rosina. "It will be fun to arrange, much of a change for us old ones as Miss Oneeil will be bringing the *chico*."

"Jaime will be thrilled when I tell him," Ricki said. "His *abuelito* means about everything to him."

She hadn't paused to choose her words, and she was aware at once of the forbidding silence that followed her remark. She bit her lip nervously, and it was quite a relief when the door opened and Alvarez wheeled in the coffee trolley. Tia Beatriz proceeded to pour, while Tia Rosina chattered away like a bird in order to relieve an atmosphere that had grown palpably tense. When Don Arturo paused beside Ricki with the *coñac* bottle, she could feel his eyes on her and she didn't dare look at him, thanking him in a strangled way as he enriched her coffee with the brandy.

She wondered, in a dull, guilty way, if subconsciously she had meant to hurt him . . . *if* she had hurt him.

Before the party broke up, the two little aunts wanted to take a peep at Jaime, who, as it happened, was lying in the lamplight with his eyes wide open. Ricki left the twins cooing one each side of his bed and ran downstairs to tell his grandfather he was awake. "Ah, then I will go up and have a few words with him!" Looking pleased, he hurried across the hall and mounted quickly to the gallery. *Every inch a pirate for a boy to love*, Ricki reflected.

"You are wondering why Jaime lives here with me instead of at the ranch of his grandfather, eh?"

Ricki turned slowly to face her employer, her eyes giving away her thoughts to him. "You're his legal guardian, of course," she said fidgeting with her chiffon handkerchief, "but there is his physical welfare to think of and he—he might be happier with his grandfather."

"Jaime is a Cazalet," the don said, and she saw him touch with a lean hand the big, embossed family Bible that stood on the reading desk nearby. "He belongs here at the Granja."

"But, *señor*, if a child is not contented—oh, I'm not saying that you don't provide every comfort, every attention, but children are funny little things a—and like grownups they have their prejudices—"

"I understand all that, and I appreciate your concern for the boy, but—" an adamant note crept into the don's voice—"I shall not change my mind."

"*Señor*—"

"You waste your breath, Miss O'Neill," he cut in. "I know what I am doing, and I really must add that you are ruled by your heart rather than your head. Jaime would be spoiled abominably at the ranch of those well-meaning old ones, and I wish before anything that he grow up a *man*. A man, Miss O'Neill, with a sense of responsibility."

"You—will allow me to take him to the ranch for a visit?" she asked, feeling defeated and chilled by the iron resolve of this particular man.

"I am not the complete ogre of the castle," he responded dryly. "When I make a promise I do not break it."

She flushed slightly, and perhaps it was a self-defense mechanism that unloosed her fingers on the chiffon square so that it fluttered out of her hand to land on the Cazalet *escudo*, still holding its colors among the foot-worn cobbles of the hall. The need to retrieve the square gave her an excuse to escape from the don's eyes, but as she bent down he bent too and their eyes met above the carved *escudo*, while their hands touched, without intention, as they reached together for her handkerchief. Her fingers fled as if from the touch of flame, and as she stood up she could feel the wild thumping of her heart. Bending down too quickly had caused it, she told herself, but knew very well the real cause.

It was a mixture of fear and fascination...for there was no denying that there clung to this man the subtle magnetism that clings to most members of an old, proud dynasty. She knew, also, that she dealt with a man who was quite implacable; one who never broke a single resolve that he made!

The Salvadoris came down from saying good-night to Jaime, and Alvarez brought a large overcoat and a pair of old-fashioned cloaks out of the coat closet in the hall. "I have informed Jaimito that you are bringing him on a visit to us," whispered Don Enrique, boomingly, into Ricki's ear. "How his eyes sparkled! He was very *thrilled*."

She smiled, and couldn't help thinking how much more boyishness there was in the old rancher than in Don Arturo, who was half his age. She walked out to the patio with Don Enrique, where his big car waited with its headlights beaming on the whitewashed walls of the outhouses and the abundant tangles of wild roses and honeysuckle that grew in various nooks and crannies. The night air had grown cool and sharp, and Ricki clasped her bare arms with her hands as she stood conversing with Jaime's grandfather. "The *chico* has a passion for my *vaqueros*," he laughed, "and I have promised they will give for him a display of horsemanship when he comes to stay for a while at the ranch. Ah, if only—"

There, with an audible sigh, the old rancher broke off and turned to ask his sisters if they were ready. Ricki gave a start as something silken and fringed landed on her bare shoulders and arms—the lovely shawl from the don's piano, accompanied by a curt comment that she would catch a chill if she stood long out here with uncovered shoulders.

"Thank you," she said and wished there wasn't always a hidden sting in his remarks to her. What was it he disliked the most, her European mode of dress or the fact that she had got on so well with Don Enrique?

She stood in the side-glimmer of the car's lights as he kissed the small, ivory colored hands of the twins and handed them into the upholstered interior of the car. Don Enrique took her own hand and lightly kissed the back of it, his piratical eye twinkling brightly at her. "If I were the *caballero* of my youth, Miss Oneeil," he smiled, "I would be kissing the palm of your hand."

"Really?" She joined in the game and smiled back at him. "Is a kiss in the palm more significant?"

"In Spain it is very significant," he chuckled. "We are a subtle people, *niña*, and our ways to the heart are more quietly ruthless than you would believe."

"A kiss in the palm of the hand doesn't strike me as ruthless," she scoffed.

"Then it is obvious you have never received such a kiss from a Spaniard," he rejoined teasingly. "What he can imply with such a kiss is really too much for those *diminutas orejas* of yours, so I will leave you to glean the knowledge for yourself."

During this playful exchange Ricki was aware of her employer standing by with a sardonic expression, while Tia Beatriz peered inquisitively out of the car window. Suddenly Beatriz could contain herself no longer and she called out, "You forget your years, Enrique. The night air is not good for old bones!"

"What can you do with such a sister!" He threw up his hands. "It is no wonder, Beatriz, that you have never received the kiss about which I speak—you have gall under your tongue instead of honey.''

"Better there, brother, than in my intentions," she shot back at him. "And now, *mi gran caballero*, please tear yourself away from Jaimito's nurse and get into the car,''

"I am coming, my *tortolas*," he said sweetly, adding with a direct look at Don Arturo, ''The boy is looking very much improved, *hombre*. There is no doubt in my mind that you have placed him in kind and clever hands.''

Ricki flushed with pleasure at the warm sincerity in Don Enrique's voice, and his *hasta la vista* was still ringing in her ears after the big car had rolled out from under the stone archway onto the road that led away from the valley, toward the open plains where the Salvadori ranch was situated.

A smile lingering on her lips, she drew about her the folds of the silk shawl her employer had flung over her shoulders. Overhead the stars swarmed like fireflies, while the dusky air was spiced with the scents of flowers and creepers that had been sun drenched all day. Then, suddenly, she alerted into a slim figure of delight as from among some nearby cypresses there came the sweet piercing song of a night bird.

She stood there, unbelieving and enchanted by the quavers and trills of the first nightingale she had ever heard singing, her head cocked toward the cypress spires where stars glinted as though hung there. "How beautiful. . .and just a little bit sad," she murmured.

"Like life. . .and love," said a voice at her shoulder.

She caught her breath, turned too quickly to hasten indoors and stumbled on the edge of a raised cobblestone. Warm, swift hands took and steadied her. "Is the wine of the pomegranate still troubling you?" said the don mockingly.

He firmly held her shoulders pinned against his chest, his hands about her bare arms under the fringes of the shawl, and her heart was in her mouth in case he was about to prove, here and now, that to challenge a Spaniard was to invite dire consequences. Then she gave a little gasp as he spun her toward him, a doll he had taken into his hands, whom he could near enough break in two if he so wished!

He tilted her chin with a long index finger and scrutinized her face in the starlight. There wasn't a hint of a smile on his mouth, but she saw something alive and taunting glimmering in his dark eyes. "Are you tired after the party," he asked, "or have you lost your courage now that you find yourself alone with me?"

She wanted very much to laugh in his face, to say defiantly that he didn't scare her in the least, but never before had she been so close to the flexible strength of the man, to the dark mystery of him in an atmosphere heavy with the scent of honeysuckle and roses, and haunted by the sad sweetness of the nightingale singing in the cypresses. She felt the pulse that beat in her throat and saw his eyes fix upon it. He was so near...intolerably near enough to take her mouth....

She went taut, her every nerve shocked wide awake and alert at so shattering a thought, and then with a laugh he said, "Are you afraid I shall kiss you?"

"Goodness, no!" His mockery was like a jet of icy water in her face, and it was even more intolerable that he should have guessed her thoughts. "I'm well aware that you're merely trying to scare me by implying such an intention," she said coldly.

"Let me remind you, *chica*, that you stumbled and I caught hold of you to steady you. Come," his tone was dry, "do I really deserve such suspicion from you?"

"No one, Don Arturo, could accuse you of being an

easy person to fathom,'' she rejoined, ''and being a woman I prefer open country to the edge of a chasm.''

''So I am to you a chasm, eh? I am full of shadows and crags and depth, and I unnerve you?'' His hands tightened for a moment on her slim arms, then slackened. ''How young you are! I forget that the British take longer to grow up than the Spanish.''

He released her suddenly, as though the game of baiting her had lost its edge. He stood aside so that she could precede him into the house, and she hurried ahead of him, in out of the scented night where the nightingale added its ''ravish'd'' notes. She removed the silken shawl from around her shoulders and handed it to her employer without meeting his eyes. ''Good night, *señor*,'' she said politely. ''Thank you for a most interesting evening.''

''*Buena noche*, Miss O'Neill.'' He inclined his dark head. ''For me, also, the evening has had its moments.''

She couldn't help but look at him when he said that, but his eyes were inscrutable and it was impossible to tell whether he mocked her or meant what he said. She gathered her skirts and walked quickly to the stairs, her heels clicking on the stones of the hall, and as she ran upstairs she was hoping that Jaime's grandfather would write soon to say that everything was prepared for their visit.

CHAPTER SIX

DURING THE FOLLOWING WEEK Ricki and Jaime used the swimming pool for the first time. Filled now with water, the mosaic tiling of the pool showed up in lovely wavering patterns, while the little house of shells looked really cozy and was well aired of ghosts, Ricki thought, since she had been in and out watering the plants, arranging in the chairs the bright new cushions she had made for them, and hanging on the walls attractive oddments such as colorful gourds which took strange shapes when they dried and became hollow.

Ricki had sent to a store in Seville for swimwear for Jaime and herself, along with inflatable rubber rings to support the boy in the water. He was excited and nervous as she dressed him in his swimming trunks—Alvarez had carried him down to the *caseta*—and when Ricki felt his fingers clenching the Gaelic floss of her sweater she suddenly unfastened the chain which held her good-luck shamrock and put it around the boy's neck. "There, now you'll be safe and protected in the water," she assured him with a smile.

"What about you, Rickee?" He fingered the shamrock and studied her with his great serious eyes. "Will you be safe without your charm of good luck?"

"I'll tell you what I'll do," she ran over to where a patch of vervain grew in the sun and plucked a sprig. "I'll wear this in my hair—there, how does it look?"

"It makes you look nice." His eyes had begun to smile. "But what is the good of that?"

"Vervain is a magical plant, my lad." She did an Irish jig for him among the shadow patterns cast on the flagstones by the boughs of the trees, and his laughter rang out, fresh and young here where his lovely mother had sat watching her admirers sporting for her amusements in the water.

Having coaxed the child into a more relaxed mood, Ricki whipped off her sweater and slacks to reveal her own swimsuit, and in a few more minutes she and Alvarez had eased the boy into the water and he was floating, all big-eyed and still a little scared, in the support of the rubber ring which Alvarez had inflated.

"Well, my pigeon," Ricki joined her charge in the water, "how do you like yourself?"

"I am floating like a duck, Rickee." He paddled with his arms and could see his own legs punily kicking about in the water, while his devoted Alvarez stood on the rim of the pool and smiled down encouragingly at him.

"It is good, this swimming," Jaime informed him, and his childish laughter mingled with Ricki's as she got up to a few of her antics and then began the more serious business of teaching him to draw in his legs and then kick out.

"Kick like a little mule, *chico*," she urged. "In, out. In, out. That's the ticket—oops, mind you don't swallow all the water!"

She allowed him only an hour this morning, as this was his first time, and after she had toweled him they stretched out in cane chairs at the poolside and enjoyed the lemonade and cookies that Alvarez brought to them.

In a while Jaime snoozed, healthily spent after his frolic in the pool, and Ricki gazed around her and recalled what she had said to the don about the laughter of a happy child being needed here to bring the place back to life. It was a grand morning, the sky an ardent blue through the boughs of the Spanish lilacs, the tapering cypresses, and the purple-trailed Judas tree. The air was motionless and scented, and butterflies skimmed from flower to vine, where trumpets of cream, purple and gold were meshed in the jade green. Pruning away of the tall weeds and tangy shrubs had revealed lemon trees, low and fairylike, and hedges of pomegranate.

Ricki breathed the pomegranates—fruit of regret for Persephone. She grinned to herself, for here in the sunshine the story could not send a cold shiver running over her skin. . . besides, there was no tall, dark man to add reality to the plot.

She closed her eyes for a catnap, and suddenly felt a shadow blocking out the sun. Her eyes blinked open, and standing before her on the flagstones was Alvedo Andres, thumbs in his belt, a lazy smile on his lips. "It is as I have thought before," he said. "There is a hint of the witch about those green eyes of yours."

"Shhh!" she indicated the sleeping boy and got to her feet. "You are here early," she added, walking with him to the edge of the pool, where the water glimmered myrtle green.

"I was at loose ends and I came to see how my pupil enjoyed his swimming lesson." Alvedo smiled down at her. "I have never seen you in a swimsuit—it becomes you."

Ricki was suddenly very conscious of the brevity of the white suit and she wished to goodness she had put on her slacks and sweater. She slipped into a sitting position at the edge of the pool and dangled her bare feet in the water. Alvedo lounged against the trunk of the Judas tree and watched her. "Is it possible that I make you shy?" he murmured.

"Not exactly shy," she rejoined. "But I'm aware that Spanish protocol frowns rather on the bikini."

"It is less—daring than some I have seen worn by tourists along the Costa Brava," he laughed. "But why should a girl hide herself away if she is shapely? My artistic eye is charmed. You are a nymph I should like very much to paint. Will you sit for me?''

"I—don't know." Drops of water scattered from her toes like liquid pearls in the sunlight. "Very soon Jaime and I are to go on a visit to the ranch of Don Enrique Salvadori—there may not be time, you see. Jaime grows stronger and more active, and soon I shall not be wanted here any more."

"You mean," he came and stood over her, "you will be leaving Andalusia?"

"I shall be leaving Spain when my work here is finished." She glanced up at him. "You didn't think I had come for good, did you?"

He gazed down at her, a sudden glint in his brown eyes. Her hair had dried in ruddy tendrils about her temples and ears. *"Qué guapita eres!"* he exclaimed, and she flushed at the compliment and shook her head.

"Don't call me pretty, Alvedo," she pleaded. "Don't—flirt with me."

"Can it be that you are afraid of falling in love?" He settled on his haunches beside her, smiling, attractive, very much the romantic Andaluz in his open-throated white shirt and narrow black trousers. "What is there about love to fear, *chica*?" His tone was indulgent. "It was the Marquis de Custine who rightly said that love is life for those who find it in Spain."

"I came here as a tourist, and then I agreed to tackle this job, but—love was not on my list," she returned lightly.

"Prudence is a comfortable chair," Alvedo laughed softly, "but one grows drowsy sitting in it. Ah, Ricki, I like very much the cool charm of British girls, their air of retreat—which is also a beckoning. I like the freckles across your small nose, and the hint of fire in your hair.

I cannot believe that you mean to be left to dress images.''

She gave a laugh, for the expression he used was the Spanish equivalent of being left on the shelf. "When one has a satisfying job—" she began.

"There is only one satisfying job for a woman." He looked at her meaningly and imprisoned her wrist with warm fingers; the fingers of her free hand clenched over the tilted edge of the pool and she felt a dart of alarm. She cast a glance over her shoulder...the boy slept on, but there were trees through which a tall figure could come striding, silently and abruptly, to see her seated here at the poolside with her hand enclosed in that of the tutor's.

"Alvedo, let me go," she whispered urgently. "I won't listen to such talk—it isn't right—"

"Of what are you nervous now?" he gibed. "Do you think there are ghosts here—or do you fear someone who is very much alive?"

She gave a little start which she couldn't control, and saw his eyes go narrow. "We are safe from Don Arturo," he said coolly. "For him there are ghosts, so he keeps away."

"I've known him to come here." She was trying to pull free of Alvedo's fingers, but they had tightened and were hurting her a little. Seen close like this, his face was dark and reckless; her nervousness and her bare white arms and legs were obviously exciting him. She wished Jaime would awake. Alvedo would not try anything like this with the boy looking on.

"You have been alone here with Arturo?" The tutor's eyes held a glitter of curiosity. "And how did he behave, like a man or an employer?"

"Like an employer, of course." Ricki was rapidly losing her temper. "It can be said about Don Arturo that he always behaves with courtesy."

"So—only with courtesy?" Alvedo's eyes were still narrowed as they took in the flash of her eye, and the color which had risen to her cheeks. "Does this disappoint you, *guapita*? Would you like to see him in another sort of mood—a passionate one, perhaps?"

"How dare you say such a thing!" Ricki brought around her other hand and fought to unclasp his fingers from her wrist, but he only laughed at her struggles and suddenly both her wrists were held captive in his hurting hands.

"There is more to Arturo de Cazalet than pride and iron, little English miss, and you cannot tell me that he has had you beneath his roof for a month without noticing that you have soft, untouched skin and eyes like tilting jades." Alvedo suddenly jerked her to her feet and, being wet from the pool, they slipped on the tiles. To save herself she had to fall against him. In an instant his arms closed around her, and as her head tilted back so that she could demand her immediate release, the tendrils of cypress and palm rustled behind her as though brushed by a wind.

She saw first the stare in Alvedo's eyes, then his arms relaxed from around her and she was free—free to turn and see her employer standing by the trees. Tall, cold-eyed, clad in a gray business suit that told her he had come straight from the conference table to see how Jaime had enjoyed his water exercises. Ricki could tell at once what he was thinking, and hot color ran up her neck to her very temples.

Then Jaime stirred in his chair, opened his eyes and gave a yawn. "What a long dream I have been having," he announced innocently.

The don strode over to his nephew and lifted him into his arms. "Come, *chico*," he said, "I will carry you to the house. It is almost time for your luncheon."

Bemused, perhaps, by his nap, the child did not protest at finding himself in his uncle's arms. "Rickee," he was actually laughing over that gray-clad shoulder, "you have such a funny look on your face."

The skin of her face felt tight now her flush had receded, and she knew she had gone white with the reactive shock of seeing Don Arturo over by those trees, so still, so dark—so contemptuous!

She shot a look of dislike at Alvedo, who was lighting a cigarette, then snatching up her slacks and her sweater she ran into the *caseta* and slammed the door behind her. She dressed quickly, feeling curiously sick and empty. A sixth sense had told her that the don might come here this morning to check on Jaime, and she couldn't help wondering if Alvedo had thought the same and had deliberately brought about that scene by the poolside. It could only have looked like a love scene. . . a particularly intimate one, she in that brief swimsuit, her hair tousled from drying in the sun.

She combed her hair vigorously and dashed lipstick over her pale mouth. Her hand was shaking, she noticed, as she snapped shut the compact she had bought here in Andalusia.

Andalusia, the place she had grown almost to love. . . now it looked as though she would be sent away, dismissed with all the contempt of which her employer was capable. "I did not employ you to dally with the child's tutor," he would probably say. "It would seem, after all, that your career is of less importance to you than the kisses of a philanderer."

Ricki nipped her lower lip with her teeth and was glad when she stepped out of the *caseta* to find Alvedo had gone.

As she made her way through the walled garden to the arched slave door, she tried to tell herself that the don was a cold autocrat who disliked emotions in other people because his own had died. She tried, defiantly, to draw comfort from this, but still it hurt to be taken for a little sensation-seeker. Twice, now, he had caught her in Alvedo's arms; it was inevitable that he conclude there was something between them.

She hurried across the patio to an archway into the house. Alvarez was in the hall and he informed her that Don Arturo had taken his nephew to the nursery-suite and was now lunching alone in the dining room. Ricki ran upstairs to her own luncheon with Jaime, visualizing that dark, lonely man eating alone in the long room paneled by cypress wood and Cazalet portraits. Then she winced as something jabbed the palm of the hand that caught at the balustrade of the stairs; she paused to take a look and saw the dark point of a rose thorn in her hand. As she hastily pulled it out and sucked the place, she thought of the bush of small wild roses she had touched on her way through the garden of the *caseta*. Her thought moved on to the single white rose in a vase on the don's desk...roses and dark thorns. The loveliness of a rose compelling the adoring hand...the sudden stab of the hidden, secret thorn.

Ricki felt herself go cold and hurried on up the stairs to Jaime.

When Alvedo came to give the boy his lessons, Ricki made herself scarce in her room. She sat out on the balcony, a book resting idle on her lap. Down in the patio there was a burst of activity now siesta was over, and Ricki watched one of Sophina's sons saddling a couple of horses. One was the big dappled gray which the don usually rode; the other was honey colored with a silky black muzzle. She was wondering who her employer was riding with, when she heard behind her the rapping of knuckles on her door.

She rose and crossed the room, quite unaware that her fingers were clenching the shamrock in the neck opening of her blouse. Upon opening the door she found herself staring up at the don. He was already dressed for his ride in a fine linen shirt, half-secured at the throat with a strip of leather, breeches, and knee-length boots, latched by a trio of sturdy straps. A broad-brimmed *cordobes* hung at the nape of his neck, the black strap across his brown throat.

"I am about to take a little exercise, Miss O'Neill," he said, quite unsmilingly. "It unloosens me after being at a desk. I should like you to accompany me."

Ricki had been out riding a few times since coming here, but never with her employer, and she felt a flutter of panic at the idea. Was this his way of getting her alone so he could dismiss her from his employ?

As she stood there in the doorway, netted in her indecision, he swung a brown hand and his whip curled round one of his boots. "Are you coming—or not?" he asked, and his dark eyes were steady on her upraised face.

"If you wish me to ride with you, *señor*, then of course I'll come." She heard the tremor in her voice and knew forcibly that she didn't wish just yet to leave this house in the valley. But his word was law here; if his decision had been made, then there was no fighting it.

"Good." The whip curled again round his boot with a whispering hiss. "I will give you ten minutes in which to change into your riding clothes. Come to me down in the patio."

"Very well," she said, and watched him stride away toward the stairs, forceful and dictatorial, yet always with that hint of loneliness about him. Ricki glanced at the little thorn wound in the palm of her hand, then remembered that he had given her just ten minutes in which to get ready.

She hastily changed into the divided skirt she wore for riding, fastened the chinstrap of her own gray *cordobes*, and arrived down in the patio in some breathlessness.

He waited with a booted foot resting on the mounting block, his *cordobes* tilted forward to aid the darkness of his eyes and his level black brows.

"What amazing punctuality for a woman!" His teeth flashed in a brief smile as he assisted her into the saddle of the honey-colored horse and assured himself that the stirrups were adjusted correctly to the length of her leg.

"This horse is a beauty, *señor*," she remarked.

"I saw him for sale just last week." Ricki felt the don's side-glance as he swung on to his own mount. "A Spaniard can never resist anything that gives pleasure to the eye."

They cantered out of the patio under the massive stone arch, as strong and time mellowed as the walls of the farmhouse. The sunshine was still quite hot but not uncomfortable, and soon their mounts stretched themselves in a gallop. Ricki decided to enjoy the sheer pleasure of riding this silk-mouthed, supple horse and to forget what was to come when their gallop was over.

Her companion seemed to be part of the big striding gray, and Ricki knew he was firmly holding his mount back so that she could keep abreast with him. She shot him a smile under the tilt of her hat and saw him answer it. A tingling shock of pleasure ran through her, and she knew that the spell of his barbaric and exciting land was upon her. Its rocks, its shadows and its fierce sun were in the blood of its people. Here it was no wonder that the mystery and passion of love were all the keener.

Eventually they halted their mounts, poised on the rim of the valley. Heat hazed the acres of wheat and barley, and Ricki thought warmly that a countryside tended by hand and plowed by oxen was beautiful beyond words. Reaped by the sickle, it had a Biblical wonder about it.

The sudden upsweep of her glance caught a look of almost pagan pleasure on the don's face as he gazed down into the valley. He wasn't just enjoying a sense of power and ownership, she realized. He was as moved by the wide and splendid view as though seeing it for the first time.

"The valley never fails to enchant me," he murmured. "I have known it all my life, yet each time I come here I am amazed anew by its wonder, and my own pleasure."

"You love it, that's why," she said shyly.

"And the pleasures of love are continually renewed, eh?" His dark eyes came suddenly to her face. "Do you now speak from experience, Miss O'Neill? You who asserted that you had no personal feeling about that many-sided emotion which we call—love?"

She flushed and looked away from him, feeling the shadow of Alvedo Andres across the sun. "You refer, of course, to that scene you witnessed this morning, *señor*." She spoke stiffly. "I do assure you that it was not what it seemed. My feet were bare and wet on the tiles beside the pool. I slipped and Alvedo—caught at me to prevent me from falling over."

"Miss O'Neill," there was the faintest edge to his voice, "if there is an impulse of attraction between you and the good-looking Alvedo, then it is your own concern. If I appeared angry this morning, it was only that I am too Spanish to care much for the courting habits of the less traditional."

Ricki felt her spine stiffening, and her fingers clenched on the bridle of her mount. "Señor Andres and myself are not courting," she said indignantly. "I did not come to Spain for *that* purpose, and well you know it, *señor*."

"The better acquainted one becomes with a woman, the less one is able to understand her. The brilliant hardness of his gaze flicked Ricki's face. "Women are creatures of extremes. There is no middle course for them—they either hate or love."

"Or feel entirely indifferent," she flashed, and she was looking right at him, uncaring in her sudden anger if he took her thrust as meant for him.

He shrugged, making it plain that he was indifferent to her personal regard for him.

"Love," she added, "is depending on another human being for happiness, and I don't think I'd care to land myself in that kind of predicament."

"So," his smile was ironic, "we agree about something. *Todo o nada*, all or nothing. It is a painful fact to face, is it not?"

Ricki glanced away from him, across this land to which he belonged in his every fibre. *España*, land of the proud. Land of those who loved with a fervor that frightened her, for it drove them to the cruel vendetta if they were crossed.

"You shiver a little." He had reached across and she felt his fingers touch her wrist, then withdraw. "We rode too hard, perhaps?"

"No, I enjoyed it." She forced a smile to her lips. "Why did you invite me to ride with you, *señor*?"

His mouth compressed into the stern line that took away youth from his face, and for a long moment he was silent. Her heart pounded. She knew that what he had to say would alter her life from this moment. A bird flew, startled, from a nearby bush. The sun was sinking a little in the west, webbed in strands of orange and saffron, and the shadows of pines were growing longer, the olive leaves were trembling a little. *A sign of rain*, she thought. The don had told her that when he had shown her around the groves the other day.

"Come—" he slipped with sudden decision from the back of the gray "—we will give the horses a rest while we talk."

He came around to her and she felt the lean, hard grip of his fingers as he assisted her from the saddle. For a strained moment she was close to him in dismounting; her arm brushed his chest and she breathed the open air and sunshine on him. She glanced up, and her eyes were wide with the fear of what he was about to say. She wouldn't beg not to be sent away. She had her pride— but oh, how it would wrench her heart to leave Jaime, and the wild beauty of the valley!

WHILE THE HORSES bent their heads to crop the grass, Ricki and Don Arturo walked over to a jutting ledge of rock above the valley and sat down on the sun-warmed stone. Nearby there was a strawberry tree, which flourishes in the south: an attractive evergreen studded with red fruits and glossy leaves. Beyond, set in the cliffs, were little whitewashed houses with their Miranda balconies, and above all the proud and rugged Sierras.

Ricki caught her breath on a sigh of mixed pain and pleasure, and beside her the don said quietly, "You are learning, I think, how to grasp the momentary joy and not to question what comes after."

She nodded, for it was true. Even as she dreaded what he was about to say, she couldn't help but thrill to the vista laid out before her eyes. "I have never seen a place like this valley, *señor*," she replied. "It is surely the most fascinating part of Andalusia."

"The sweet breath of life is in the very air, is it not?" He lifted his face to the warm gold of the sun and her eyes dwelt on the strong, sculptured cheekbones, the hard imperious mouth, with its shading of sadness.

"To be Spanish, *señorita*," he murmured, "is to be touched a little by the fatalism of the East. Here we believe that each man is a slave of his destiny."

"And what of the women?" she heard herself ask.

"They, in the main, are the slaves of love," he replied, and his eyes flashed round to meet hers, penetrating and searching. "I angered you in speaking of your—

friendship with Alvedo Andres. It is no more than that? I demand the complete truth.''

"I never speak less than the truth, Don Arturo,'' she retorted, stung.

"Ah, how the green eyes flash!'' He gave a sudden, surprisingly warm laugh. "You have quite a temper, *la inglesa*. But what is a woman without a temper?''

"You, *señor*, have quite a talent for exploding my temper.'' She smiled, and then it wavered on her lips. "Do I take it that you might reconsider *not* giving me my notice?''

In a second his eyes had narrowed and she heard him draw in his breath. "We talk at cross purposes, I think,'' he said quickly. "You thought I meant to dismiss you—for indiscreet behavior?''

She flushed slightly at his choice of words. "I know you thought your nursing attendant had lost all sense of discretion,'' she said wryly. "But you must admit, *señor*, that circumstances sometimes appear to be what they are not.''

"Too true.'' A smile, cynical and thoughtful, flickered on his lips. "You appear reluctant to leave our valley, Miss O'Neill. Can it be you have developed a feeling of attachment for—all this?'' He gestured widely with the lean hand on which gleamed the crested ring of the Cazalets.

"Yes, I have grown fond of the valley, and of your nephew,'' she admitted. "It would come hard—it *will* be hard to leave.''

"But you need never leave,'' he said quietly.

"I—don't understand—'' her eyes, wide and wondering, were fixed on his face, and all was still but for the clouds now scudding across the sun and dimming the landscape.

"Then, to be more explicit,'' he suddenly took her hand and, dark head bent, he examined its paleness in contrast to his own sun-bitten skin. A smile quirked his lips and Ricki caught herself staring at the shadows of his lashes. "Do you recall what I once told you, that way back in my ancestry there is British blood? This is interesting, no?"

"Please—" her fingers moved restlessly in his "—what has your past to do with—with my future?"

"I am, perhaps, pointing out that our basic backgrounds are not so very different." His eyes took in deliberately every facet of her upraised face, they dwelt on the tension outlining her mouth. "Miss O'Neill, would you consider becoming my wife?" he asked.

The big, life-moving, shattering things are not grasped all at once. They have to be absorbed by the heart and the nerves, and in this instance they had to be absorbed by someone braced for a dismissal rather than a proposal. Ricki's gasp of surprise, a choked little sound, seemed locked in her throat so that further speech was not possible for long moments.

"You—are speaking seriously?" At last she could speak.

"Where marriage is concerned no Spaniard plays about." His eyes were fixed on her pale, almost shocked face. "I am seriously asking if you will marry me."

"But—why?" Her riding crop was shaking in her hand, and suddenly it slipped from her nerveless grasp. She leaned over to pick it up, feeling confused and unreal. A girl looked gratified or prettily flustered when a man proposed to her—she didn't behave in this clumsy way. Ricki swallowed dryly. "Why?" she said again.

"Why not?" He spoke without expression. "You assure me you have no other commitments of the heart. You like the valley and have settled down to our rural life very well. You are fond of Jaime, and he of you...."

He paused there, significantly, and in her mind Ricki

filled in the remainder of his sentence: Jaime needed a mother! She stared at the don, her hands clasped tightly over her riding crop, her thoughts tumbling through her mind as though on a treadmill. Don Arturo needed to make amends to Conquesta's child, and he saw her, Ricki, as the perfect sacrifice. Jaime loved her, so Jaime must have her in place of the mother whose death was on the don's conscience....

There, at that point, Ricki's thoughts grew unbearable and she jumped to her feet. "I'll stay here with Jaime for as long as you want me to," she said. "But I can't—marry you. I can't!"

He got to his feet as well and they faced each other in that clouded glory of the sun's waning. A breeze plucked at Ricki's hair, and her throat hurt where the strap of her *cordobes* was stretched across her white young throat.

"You need not fear that I would expect love of you," he spoke with cold, almost savage frankness. "I speak of a marriage of convenience only. For the child a mother, for you a home and a position of some importance in the community. Are they not fair exchange for a career that, if you remain unmarried, will peter out in the end to a small pension and an impersonal apartment?"

"I know well enough what an unmarried woman can expect from the future, Don Arturo," she said. "I know that in the end all she has is the memory of service well rendered and none of the comforts of children grown and grandchildren in whom to renew herself. It's a cold prospect, but one I'd sooner face than—"

"Marriage with a man you do not love." His words were edged by ice. "It is a brave and admirable sentiment, Miss O'Neill, but the young are brave and at your age the lonely future seems as distant as the polar regions. And like all women, despite your independent talk of wanting only a career, you are confident in your heart that an exciting lover will stride into your life one day and sweep you off your feet.''

He swept her youthfulness with his dark, very adult eyes. "You would not know what to do with such a man if he came along. He would frighten you with his feelings, for in many ways you are still very young. It is that in you to which Jaime responds.''

"He will not always be a child," she said, her heart hammering from his look and his words. "He will grow and branch out, a—and we too will be left with each other—and our lack of love.''

Something flicked across his face when she said that, then was lost behind the sudden blankness of his eyes. Ricki saw it and felt sure he restrained the impulse to shake her into submission to his desire—his loveless desire to make recompense to the woman he had loved.

"I can't marry you." Ricki spoke clearly, and it was so quiet just here that her statement sounded even more emphatic. "I can't do it, even for Jaime's sake.''

"Then we will forget I ever mentioned a subject so distasteful to you." His smile was a lash of irony, flickering on the fine scrolling of his lips and dying before it reached his eyes. "But would you not like to see the betrothal ring I would have placed on your hand?''

He was looking at her as he took a small box from the pocket of his breeches and sprang the catch. The clouds had parted from the sun and in the orange gold of its last rays the rubies of the ring glowed red as blood. Ricki's throat seemed to have fingers digging into it as she stared dumbly at the ring; she was picturing the don's long fingers holding Conquesta's hand as he slid the ruby ring on to her finger.

"This," he said deliberately, "is the betrothal ring of the Aguinardas. My mother was the last woman to wear it.''

Not Conquesta? That was the question in Ricki's green eyes as they lifted quickly to his face.

"Conquesta preferred the Cazalet emerald," he said in answer to her unspoken question.

Beautiful as she, Ricki thought. Fiery and tempestuous, not still and glimmering as the rubies were. Then, abruptly, he took a step closer to Ricki, his fingers captured her wrist, and he held the antique ring in contrast against her white hand. "You have the skin for rubies, *chica*." He spoke crisply, no hint in his voice or his eyes that he found her skin pleasant, perhaps inviting to touch.

But then, Ricki thought wildly, she was not a woman to him, merely an obstinate pawn in a game of make-believe. First he used Jaime as a gambit, now he attempted to entice her with the family rubies!

"If you think I can be bought, then you're very much mistaken," she said coldly. "You can't buy people, Don Arturo. Haven't you learned that from Jaime?"

It was the cruellest thing Ricki had ever said to anyone, and she caught her breath as she felt the painful grip of his fingers and saw anger leap like flame in his eyes.

"You know even less of the world than I had supposed." He spoke with contempt. "There are many people to be bought, so why should I suppose you any nobler, my English miss? Any less self-seeking—"

"L-let me go!" She tried to break the grip of his fingers about her wrist, but they were much too strong for her and she was left gazing helplessly up at him, her heart racing with the sudden panic of a hare in a trap.

"You—you judge all women alike," she said shakily. "It isn't fair to do that—"

"You think I compare you with Conquesta?" His voice was menacing in its softness, and the sudden queer light of the sun played over his face so that there seemed savagery in his cheekbones, and a leaping, barely reined devil in his eyes. "How quick you are to draw conclusions out of the very air!" he mocked. "I assure you there is no comparison."

"You know what I mean." Ricki flushed under the mocking probe of his eyes. "She treated you badly a-and made you bitter towards all other women."

"And is that why you refuse to marry me?" His eyes narrowed. "You are afraid of the things of the past—and of me?"

She gazed back at him, magnetized by the eyes that were dark as the valley when night fell. . . eyes in which dark secrets could well be hiding. Ricki needed, then, an armor against him, a defense that would stop him from coming any closer to her. "I—don't love you," she said. "It would be wrong to—marry you."

He didn't let her go, and he could surely feel the thud of her pulse as he subjected her to a small ordeal of silence. "My peace of mind is shattered," he drawled at last. "How shall I bear up under such a blow to my feelings?"

"To saddle yourself with a wife just for Jaime's sake would be going a bit far," she said, stung. "And there's no guarantee that he would accept me as a—a mother, even if I were prepared to fall in with your scheme."

"And you are not prepared to fall, eh?" He turned over her wrist very deliberately and quizzed it.

"Throwing the rope after the bucket never drew any water from the well," she pointed out.

"They only sink together, eh?" He gave a brief laugh, then shrugged his shoulders. "Have patience, we say here in Spain, and the mulberry leaf will become satin. If I strive for a little more patience, the love I want may perhaps grow like silk out of the green leaf—but what if it does not materialize?"

Thou are more deep damn'd than Prince Lucifer!
leaped into Ricki's mind. But still she couldn't marry
him! As she had pointed out to him, there was no
guarantee that by doing so she would ease the burden of
his nephew's dislike; also the idea of sharing with Arturo de Cazalet the cold fare of a loveless marriage was
appalling.

"I'm sorry, *señor*," she said as gently as possible. "I
can stay on at the Granja only as Jaime's nurse."

"There is nothing for you to be sorry about." He was
looking again at her wrist; his other hand thrust the
ruby ring out of sight in his pocket. "I appear to have
bruised you, Miss O'Neill. How do I make amends for
my savagery?"

"I—I angered you," she met his eyes confusedly.
"Please let's forget about it."

"I am not quite that savage." He smiled gravely and
ran a finger over the bruises. "Will it salve these to hear
that you are to take Jaimito to the Salvadori ranch in a
week's time?"

"Why, Jaime will be thrilled," she exclaimed, her
own feeling one of deep relief at the thought of getting
away from the Granja for several weeks.

"Because his *abuelito* means so much to him, eh?"
The don released her wrist. "Again I apologize for the
bruises—but in the heart of every Spaniard there is a
sleeping devil, you know."

"And I aroused him at my peril," she smiled shakily.

"You roused him—at the peril of both of us." Don
Arturo gazed down into the darkening valley; the sun
had flared and gone and the promise of rain was bringing a tang out of the earth. Here and there stars were
studding the filmy lace of the sky, and dark hawks
winged across the mauve path down which the sun had
gone home.

The bold line of the don's nose and jaw was outlined

against the dusky sky, and Ricki gave a sudden shiver. She felt cold and a little tearful, and she wanted with all her heart to be gone from this spot.

"Come, let us go home," he said, and his fingers held her elbow very lightly as they walked over to the horses. He assisted her, and he must have sensed the sudden depression in her.

"Please," he said, "dismiss from your mind all that we have said this evening. It was of no real importance, you know."

"Of course not," she said, yet as they rode home to the Granja she wondered if it would be possible for her to forget and to stay here, as she had promised, when she and the boy returned from their visit to his grandfather's ranch.

Could things ever be the same between her and the don? Could either of them dismiss all thought of his proposal of marriage, even if it had been one of convenience only?

She had dinner with Jaime that evening, then they played snakes and ladders, and when he grew drowsy she sang softly to him until he drifted off to sleep. She had not yet told him that their visit to the Salvadori ranch had been arranged; tomorrow would do for that momentous piece of news.

For a long while she sat on beside his bed, watching him sleep in the soft glimmer of the lamp. Tenderness gripped her throat as she took in each detail of his finely etched young face and that absurd replica of the point that centered his uncle's thick dark hair. She sat there, helplessly magnetized, then she glanced down at her wrist and saw the dark bruises from the don's grip. Sudden, inexplicable tears stung her eyes and hung wet and heavy on her lashes. How deep had lain his love for Conquesta, that he could think of marrying for the child's sake only?

Ricki drew a sigh and heard it with faint surprise as she rose quietly to her feet and leaned forward to touch a kiss to Jaime's dark hair. Then she went to her own room where the *brasero* was glowing and sending out its tangy smell of crushed olive stones. She undressed and slipped into bed with a book, but the story could not hold her. She kept thinking of her ride with the don and his proposal of marriage there above the valley—his valley.

She set aside the book on the bed table and eclipsed the lamp, and the fall of darkness brought more clearly the patter of rain on the vines that meshed the ironwork of her balcony. She recalled what she had thought upon first seeing those cages of wrought iron—that they made her feel like a captive of Don Arturo de Cazalet.

She was no captive. She still had her independence, and, much as she cared for Jaime, much as she felt the magic of this place, there had never been any doubt in her heart that it would be wrong to surrender her freedom for security alone. Security was certainly worth a lot, but Ricki knew that love was beyond price...and the don had not offered his love.

IT WAS A RELIEF during the remainder of that week to have the pool in which to occupy herself and Jaime. He quickly developed a love of the water, and upon a couple of occasions his uncle came to watch him at his exercises. The don would quietly smoke a cheroot, not speaking after the initial formality of his greeting, and after watching them in the pool for about ten minutes he would turn and go away. Ricki would then relax from the tenseness that had begun to stretch her nerves whenever she saw him, and she was more than glad when Sunday came at last and it was time for her and Jaime to set out on their trip across the plains to the Salvadori ranch.

Don Arturo was to drive Jaime and herself to the ranch, and Ricki strove to appear nonchalant when she and the boy, along with their suitcases and the folding wheelchair, were settled in the station wagon.

Looking cool and courteous, the don placed a cushion at the small of her back, then he leaned over to his nephew and said gently, "You are quite comfortable, *chico*?"

"Yes, thank you, *señor tio*." The boy gave the man a tentative smile and did not shrink back when the lean brown fingers gave his chin an affectionate tweak.

"You are happy to be getting away to the ranch of your *abuelito*, eh?"

The boy nodded and slipped a hand into Ricki's, made a trifle shy, she thought, by his own unexpected response to his uncle. The don was looking lean and distinguished in a suit of light gray. His shirt was very white, his tie a dark wine red, and when he took the driver's seat in front of Ricki, she saw in a shaft of sunlight a few silvery threads running through the raven darkness of his hair. She was curiously touched. He always seemed so strong and armored, yet he was but a man like any other man. He had had his dreams and his hopes, and now youth was slipping away. Whatever the truth behind the Cazalet tragedy, Ricki no longer felt any fear of the man who would drive Conquesta's child and herself down past the Devil's Tears.

The road that wound around the valley was a corniche of sheer twists and turns, until they seemed poised above a great green bowl. The dramatic beauty of the scene made Ricki catch her breath, as always, while Jaime's eyes looked big as brown pennies in his small olive face. She wondered, with a catch of her heart, if he was reliving another ride, with two other people, and felt the tensile clinging of his hot young fingers.

The don drove with smooth speed, and soon they had

left the valley behind and their wheels were throwing up the red dust of the road through the plains. They saw the chalk green cactuses that dotted the land and giant aloes bristling with small yellow flowers. The spacious, sun-hot plains reflected the great clouds that rolled over them. They exhilarated and yet took the breath away. They were endless as the sea, backed by a tapestry of wild mountains rising up into ice-capped crests.

The only traffic they met on this road was that of farm carts with wooden frames and sides made of braided rope. They were pulled by mules or oxen, and the brown-faced drivers called a friendly greeting as they passed by. These greetings were in the broad Andaluz to which Ricki had become accustomed, and it came to her anew that it would be hard to leave this land of rocks, of strange-shaped olive trees, a sun that sometimes scorched the earth, and a people who were untouched by the discontent of those who dwelt in cities.

They came to a scattered village with a stream rushing over dark boulders, where the women were washing clothes and spreading them in the hot sun to bleach. And they passed by an old threshing floor, and Don Arturo stopped the car so Ricki and Jaime could watch the corn being ground between stone mills which a blindfolded mule slowly turned. Dust hung on the air, and there was a sense of time standing still as the old ways went on in the new world.

The brown-faced *patrón* of the old farm began to approach the car. He was clad in the country smock and leggings, and Ricki thought how medieval he looked and how out of place she, at least, must look in such surroundings as these. She was wearing her smart, bronze brown jacket and skirt with a chiffon blouse in a honey shade; since coming to the Granja and being out of touch with a city hairdresser, her hair had lengthened into tawny scrolls at either side of her gamin face.

The farmer spoke with Don Arturo in Andaluz, and Ricki was delighted to learn that the three of them had been invited to share a meal with the man and his family.

"You would like this?" Don Arturo had turned around in his seat and was surveying Ricki with his grave smile. "Ah, but of course you would! Strange how in some things we understand each other without words—there is some *simpatía*, eh?"

"You know I can't resist these old, lost-in-time places," she laughed back at him.

"Quite so." He directed his smile at his nephew. "And how about you, *picaro*? Shall we join these good people for lunch, or are you eager to get to the ranch?"

"I like to do whatever Rickee likes," Jaime replied, so gallantly that Ricki all but hugged him, while the don's left eyebrow described a quirk above eyes that held—for a fleeting moment—a flash of sheer love. *Oh, Jaime,* Ricki thought, *this man could never have hurt your mother. I know it! I feel it!*

"We will be happy to accept your kind invitation, *señor*," Don Arturo said to the farmer.

"I will go at once and inform *mi mujer* that we have guests for lunch." The farmer smiled and bowed at Ricki and hurried away toward the big kitchen door of the whitewashed farmhouse. There were hens, chickens and small podgy pigs grubbing about in the yard, and a wall-tangle of morning glory added to the rustic charm of the place.

Don Arturo got out of the car and opened the door beside Ricki. She felt the lean strength of his fingers as he handed her out, and she stood watching as he lifted Jaime and with casualness swung the boy to his shoulder as if to make it less obvious to the children in the yard that this particular child could not run about as they did.

They were dashing about after a piebald dog that kept filching their ball, and Jaime turned his head to watch them. All at once Ricki saw him break into a smile. "Can you swim?" he called out in Andaluz to one of the boys.

The boy slowly shook his head, and Jaime added importantly, "I can—almost."

Ricki felt the glance which the don shot at her, and as she met his eyes they shared a smile that was both amused and thankful.

You see, Ricki wanted to say, *the child will grow and flourish, and there was never any need for you,* señor, *to take for his sake a wife you could never love.*

They spent a couple of very pleasant hours at the Andalusian farm and reached the *ganaderia* of Don Enrique about an hour later.

Don Arturo stayed for a glass of the ranch's manzanilla, and long enough to exchange greetings with the twin aunts, then he prepared to leave and bade his nephew and Ricki enjoy themselves.

"*Amigo mio*," cried Don Enrique in his deep voice, "you must promise to attend my birthday party on the twenty-third. It will be an occasion to remember, with the young *picaro* here, and Señorita O'Neill, and flamenco dancers from Seville. It will be such a happy gathering, a real *verbena*. We will have wine and song, and also the bullfight dance for my friend Juanilo, the famous *espada* who comes to celebrate all the ears he has won in South America and Mexico. There will be *estepona* on the menu—wild roast swan, a dish fit for Spanish kings!"

"The twenty-third, you say." Don Arturo wore a quirk of a smile. "That will be Midsummer's Eve, the night when young girls see the faces of their future husbands."

"Arturo—" Tia Beatriz gave him her caustic smile "—I never thought you a man of romantic beliefs."

"*Al contrario*," his smile grew faintly wicked, "the pagan world has always intrigued me—and not me alone," he added with a low-throated laugh that told Ricki he was referring to the pomegranate wine they had shared, and his reference to Pluto, who snatched Persephone at her play and carried her away to his kingdom.

"You must come for the party, Arturo." Tia Rosina touched a birdlike hand to his sleeve. "Promise before you go that you will come."

"I will see, *tia*," he replied. "If I can spare the time I will come."

A few minutes later he said goodbye, and when the station wagon had gone out of sight in a cloud of dust, Don Enrique hugged his grandson yet again. "How good to have you here, my small *picaro*," he said huskily.

The boy wrapped his arms about his grandfather's neck and put his smooth young cheek against the rugged, sun-scorched one. Ricki couldn't help but smile at the two of them, though all at once she felt a little sad.

"Come, we will show you to your room, Miss Oneeil." Tia Beatriz spoke briskly. "Leave my brother and the boy to themselves."

Ricki saw that Jaime had quite forgotten her for the present, and she had a confused impression of dark beams, massive furniture and iron carved as though it were wood as she went upstairs with the two aunts. Tia Rosina chatted away, but her sister had fallen silent and Ricki felt the jetty eyes upon her more than once. She wondered a little whether Beatriz had wanted her there.

Her room, which adjoined the one Jaime was to sleep in, was large, with whitewashed walls, a casual scatter of rugs, a bedspread of bright squares, and dark, highly polished Spanish furniture. It smelled of crushed rose-mary, and there hung on the wall a picture of the Madonna and Child.

"We will now leave you to freshen up after that dusty drive, Miss Oneeil." Tia Beatriz bustled her sister to the door.

"I do wish you a pleasant and enjoyable stay with us—Veronica," Tia Rosina said shyly. "I may call you by your name?"

"I'd love you to!" Ricki flushed a little and realized that her employer must have referred to her as Veronica in private conversation with these people.

It was curiously disconcerting to think of her first name on his lips!

CHAPTER SEVEN

THE RANCH WAS BIG, stone-walled, with acres of pasturage stretching beyond its feed sheds and the large bunkhouse where the *vaqueros* lodged.

Jaime was thrilled by these tough, sun-dark men, many of whom were scarred by their hazardous work among the bulls. Several of them were Gypsies, sons of the stars, said Don Enrique, who had a stern but affectionate control over his band of bullherders. Jaime would watch them, fascinated, as they played a game in which flat pieces of stone were tossed on to explosive caps. Or as they drank wine from the red clay *jarras*, which had spouts that shot the red wine down the throat from way above the mouth.

They had about them a rough kind of courtesy, though there were times when Ricki caught one or two of the younger ones eyeing her with an interest that warned her to keep out of their way when she was not with the boy. She was *inglesa* and therefore different from their own plump, olive-skinned girls; though their curiosity was probably quite harmless, Ricki steered clear, when alone, of the yard where the men smoked their Rumbo cigarettes and played their various gambling games.

One of them had a rather fine voice and at night Ricki often heard him singing and playing the guitar. It was a very Spanish sound, intensifying at times the curious sense of loneliness that had begun to steal over her since coming to the ranch.

She began to wonder if she was getting homesick for England and her father, yet she and Tynan had not seen all that much of one another in the past few years, and she wrote regularly to him. He replied haphazardly to her letters and was full of the work he had recently found on Eire television, acting in a historical serial. Ricki was naturally pleased for him, but she couldn't help but feel anew that he had no real need of her, even if she decided, when no longer needed here, to find employment in a hospital in Ireland.

Anyway, whatever her private misgivings, she found the Salvadori ranch a place of immense interest. Don Enrique was a man of great vitality despite his age, and there seemed no end to his delight in having Jaime under his roof. Toys from Seville filled the playroom that had once been Conquesta's, and Ricki could well see why her employer had said that the boy would become spoiled if he lived at the ranch. Apart from the pony he had been given, he was also presented with a baby bull black as coal, with a dewy muzzle, a rough furry coat and aggressive little horn buds which he butted against anyone who came near him. "He will be a real demon when he grows up," laughed Don Enrique as they watched the baby bull chasing a *peoncito* round one of the corrals. Jaime sat upon the shoulder of his grandfather, calling out, "Huy, *toro*, take him for a ride on your horn!"

Don Enrique laughed again, richly, and then he caught Ricki's eye and his mouth assumed a mocking slant. "What is it, *niña*?" he asked indulgently. "Do you fear that I am teaching the boy to like the terrible bullfight?"

"He's Spanish," she replied. "It's natural, I suppose, that he respond to the impulses that are in his blood."

"Do you find Spanish impulses very unnerving?" he said jovially.

"Not at all," she rejoined. "They're interesting in that they are less restrained than—ours."

"Those of the British, eh? Well, if in my turn I am somewhat perplexed by your restraint in certain matters, I admire your patience and skill. The small *picaro* has become a new child in your care, *señorita*." He glanced up fondly at his young grandson, who wore a junior-size *cordobes* with silver neckcords, and a gaucho belt encircling the waist of his jeans. The boy did indeed look hardier than ever before, and last night he had managed to get out of bed unaided and use the *vase de nuit*. He had announced this proudly at breakfast, to the vast pleasure of his grandfather and the fluttering amusement of Tia Rosina. Tia Beatriz, who supervised things in the kitchen, had not been present. She was a taciturn woman at times, and Ricki got along much better with Rosina.

The little aunts had their own private *sala*, where they sat working at a circular table, using vivid embroidery silks, sewing hundreds of glittering sequins on purses and painting flamenco scenes on lampshades. Ricki couldn't resist lending a helping hand, though she was much slower at the intricate work than they. Tia Rosina sometimes mentioned the past in a soft, troubled voice. Tia Beatriz would frown then, until her sister took the hint and changed the subject. But one afternoon Tia Beatriz opened a drawer of the mahogany bureau and took from the very back of it an old cigar box with a picture of a flamenco dancer on it. She came back to the table, sat down and opened the box to reveal quite a hoard of family photographs. One by one, frowning in that way of hers, she passed them to Ricki. Tia Rosina, her eyes soft with memories, pointed out who the various people were. Ah, yes, that was herself when a girl of Ricki's age. And that was her brother at the time of his betrothal to Conquesta's mother—yes, they did make a handsome pair, did they not? It was, of course, a pity about the patch over Enrique's eye, but, always a wild one, he had lost the eye when a boy, fighting with the young bulls.

"The old *gaucho*," muttered Tia Beatriz, passing to Ricki a photograph on which her fingers abruptly clenched until the tips of them showed white.

"Yes, that was Conquesta," murmured Tia Rosina. "*La fiamma e bella*!"

"No matter how beautiful a flame, it burns!" snapped Tia Beatriz. "Far better a warm, abiding glow."

"I do not argue with you sister." Tia Rosina looked distressed, while Ricki gazed for long moments at the face of the girl who had defied her father, denied Arturo and eloped with Leandro. The photograph showed her in the Andalusian riding habit, which took on an added charm on her slenderly curving figure. The tilted *cordobes*, the strap dark against her creamy skin, gave her an attraction beyond words. She smiled down from the saddle of a horse, and there was a masculine hand on the bridle—someone had cut off the rest of that male figure.

"That photograph was taken before Conquesta's marriage," said Tia Rosina.

"At the time of her betrothal to Arturo," put in Tia Beatriz sharply. "Arturo was with her in the photograph, and it must have been her hand that cut him off. The photograph, you see, was found among her private papers after—the accident."

There was a sudden brooding silence which, after a minute or so, Ricki felt compelled to break. "Why," she blurted, "does everyone mention the accident in such meaningful tones? It *was* an accident."

Tia Beatriz raised her eyebrows at this outburst. "It is hoped it was only that," she rejoined. "There was doubt and speculation, but the Cazalet name is a much respected one and so the business was hushed up.''

"It is unfair to use that term,'' gasped her sister. "It implies that there was something sinister about the way those poor children died.''

"I believe there was,'' Beatriz said deliberately. "I have always thought so.''

"Oh, how can you say such a thing, Beatriz?''

"I have said it, little sister.'' Beatriz shrugged and packed the photographs back in the cigar box. Ricki watched the deft movements of her hands, and felt the trembling of her own. Beatriz rose and returned the box to its hiding place at the back of the bureau drawer. "The wound that bleeds inwardly is the most dangerous,'' she said, without turning around. "And now shall I ring for some refreshments?''

Ricki jumped to her feet. "I—I have to go and see if Jaime is awake from his siesta,'' she said, and her legs felt drained of all strength as she hastened out of the *sala* and crossed the big, shadowy hall to the staircase. It wasn't true! It couldn't be true! Tia Beatriz was old and her mind was not as it had been—that was the explanation.

Ricki's face must have been white when she entered Jaime's room, for as he roused out of his nap he gazed at her with questioning eyes. "Are you not feeling very well, Rickee?'' he asked.

"I'm all right, my pet,'' she assured him, forcing her lips into a smile. "Come, I'll dress you and then we'll go downstairs and see your pony. Have you decided yet on a name for him?''

"Yes.'' Jaime gave her a smile of mischief as she unbuttoned his pajama jacket. "I am going to call him Paddy Fair.''

"To remind you of me?'' she joked.

He looked away then, his eyebrows pulling together

above eyes that had sobered. "I know you will go away when I am quite better," he said, "and it makes me sad to think of it."

"Ah, but soon you will be going away to school," she said bracingly. "You will be with other boys and that will be great fun."

He nodded, then pressed his forehead against her shoulder. "I shall miss you," he whispered. "I shall miss all your stories and the way you laugh."

She pressed a hand to the back of his head and felt a lump in her throat. "I shall miss you, my poppet, but your uncle needs you, you know. He's a lonely man and he has much love for you, *chico*. You must believe that he was in no way—*no way*—" her voice grew firmer, as though fed by some inner belief that could not be shaken "—to blame for the accident that hurt you and—killed your mother and father. Jaime, was it Señor Andres who told you—those lies?"

He nodded against her, then drew back quickly. "He was my father's friend, and he—he said Tio Arturo was jealous of my father."

"I think your Tio Arturo is too big a man to stoop to the smallness of envy, *chico*. Can't you see that for yourself? Don't you feel it?"

"He is a proud man," Jaime admitted.

"A man to look up to—oh, so you want to put your own pants on, do you?" She gave a laugh that was husky and yet triumphant. The past and its fetters were breaking their hold on the child—if only the same could happen soon for the man!

A FEW DAYS LATER there was a lot of excitement at the ranch owing to the arrival of Juanilo Esteban. He came in a great, glistening car, accompanied by much luggage and several servants. He swept off his *cordobes* with a flourish and bowed with lithe-bodied grace to the twin aunts, and then to Ricki. He had the thin-lipped, glittering smile of a tamer, and there was flashing diamond links at the cuffs of the frilled shirt under the short Andalusian jacket that fit him as though pasted on. He was everything Ricki had expected an *espado* to be, and she could well imagine the dashing figure he must cut in his *traje de luces*, pointing his curved sword at the bull when the moment came for the kill.

The moment of truth, he told her that evening, when they all sat out on the lamplit patio after dinner. He and Don Enrique were drinking Soberano, a strong Spanish brandy, and smoking long dark cigars.

"Our young *inglesa* does not care for the bullfight," laughed Don Enrique.

"That is understandable, I think." Juanilo gave her a steady look; he was not as young as his lithe figure suggested, but here in the tawny light of the patio lamps the lines were less noticeable in his dark gypsy face. "To see beauty in the paganism of the bullring, one must be of Latin blood, and Señorita Oneeil is a flower of the north."

She smiled, unable to resist the poetry that seemed inborn in these men of Andalusia. "We of the north aren't angels," she conceded. "We chase foxes and deer with hounds, hook sunfish out of our streams, and trap the playful otter. Man the world over is a fundamental hunter, I suppose."

"You have expressed it very shrewdly, *niña*." Juanilo tapped a finger against the side of his hawk nose. "Needle and thread for the woman, we say here in Spain, horse and lash for the man. While in America I could not help but notice the aggressiveness of the women there. How they can talk, as though wound up, but they have not the *sal* of Latin women. Perhaps only here in the south do women remain content to be primeval, warm, the center of the home."

He waved cigar ash off the end of the dark brown cylinder, and his eyes glittered in a narrow smile as they held Ricki's. Her wide, tilting eyes were a deeper green in the lamplight. "Are you like the women of America, *señorita*? All for education and the career? Does your heart not yearn for a hearth of your own, and many small ones to make your husband proud?"

"You Spaniards!" she exclaimed laughingly. "Is a woman made only to be a wife and a mother?"

"But of course!" There wasn't a fraction of doubt in Juanilo's voice. "Woman is the shape of love. She should feel proud of being so. Enrique, my friend—" he flashed a smile at the other man "—we should do something about finding this pretty *niña* a young man of Andalusia for her *novio*."

"Spare me!" she protested amusedly, though a warmth stole to her cheeks.

"You do not fancy a Spaniard for you *novio*?" Juanilo was enjoying this game; his eyes were dancing with glee, while Tia Rosina was smiling gently over her cognac and coffee. Tia Beatriz had retired to bed with one of the bad headaches from which she suffered now and again.

"I doubt very much whether a man of Andalusia could swallow the emancipated views of someone like me," Ricki rejoined. "Here in the south you people tend to cling more to the old ways, don't you?"

"Because so many of those old ways have an intriguing charm about them," Juanilo asserted, with a hint of Spanish passion. "You are not unmoved by these ways, *señorita*. I sense it when you speak. There is in your voice a note of awe, and warmth. Come, why pretend you are all for civilized veneers when below the surface you respond to the same things that thrill our women?"

"You have only just met me, Señor Esteban." She

laughed yet was shaken anew by the perceptivity of the Spanish male. How well these men understood women! How shattering it was—and yet exciting—to be with men who had fathomed women to their complex depths!

"With some people one is always a stranger," he said dryly. "With others one is a friend from the moment the first greetings are exchanged. The eyes meet, thoughts are exchanged, and the *simpatía* is established. Many of your countrymen and women visit this land of ours, a good few of them stay to set up homes here. There are industries run here by your people, but it is only to a few of them that one can say they have what we call *espanolismo*. You know what the expression means, Señorita Veronica—ah, an interesting name, that!" He snapped his fingers, delightedly.

"You mean you think I have an understanding of the Spanish," she said, her cheeks warm from the compliment.

"Exactly so. Don Enrique agrees with me, eh, my friend? He informs me that the young Jaimito has flourished in your care for more reasons than that you are skilled in your work."

"Veronica has done wonders for the child," Tia Rosina said happily. "She has eased fear from his mind and stolen away his grief. Already he is walking a few steps each day—how it does my heart good to see that! Arturo is greatly pleased with his nephew's progress."

"Ah, Arturo!" Juanilo's voice had changed, grown more sober. "He, too, should forget. To court regret and sadness will always cast a dark shadow over his life, and always people will say of his house that it is *aquella soledad*."

That lonely place! The words went through Ricki, and she was deeply relieved when Juanilo abruptly changed the trend of the conversation. He turned to her, smiling. "Talking of the old traditions of Spain," he said, "are you familiar with those associated with our marriage customs, *niña*?"

"Please enlighten me," she said lightly.

He proceeded to do so, and she was much taken with the one which still survives in the south, that of waiting with a lighted candle for the bridal pair at the threshold of their new home. The candle is held by a relative—the fire of the new hearth. There was a rustic warmth about the idea of guiding a young couple to romance with the soft glimmer of a flame, Ricki thought. Between them they could keep it burning and steady, or they could quench it. It all depended on the strength of their love.

In a while Ricki noticed that Tia Rosina was nodding in her chair, and she gently touched her to wakefulness and suggested they go to bed and leave the men to their moontalk.

Noche buenas were exchanged, and Ricki and the little aunt went indoors and upstairs to their rooms. Before they parted, Tia Rosina expressed the wish that Ricki would remain a long time in Spain.

"I'm afraid that's a promise I can't really make." Ricki bent her head and kissed the faded-petal cheek of her favorite twin. "I'll stay for as long as I'm needed, anyway, Tia Rosina."

EACH NIGHT the southern moon peeled off one more veil to reveal its golden glamour, and Ricki was awakened one night both by the shafting moonglow through the windows, and by the moist feel of tears on her cheeks. It troubled her to find she had been weeping in her sleep, and she wondered again if she was subconsciously pining for her father. She had so looked forward to this stay at the Salvadori ranch, yet since coming here she hovered between pleasure in her surroundings and a melancholy disquiet. Like a fitful sunshine her happiness came in spells: one moment she felt quite gay, then the next she was plunged into shadow.

The little aunts had been wanting for days to take Ricki and Jaime to see Seville. " '*Quien no vista Sevilla No la vista maravilla,*' " quoted Tia Rosina, so much more romantically inclined than her sister, though even Beatriz was inclined to praise Seville, the heart of Andalusia.

But since Juanilo Esteban's arrival at the ranch, Jaime was less inclined for female company, and Ricki reluctantly agreed that he could stay and watch a *tienta*, a testing of local youngsters who wished to fight the heifers, while she drove into Seville with Don Enrique's sisters for a shopping and sight-seeing tour.

"The small one will be fine with us," Don Enrique assured her. "Go plunder the shops, you females, while we men enjoy ourselves in our own way."

"Please remember, *señor*, that Jaime is not yet as strong as your *peons*," she pleaded. "If anything happened to him—Don Arturo would never forgive me."

"I am the boy's *abuelito*." Don Enrique drew himself up, offended. "I would sooner be trampled by my bulls than permit any harm to come to Jaimito. He is the little son of my heart, a small lingering ray of the sunshine that was extinquished when my Conquesta died."

The old don rarely mentioned his daughter, and Ricki guessed that it hurt him to do so. She touched his sleeve. "Forgive me. Of course you'll look after Jaime and see he comes to no harm. It's just that he has not been out of my sight for a whole day since Don Arturo placed him in my charge. I," she smiled and shrugged, "I am overburdened with a sense of duty."

"You are overburdened with too much heart, like a lot of women." The old don touched a gnarled hand to her soft young cheek. "Enjoy yourself in Seville, my child. Forget care and responsibility for this one day and be only the pretty *turista* from England. The shops of Seville will enchant you, and the wonders of the Alcazar will put stars in those green eyes.''

He paused and studied her shrewdly. "There have been a few shadows in those eyes, *pequeña*. You are sad, I think, that your work is almost over.''

"Yes, that's why I'm sad," she agreed, knowing it to be only part of the truth.

SEVILLE WAS RIGHTLY NAMED the heart of Spain. The atmosphere was one of gaiety and beauty, with a zest for living in the eyes of the people and palms standing golden and green in its gardens. This was the city of seven hundred streets, and the most famous was the Calle de las Sierpes, gay with cafés where the tables stood on the pavement and shops where all manner of goods were for sale. Ricki bought a dress and a pair of evening slippers for Don Enrique's birthday party, then the three of them went farther along the busy street to a shop where antiques were sold. The sisters wished to choose their brother's present from the paintings and ornaments on display and while they were in consultation with the manager, Ricki wandered to a side counter on which less valuable but even more intriguing objects were set out.

Her eyes widened with sudden delight and she picked up an old and amusing music box. Upon the lid sat a monkey, and facing it was an organ grinder. When the music started the monkey danced about. Jaime would love it, Ricki thought at once, and she turned to a hovering assistant to ask the price. It was within her means and she bought the music box, which made even Tia Beatriz laugh when she saw the monkey in action.

It was now close to lunchtime and they passed the pavement cafés on their way to a more discreet restaurant. Lean, good-looking Sevilians sat at the outside tables, drinking strong coffee or *aguardiente*, smoking dark cheroots as they discussed business or the bullfight. Bold dark eyes appraised Ricki's slender legs and ankles as she passed by, and more than once there was an audible murmur of appreciation. Nowhere else in the world is a well-turned ankle more appreciated than in Andalusia; perhaps a lingering instinct in the blood of a people whom the Moors once ruled, when women wore veils and the ankle alone was the outward sign of attraction.

Ricki was quite hungry by now and she thoroughly enjoyed a lunch of *langostinos*, giant shrimps with a piquant sauce served in a lobster shell, veal kidneys with a selection of vegetables, then juicy loquats with cream, followed by two cups of wonderful Spanish coffee.

"You wish, of course, to see the Alcazar?" remarked Beatriz.

"Yes, please." Ricki was in no doubt about that. When she left Andalusia, she might never return to see the colorful palace that was said to be straight out of the Arabian Nights.

"The road to the palace winds uphill from here." Tia Beatriz rose briskly and gathered up her purchases. "So we will take a carriage and not bother to walk back to the parking place to the car."

Their carriage had a tasseled canopy, and the horse's harness was decorated with small bells and blue beads. Seville was quieter now a good portion of its population had retired for siesta, and the gardens of the alcazar were peaceful and lovely. Ricki wandered with the sisters through orange groves and beneath tunnels of roses. The little Moorish pleasure houses delighted her, also the carved fishponds shaded by lovely magnolia trees. The palace, seen from a sunken garden, was old and romantic-looking, turreted, with a colonnade of archways and palms spread green and dark against the sky of blue.

The mazes and groves had an air of mystery and be-witchment about them, and Ricki could well believe all the stories that were whispered about the alcazar, palace of Pedro the Cruel.

Cries were still said to echo from the dungeons beneath his private apartments, where the beauties who resisted him were locked up long ago.

The interior of the alcazar was fabulously carved and tiled, with columns of marble where odalisques had once posed, and corridors down which the ankle bells of slave girls seemed to tinkle. Ricki, a true Gael of Erin with a vivid imagination, could have spent hours, days, wandering about this old palace and its gardens, but dusk was falling and the time had come for them to return to the ranch.

During the carriage drive into town where the car was parked, Ricki sat quiet, spellbound by the strange, cruel beauty of the Spanish past...the past which intrigued Don Arturo, and which he read about in those many volumes that lined the walls of his study. She pictured him, passing the long, quiet evenings alone in his study, the lamplight playing over the strong, El Greco planes of his face, the smoke of a cheroot drifting in blue spirals past the unfathomable darkness of his eyes.

She gave a little shiver and Tia Rosina at once pressed her hand and inquired if she felt cold. "When the sun goes down, our evenings do grow cool," she said.

A symbolical contrast, Ricki thought. Fire and ice, not mingling to produce a moderate warmth, but each a separate force that made these people both gay and alarming, emotional and yet aloof, superstitious in some things and adult in others from childhood.

Ricki felt a gladness shot with pain as she reviewed the weeks she had spent working in Andalusia. Here she had really grown up, and learned that her warm heart wanted more fulfilment than a career could ever give her.

DON ENRIQUE'S BIRTHDAY had drawn very close, and it was inevitable that Ricki should wonder whether her employer would come to the festivities. She wasn't quite sure whether her disquiet was caused by the thought of his coming or staying away. Anyway, she was so restless one afternoon that as soon as she had settled her charge for his siesta, she changed into riding clothes and went down to the stables to saddle the horse which Don Enrique had put at her disposal.

A farmhand was sprawled asleep in the shade of a tree, but the tramp of hoofs disturbed him and he awoke and pushed his straw hat back off his eyes. "The *solano* blows, *señorita*," he exclaimed. "It is not wise to go riding."

"The wind isn't too bad as yet." She cast him a confident smile from the saddle. "I shall not be out very long."

Her mount cantered out of a side archway that gave on to the plains rather than the stretches of pastureland where the bulls of the ranch roamed black and sleek. Out in the open she at once felt the sultry breath of the *solano*, which had been blowing since early morning. She was aware that a particularly heavy blow from the east could cause a dust storm, but so far this one seemed but a high, hot wind that made her feel a trifle breathless. The horse huffed a bit when she first set him into a gallop, but she felt a need right now for some fast riding; it would settle her restlessness, and there was peace in being entirely alone for a while.

How different the sunburned *vega* from the random hills and green sweeps of Ireland, where she had learned to ride with her father. They had rented hacks from a local riding stable, but there had not been in them a quarter of the speed that was in this particular horse. His pace was a good one despite the heat and the growing sting of dust in the air, but Ricki didn't want to overtire him and in a while she slowed him down and glanced around for shade where they could rest before riding back to the ranch. A stranger to the plains, she could not get lost, for Don Enrique had supplied her with a horse that would always take her home to the ranch if she was in any doubt of its location.

A patch of gray green shrub and prickly pear showed ahead and she made for it. There she slid from the saddle and looped the bridle around a branch of the shrub. She contemplated resting awhile with her back against a boulder that reared above the turf, but she had done this once before on a solitary ride and had been attacked by the spiteful and tenacious ants that belonged to this part of the country. She wrinkled her nose and scratched her hand in distasteful recollection, wandering instead to the edge of the shrub to gaze upward where an elevation of rock gave back in the stillness the sound of trickling water. She guessed there was a fall or a stream up there and was about to make for it when another sound caught her attention.

She swung around sharply and listened again. Now she heard it plainly, the angry, frightened bleat of a goat, and when she hastened around the ungainly shapes of prickly pears that were taller than herself, she saw a goat, shaggy and brown, with one of its front hoofs trapped in a groove that the hot sun had opened in the ground.

Ricki approached the animal, then paused, uncertainly, as it lashed out with its hindlegs and looked dangerous in its distress. Its eyes, green and malignant, glared at her, and she realized that it would be the height of folly to go forward and attempt to help the infuriated goat get loose. But she couldn't leave the animal bleating and straining like that, and after gazing thoughtfully at the groove that imprisoned the hoof, she decided that if the groove was drenched with water and became slippery with mud, the goat would be able to get free on its own.

A minute later she was clambering up the rocks toward the sound of running water. It was a small fall running into a narrow stream, and for the next quarter of an hour, it might even have been longer, Ricki proceeded to fill her stiff *cordobes* with water and to carry it down to the sungroove where the goat was imprisoned. It was hot work scrambling up and down the rocks, but eventually Ricki returned with yet another hat full of water to find the goat had freed himself and made a hasty retreat.

Ricki smiled her relief and pushed the damp hair back off her perspiring forehead. Her riding shirt was clinging to her, and she took a sudden alarmed look at the sky. A reddish haze lay over the sun, and eddies of dust were being whipped across the plains by a wind that had increased in velocity and now felt as though it were blowing off a furnace.

She decided hastily that it was time to go and approached the shrub where she had tethered her mount... who no longer stood there, brown and large and sure of the way home!

Ricki's throat went dry and she quickly scrambled up the rocks to see if he had slipped his tether in order to seek a drink. But the stream babbled on between the rocks and there was no reassuring horse with its head bent over the water. Sometime during her rescue operation, perhaps unnerved by the wail of the wind, her mount had slipped the tether she should have made more secure and gone home without her.

It was frightening, standing there all alone, lost on the wild plains with a dust storm coming on. Ricki replaced her *cordobes* with a shaking hand and tied her neckerchief across her mouth to keep out some of the dust. She would have to stay here until the storm blew itself out.

There was at least a bit of shelter among the rocks, and water nearby to keep thirst at bay. From all accounts a dust storm could last from one hour to several, and she could only hope that this one would soon blow itself out.

She settled herself in the shield of a boulder, braving the ants in preference to the wind that was howling and puffing dragon breaths of dust and heat ahead of its fury. It had been crazy of her to ride out and chance this, Ricki berated herself, knees drawn up and head tucked well down so that she felt half-stifled by her scarf and her *cordobes*. The air grew choking, and her limbs began to feel as though they were dissolving in the heat.

Time became a vacuum—a dust vacuum—in which she was held in her crouching position until her hazy mind took in a sudden deathly stillness and she realized that the storm had dropped as suddenly as it had arisen. She tore the scarf from her dry mouth and rose out of her cramped position. With stinging eyes she took in the plains that looked wilder than ever. Shrubs had been torn out of the soil and carried for miles, and the strange prickly pears were gray with dust.

Ricki made for the stream and knelt down to wash the dust from her face and arms. A scum of dust floated on the water, but she was feeling too dry to be fussy and she drank several handfuls.

Feeling a little cooler and less parched, she stood up and took stock of her situation. The arrival at the ranch of her riderless horse would have caused concern, and by now Don Enrique would have his men out looking for her. In view of that, it would probably be wiser to remain here than to attempt to find her own way back to the ranch. The plains stretched around her like a desert, and with dusk coming on she was very hesitant about leaving her rocky haven. She gave a little shiver. The fierce, living tones of the plains were lost in growing

shadows, while the only sign of life was the dark winging of a hawk overhead. It circled, dipped, then suddenly flew out of sight, leaving Ricki feeling more alone
than before.

She thought of the goat she had helped release and
wondered if the flock and its shepherd could be anywhere in the vicinity. Though more than likely the
animal had become trapped hours ago, even yesterday,
when the flock had passed this way. There wasn't the
faintest sound of neckbells, only a growing creak of
cicadas and an occasional honk of a frog near the
stream.

Darkness was spreading and there was a coolness in
the air now the hazy red sun was slipping lower in the
west. Ricki glanced at her wristwatch, but the dust had
clogged the hands and she could only guess that it was
some time past six o'clock. What should she do?
Chance finding the way back to the ranch, or stay here
in the hope of spotting Don Enrique's men from a van-
tage point? She could light a fire of dried shrub! The *vaqueros* would be bound to see a fire from here, and it
would help keep out the chill night air.

Ricki dug into the pocket of her riding skirt and
brought out several odds and ends, including a roll of
fruit drops, a lipstick, and a small box of waxed
matches which she had confiscated from Jaime the
other day and absently put in her pocket. Her smile was
thoughtful as she gazed at the Spanish castle depicted on
the box. She had quite forgotten she had them until
now. Jaime had said he wanted the picture of the castle;
she must remember to let him have it.

After collecting several fairly large stones, she arranged them in a rough circle and filled it in with dried
shrub. She wouldn't light her beacon until it grew cold,
for the dry shrub would soon burn out and her small
stockpile not last long.

The little twilight of the south had given way to night and stars were beginning to glow in the sky. There was a breeze blowing, and Ricki found herself searching the heavens for a glimpse of that solitary dark hawk. But he had gone. She was all alone. . . and quite lost.

She bore the increasing coldness for as long as possible, then struck several of the little waxed matches and set them among the brush of her fire. Cheery flames leaped at once and dispelled the darkness, and Ricki knelt on the turf and held her hands to the warmth. It was amazing that only a couple of hours ago she had been stifling in the heat and dust of the *solano*; now her thin white shirt gave her hardly any protection from the cold. She sucked another candy and as the fire burned down to a red glimmer, she sank back on the turf and looped her arms about her knees.

The darkness is an ally of restless thoughts, and it is only natural for a girl alone, and a little afraid, to think of happier times. That journey to the ranch in Don Arturo's car had been a lighthearted one, and Ricki smiled wistfully at the memory of being accepted by him as a friend rather than an employee. There sprang vividly to her mind the moment when he had turned to ask Jaime and herself if they would like to lunch at the old farm. In that moment his eyes had not been inscrutable. She had seen them brilliant with love. . . for Conquesta's child.

Ricki let her glance wander the plains all around her. *Sierra de luna*, she thought, with that ragged fringe of mountains shutting out the stars. And those odd-shaped prickly pears, looking in the shifting darkness just like the weird plant life of science fiction.

She renewed her fire with a couple of handfuls of shrub and was grateful for the cheery crackle and flare that died all too soon. It must now be very late. Once or twice in the distance she heard the howl of a dog. It wasn't a friendly sound and she knew it could be a sheepdog that had turned wild and was night stalking. Her skin crawled at the thought of confronting a big, rough dog bristling with teeth and temper, and she made up the fire again. She sat very still, listening to every sound with her heart pounding, but the howling gradually died away and now the wind seemed to be sighing something. She strained to catch it, almost heard it, a name, and then all was still again.

She drowsed, her head nodding forward onto the hillock of her knees...and then, not in a dream but in reality, a deep and unmistakable voice called her name.

"Veronica.... Veronica...!"

Her name rang out over the plains, and she was on her feet, standing slenderly outlined by the leaping flames of her last handful of brush as a horse rode out of the night into the play of firelight and she saw clearly who the rider was.

For long seconds she stood looking down into eyes fierce as a hawk's, then he gentled his mount and slid from the saddle. The nostrils of the horse flared and huffed—it had been hard ridden.

Ricki stood unmoving as Don Arturo tethered the horse, then came bounding with long strides up the rocky slope to where she awaited him. She could feel the frightened race of her heart. She had seen the storm lights in his eyes and knew he was angry with her for causing concern and anxiety to those at the ranch.

"You might well look at me with apprehensive eyes." His voice was velvet wrapped around steel. "Did you choose on purpose to ride out in the *solano* because you knew I was coming today to the ranch?"

"I—I didn't know you were coming—nobody told me—" Her voice shook, for it hurt that he could not show her any kindness after her ordeal of being lost in the dust storm and being stranded here on the plains for several lonely hours.

"Don Enrique did not tell you I was coming to spend the weekend for his birthday party?" Arturo's eyes had lost some of their glitter. "I thought—but no matter!"

He came a sudden step closer and caught her cold hands in his lean, warm hands. "*Chica*, you are cold as a small frog! You must at once wear my coat." He whipped it off, a rough sheepskin, probably borrowed from Don Enrique, and briskly helped her into its enveloping warmth. "Was it practical, little one, to ride out with a *solano* blowing?" he murmured, his knuckles warm at her throat as he buttoned the coat. "Whatever induced you to do such a thing? When your horse returned riderless to the ranch there was much concern. Several of the *vaqueros* rode out with me to search for you. About ten minutes ago I thought I saw the flickering of a fire and said I would ride in this direction to see whether it was a fire you had lit, or one belonging to a hill shepherd."

"I—I'm sorry to have caused so much trouble." Ricki huddled into the sheepskin coat and felt like weeping. "I was resting here after my ride—there was a goat caught by its hoof in a sun crack. I had to help the poor thing, and while I was carrying water to the groove to make it muddy and easier for the goat to get free, my horse slipped his tether—"

"So you were being the Good Samaritan again?" An oddly tender note had come into Arturo's voice, and when Ricki raised her eyes to his face, she caught her breath at the look in his eyes. Their gravity was lit by a burning, tender hunger, and the sternness was gone from his mouth. Beside it pulsed a nerve against which—the awareness was shattering—she wanted to press her lips.

For a moment she was without breath, emotion tore

through her, breaking down every barrier she had built against him... love rushed in like a great tide, and she had to turn away from him in case it was only a fondness he felt for her and he read in her eyes the storm of longing that was surging in her heart.

She felt his hands close hard on her shoulders, holding her with her back to him.

"What is the matter," his voice was amused yet rough, "are you afraid of me since I asked you to become my *bellisima esposa*?"

"I'm not beautiful, Arturo," she replied shakily.

"You have the beauty that shines out of a truly kind and generous and spirited heart, Veronica." His voice had deepened, his hands tightened. "If you fight me now, *mi vida*, then I shall not be responsible for what I do."

Mi vida—my life!

She could not believe she had heard him say it, yet— yet now he was turning her to face him, drawing her against him with such exciting deliberation. "Why did you insist that you could never marry me?" he demanded.

"I thought you loved Conquesta still—and could never love me," she whispered, knowing now beyond any doubt that it was the truth. "I could not accept marriage without love, Arturo."

"And I thought that once you came to trust me, you would grow to love me." His dark eyes were searching hers. "Dare I believe, *amiga*, that you loved me and would not have been afraid had I declared my feelings?"

"I should not have been afraid, Arturo." She pressed her cheek against his heart and there was no fear in her, only a great and wondering thankfulness and tenderness. If she could have the future with him, she would not begrudge the past that belonged to Conquesta.

Now, so close were they in spirit that it was inevitable he guess what was passing through her mind. He led her to a boulder near the fire and they sat down side by side, her left hand held fast in his. "Everything must be made clear between us, *chiquitita*," he said quietly. "All the shadows must be dispelled for always."

He paused, and she waited, her eyes on his fierce, fine profile in the glow of the fire. Her fingers twined among his and gripped, encouraging him to go on, assuring him she was not afraid any more.

"With regard to Conquesta," he drew a deep breath, "I was a fraud! She came to realize that I was marrying her just to please my father—and this was true! My father was a sick man and he had set his heart on the match. How could I hurt him? And though my heart was not excited by the thought of marriage with Conquesta, I resolved to go through with it. But she knew. Instinct told her that I only played a game of love."

He sighed, then put an arm around Ricki and drew her close to his side as though the loving young feel of her helped him to go on.

"Conquesta was very beautiful. It should have been easy to love her, but love is a mysterious force over which we have little control. We quarreled one evening in the little house of shells. She accused me of coldness toward her. She said she would do something desperate—but I did not believe she would go as far as to elope with Leandro...."

"My father, unfortunately, was the first to find the note she left. He had a second stroke and he died. That was the fountain heart of my bitterness, that women do not fight face to face in these matters. I had hurt Conquesta by being unable to love her in the infatuated, beauty-struck way of other men, so she chose Leandro as the weapon with which to overthrow my pride. Everyone would think—and they did—that she had left me high and dry. She had her revenge, but she never took into account what her folly would do to my father, and eventually to Leandro.''

Arturo sat very still for long moments. The fire had died to ashes, and the stars were very low in the velvety southern sky.

''There's no need to say any more, Arturo,'' Ricki whispered.

''Isn't there, my love?''

''Not ever,'' she assured him, for she knew, as he did, that Leandro had known the brakes of his brother's car were faulty when he had taken his wife and his son for that fateful drive. Loving Conquesta, he had been unable to face the fact that she did not love him.

Love, how strong indeed were its forces.

Ricki and Arturo sat quiet for several minutes, then she felt the tightening of his arm and turned to look up at him. The force of his love for her was there in his eyes for her to see, a flame that burned and beckoned, a glow that held a hint of tears. She felt his arms gradually enclosing her, and she went close to his chest and was locked there, against his heart—for always.

''Well, my darling Veronica,'' he murmured, ''what of that career now?''

''Blow my career.'' Her arms stole up around his neck. ''I'd sooner be your dear, dominated wife.''

''It is not I who dominates you.'' He laughed softly at the idea. ''It is love that dominates both of us.''

''Really, Arturo? Even when you seemed so distant—and cold?''

''If I had shown the warmth of my feelings you would have run away from me.'' He laughed softly and kissed her eyes. ''Like everyone else you thought me a devil, eh? You believed the whispers, the innuendoes.''

''Only for a while.'' She could have wept for ever doubting him. ''Arturo, there will be no more whispers.

I shall love you so much and show the world how I love you, and everyone will say that only a saint could be so adored.''

"Ricki,'' he smiled down rather wickedly into her eyes, "I am but a man, and a rather impatient one. We will announce our intention to marry at the party tomorrow night, and Jaime can stay with his grandfather while we take our honeymoon. Where would you like to spend it, eh?''

She thought of Ireland and the heather lands and knew she must show him the places of her childhood before they settled down to life together in the valley. She whispered that he should take her there, and she thrilled as never before when he sealed his promise with a kiss that held love and longing and all the pent-up passion of a man who had suffered and was now hers to heal.

The night enclosed them and the stars seemed to smile in the Spanish sky.

BELOVED CASTAWAY

Beloved
Castaway

Shipwrecked or not, there was no way Morvenna wanted to stay on a remote Brazilian island.

Unfortunately, with the next steamer a month away, there was no way she could get off Janaleza.

It was a time to make the best of things. But how did you make the best of a situation that included the autocratic overlord, Roque de Braz Ferro?

CHAPTER ONE

THE SKY WAS a dazzling blue, and the wings of tropical birds flashed in the sun high above the dense green masses of trees and giant-fronded ferns.

Within the heart of the forest, long-tailed monkeys flung through the trees and peered down through the mesh of boughs to the distant glimmer of a sandbar that forked out into the blue ocean. Their keen little eyes were full of wonderment. And gay green parakeets cocked their heads as through the green shadows crept yard upon yard of speckled snake. All at once the parrots shrilled into a frantic clamor and flew from their treetop perches into the depths of the forest.

Far below on the shore, where the sands were as tawny as the pelt of a jaguar, lay a girl. She lay very still, her torn dress shimmering with dried sea salt and bound around her body like the scales of a mermaid. The hot sun played over her as though in curiosity, touching the silvery tendrils of her hair, her bare white arms, her hands clenched in the sand.

The sand pricked her cheek, and she heard as in a shell the murmuring of the surf, mingling with the pounding at her temples. She was too spent to move, but as consciousness slowly returned she became aware of nausea. Suddenly it gripped her, arched her slim young body, and she began to retch. She hardly knew that she was making whimpering little sounds of distress.

"That's it." A hand pressed between her shoulder

blades and a strong arm held her. "Get rid of what you've swallowed."

When it was over, the sea water expelled, she lay in the strong hands wearily, a cold perspiration drying on her body in the heat of the sun.

"Better?"

She knew the voice and it compelled her to open her eyes. She blinked at the merging of bright colors all around; they dazed her and brought tears to her eyes. The face bent above her was hazed by her tears.

"Yes, I'm real." She knew the rough auburn hair, sardonic drawl in the man's voice. "We're both very much alive."

"You...pulled me out?" Her voice was husky, with a faint musical intonation.

She lay looking up at him. The sun was unbearable and she raised a hand and shielded her eyes from the glare. This brought his face into clearer focus—tough, square, made attractive by a pair of swashbuckling eyes. She was about to smile her relief that they were both alive and safe when, blindingly, she realized that they had not been the only two on the yacht.

"The others?" She reared up, clutching his arm. "Where are the others? Did we all get away all right?"

He didn't answer—he didn't have to. She saw now that his tanned face was weary from something other than physical exhaustion.

"Are they dead?" There was horror in her eyes.

"Yes." He helped her to sit up, kneeling in the sand and wincing as he pushed the tousled hair out of his eyes. She didn't notice his wince of pain, all she could think of was beautiful, luxury-loving Poppy cold in the sea—gone to the sharks. She gazed over Leird's shoulder at the sea, saw the rampart of coral rocks where the *Sea Panther* had got herself ensnared like a cat in a trap. Just before that rending of the yacht's side they had seen the sharks, their fins cutting through the steel blue of the sea's surface.

Leird and Poppy's husband had been planning to "take" a couple of the sea tigers. Poppy had stood shuddering theatrically, her emerald green slacks a splash of color below the spread sails of the yacht. "You'll be careful, honey," she called out to Gerald, her long, lazy eyes on Leird. "Now promise me you won't go falling in there among those fearful creatures."

Gerald had turned from the tiller to laugh at her, and that was when the crash had happened.

The whole scene sprang back before Morvenna's eyes. The shocking rending of the yacht's side, a high scream, a flash as something brightly emerald disappeared over the side. Then the shock of being thrown herself, of hitting the deck, the palms of her hands and her knees striking the planking as she tried to save herself. All horror in the crash was swamped in the horror of seeing Poppy thrown into the water among those ghastly sharks.

Morvenna crouched in the sand like a small, wounded animal. "Poor Gerald went after her, and the sharks went after both of them," she whispered. "That's how we managed to get away, isn't it, Leird?"

"Yes." His eyes were bleak as he looked at her and then out toward the reef, as though he saw it all with dreadful clarity—the yacht under those rocks, and the seawater washing all the gaiety from Poppy's face.

A rim of foam washed around those guardian rocks, and flecks of it were in the surf, splashing sand from small stones and fanned shells, bringing them to the light so that their colors winked in the tropical sunshine.

"Where are we?" Morvenna gazed around her and saw the high mass of jungle vegetation, heard the raucous cries of forest birds above the sound of the sea. She looked at Leird and then gave a small cry of alarm as he suddenly pitched forward on his face in the sand, as though struck by a blow on the head. She leaned over him in concern and saw the congealed blood of a wound at the back of his head. It had been concealed from her by the dark red color of his hair.

"Leird," she whispered, and she stroked his cheek, grooved by the wind and sunshine of a dozen lands.

The call of a bush bird rose to a squawk in the jungle growth behind her. She turned to look in instinctive awareness of a presence, and she tautened and was filled with apprehension as the bushes parted and men appeared.

They stood in a group, gazing down the beach at Morvenna and the large, sprawled figure of Leird Challen. They looked like Indians: short, wiry men who were regarding her with looks of superstitious awe. "*Kurumi?*" she heard them mutter. It sounded more like a question than a statement that she was a woman.

And a frightened one, needing help for Leird but possessing only a very basic knowledge of the Brazilian language. She was gazing at the Indians, Leird's head in her lap, when the group broke apart to give passage to a much taller man. Without a moment's hesitation he came striding down the beach toward Morvenna, and a few seconds later he stood over her, his booted feet deep in the sand. Lean, haughty, hammered out of copper, he had the features of an Aztec warrior and hair black as jet above eyes of *blue*.

His eyes held her captive, fierce as the blue seen on the edge of a flame, or the wing of a kingfisher as it arrows down on its prey. A slash-throated shirt covered considerable width of shoulder. He was a man of Latin blood, Morvenna guessed, with a great deal of authority in this remote part of the South American continent.

He looked at the man she cradled in her arms, then

swift as flame his gaze ran over her face, taking in the freckles that spattered her slender nose, and the silver gilt hair that clung to her head like a cap, peaked at the center of her forehead above eyes the color of sea lavender.

"You are British—both of you?" His voice was deep pitched, his accent Brazilian, his command of English easy and educated.

She nodded, for this was not the time to add that she was half-Welsh and very proud of the fact.

"Who is the young man?" A lean brown hand gestured at Leird and the sun struck the heavy gold ring on the middle finger—a coiled serpent, tail in mouth.

"A friend, *senhor*. He has a bad cut at the back of his head that needs attention—"

"Allow me to have a look." As the tall man hunched down beside Morvenna and carefully inspected Leird's injury, her gaze dwelt with awe and curiosity on the proudly defined profile. The nose jutted in a straight line from the broad forehead, the lips were cut to express every nuance of command. It was a face, she thought dazedly, out of the days of the *magníficos*.

"The wound is deep but not too dangerous." Morvenna gave a start as the man fixed his arresting blue eyes upon her. "I am informed by my Indians that a small yacht ran onto the reef early this morning. You and your friend were alone on it, *senhorinha*?"

She gave a little shudder and told him wearily what had happened.

"The *tubarao*," he muttered with a frown. "Sharks are not hunters of men, but the sinking of the yacht and the panic of the people you mention could have caused the *tubarao* to attack. However, there is a remote chance that your companions managed to swim ashore, so I will send some of my men to search farther along our coastline."

"Thank you, *senhor*." Her feeling of exhaustion made her eyes look like lilac shadows in her white face. Her eyelids felt heavy and she wanted to sink down and fall into the forgetfulness of sleep. Perhaps she was already asleep and dreaming all this.... But no, the voice beside her that rapped out sudden orders was too alive to be part of a dream.

"Where is this place?" she managed to ask.

"The island of Janaleza." The Indians lifted Leird and she was vaguely aware that they carried him carefully away toward the trees. Then she was lifted herself out of the crushed gold of the sands; her head fell back against a shoulder like iron, and blue eyes gazed down at her weary face.

An island, and the man who carried her was lord of it. Tired in mind and body though she was, she had no doubt that she had fallen into the hands of one of the feudal *fazendeiros* who ruled in these remote parts.

"My name," she heard him say in his deep voice above her head, "is Roque de Braz Ferro. I am taking you to my coffee plantation, where you and your friend will be looked after."

Green shadows enclosed them, along with a scent of lush tropical flowers. Morvenna felt the shadowed coolness on her face, in contrast to the warmth of the arms that bore her along under the giant trees. The sun no longer shot daggers through her head when she opened her eyes, and for the first time she was having a real glimpse of the Brazilian wilderness into which her father had so often ventured, following the beckoning magic of the emerald, or the hidden fire of diamonds.

Most of his life her father had been searching for a pot of gold at the end of a rainbow, and some months ago he had written to her from Manaos, a jungle city on the Brazilian coast, enclosing with his letter a copy of a map pertaining to the treasure trove of an ancient Aztec tribe. The tribe was said to have fled to this region to escape the Spanish invaders. Morvenna's father was sure that at last he was on the track of the real thing, and she had read his letter with an indulgent smile. He was happy exploring faraway jungles for his pot of gold, and though she often missed him, she was resigned to his long absences from England.

Her mother had died when Morvenna was fifteen, and she had brought herself up. There were wandering Celtic minstrels in her ancestry, and she not only worked in a music shop but had a flair for folksinging and playing the guitar.

A prolonged silence had followed her father's letter and map, and then had come an official letter from the authorities at Manaos. The canoe in which Llew Fayr had set out on his expedition had been found abandoned, along with his rifle and his canned supplies, cast upon the shores of a creek inhabited by crocodiles and *piranha*, a voracious type of fish that left little of a man to float downriver if he fell a victim to them.

The letter had shocked Morvenna, left her with a numb feeling of disbelief. Llew had always been so big and vital, so sure that one day he would find his pot of gold, that she couldn't accept the fact that he was lost to her, accounted dead in some faraway jungle.

She had left her job, and taken to a jeweler the half-dozen unflawed beryls her father had found long ago and given to her. "They should fetch a fair price," he had said. "Use them for your trousseau when the time comes."

They had fetched enough for her fare to Brazil, and a stay of about six weeks, during which time she hoped to find out more about her father's disappearance. It was at Manaos that she had met Poppy Tyson and her husband. They had shown immediate interest in the map, which she hoped might lead to her father, and Gerald

Tyson had suggested that they form an expedition and hunt for her father, and possible treasure, in his yacht, the *Sea Panther*.

Leird Challen, a rover who also earned quite a comfortable living as a photographer of wildlife, had been conscripted into the expedition by the vivacious Poppy.

It was obvious to Morvenna right away that Poppy was bored with her husband, and she didn't take much trouble to hide it. Leird's rugged charm and footloose nature had reminded Morvenna right away of her father. She was soon on good terms with him, but she had no illusions about him—Leird, the Red Lion, as Poppy had called him.

Morvenna shuddered against the hard shoulder of Roque de Braz Ferro. She seemed to hear again that scream of Poppy's as the *Sea Panther* struck rock and went down. She wondered if it was true, the legend that those who sought Aztec treasure aroused the wrath of their pagan gods.

Her heart beat wildly and she pulled suddenly away from the shoulder of the stranger who carried her to his plantation house. He glanced down at her and the shadows of leaves played over the strong molding of his cheekbones, the bold curve of his lips, and the indomitable set of his chin.

She had a wild impulse to escape from his arms, and he must have sensed this in the rigidity of her body, for his black brows drew together in a frown. The jungle trees closed in around them and it was as though she and this dark stranger were entirely alone.

"Silence is more eloquent than words," he said. "What is the matter? Do you fear that you and your friend have been cast up on the shores of an island inhabited by savages?"

He carried her with ease along a track cut through ranks of tiger gold bamboos, wild palm and tamarisks.

His booted feet crunched the dry foliage underfoot, and the buzz of insects and the chirr of cicadas was as constant as the beat of the pulse under the tanned skin of his throat.

"This seems to be a large island, *senhor*, and my father once told me that as fast as a man tames one section of Central Brazil, another returns to its state of wildness."

"Your father must have been speaking from experience, *senhorinha*." There was a shimmer of blue behind black lashes as he looked at her.

"Yes." A lump came into her throat and she had to struggle to control her voice. "He's Llew Fayr. He set out on a treasure hunt seven months ago, and then was reported missing. I . . . I came to find him. Now my map is at the bottom of the sea—"

"The authorities told you he was . . . missing?" The blue gaze was keen rather than sympathetic; his tone of voice imperative.

"Yes, I had a letter from the officials at Manaos." She felt hurt by his brusqueness. "My father's canoe was found abandoned along with his rifle and supplies. A search was made of the area, and in the end it was assumed that he—"

Morvenna broke off with a choked little sound. She fought against the tears that would not move this man of Janaleza. Roque— How well the name suited him! Rocklike to touch, with no doubt a heart to match!

"Indian trackers would have been used in the search for your father," he said. "If they could not find him, then no one could find him."

"Please, don't say that." She looked at Roque de Braz Ferro with a desperate appeal in her eyes.

"Truth is like surgery; it cuts but cures." He held her strongly in the circle of one arm as he brushed a great plumy fern from their path. Then as his arms encircled her again, she became aware of the torn state of her dress, through which she could feel his arm.

"It would seem that you have taken a long and foolhardy journey, Miss Fayr," he added.

"Meaning that it is foolish to love someone, I suppose?" A flash of antagonism came into her eyes as she met the blue gaze that had not softened at her story.

"Always foolish, but unavoidably human." It could have been anger or amusement that flashed in his eyes, and she lay still in his arms, trying not to feel their hard warmth. "You spoke of a map at the bottom of the sea—a treasure map, I take it?"

She nodded tiredly and wished this interminable trek through the forest would end and his arms not be around her a second longer. "It wasn't any interest in possible treasure that brought me to Brazil," she said. "I only wanted to try to find my father."

"But I assume that your companions on the yacht were interested in this treasure—which was bound to prove a myth?"

"You would be the sort to assume that people are more mercenary than merciful," she flashed. "Good heavens, how far is this coffee plantation—in the depths of the jungle?"

"Not quite." A thin smile edged his lips. "We approach the tamarind grove in which the *fazenda* is set. Breathe deeply and you will catch their spicy scent."

"All these trees smell alike to me," she said offhandedly.

"At first," he agreed. "After a while you will grow used to their varied scents and be able to distinguish between them. The sandalwood, the oleander, the camphors, and breath-of-heaven."

"I don't intend to stay that long," she rejoined.

"Who can tell what is intended for any of us?" He glanced down at her and his eyes, though so blue, were the most enigmatic she had ever encountered. "The yacht of your companions is under the reef, and the steamer that visits Janaleza once a month is not due for almost a month. It therefore looks as though you will have time to grow accustomed to our Janalezan ways as well as our trees."

She caught her breath sharply at what he said—that for a month almost she would be marooned on this faraway island among strangers. Even Leird Challen was comparatively unknown, though a little more civilized in looks and in outlook, she was sure, than Roque de Braz Ferro.

"Do you live on this island all the time?" she asked incredulously.

"Where else would I live, *senhorinha*?" There was a deep note of amusement in his voice. "What can the world offer that providence has not already supplied me with here on Janaleza? Long ago an ancestor of mine discovered the island when his ship came to its shores searching for fresh fruit and water. He was a *conquistador* sailing under letter of *marque* for booty he shared with the crown—a piece of information that does not surprise you, eh?"

Her eyes rested on him with a gravity almost childlike. "An ancestor of mine was a Welsh witch," she said. "She had a lover in the king's army and nearly got burned at the stake because she went to war with him, dressed as a drummer boy. The officer loved her, so they let him marry her. The king was supposed to have said she was too comely a wench for burning in fires other than those of love."

"And what was she called, this sorceress who charmed a king?" The brilliance of the sea was in the eyes of Roque de Braz Ferro, a heritage from the man who had roved and plundered it.

"Morvenna," she said. "My father always liked the story, so he called me Morvenna."

Her eyes grew shadowed as she mentioned her father, for a month of her search would be lost while she was marooned on Janaleza.

"Your Indians have canoes, *senhor*, the words broke from her. "Won't you let them help me search for my father?"

"Where will you look, Miss Fayr?" He spoke almost harshly. "Brazil is a continent. Its rivers are numerous, its jungles vast, and its killers range from fever to the *piranha* and the jaguar."

"I know all that," she said, "but something must be done."

"A search was undertaken, was it not?"

"Yes, but I . . . I have to be sure."

"First, you have to rest after your ordeal in the water."

He strode with her across a compound, under the shade of giant trees, and Morvenna caught her breath as the *fazenda* came in sight. The thatch of the high-pitched roof was a deep shade of saffron. There were wide verandas at either side of the house, reached by twin flights of steps and shaded by the overhanging eaves of the roof. Masses of purple and flame bougainvillea encrusted the walls, and doors and shutters were of carved teakwood. Its proportions were immense, due perhaps to the fact that the *fazenda* was one-storied.

There were two or three people on the veranda, but Morvenna had only a tired glimpse of them as she was carried into a large cool room where a fan purred in the ceiling. Her limbs were aching for the solace of a mattress, and within seconds of being placed beneath the netting of a big bed she was deeply, dreamlessly asleep.

CHAPTER TWO

MORVENNA STIRRED AWAKE after a long time. She opened her eyes and saw moonlight streaming in a barbaric way through slatted blinds. Where on earth was she? She sat up, the light sheet slipping from her, and gave a frightened gasp as something laughed jeeringly in the treetops outside.

It was a bird of the jungle, reminding her with a jerk of where she was and how she came to be here. As she grew more accustomed to the strange room, she drew aside the netting that was suspended from the head of the bed and felt for the switch of the bedside lamp. The slight click and the soft blooming of light under the topaz shade made her nerves shrink and expand, as they might at a sudden pain.

The merciful numbness of sleep had ebbed away and she was fully awake once more to the painful events that had brought her to this place.

A jungle *fazenda*, home of a man named Roque de Braz Ferro. A Brazilian of means, judging from this room. The bed in which she had slept so soundly had a cane headboard and carved foot posts. There was a dressing table and matching cupboard of jungle mahogany, bent bamboo chairs, and a magnificent jaguar pelt spread upon the tropical inlaid wood of the floor. The walls were color-washed in pale green, and a screen painted with tropical birds and flowers concealed a washstand.

On the night table was a plaited bowl of green gold

papayas, a couple of alligator pears, and a handful of tiny bananas called fingers-of-gold.

Morvenna realized that she was thirsty, and she took a papaya and bit into the juicy fruit. Mmm, that was good. She dropped the black stone into the fruit basket and noticed on the palm-wood table a carving of a jungle cat. She stroked a finger along the smooth tawny muscles and was reminded vividly of her encounter on the sandbar with the man who owned this house, and possibly half the island.

He had stepped out of the bush as though out of some old pagan legend, and she remembered the shock of his eyes upon her. Arresting, almost an assault on the senses, to see eyes so blue in a face so sun-dark and autocratic. So must the Eagle Knights of the Aztecs have looked, and as she pondered the pride and strangeness of the man, she thought it possible that in his blood ran an exotic whisper from the lips of an Aztec princess, taken as wife or concubine by one of the *conquistadors* who invaded the Aztec kingdom long, long ago.

She was smiling faintly at her own flight of fancy when she heard footfalls outside the long windows facing the foot of her bed. She went taut, her every nerve shocked wide awake as the slatted doors were pushed open. Alarm of a primitive nature ran through her blood as Roque de Braz Ferro stepped into her bedroom. The room seemed darkly filled with the shadow of him. He towered there in the veranda doorway, wearing a white silk shirt deeply open at the throat, and dark trousers that emphasized his lean length of leg.

Morvenna's heart seemed to beat in her throat. There was a look of wild uncertainty in her eyes as she caught at the abundant bed netting and drew its veiling around her bare shoulders. Her dress had been half-ripped from her body when the *Sea Panther* had flung her across its decks. It had not mattered down on the beach, but right now she was unbearably aware of the bed on which she lay, and of the blue eyes raking the soft pallor of her skin and the thick, soft fairness of her sleep-disordered hair.

Her lips, half-parted because of her rapid pulse, had sung often enough about "kisses sweeter than wine," but they had not yet known any.

"You really do believe that this is an island of pagans, eh?" There was an amused curl to his lips as he came and stood beside her bed. He took hold of her wrist and checked her pulse. "You look less fatigued, but your pulse is racing. Are you afraid of me?"

"I...I should imagine that most women are." A blush ebbed into her cheeks as she noticed the dark hair curling crisply under the white cuff of his shirt sleeve.

"Women are creatures of curiosity." He captured her gaze and held it. "What they fear, they like to investigate."

"I have no intention of investigating you," she gasped.

"Really?" A black eyebrow quirked above a vivid blue eye. "And you such a venturesome female!"

"I had a reason for venturing out here," she said and wondered if she dared pull free of those lean and steely fingers. "Are you a doctor, *senhor*?"

"I am a *curandeiro*, Miss Fayr. A bonesetter. It was a skill I was born with, and I undertook a few years' training in Brazil, which makes it quite respectable for me to take the pulse of a young lady in bed. How did you sleep?"

"Like a log," she said and wondered just how many facets there were to the amazing personality of this man. "How is Mr. Challen, *senhor*, the man who was with me down on the beach?"

"I had to put a few stitches into the cut at the back of his head and he should be all right in the morning, apart from a headache. He was awake a couple of hours ago and he gave no signs of a concussion. He is a tough young man, Miss Fayr.''

She caught a glint of curiosity in the blue eyes of Roque de Braz Ferro and decided not to reveal how slight was her acquaintance with Leird. Janalezà was cut off from the rest of civilization, and despite the culture and medical skill of its overlord, there were elements to the man that were not entirely reassuring to a girl. He was jungle-lithe, with a definition to his features that was almost ruthless; a vibration to his voice that made it the most masterful she had ever heard.

"Leird pulled me out of the sea." She looked directly at Roque de Braz Ferro. "Is there any hope for the Tysons, *senhor*?"

He gazed back at her, the topaz lamplight playing over his lean face and wide shoulders. "It would seem unlikely, Miss Fayr. The only consolation is that they were together.''

She gave a sad little nod and tried not to remember Poppy's impatience with Gerald, and the way she had hung around Leird during the few days Morvenna had known her.

"You must be feeling hungry, *senhorinha*.'' He strode to the cupboard carved out of jungle wood and took from it a robe, which he brought to Morvenna. "You will wish to make yourself tidy while I go and fetch your supper tray. My servants are Indians, so tonight I will spare you their curiosity.''

"Thank you, *senhor*.'' Her voice was low-pitched, gravely musical. Welsh valley music, strange to hear in this room of dusky jungle woods and pelts.

She slipped out of bed and felt the velvety smoothness of the tawny pelt under her bare feet as she removed her torn dress and put on the silk robe. She rolled up the sleeves, and the heavy dark silk trailed around her ankles as she went behind the tall screen that concealed toilet facilities.

She was back in bed, looking clean and combed and small in the dark robe, when her host came in through the veranda doors carrying a bamboo tray. He stood it across her lap on little legs and removed the cover from a plate of delicious-looking chicken on a bed of saffron rice.

"Do you like Latin food?" he asked, flicking his eyes over her smallness in the robe that was evidently his.

"I find it very tasty," she admitted and felt hunger stir in her as the aroma of saffron wafted to her nostrils. She bit her lips at the ruthlessness of life. Here she was about to partake of food, while poor Poppy....

"Come, eat your food. It will make you feel better." That crisp, commanding voice made her pull herself together, and with a sigh she obeyed him. The merciless demands of the body were beyond her control, just as the forces of destiny were beyond it.

The meat was so tender that it melted in her mouth, and with a blink of her lashes she saw that the *senhor* was pouring wine into a pair of stemmed glasses. In the topaz light of the lamp his long fingers and the wine had a tawny gleam as he handed her one of the glasses.

"I have to drink it, of course," she said.

"Of course." A sardonic smile gleamed in his eyes. "Think of it as a medicine."

She took a sip and found the wine evasively sweet. How pagan, how dangerous, to be drinking wine in a strange bedroom, with a man who looked such a law unto himself. He lounged in one of the bent bamboo chairs, his long legs stretched across the jaguar pelt, the lamplight outlining his high cheekbones, high-bridged Latin nose, and the fleshless angle under his chin.

There was a boundless assurance and authority about the man, a teak-hard masculinity that made her wonder if he had a wife. Surely if he had one, the *senhora* would have appeared before now to satisfy her feminine curiosity about the girl-stranger under her roof? Also, as Morvenna felt the sleeve of the robe fall back along her bare arm, she would have been able to supply a garment less roomy.

"Your dessert is in that other dish," he said, a note of firmness in his voice.

Slices of honey-sweet pineapple and custard spiced with cinnamon. "This pineapple is delicious," she said. "Do you grow your own, *senhor*?"

"We have our own pineapple beds, palm-oil groves and mill, banana-tree plantation, several other varieties of fruit, and then the coffee, which is our main industry here on the island. Shall we have a little coffee now you have satisfied your hunger?"

She poured it, dark and rich, from the little silver pot into the cups he had provided. "Cream, *senhor*?" she asked.

"Sugar only, *muito obrigado*." He took the cup and saucer she held out to him. "A Brazilian, *senhorinha*, likes his coffee as black as a curse and sweet as a kiss."

"So I see." A faint, faint flush tinged her cheeks, for to talk of kisses with this man was to be aware all through her being that she had never been kissed. He looked as though nothing about life and women could offer him any more surprises.

Her eyes concealed by her lashes, she watched him drinking his coffee. Ruthless lips, she thought, somehow matched by his lean hands.

In through the partly open veranda doors crept a dusky scent of tropical trees and creepers. There were sounds alien to her: a persistent chirring, the distant cough of a prowling jaguar, now and then that jeering bird laugh.

He saw the little shiver she gave and told her that the bird was the *mae da lua*, known in the Brazilian forests as the goddess of the moon.

"Our moon is a barbaric one," he added. "Here on Janaleza, Miss Fayr, you will see nature at its most awesome. The island as you guessed is a large one. There are untamed regions, and a rain forest at its heart where the Indians live almost as wildly as in the days when El Draque, my ancestor, discovered the island."

"Haven't you tried to change all that?" she asked, for he looked a man who would reap great satisfaction out of seeing all the island under cultivation and its people well fed and actively employed.

"A wise man does not interfere with nature." His glimmer of a smile informed her that he had read her mind. "Where we are able to cultivate maize, fruit, coffee and vegetables, we cultivate, but the people of the rain forest are part of the wildlife of the island and I would no more try to tame them than I would attempt to tame a jaguar, or shoot the shadow spots off a fawn."

"You feel they are happy living wild, *senhor*?"

"Far happier than the people of cities, *senhorinha*. I give them medical aid, naturally, but they are proud and independent and recognize only the authority of their own *chefe*."

"But everywhere else on the island, you are the chief." she said.

"I have that honor." He gave her a look of cool, saturnine amusement. "In all communities there must be someone in authority, Miss Fayr. Do I not meet with your approval as the *patrao* of most of the island?"

"It is not for me to approve or disapprove of the feudal chief of an island I knew nothing about until fate threw me upon its shores."

"Fate is the master of us all." An oblique smile lifted

one corner of his mouth as he surveyed her in the big jungle-wood bed. "In the blood of a family is written what we will be. In the stars is written what path we shall follow. You are venturesome, Miss Fayr, and follow in the footsteps of your father. Has he always followed the trail of mythical treasure?"

"Is it always mythical, *senhor*?" She bristled in the large bed like a small, fey-eyed cat.

"More often than not, *senhorinha*." It seemed to amuse him to address her in the Latin way each time she bristled. "Diamonds can be as magnetic to some people as love—and just as brittle should a blow befall them. In all his wanderings what has your father accomplished, or found?"

"Freedom, adventure—" she bit her lip to steady her voice "—a few beryls, which enabled me to get the money to come out here. I . . . I can't believe that Llew is lost to me. . . ."

"How often was he at home to be a father to you?" The eyes of Roque de Braz Ferro were suddenly as cold as blue ice. "Are you not in search of a dream—of treasure you may never find?"

"Is that any business of yours, Senhor de Braz Ferro?"

"Yes, while you are a guest on the island of Janaleza." He rose to his feet and, after placing his coffee cup on the tray she had slid onto the bedside table, went to the veranda doors and stood tall there, looking out at the moonlit jungle night. The breeze that rustled the tamarinds and palms wafted into the room a scent that was dizzying in its sweetness. A breath of magic, poignant enough to bring the sting of tears to Morvenna's eyes. She didn't like the man to whom she must be indebted for the next few weeks. She felt him to be hard, unfeeling toward anyone whose ideas and ideals clashed with his own.

She watched him go out through the veranda doors and thought resentfully that he might have wished her good night, but a moment later he returned carrying a spray of clustering, pagoda-shaped flowers, softly pale as the skin of Morvenna's throat and arms. Their scent filled the room as he brought over the spray and handed it to a startled Morvenna.

"The flower belongs exclusively to this island," he said. "It is called Virgin's Pagoda. Strange, eh, that flowers so delicate should flourish in our barbaric soil?"

"They're very lovely." She touched her fingertips to the spray and could imagine it pinned among the raven dark waves of a *senhora*'s hair. She glanced up at the man who towered, copper skinned and jungle-lithe, beside her bed. His presence there was an assault on her nerves. What did she know about him? Only that he was the feudal chief of the island who answered to no one for his actions. . . .

"This man Challen—are you romantically attached to him?"

It was a moment or two before she took in the full impact of the question, then his cool assumption that he could ask it and expect an answer set her temper afire. Pink warmth stung her throat, cheek and temple hollows. Her lips parted and she was about to tell him to mind his own business, when he leaned slightly forward so that his face came out of the shadows and she saw how impersonal his eyes were.

"I ask," he said coolly, "because you are young, you are out in the world on your own, and a romantic who finds it hard to accept reality."

"You did say you were a bonesetter, didn't you, *senhor*?" She heard the note of defiance in her voice. "Perhaps I misunderstood you and thought you said you straightened out the minds of mixed-up females."

"You have the look of an untouched infant, but that does not mean that you are in no danger of falling into an emotional involvement with a man." He swept his eyes over her, then touched a long, aggressive index finger to the flowers he had called Virgin's Pagoda. "The true flower of passion is a pale one, *senhorinha*."

To her chagrin, the color deepened in her cheeks. "The schoolgirl you take me for would hardly know about... passion," she said tartly.

"On the contrary, the most innocent of females are often the most dangerous to males. Take the mantis, for example." He gestured at the topaz shade of the lamp where one of the strange insects clung in a praying attitude. "The mantis prays, you might think, for absolution from the sin of killing the beloved."

Morvenna looked at the spidery front legs of the mantis, clasped as if in an agony of remorse. She gazed fascinated at the cruel, beautiful thing.

"Yes, all that is fascinating has something of the sinister in it," said the *senhor*. His profile was outlined strongly against the lamplight, stamped with autocracy, shaded by the pagan past, and then with a movement almost savage he lifted the tray from the night table and sent the mantis winging ahead of him out of the veranda doors.

"This house has no *dona de casa* from whom I can borrow some night attire for you," he said. "I hope, however, that you will be able to manage until tomorrow. There is a store that provides clothing for the women of the island, and in the morning I will instruct my servant Toriano to bring you whatever you immediately require. Toriano is the father of several girls, so he will know what to bring."

"Thank you for your hospitality to Mr. Challen and myself," she said. "How I'm going to repay you I don't know—all my things, my money, are at the bottom of the sea.''

He stood a moment looking at her, haughty and expressionless. ''Repayment of hospitality is not required,'' he said. ''But it may be possible to salvage some of your belongings, as well as those of Mr. Challen. I understand that he is a photographer and that he was carrying equipment in a steel box. He was much concerned for it, and I promised to send down divers to see if it could be recovered.''

''If there really is a chance of saving my things—'' Morvenna's eyes had lit up and her fingers crushed the pagoda blossoms in her excitement ''—then my map will be among them. I stowed it away in a small leather writing case, which I've had for years. It's strong, and if your divers go down tomorrow, *senhor*—''

''They will go down tomorrow,'' he promised, ''but don't set your hopes too high, Miss Fayr. Below the reef there are deep coral canyons into which a torn-open ship could sink with its contents, making recovery of them impossible for days. Within days your writing case could suffer beyond repair, and your map beyond recognition.''

''I realize all that—'' her aroused hopefulness was not to be damped at this stage ''—but at least there is a good chance of the map's being recovered. Senhor de Braz Ferro, don't you realize how much even that small hope means to me?''

''A small hope will not lessen the large hurt if this Aztec treasure map is not recovered,'' he said dryly.

''I'm not interested in the treasure, *senhor*.''

''If you were, *senhorinha*, I would make no attempt to try to recover it for you. I would leave it where it is.''

''You are superstitious, *senhor*?'' Her eyes held challenge and a hint of curiosity. ''I met an old diamond hunter at Manaos who knew my father, and he spun me a tale about Aztec gold being guarded by their pagan gods. He said anyone who sought it was in peril. Do you believe such stories?''

''The fact that you are here, Miss Fayr, would appear to verify the fantasy.'' His brief smile was tinged with something indefinable. He pushed open the veranda doors with one hand and she saw the moon blazing through the treetops like an Aztec shield. He was used to the pagan moon and accorded it only a moment's glance before giving her a brief Latin bow.

''*Bona noite, meninazinha.*''

''Good night, *senhor.*'' .

The doors closed and the tall shadow of him passed in front of the slatted blinds. Morvenna was alone, clutching in her hands the spray of Virgin's Pagoda, which grew so delicately out of the barbaric soil of Janaleza.

A strange interlude had begun for her, and until the steamer came to take her to Manaos she must make some attempt to enjoy it. She set aside the vividly scented flowers and hesitated a moment before plunging the room into moonlit darkness. Cicadas chirred out there among the jungle trees, a million hidden wings that finally carried her off to sleep.

CHAPTER THREE

A LONG TONGUE of sunshine licked into the room, and Morvenna blinked at its brightness as she opened her eyes. A blue-headed lizard crouched on one of the carved posts at the foot of her bed, and she absorbed anew the strangeness of this room and the scents that came in with the tropical sunshine.

She caught the tang of coffee and sat up eagerly. She disentangled herself from the ample folds of netting and poured out a cup of the coffee someone had been good enough to bring her. It was still hot and fresh, Brazilian nectar from the estate of Roque de Braz Ferro.

As the coffee woke her up more fully, she noticed a selection of garments arranged neatly across the back of a chair. She guessed that the Indian servant of her host had put them there in readiness for her. In daylight she could appreciate the kindness, but the pagan moon last night, the wine, the ruthless events that had thrown her on the mercy of a stranger, had made his smallest kindness appear in the light of a seduction.

The sanity of sunlight was good, warm on her skin. The motionless clinging of the lizard, the rapid beating in the tiny throat matched the beating of her own pulse. She was excited, not alarmed. Today the *senhor*'s divers would go down under the reef to try to salvage what they could of her belongings. Again she might hold the roughly drawn map that she had carried with her all the way from England.

How far away England seemed at this moment! Cool and distant, where the sun shone coyly, ebbing and flowing like the blush of a girl who was warm at heart.

Her coffee finished, Morvenna slipped out of bed and took a look at the clothing Toriano had brought her from the island store. A cotton top and panties, matador denims in a rather noisy shade of pink, a fawn shirt, and best of all, a pair of sandals. They were the sort made in England for schoolboys, but they fitted her and that was all that mattered.

She washed and dressed, and had a good laugh at herself when she looked in the slightly damp-spotted mirror of the dressing table. The pink denims were a little too tight, the shirt a couple of sizes too large, and combined with her soap-shiny face and freckles they made her look the picture of an urchin. Her London friends would have a pink fit if they saw her, and with a thumb in the pocket of her denims she sauntered out onto the veranda. It was paved, furnished with rattan chairs and tables, and ran the length of this side of the *fazenda*. No one was around, and she stood for a minute looking at the moth-sized flower-kissers, the brilliant splashes of bougainvillea, and great shade trees—the palms with their leaves like human hands, the dark and spicy tamarinds, the strange calabash with gourds clustering on the trunks, the soft and feathery plumes of the giant ferns.

Near her hand, as she went to the veranda coping, hung a cluster of the pagoda blossom that seemed less scented by daylight.

Where was everyone? She turned to study the line of shuttered veranda doors and wondered in which room Leird Challen was lodged. She longed to see Leird so she could discuss with him the rather alarming fact that they were marooned here for almost a month. Leird might not mind too much, if the divers managed to salvage his photographic equipment. The island teemed with wildlife, and she knew he could sell his startlingly good photographs and articles to any of the big magazines.

She was the one who would fret until that steamer from Manaos heaved into sight. For months she had been haunted by the belief that her father was still alive, lost and ill, perhaps, somewhere deep in the jungle where his wanderlust had led him. And now, by a cruel quirk of fate, she was cast up on a jungle island, with little hope of continuing her search for several precious weeks.

She gazed across the compound of close-cut lemon grass, silvery under the sun, and on impulse she ran down the veranda steps and crossed the compound toward the forest. A thousand subtle colors beckoned her—blossoms bright and strange; leaf and flower shapes that left her bedazzled. Here the sunshine was diffused, the air much cooler. The jungle smells were cloying in their sour-sweetness, yet curiously enticing.

Morvenna felt herself succumbing to the pleasure of the moment, for the forest was full of songbirds, large gaudy butterflies, and long-tailed monkeys who made scolding noises as she passed beneath the trees where they lived in family groups. Her father had talked so warmly about the jungle whenever he was at home that she felt she knew and understood it, a little. Because of this feeling for the wilds, which his tales had implanted in her, she had been quite unafraid to come searching for him.

She plucked a wild banana and sat down on a tree stump to eat it—a small girl in gamine attire, who sat alone in a jungle glade as innocently as though she were in an English wood, relishing with youthful hunger a banana plucked straight from the tree.

Several minutes passed before she grew aware that someone was watching her from among the trees at the other side of the clearing. She glanced up and felt her pulse quicken as the figure stepped out into the open. He was clad in sun-faded trousers only; his upper body was the color of copper. His thick black hair caught the sun as with the gait of a young puma he came toward her. A hunting cur ran at his heels.

The animal grace, the smooth copper skin, the tensile feet in thong slippers, were enough for Morvenna. She jumped to her feet, convinced that he was a wild young Indian.

"*Bon dia, senhorita.*" His accent was one she had heard last night, in her bedroom at the *fazenda*. His eyes were a dark contrast to flawless white teeth. "Did you think me a *brabo*, a wild Indian?" he laughed.

"Yes, for a minute." Relief made it easy to smile back at him. "You are a Brazilian, of course."

"*Sim, senhorita.*" He gave her a rather unpolished bow. "My name is Nuno Sebastian. I hunt and fish for the household of the *donatario*, and I know you are the Senhorita Fair from the yacht that sank yesterday."

"My name is Fayr," she corrected him.

"Just so, Senhorita Fair." An imp of devilry danced in his eyes as he looked at her hair, which seemed to throw off a beam of light as the sunshine caught it. "You have wandered rather a long way from the *fazenda, senhorita.* This is where I live."

"Here?" She gazed around her, but saw no sign of a dwelling. "Do you mean you live out in the open—like Tarzan?"

"Tarzan?" He quirked an eyebrow, a mannerism probably picked up from his employer. "I have read about him—in the English language. The *donatario* had me educated, but before that I lived among Indians of the rain forest and I had grown too used to the forest

and being a hunter to become altogether law-abiding.''
There was a flash of white, flawless teeth, and then a
quick command in the Indian dialect as the hunting cur
sniffed around Morvenna's ankles.

Morvenna looked at the animal and thought she had
never seen such a scruffy object.

"I live up there." Nuno Sebastian pointed upward,
into the branches of a great, buttressed tree. "It is a
bamboo tree house, and I would be honored if you
would like to see it, *senhorita*."

"A tree house?" She gave him a look of incredulity.
"Are you serious?"

"Of course. Have you never seen such a house?"

She shook her head, but was admittedly intrigued by
the thought of seeing one. "Do you mean that you live
and sleep up there?" She gazed up at the impenetrable
mass of branches and creepers that kept out most of the
strong sunlight.

"It is my *cabana* where I cook for myself and have
privacy when I want it. Do you think we are *que bar-
baros*, here on this island, *senhorita*?"

"Barbarians?" She smiled a little as she thought of
her reaction to the island's overlord. "Let me amend
that to individualists, Senhor Sebastian."

"You must call me Nuno." His smile would have
kindled warmth in the most frigid of female hearts. "Do
you think it wrong that men should be lions rather than
sheep, *senhorita*?"

"I am all for men being lions, so long as they don't
growl and pounce too often." She gave her husky,
rather shy laugh. "Are all Brazilians so unusual and
outspoken, Nuno?"

"We are not shy, I think." He gave a Latin shrug.
"And we don't care to be defied. We take more notice
of our instincts than the Nordestino, who is slower to
sense danger, and slower to fall in love."

Morvenna blinked, and was about to suggest that he show her the way back to the *fazenda, pronto*, when he gave her such a direct look that she was compelled to await his question. "Will the Englishman mind if I invite you to my house?" he asked. "Is that why you hesitate, or do you think it would not be proper to be alone with me?"

He spoke so formally and looked so gravely Latin that in an instant she was ashamed of doubting his good intentions. "I would enjoy seeing your tree house very much, Nuno," she said. "How do we reach it—by ladder?"

"Monkey ladder." The smile was back in his densely lashed eyes. "It is made out of jungle creepers and is very strong. You will not fall, *senhorita*. And if you do, I shall be right behind to catch you."

She walked with him across the forest clearing to the massive tree he had pointed out to her. Chains of red blossom had bound themselves around the immense trunk, and petals fell like rain as Morvenna was helped to climb the swaying ladder of creepers, thick as Nuno's muscular arm and strongly bound with pliable liana.

It was in more ways than one an unnerving experience for Morvenna, and once she missed her footing and slipped right into Nuno's arms. Swiftly, before she could come to harm, she was caught close against his warm, supple body. He laughed against her hair and murmured something in his own language.

"I—I'm sorry to be so clumsy," she said breathlessly.

"No, you are doing well for a novice." Now they were right in among the leaf-laden branches of the tree. "A few steps more and we arrive."

She breathed a sigh of relief as she felt the sudden firmness of the platform on which the tree house was erected. Nuno swung to the platform beside her, and she saw with amazement that the thatched beehive was fairly large and cleverly constructed between the tree they had climbed and another that stood a few yards away.

"Up here among the trees I have, as you see, a flower garden." Nuno indicated the many flowers that grew high up, seeking the sun: the wild orchids that clung like live things to the hairy palm trunks, the garlands of gay lianas. Iridescent birds flew in pairs, as did the crystal blue butterflies. It was as though the island was Eden itself, where love was wild and innocent.

"They love on the wing," Nuno murmured. "What could be more beautiful?"

"Surely you don't live up here all the time?" Morvenna said prosaically. "I shouldn't imagine it would be very comfortable when the rains arrive."

"It is a fair-weather house," he agreed with a Latin shrug and smile. "You would like to see inside, no?"

"Yes, please."

"My house is your house, *senhorita*." He swept aside the bamboo strip curtain and bowed her in gallantly. Light came in through a small window, and she saw that the one room was walled with palm bark. Palm posts supported the roof, and the floor was of resilient split bamboo. There was a table of bamboo, a hammock slung between the roof supports, a couple of stools, a Primus stove and a shelf of cooking utensils.

"I have books, as well." He proudly indicated a shelf of paperback romances and thrillers. "My sister likes to read the romances—love, you understand, is all she has in her head."

"You keep surprising me, Nuno." Morvenna gazed with fascination at some Indian dancing masks that he had hung on the wall as decoration. The masks were carved from a kind of soft, dark wood and were very demoniacal. "Where does your sister live?"

"Raya has her own house in the village. We are of independent nature and much alike, for we are twins.

Would you like a drink, *senhorita*? This is made from
jungle fruits and is very refreshing.''

"Thank you, Nuno." She accepted the fruit drink,
which he poured out from a calabash into polished
coconut cups. He touched his own cup to hers and murmured, *"Salud."*

She drank, and was astonished at how good the
jungle juice was. In coconut cups, indeed. Nuno Sebastian was a romantic! Perhaps all Brazilians were, behind
their facade of ruthless good looks and dominant
assurance.

A bright macaw fluttered in through the window and
perched on Nuno's shoulder. It cast cheeky glances at
Morvenna, then squawked, *"Ate a vista. Ate a vista!"*

"Be quiet, you old sinner," Nuno said with a laugh.
"The young lady has only just got here."

"He's a gorgeous color," Morvenna said admiringly.
"Does he say anything else but 'good-bye for now'?"

"Give him one of those bananas, *senhorita*, and he
will thank you." The macaw strutted on his perch and
spread his cluster of bright feathers as Morvenna peeled
a banana and held it out to him. He pecked at it, gave
her the eye, then said clearly, *"Ate a vista."*

She and Nuno laughed together. "So you have a twin
sister," she said. "Did you both live with the Indians?
Really? How did it come about, Nuno, if you don't
mind my curiosity?"

"I am honored that you are interested, *senhorita*."
He gave her one of those charming Latin bows. "Twenty years ago the mother of Raya and myself was carried
off into the bush by Indians. She was a white woman—
my father, also. He had a rubber plantation, but this
chief of the Incalas had seen my mother and wished to
have her, and in those days there was more wildness in
the people of the island and the chief was not like the
one they have now. My father put up a fight, but an

arrow from a blowpipe killed him and my mother was carried off to the camp of the Incalas.

"As she was a white woman, her condition was not realized until at the camp she collapsed and gave birth to a boy, and then to a girl. White twins were *icaro*, magic, you understand, to the Indians, and one of the wives of the chief wanted us for her own. Our mother died, you see, and for a long time we lived at the camp of the Incalas until one day the Senhor Roque came to the camp.

"He was now the *patrao*, for his father had succumbed to fever, and when he saw a pair of white children at the Indian camp, he immediately bargained for us. I did not wish to leave, for I had grown up wild, like an Indian boy, but he was insistent. He told the chief he would give him so many goats, so many pigs, so many pots and blankets and strings of beads for the two *gringas*. The chief demurred. He wished to marry Raya to his son, and his son would not give up the girl.

"Right away Senhor Roque said he would fight for the girl. Even then he was the *hombre de heiro*," Nuno added admiringly. "He knew that in offering to fight an Incala he would be given the steel machete to fight with. The machete is a deadly weapon, *senhorita*. The clash of naked steel blades in the forest, the silence of everyone as they stand watching, is enough to turn the blood to ice. It takes much raw courage to fight a machete duel with an Indian, and great skill, for no quarter is given.

"Can you picture it, *senhorita*? The circle of primitive Indians. The animals and birds as silent as they, the trees all around the camp like sentinels, and the white man stripped to the waist, his skin agleam with sweat as he parries the swing and chop of the machete in the hands of his opponent."

Morvenna gave a shiver, for Nuno painted a vivid picture of the event. Last night she had glimpsed a remorseless kind of strength in Roque de Barz Ferro, and the fact that Nuno and his sister were now living under his protection was answer enough to who had won that duel in the jungle.

"Did he—how did the fight end?" she asked quietly.

"Senhor Roque is a Brazilian, not a Spaniard." Nuno looked at her knowingly. "He did not kill the bull after he had defeated him."

She smiled at that, "And so he brought you and Raya out of the wilds and had you educated. I should imagine you fought against that."

"Like a *tigre*," Nuno grinned. "But he was right. Education gives a person dignity, and when I returned to Janaleza he did not insist that I wear a white collar and sit at a desk. He knows my heart is happy when I am in the forest."

"What does your sister do, Nuno?"

"She is a nurse," he said, surprisingly. "She helps Senhor Roque care for the islanders, though the more serious cases are taken across to Manaos to be cared for at the hospital where Raya did her training."

"The *senhor* seems to have all your lives organized," Morvenna said dryly. "I wonder what job he will decide to give me? Back in England I sing for a living, but I am sure he would consider that a rather unimportant accomplishment."

"I don't," Nuno said with a smile. "I would enjoy hearing you sing, Senhorita Fair."

"*Toledia. Toledia!*" sang out the macaw.

"Now he is saying you are nice." Nuno's glance dwelt on her hair with open admiration, and she turned in shyness to the window and saw an entire monkey family squatting along a branch of a nearby tree. It was a funny sight. They were so like an audience in a theater.

"Do you like my house in the trees, *senhorita*?" Nuno asked.

She felt him at her shoulder, lean and lithe as a young panther. "I like your treetop garden, and your neighbors," she answered smiling. "This has been a nice visit, Nuno, but now I think I ought to be going back to the *fazenda*. Senhor Roque must be wondering where I am...."

"That is hardly likely, *senhorita*." There was the hint of a knowing smile in his voice. "The *patrao* went early with several of his Indians to inspect the position of the wrecked yacht and to make another search for the others who were on board. He is one of those who feel that a job of work is done better if they are there to supervise it."

Morvenna turned quickly to face Nuno, and her eyes were a sheer violet in that moment. "You know the reef and the ways of the sharks—do you think there is a chance that my other friends got to safety?"

"It is almost a day since the yacht struck the reef, and a search of the area was made yesterday." Nuno shrugged eloquently. "Strange things happen, *senhorita*, especially in this part of the world, but it is best not to be too hopeful. In the meantime, I invite you to take breakfast with me. I cook very good."

He also looked so charmingly eager that Morvenna couldn't refuse him. "I am rather hungry," she admitted. "Can I help you at all?"

"You can sit and look at me while I fry eggs and make banana chips," he grinned. "That will be very pleasant for a man like me who is often alone."

"Doesn't your sister come and cook for you, Nuno?" Morvenna watched him light the Primus stove and spoon rich ground coffee into a cooking pot. He set it to boil over the ring of blue flames and took from his wall larder a basket of eggs that looked like dented Ping-Pong balls.

"Raya has her life, I have mine," he said. "Living

among the Indians we learned to become independent of each other, for Indian boys and girls do not mix together very much. We are friends, and it is better to be that way. These are turtle eggs, *senhorita*. Have you ever had them?''

She shook her head. "Are they nice?" She was very intrigued by this self-contained young man and his twin sister, who must be exceptionally pretty. Roque de Braz Ferro had fought a duel for her, a highly dangerous and romantic proceeding that made Morvenna very curious to meet Raya Sebastian.

"Anything tasted for the first time is either pleasant or disappointing. I like the eggs of the turtle, and I watch where the foolish creature buries them and I dig them up for my breakfast." His teeth flashed in a smile as he sliced bananas. "Law of the jungle, *senhorita*. The strong and wily take precedence over the slow and the weak."

"A law of the world all over," she rejoined. Her gaze dwelt on the bale of hides and pelts that filled one corner of Nuno's tree house.

He saw her looking and said quietly, "I also collect medicinal herbs for a big company that makes ointments and remedies and painkilling drugs. There are many healing herbs in the jungle, known only to Indians, and I was one of them for a long time."

The sliced bananas sizzled in the pan, and that delectable smell of Brazilian coffee filled the room. Nuno added the soft brown sugar that made nectar of the drink.

They had finished their breakfast and were talking as they enjoyed a second cup of coffee, when Nuno suddenly stopped talking and cocked his head to listen to a sudden throbbing sound out in the forest. Morvenna's heart gave a throb. Drums... pounding out a rhythmic message!

"What are the drums saying?" She had heard that jungle drums relayed a kind of bush telegraph, and she knew from the look on Nuno's face that the message was an important one.

"A woman has been found," he said tersely. "She is from the yacht and is being brought at once to the *fazenda*."

CHAPTER FOUR

MORVENNA FELT DWARFED by the great thatched roof that overhung the wide veranda. She reached the slatted doors of Poppy's room, carefully opened them and peered in. "Hi, there!" Poppy opened her eyes at once and smiled. "Come in and talk to me."

"I won't be disturbing your *siesta*?"

"I wasn't sleeping, I was just lying here thinking."

Morvenna bit her lip when Poppy said that, and came and sat near her bed in a comfortable cane chair. Several days had passed since Poppy had been brought to the *fazenda*, exhausted and badly bruised, but now the color was returning to her cheeks and she swore that the Indian poultices of the old woman who had found her had helped her bruises to fade more quickly.

"I hate being marked," she said, holding up a honey-tanned arm and inspecting its contours. "One of the things Jerry liked so much about me was my shape and my smooth skin."

"You...must miss him a great deal," Morvenna said quietly.

The ceiling fan purred as Poppy reached for one of the golden limes in the fruit bowl beside her bed. The gold mesh wedding ring looked very expensive on her hand.

"An extravagant person has to marry money," she said, the juice of the lime on her lips. "Jerry had plenty, until the textile slump and the sudden closing down of the Tyson Mills. The yacht was about all he had left, did you know that? He was getting desperate for cash, and that was why we agreed to go on that treasure hunt with you. What became of the map? Was it among the things the Indians managed to salvage?"

"The map wasn't found." Morvenna leaned forward and cradled her knees, her sharp ache of disappointment no better than it had been when her writing case had not been among the pile of sea-wet articles brought to the *fazenda* by the *senhor* and his divers. Leird's cameras and the rest of his equipment had been undamaged in their steel box with the insulated cork lining. A trunk of Poppy's clothes, shoes, and jewelery had been recovered...but not Morvenna's precious map.

"So the treasure hunt is off?" Poppy's eyes narrowed as she studied Morvenna. "You look a bit white around the gills, my pet. Shocked by what I said just now about Jerry and me?"

"The poppy is the flower of forgetfulness, I believe?"

"Now don't be cynical, it doesn't become you." Poppy was too lazily self-loving to really care what anyone thought of her, and with a sigh of luxury she stretched her tawny body in a silk kimono. "I shall get up this evening, kitten. It's about time I inspected the rest of this palatial jungle house, and showed the master of the establishment how nice I look in a dress. Did that turquoise sheath of mine iron out all right?"

Morvenna nodded. "Some of your other things got sea-stained, but you came off luckier than I did. My suitcase wasn't made of pigskin."

"Poor pet," Poppy said carelessly. "You must borrow a frock of mine, if one will fit you."

Morvenna thought this unlikely, for Poppy was built on sleek but generous lines and she dressed in a highly sophisticated manner.

"The island store stocks my size," she said with a

faint smile, "and I hardly think that Senhor ~~de~~ Braz Ferro takes notice of what I wear of an evening."

"How formal you sound." Poppy pushed a lazy hand through her hair, as thick and long as ripe wheat. "I should think he's the kind of man who notices everything about a woman—but perhaps he doesn't regard you in quite that light. You're the eternally youthful sort, and in store dresses with that Joan of Arc hairstyle you must look a mere kid to a man of his temperament."

Morvenna ran a defensive hand over her cap of silvery hair, and Poppy laughed at the action.

"You don't like him very much, do you?"

"He's too sure of himself," Morvenna rejoined. "He likes people to bow down to him."

"You make him sound exciting," Poppy drawled. "Have you got a funny idea in your head that here on this island the men still take by force the things they want?"

"They used to, and that wasn't so long ago." Morvenna flushed sensitively and wondered how Poppy could show such obvious interest in another man so soon after losing her husband. Morvenna's own sense of devotion felt violated.

"There's no such thing as love imperishable, my pet." Poppy gave a shrug. "It's a dream, a fairy yarn spun by romantics. The truth is that men and women are opponents. This can be exciting, but Jerry gave in to me too easily. He wouldn't fight with me, and in the end I got bored. The little zing of danger was missing. Now, Roque de Braz Ferro has the kind of personality I could get really interested in. Iron charm. Magnetics. And that autocracy you dislike, Miss Prim, is natural to his nature, inborn."

"There's a streak of savagery in him, as well." Morvenna tilted her chin in scorn. "He's very handy with the machete, so I've been told."

"What a man!" Poppy gave a chuckle. "It's a proof of your innocence, my pet, that you don't yet know that most women like to think there's a whip in the hand of the man who kisses them. Mmm, I could get more than interested in that noble savage. By the way, what does Leird find to do with his time?"

"He's got interested in the wildlife of the island."

"Including that jade-eyed charmer, Nurse Raya." Poppy gave a cynical chuckle. "She's no dedicated carrier of the Lamp of Vigil. She's far too attractive for one thing—the brother's darned good-looking, as well. I noticed him out on the compound with you this morning. He's taken with you, isn't he?"

Behind Poppy's teasing there was a sudden keen curiosity. She looked Morvenna up and down, as though searching for the hidden sorcery that enchanted the handsome Nuno. "My pet, you're blushing like a milkmaid," she jeered. "Come on, do you like him?"

"Yes, he's easy to like," Morvenna said defensively. "He's my own age and full of interesting tales about the island and its jungle interior. Tomorrow he's taking me fishing in his canoe."

"Well, I'm glad to hear that you've found someone who finds you amusing." Poppy raised a curvaceous leg and surveyed her toenails. "Be a pet and fetch me that peach nail polish." She waved a hand toward the dressing table, and when Morvenna had located the bottle among all the other jars and tubes and flacons, the incorrigible Poppy asked her to apply it. "I'm not up to bending that far. My hip is still a trifle stiff."

Morvenna caught her bottom lip between her teeth. She wasn't the lady's maid around here, and Poppy

could manicure her own toenails and press her own
dresses as soon as she was up and about.

Beware of being too tenderhearted, her father had
once said. People who are not tender will take advantage, and hurt you.

Poppy was certainly the type to take advantage.
Already she had forgotten the man to whom she had
been married and was casting around for a way to catch
Roque de Braz Ferro. Was he the type to like painted
toenails? Who could tell? The only certain thing was
that gay and vibrant creatures like Poppy Tyson were
not frequent visitors to the island of Janaleza.

"There!" Morvenna applied the final coat of polish
and screwed the cap back on the bottle. When she
glanced at Poppy she saw that the other girl had dozed
off to sleep. Her wheat-ripe hair was spread over the
pillows, and the silk kimono had slipped off her
shoulder to reveal its honey curves. She looked so innocent in sleep that Morvenna could hardly believe that
she had not shed a tear over Gerald.

Perhaps, like a good many people, she hid her most
secret feelings and only pretended to be as hard as
the many gems she carried around with her, and which
had been found safe in her trunk. Morvenna hoped
so, and her eyes brightened as out on the veranda she
came upon Ringo, a ring-tailed *coati*, with a furry muff
of a body, barred with black and honey stripes. Ringo
had a long, curious nose, and small curved ears, and he
made no demur when Morvenna picked him up in her
arms.

He snuffed at her shirt as she petted him, tame as the
baby puma that ran in and out of the house, and the
many colorful birds that perched on the great thatched
roof. Morvenna loved animals, and it had been a real
delight to her to find that so many of them had the
freedom of the compound. Long-tailed monkeys, green

parrots, and even tapirs were to be seen in the vicinity of the *fazenda*.

Surrounding the great house were the various plantations. The vivid green banana jungle, the rows of trees bearing peachy mangoes, papayas and guavas. Then there were the pineapple beds, and the eucalyptus groves, where the golden, pungent liquid was drained off into little cups attached to the slender trunks.

And over all the spicy scents hung that of coffee, rich and permeating, drifting from the ranks of tidy, brown gold trees. They sheltered under graceful, palmlike trees, and derived breeze and shade from the feathery crests overhead.

The many islanders employed by the *senhor* were housed in long rectangular houses built of bamboo with banana-leaf thatching. The men wore dun-colored trousers and bright shirts. The women liked swathings of vivid material, and looked less gay and appealing in the cotton dresses sold at the store. The store was run by Flavio, a young Amerindian who wore a single gold ring in his left ear and was very popular with the young girls.

Each morning the *senhor* held sick call on the veranda that fronted the living rooms of the house. With the assistance of a white-uniformed Raya he would treat eye infections with ophthalmic drops, give doses of worm medicine to the giggling, cocoa brown children, and shots of penicillin and vitamins. The Indians weren't a bit afraid of the needle. Broad smiles would crease their brown faces. There was more magic in being pricked than in swallowing a pill.

Morvenna liked the *fazenda* Indians, with their triangular dark eyes and graceful bodies. She wandered among them quite unafraid, though girls of her coloring were not a familiar sight to them. Dark hands often reached out shyly to touch her hair, as though some special *icaro* might be imparted from it, and the other day the *senhor* had smartly reprimanded one of the youths for doing this.

"Wear a hat when you are out alone." he advised her curtly.

Morvenna crinkled her nose and caressed Ringo's ears with her finger. His muff of a body quivered with pleasure, and clambering onto her shoulder he snoozed with his long nose pressing against her neck. He stayed comfortably in that position as Morvenna took a walk. Like all wild things he responded instinctively to genuine tenderness.

She wandered around the side of the *fazenda* and then stood very still, poised for instant flight. Roque de Braz Ferro was sitting in a fan-backed chair under the shady eaves, a slim cigar in hand, a lazy air about him. On the rattan table in front of him stood a jug of fruit juice and a dish covered by a snowy napkin.

Morvenna gazed for a startled moment at his profile, and the dark peak of hair that stabbed the bronze skin of his nape. Even in repose there was a taut strength about the man that suggested a jungle cat, ever on the alert. Even as Morvenna retreated with a natural delicacy of movement, those alert instincts of his warned him of a presence.

He swung around in his chair and his glance was like a flash of blue mercury. Bees droned and jungle scents drifted across the compound on the somnolent air.

"Won't you join me, Miss Fayr?" He rose to his feet and invited her with a gesture of a lean hand to take the chair at the other side of the rattan table. His eyes took in the *coati* that drowsed on her shoulder and he added dryly, "You may bring your friend."

She approached him reluctantly, for though he was clad with his usual daytime informality in a bush shirt and canvas trousers, there was little humility about the rest of him. He drew out the chair for her and she sat down. She felt Ringo stir against her as a lean, bronzed hand stroked him.

"You are fond of animals, eh?"

"I have always found them easy to get along with, *senhor*." She was tense in the fan-back chair, unable to relax with those keen blue eyes upon her. "All an animal asks of one is a little loving kindness and in return he gives his heart. He doesn't care if you sweep roads. If your house is poor, he finds it a palace."

"You think that too many people have lost their sense of values, eh? Nowadays they respond not to loving kindness, but to money, position, and appearance?"

"They are less merciful, *senhor*. You said it yourself."

"Yes." His gaze dwelt reflectively on her, then he indicated the jug of fruit juice, cooled by a tube of ice fitted inside. The *fazenda* was supplied with ice from the big refrigerator that was fed from the estate generator. "May I pour you a glass of pineapple juice, and offer you some maiden's kisses?"

"What?" She looked at him in alarm, and he was laughing as he whipped the table napkin off the dish on the table. It held a selection of tasty-looking pastries.

"Maiden's kisses," he said. "I am rather fond of them."

She didn't doubt that, and said demurely that she would like a pastry and a glass of fruit juice. Ringo stirred instinctively at the mention of eatables, and she shared her pastry with him as her host sat smoking his cigar, long legs crossed, his eyes faintly amused as he watched her with the *coati*.

"Have you been wandering around again without a hat?" he asked.

"I always seem to forget it." She wished to goodness he would. "Anyway, I didn't go beyond the compound. I had a chat with Poppy until she fell asleep. She feels a lot better and intends to get up this evening."

"Your friend has made a quick recovery in the circumstances, and I am sure she will be sensible enough to regard this interlude on our island as a holiday." Cigar smoke veiled his eyes, but Morvenna was sure the slight hardening of his voice was meant for her when he added, "I advise you to do the same, Miss Fayr. The time will pass much more quickly if you try to enjoy your stay on the island instead of just marking time until the steamer comes to call in three weeks' time."

"The island is very interesting, even lovely," she admitted. "An earthly paradise, *senhor*."

"But you have no taste for paradise at the present time. You want to go through the hell of a jungle search?"

"It would be worth it, even without a map." Her violet eyes fenced with his. "I have to know one way or the other whether my father is alive or dead. He meant a lot to me, with his big laugh and his rough diamond charm, but I'm sure you wouldn't understand my feelings."

"I had parents, Miss Fayr, and don't presume to be sure about me, or my motives, after only a few days' acquaintance." His mouth was imperious, his brows a dark bridge above the brilliant eyes—eyes that might probe another person's mind without revealing *his* thoughts and feelings. "The jungle is full of hazards and I would not dream of exposing a girl so young and inexperienced to the heat and the rains, and the bite of fever-carrying mosquitoes."

His eyes flicked her boyishly cut hair and her vulnerable young neck. "I admire courage and spirit, *senhorinha*, but not obstinacy."

"It isn't obstinacy." She felt a sudden angry trembling through all her slim body; even her lips trembled. "If I had been able to weep for Llew, then I should have known that I had lost him for always."

"Your reasoning is that of a child who has been left too much alone," he said crisply. "I know the jungles of Brazil only too well, and though to a stranger they might appear to be cut off from all contact with the outside world, this is far from the truth. The drums of the Indians "talk" constantly. They relay the jungle news as regularly as any broadcasting system, and if a white prospector had been found in the bush, suffering from fever or an injury, then I would have got to hear of it."

"White people have been kept prisoner in the bush," Morvenna blurted. "Nuno and his sister were—"

"They were brought up as members of the Incala tribe," he said patiently. "Even hostile Indians would be unlikely to harm a pair of children. Miss Fayr, will it set your mind at comparative rest to know that my Indians are keeping their ears to the ground? Any unusual item of news will be reported to me, but I warn you again that the chance of your father being still alive is a remote one."

Morvenna gazed for a long moment at the inscrutable face of Roque de Braz Ferro, then she relaxed with a little sigh against the fan back of her chair. "Why couldn't you have told me before that something was being done, *senhor*?"

"Perhaps I took it for granted, *senhorinha*, that you would credit me with a little humanity." His smile was faintly mocking. "In any case, the Latin is not as blunt as a British person. It is a quality that we find disconcerting."

"You prefer to wrap everything in secrecy?"

"Woman herself is a secret, *senhorinha*. Few men understand even the woman they choose to love, for it is our instincts, not our intellect, that sway us toward one person rather than another."

"Meaning there are people who love someone against

their better judgment?'' People like poor Gerald Tyson, she thought.

"A prosaic way of putting it." She saw the muscles tauten against his shirt as he leaned forward to stub his cigar. "Love is a sweet and savage combat, more so in a land such as mine, and that is why I warn you to keep your hair covered. The men of Janaleza are not used to girls with dawn silver hair."

"This?" She put up a hand and touched her hair in amazement. "Poppy thinks I look like Joan of Arc."

"The young Amazon maidens were said to look like silver-haired boys." His smile was a flash of strong white teeth. "All the same, you are not a boy, despite the matador pants and the shirts."

"They're comfortable," she said defensively, "if not exactly glamorous. Poppy will provide all the glamour that I can't."

"Has your association with Mrs. Tyson been of very long duration?" The keen note of interest in his voice did not surprise Morvenna unduly. He might be the overlord of Janaleza, but he was still a man—very much a man—and bound to be attracted by Poppy. Her warm, ripe looks blinded men to the cool, calculating heart inside her shapely body.

"We met at Manaos soon after my arrival there. Mr. Tyson was kind, and interested in the search I wished to undertake. Poor Gerald—" Morvenna looked stricken "—he might still be alive but for that meeting with me."

"My dear girl—" a hand fettered her wrist on the table and gave it a shake "—you can't go through life with a bundle of regrets on your shoulders. They will never stand the strain. You are too much alive, I think, to the fears and hurts in other people. You need protection against your own softness of heart."

"I—I can take care of myself, even if I have got a soft heart." She tried to wrench free of his hand, but only succeeded in dislodging the *coati*. He scampered off her shoulder, leaving her alone and at the mercy of Roque de Braz Ferro.

"You are so easy to bully," he taunted. "What on earth would you do right now if I were not your host but a *seringueiro* who had not seen a woman for several months?"

Even as she looked at him, startled, he yanked her to her feet and she found herself imprisoned by an arm that felt like a steel band. In a panic she raised her left hand to fend him off, and instantly he caught hold of her hand and held it disconcertingly close to his warm throat.

"Is this how you prove your ability to take care of yourself?" His blue eyes mocked, his lips were within kissing distance of her own. "You could scream, kick, even bite, but you do none of these things. Are you too polite, Miss Fayr?"

"This... is only playacting," she said breathlessly. "You are not a real *seringueiro*."

"Ah, but I have a rubber plantation at the other side of the island, so what makes you so sure this is playacting, as you call it?"

Her heart beat furiously. Temper was growing in her that he should bait her in this way. "I would hate to chance my teeth on you," she said fiercely. "I'd probably lose a couple."

"You consider me as tough as boot leather, eh?" Laughter made lines at the edge of his eyes, and close to him like this she saw more than strength in his features. She glimpsed a certain whimsical tenderness, and knew him to be totally aware of how vulnerable a woman was—vulnerable as no man had ever been, or could ever feel. Morvenna felt strangely shaken that this man understood.

He let her go and watched quizzically as she drew

quickly away from him. "Don't be polite, Miss Fayr, the next time you find yourself at the mercy of a man. Don't, in fact, wander too far beyond the village when you are alone. There are *seringueiros* in the bush who work the rubber, and they are not nearly as polite as I am."

His bow was a slightly mocking one, and a moment later he was crossing the compound, tall, lithe, striding as though the muscles of his feet enjoyed the pressure of the ground—the island soil from which sprang the tall trees and the ardent plants that grew everywhere like live things. The place was in his blood, at the very core of his being, and as Morvenna watched him he became one with the trees and the compound looked strangely empty.

CHAPTER FIVE

THE DRESS Morvenna wore that evening was from the island store. It was of white cotton, with a plain sleeveless top and a floral-patterned skirt—cool, crisp, youthful. But it needed a necklace, and as she stood at the dressing table she fingered the coral on a fine chain that Nuno, with casual shyness, had dropped into her hand the other day.

A flush pink coral, which he said he would like her to have because all her belongings had been lost in the sea. She fastened the chain around her neck and was pleased at the effect.

Nuno was such a nice boy, she thought, kinder at heart than his exotic twin sister. There was about Raya a demure insolence that became more apparent when she discarded her nurse's uniform for one of her wild silk sarongs. She liked wearing flowers in her dark hair, and referred to her house in a grove of feathery palm and papaya as the "house of the ransomed one." Chains of shells and red coral hung in her porch, and the roof was pagoda-peaked.

Leird was bewitched by her, and curiously morose these days when in anyone else's company. Morvenna, who was doomed to worry about other people, was concerned for Leird. He had helped her to swim ashore when the yacht had wrecked itself on the reef, and she liked him as she might a cousin. She had never known a cousin, for her mother had grown up in an orphanage and her father had run away from his Tiger Bay home many years ago.

Love—the sweet and savage combat, as Roque de Braz
Ferro had called it. Did he speak from experience, or was
it another of his Latin philosophies? He seemed to have
quite a collection of them, and somehow he did not strike
her as a man who had ever let a woman into his heart. He
would have to conquer, and was a trifle cynical about
women because he had learned, probably as a boy, that
they were too eager to run to him at a snap of his fingers.

Morvenna shrugged. Most of her own knowledge of
love was bound up in her folk music. She had not experienced romance, though she had been aware when
playing and singing a poignant song that love could be a
thing of magic.

She met her own eyes in the mirror and was struck by
their faintly wistful expression. Her hair fitted her head
neatly and shiningly. She felt slick and cool all over, for
she had showered in the little shower house at the rear of
the *fazenda*, on the lookout all the time for the saucer-
sized spiders that came up through the drain in the
center of the cement floor. Her skin was fresh from the
eau de cologne she had dabbed on, with its tang of men-
thol.

She had better go next door and see if Poppy needed
her.

Poppy was being waited on like a queen by an Indian
woman whose face was lined all over like ivory when
aged. Her eyes were quick and obsidian dark, full of a
lively curiosity as they dwelt on Morvenna.

"Darling—" Poppy turned to give Morvenna a dazzling smile "—isn't the *senhor* a pet? He has sent Isidra
as a maid for me—the old lady who found me on the
beach and who looked after me so well all through that
ghastly night. She doesn't speak a word of English, but
she knows how to be a lady's maid because she worked
for the *senhor*'s mother, ages ago, when he was a boy.
See how she's arranged my hair?"

Poppy's hair was swept up in tawny loops and held in place by tortoiseshell combs—a Latin style, with which she hoped to impress the *senhor*, no doubt.

"It looks very attractive." Morvenna took a step backward out of the room, feeling an interloper as Isidra fussed aroung Poppy as though she were the mistress of the house. "Well, if you don't need me...?"

"I don't, darling, not now," Poppy said complacently. "Do run along and get smart yourself."

"But I...." Morvenna glanced down wryly at her cotton dress and the embroidered Indian slippers that had to serve as evening shoes. "I'll see you later, Poppy."

As Morvenna turned and walked away, her wry little smile still clung to her lips. She knew she looked far from glamorous in the cotton dress, but there had been no need for Poppy to rub it in. It was funny, but it always stung more when another woman dismissed one as plain and awkward and badly dressed.

Morvenna came to the doors of the big living room of the *fazenda* and was relieved to find the room unoccupied. She entered and was immediately aware of the musk of flowers. She looked around and saw the vase of jaguar flowers, with tawny splotches on the pointed petals; and the great spray of violet jacaranda, arranged in a brass bowl on one of the low tables carved from jungle wood.

Each time Morvenna set foot in this fascinating room it cast its spell upon her. The corner lamps under their golden shades were switched on, casting pools of light on the inlaid floor, islanded here and there by velvety puma pelts. Antique fans clung to the ceiling like big, purring moths. The walls were paneled in richly grained wood, against which snarled a magnificent jaguar head. The great paws of the beast held ashtrays on the elbow

tables set beside armchairs. On a handsome sideboard
hewn out of jungle mahogany there stood an antique
tantalus, the old sherry and brandy gleaming through
heavy cut glass. A pair of golden Aztec masks guarded a
painting of the woman who had given birth to Roque de
Braz Ferro.

Morvenna stood amid the fantastic shadows and
glimmering pelts of this room in this jungle island house
and studied the face of the Brazilian girl who had come
to this house as a bride; who had borne a son and passed
on to him a pair of eyes as blue as aquamarines. The
sculpturing of her brow was more delicate, and the
straight nose did not arch at the nostrils, but her hair
had been as raven dark.

Nuno Sebastian had told Morvenna how she had
died.

Fearlessly at home in the jungle, she had gone out
with her husband to hunt a killer jaguar who had been
terrorizing the people of the village. By nightfall the big
cat was dead—and so was Rosa de Braz Ferro, her long,
lovely neck broken when the tawny killer sprang upon
her from a broken column of the temple ruins where it
had its lair.

Morvenna rubbed the goose bumps from her arms,
and against her will her gaze was drawn to the jaguar
head on the opposite wall. A thread of shock ran
through her, for as silently as any jungle cat Roque de
Braz Ferro had entered the room and was standing
beneath the snarling head of the beast that had killed his
mother.

He wore immaculate white drill, which threw into
prominence the dark virility and pagan distinction of his
looks. His blue gaze was on the nerve that beat visibly in
her throat, and she tensed as he crossed the room
toward her.

"Good evening." He gave her a brief bow, and something, which might have been a smile, flickered on his mouth. "Whenever I approach you, Miss Fayr, you stiffen as though I bite. Do you think I bite?"

"Y-you startled me, *senhor*." A flush stole into her cheeks, for as always he took her composure and snuffed it as he might a candle flame between his hard fingers. "I didn't hear you come in."

"I think I had better give you something to settle those easily startled nerves of yours." He strolled over to the tantalus on the sideboard and withdrew the glass stopper from one of the decanters. He filled a pair of fluted glasses and joined her again beneath the portrait of his mother. "This is a very old wine from the cellars of Oporto." He handed her one of the fluted glasses. *"Salud, senhorinha."*

"Salud." She took a cautious sip at the wine.

"You will feel it in your heart, not in your head," he said sardonically. "Wine is like life, an acceptance of the bitter with the sweet, but I am sure you will agree with me that this is a happy wine."

"It is very pleasant, *senhor*, but I am no authority on wine."

"Who is an authority?" A dark brow quirked above a vivid blue eye. "A wine, like a woman, changes with the atmosphere of a room, or the mood of the moment. As the gods sometimes smile and give a woman charm, so it is with wine."

Morvenna cast him a wary little glance under her lashes and wondered who the woman was to whom he referred. Was it Poppy, with her ready wit and her tawny glamour? Or did he refer to Raya, the girl he had ransomed with the skillful, flashing blade of a machete?

"Have you no opinion of men?" he asked. "After all, you are often in the company of young Nuno."

"Do you mean Latin men, *senhor*?"

"Yes, let us say Latin men." His smile was tinged

with something indefinable. "Your opinion should be an interesting one, for I am sure you know that our history has been a stormy and a colorful one, splendid and devilish. As plants are conditioned by the soil in which they grow, so are people conditioned by the lives and actions of their ancestors. They implant in our bloodstream our responses to life."

"*Conquistadors*—and witches?" She smiled.

"I am sure the flaxen-haired Morvenna of long ago was a sorceress whose magic was not distilled over a cauldron."

"I am sure, *senhor*, that you are exactly like the man who found this island and took it." Morvenna tilted her chin and met the glinting blue eyes in the wickedly lean face. "I think that Latin men at heart would like to lock up their wives and keep them secret and veiled."

"Only Latin men?" he taunted. "Surely all men are possessive of what they love? Love, after all, is a primitive and powerful emotion."

"I prefer to think it a tender emotion, a compassionate one," she argued, and looked a little askance at the wineglass in her hand. A wine, indeed, that you felt in your heart!

"Of course for some there is more compassion in what they feel than passion." He shrugged and added impatiently, "*I* would not call that love. The whole heart must be seared. It should be as a flame, one that goes on burning through storm and calmness; with distance between—and when closeness allows, of no distance at all."

"You make love sound very ruthless," she said.

"That you speak with surprise at its ruthlessness, Miss Fayr, is proof that you have never been in love."

It was a statement of fact, not a question. A flick of his eyes and he saw lips that had never been kissed, and skin that had not yet thrilled to a loving touch.

"Women might deny it to themselves, but they like to be mastered," said this man whose wooing would never be like that of other men. "Mastery is not tyranny, *senhorinha*, and I am sure that one day a man will prove it to you."

He tossed back the remainder of his wine and placed the glass on a table. "What do you think of my house?" he asked abruptly. "Do you think a woman would be content to live here?"

"Your mother lived here, *senhor*." Morvenna gazed at him with wide and startled eyes, eyes the color of the violet jacaranda that spread its plumes behind her fair head.

"My mother was an unusual woman." He gazed up at her portrait with a somber expression on his face. "She was a Latin, reared to the idea that she should follow where her husband led. I speak of a woman born to other ideas, other cultures. Do you understand?"

A woman who was not a Latin! A woman like Poppy, tawny as a tigress, but with an undisputed love of civilization. A need for lovely clothes, bright lights, the admiration of the crowd.

"I couldn't answer for other women, *senhor*," Morvenna said quietly. "To me this island is like a kingdom of fantasy."

"And this house my Aztec palace, eh?"

"Perhaps." She met his smile with an uncertain one. "The pelts, the jungle flowers, the dusky timbers—the allegiance of your Indians."

"I am their guardian, their *patrao*, that is all." Still smiling in that faintly sardonic way of his, he bent to a table and picked up a carving in rock crystal—a strange, primitive, heart-shaped carving, agleam in his dark hands. Hands, she had noticed before, with all the ruthless beauty of those to be seen in old paintings of men of the sword.

"What do you think of this?" he asked.

"I don't know." She came a step closer and studied it. It was oddly anatomical, she thought. "I have always wondered how an expert, or connoisseur, can tell whether a work of art is the real thing or not."

"It has a certain quality, almost identical to that in certain people," he explained. "A sincerity of purpose, a beauty within. Integrity is the best term, perhaps."

She touched a finger to the primitive carving. "Open your hands," he ordered. She did so and he placed the piece within them. "That, Miss Fayr, is the exact weight, size, and shape of the human heart. How does it feel to hold a heart in your hands?"

She caught her breath. The heart fitted snugly into her palms and was warm from his touch. It almost seemed to throb, until she realized that her own quick pulse was animating the heart.

"I'm very prosaic." She met his eyes through her lashes and gave a nervous laugh. "I prefer to see a heart as a locket on a chain."

His gaze dwelt on her coral pendant as he took the rock crystal ornament and replaced it on the table. "Were you wearing that—" he flicked a finger at the pink coral "—when we found you on the beach?"

She shook her head. "Nuno gave it to me."

"I see." He gazed down at her consideringly. "I am sure you are unaware that the Indians attach significance to the giving of a gift to a girl. Nuno is not one by birth, but he lived among them during his most formative years and he absorbed quite a few of their beliefs. When a young hunter gives a girl a necklace or bracelet that he has made himself, he is telling her that his designs are serious. Has Nuno seen you wearing his gift, *senhorinha*?"

She shook her head dumbly.

"Do you wish him to see you wearing it?"

She shivered at the relentless tone of voice and half turned away to avoid the blue gaze that cut like diamonds. "I...I only put it on because I thought it pretty, and Nuno wanted me to have it because all my things were lost—"

"Remove the pendant, Miss Fayr. I will give you something else to wear in its place."

"That isn't necessary." She unfastened the chain with fingers that trembled. "Please don't bother—"

"It is no bother." He strode to the mahogany sideboard and opened one of the cupboards beneath. He took out a box of old dark wood and lifted the lid. Something gleamed in his fingers as he rejoined Morvenna. "You need not be afraid of my motives," he said dryly. "You need not even wear the thing if you don't like it—I shall not force it around your neck."

It was a short necklace of silver shells with tiny chains of seed pearls looping each shell together. It couldn't be a family heirloom, she reasoned. He would not leave an ornament of value to him in an old, unlocked box.

"This fastener looks a little awkward, so will you please turn your back to me." She did so, meekly, wondering as the silver shells settled against her skin and she felt his fingers brush her nape whether anyone ever dared to defy him.

"Poppy will wonder where I got the finery from," she said, and the words came out rather breathlessly.

"My dear Miss Fayr—" his voice mocked her from way above her head "—one would think that I had adorned you with diamonds instead of an old shell necklace."

"You would have had to force me to wear diamonds," she said, and she put space between them as high heels sounded on the wooden platform of the veranda and the rustle of satin preceded Poppy's entrance into the room.

She hardly looked a widow in her turquoise sheath. Apple green jade hung from her earlobes and glinted chunkily around her honey throat. Her hair was piled and looped, and shining with renewed vitality. Her smile was seductive as she presented her hand to Roque de Braz Ferro. She almost purred aloud as he brushed his lips across the back of it, where a cone-shaped diamond blazed with fire.

"You are looking in excellent health, Mrs. Tyson," he said.

"Thanks to my excellent doctor," she purred. "Please do call me Poppy, *senhor*. Being called Mrs. Tyson makes me remember the things I must learn to forget."

"The formalities are discarded." He smiled down at her. "May I offer you an aperitif, Poppy?"

"I would love a dry white port, with ice and a slice of lime," she said, and while he prepared the drink for her, she stared inquisitively at the silver shells that glinted against Morvenna's throat—a slim, white throat, which the sun seemed reluctant to touch.

"I...I wonder where Leird has got to." Morvenna strove not to cover the shells with her hand, and wondered why she should feel guilty about wearing the necklace. She hadn't felt like this about Nuno's piece of coral—but Nuno, of course, was not the man whom Poppy admired.

"Raya is joining us for dinner." The *senhor* handed Poppy her drink. "I expect she asked Mr. Challen to call for her."

"Leird is smitten with her," Poppy said with an indulgent laugh, no longer interested in the "Red Lion" now she had met more interesting game. "Raya is a very pretty girl. Poor Morvenna—" her red lip petaled the rim of her wine glass "—you like Leird such a lot, don't you, my dear? But that's men all the world over, they always prefer a pretty face to a kind heart."

Morvenna knew she wasn't pretty, so it wasn't that part of Poppy's remark that left her speechless—it was the honeyed implication that she more than liked Leird, who had not lost interest in her because of Raya. It had been Poppy who had flirted with Leird on the yacht, and Poppy knew, cleverly, that Morvenna wouldn't have the cattiness to say so.

"I hope that as a Latin, *senhor*, you don't think it unfeeling of me not to be wearing widow's weeds?" Poppy gazed up at him, frank and limpid as an angel in blue. "Gerald wouldn't want me to look drab. He loved bright colors and gaiety, and all I can do for him now is to dress as he loved me to, and not wear my grief on my sleeve. You do understand—Roque?"

She held out a hand to him and he took it—a pampered little hand, crowned by a diamond that looked too heavy for it, capable of nothing but being crushed in the lean, steely fingers of the *senhor*.

The blue angel and the prince of darkness, Morvenna thought cynically. Her smile, as Nuno came through the veranda doors into the room, was full of welcome. His handsome young face, his fawn gabardine suit, his smoothly brushed hair with a gleam of wetness to hold down the waves, were honest as good brown bread, and Morvenna wished belatedly, as his eyes sought her throat, that she wore his boyish gift instead of the chain of silver shells.

He smiled at her, but looked faintly puzzled, as though he couldn't reconcile the radiance of her welcome with her obvious rejection of his gift. "You look nice," he murmured. "There is only one thing about you that I don't like."

She pretended not to understand him, and when he turned from her to pay his respects to Poppy and the *senhor*, she found to her dismay that the coral pendant was gone from the elbow table on which she had laid it.

The *senhor* had obviously picked it up and slipped it into his pocket. Nuno's token of admiration for a girl his guardian did not approve of!

He could not approve when he had been so firm about its removal—which seemed to suggest that Poppy might have found other occasions in which to insinuate that Morvenna cared for the man whose arms had carried her ashore when the yacht went down.

CHAPTER SIX

ALL THROUGH THE EVENING that followed, Morvenna was conscious of the crosscurrents of tension that ran beneath the conversation at dinner, and later when they returned to the lamp-lit living room.

The source was Poppy. She had a talent for making people conscious of each other, and reveled in an atmosphere that held elements of storm.

Tango music came through on the radio, accompanied by some static that did not stop Raya from dancing with Leird. "How well they dance together!" Poppy reclined against the upholstery of her chair, mingling her tigress limbs and her tawny hair with the velvety pelt. "A man always looks so dangerously masculine when he holds a lovely woman in his arms. Don't you agree with me, Morvenna?"

Morvenna cradled her pineapple drink in her hands and wondered why Poppy had her claws in her tonight. "When I look at a man I don't look for danger," she said. "I prefer kindness."

"Of course, my pet." Poppy smoked her cigarette with relaxed enjoyment. "It's just as well for a girl to expect only the emotions that she is capable of arousing. I remember Gerald saying that you were the sort of girl a man had to be kind to."

She made kindness sound like an insult, which Morvenna supposed it was to a woman who preferred to be desired.

"Your type reminds me of a certain West Indian plant

that curls up when you touch it." Even as Poppy spoke, the quality of her smile changed as Roque de Braz Ferro came striding in through the veranda doors, followed by Nuno. An Indian had come in agitation to say that there was trouble in one of the houses, and the *patrao* had marched off at once to settle it.

"It was over a woman." He brushed a black strand of hair back from a frowning forehead. "These things have to be settled at once, otherwise all the relatives get involved and we end up with a family feud on our hands."

"How has it been settled, Roque?" Poppy was leaning forward, intensely interested.

"A wedding has been arranged," he said laconically. "It will take place at the weekend."

"What have you done?" Poppy's voice was silken. Raya and Leird had paused in their dancing to listen. Morvenna leaned back in the shadows and watched the fair faces and the dark ones, and felt curiously left out of the love tangles and dramas.

"I merely provided the livestock that a poor boy could not pay a greedy father for his daughter." The *senhor* gave a lazy laugh. "Bartered brides are common on our island, *senhora*. Are you shocked?"

"It's savage, primitive," Poppy breathed. "What will happen at the marriage ceremony?"

"The girl's dowry of pigs will be paid to her father, then she and the boy will go into the jungle together. The village will celebrate with a feast of roast pig, palm wine and dancing."

"I must see it all." Poppy's eyes were glittering. "Will that be possible, Roque?"

"Of course." He gave her a brief bow that indulged her whim. "A wedding is a public affair among the Indians, and certainly an interesting spectacle for visitors to our island. Mr. Challen and Miss Fayr will also find it intriguing."

"I hope, Morvenna, that you won't find it too primitive," Poppy said with mischievous relish. "Do the Indians wear masks and feathers?"

"All the trimmings, Mrs. Tyson." It was Nuno who answered, and his face was tautly drawn with distaste as he looked at her. "It is little different from a so-called civilized wedding, except that the boy and girl are often far more in love. The villagers build them a thatched house while they are alone in the jungle, and stock it with fruit and fish and flowers for their return."

"Will they do that for you, Nuno, when you marry?" Poppy flicked cigarette ash into one of the jaguar-paw ashtrays. From where Morvenna sat she could see the long, ruthless line of Poppy's profile and her upswept, darkened eyelashes. She knew with fellow sympathy that Nuno, who was so at home in the menacing jungle, was no match for a woman who cared for no one outside her own skin, but who was clever enough to make it seem a sophisticated virtue. Combat with her would leave him as defenseless as it left Morvenna.

"That radio makes more noise than music." The crisp voice cut across the room like a whiplash. "Please turn it off, Raya. We will ask Miss Fayr to play for us— Nuno, will you be good enough to fetch the guitar that hangs on the wall of my study?"

Morvenna had not known that the *senhor* possessed a guitar, and she felt a tingling in her fingers to hold one again. She glanced up as the radio was switched off and silence fell over the room for a moment. "You will play for us, honey?" Leird stretched his spare, rangy form in a chair, and his smile slid away from her and followed Raya. The smile died to a small frown as the girl struck a match across the seal of the *senhor*'s ring and carried the flame to the cheroot he had just placed between his lips.

"Thank you, little one." He gave the girl a smile of

lazy affection. Then he glanced at Leird. "You would like a drink, *senhor*, after being put through the convolutions of the tango?"

"That would be nice. Raya knows what I like."

"And the ladies?" The blue eyes dwelt on Poppy, then on Morvenna.

"I'd like a brandy with a dash of *crème de menthe*," Poppy drawled. "A barbaric mixture, but I love a dash of fire and ice."

The hidden meaning in Poppy's remark was not lost on Morvenna, nor on the *senhor*, she was sure of that. As cheroot smoke curled up around his eyes, she glimpsed the amusement in them. "And you, *senhorinha*," he said to her, "will you try this combination of fire and ice, or do you prefer something more temperate?"

"I still have my pineapple, thank you." She sounded like a prosaic schoolgirl and wasn't surprised when he quirked that left eyebrow of his and flicked a glance from her Indian-slippered feet, set demurely side by side, to her slim hands cradling her long glass of juice.

"Morvenna likes her drinks sweet and her men kind." Poppy's side-glance was maliciously amused. "She would sooner be chaste than chased, wouldn't you, pet?"

"Morvenna isn't all that timid," Leird put in. "She came alone to Brazil, toting a suitcase, a map, and a dream. Would you have that much courage, Poppy, without a man to sail your boat?"

"I wouldn't have that much folly," she rejoined.

"Cautiousness is calculated," Leird shot back at her. "Chasteness is innate."

"No doubt." Poppy gave a silky laugh. "But I bet you don't place it top of the list when you look at a woman. You aren't the type, Leird. You've seen too much of the world and lost too many of your illusions."

"I had them to lose," he said, narrowing his eyes. "I could learn to find them again." He glanced up at Raya as she came over to him with his drink, and for a moment his eyes were naked with what he felt for the girl. Poor Leird! Morvenna's heart was anxious for him. She hoped he wasn't harboring illusions about Raya. She was exquisitely pretty, but there was something primitive about her that would demand the heat and spice and danger of the jungle in the man she chose to love. Leird, for all his manliness, was very sophisticated. Raya was as exotic, inside and out, as a jungle flower.

The guitar that Nuno handed to Morvenna was a lovely instrument, with mother-of-pearl inlay and a tone that sang on its own.

Morvenna was rather shy of people until she held a guitar in her hands. Then, like a shield, it protected her sensitivity. Like a talisman it awoke in her the curious magic that the true folksinger possesses.

Her guitar strings murmured, and half in shadow her eyes were a mysterious purple, and her hair was a medieval cap of silver. The song she sang was old as the wild hills where the sorceress in her blood had roamed with her lover. She sang in Welsh, to suit her mood, and her awareness of being far from all she knew and was part of.

Never in her life before had she sung in so strange a setting, to people whom a tragedy had thrown together for a few short weeks. They stood or sat around, transfixed like figures in a dream. A girl in a garment of gold silk, reaching to her ankles and leaving the golden pallor of her shoulders quite bare. Her eyes slanted in a secret smile. A single gold ear pendant hung against the dark sheen of her hair; her small feet arched in slave sandals with tiny beads across the ankle straps. She sat at Leird's knee like his handmaiden—but whose kisses did her red lips remember as Morvenna sang in her sweet husky voice of love and its strange enchantment?

Strong shoulders stretched the immaculate white tussah that covered them. There was a glint behind the dark lashes, like fire seen way back in a forest clearing. Smoke rose up and veiled the blue flames. He stood only a few paces from Poppy. She had only to stretch out a bejeweled hand to touch the *senhor*.

Six people, each one wrapped in personal mystery. Each one affected in a different way by the music and its evocations. "Again!" Nuno pleaded when the song died away. "Sing for us again, *carestia*."

Something winged across her vision like a dart of blue. Poppy stirred out of her languor, and Raya turned her head and gave Morvenna a catlike stare. "So," that look seemed to say, "there is more to you, Little White Mouse, than meets the eye."

"Please sing and play again, Miss Fayr." It was the *senhor* who spoke, his face as carved as the Aztec mask beyond his shoulder. "That guitar has not been played so well for years. It belonged to my mother."

She had known because of the faded scarlet ribbons that hung from it. They trailed her arm like a ghostly touch as she sang once more. The jungle pressed in closer around the house as the night deepened; moths clustered around the lamps, and a green mantis prayed on the violet jacaranda.

"No—no more." She brushed past Nuno and went out onto the veranda to its farthest end. The darkness was warm and breathing, full of the strangest sounds, low as a pulse beat, and the next moment high as a sobbing scream—or was it a jeering laugh?

Morvenna ran her hand along the smooth railing, and her fingers hastily retreated as they met another's. Nuno had followed her.

"You sing as though your heart is afraid of happiness," he said. "Have you not known much happiness, Morvenna?"

"The best part of happiness lies in being needed," she murmured, "and I supposed that is why I came all this way, toting a map and a dream. For the first time I felt as though I might be needed, but the *senhor* seems to think that my quest has been a hopeless one. He told me the Indian trackers would have found some sign of my father—if he were still alive."

"You are alive." The words brushed her ear. "Your life is ahead of you, and there will be someone else who will give you the best part of happiness by needing you . . . by cherishing you."

She caught her breath, for to every woman the word *cherish* is probably the loveliest, the most promising in all the world. To be adored put you on a pedestal, where you were out of reach, but to be cherished made you companion, lover, and beloved child.

"Are all Brazilians as full of charm as you, Nuno?" She spoke lightly because the music she had played, the strange glamor of the night, and the sympathy of a handsome boy made her vulnerable and more afraid of herself than of him. To be cherished—how she longed for just that.

"The *patrao* is a Brazilian." Nuno's warm hand crept over hers again. "Don't you think him charming?"

"He seems as fierce and unpredictable as the jungle itself." The words had been in her from the moment she had glanced up from Leird's unconscious face into the dark, fearlessly molded face out of another century, another time, meeting eyes that seemed to burn like cold blue flames.

"Sometimes when he looks at me, he makes me cold to my spine." Her words were a whisper in the night, mocked by that jungle laugh that echoed across the dark compound from among the giant trees.

"Do you think him a tyrant?" Nuno could laugh because he was male and would never feel the same kind of fears as a woman. "Tyranny means cruelty, and the people of Janaleza are too loyal to the *patrao* to be victims of his autocracy."

"I . . . I don't mean that he goes around the island with a whip in his hand. It's more complex than that, Nuno. For instance, I can't be relaxed with him as I am with you. He's so armored, so unconquered, so infuriatingly sure of himself. You could never imagine him tripping on a vine and falling on his face; and as for falling in love . . . !" She gave a nervous laugh. "Can you imagine the Senhor Roque de Braz Ferro ever humbling himself to a mere woman? He will merely snap his fingers and she will run to his knee like his latest jungle pet."

"When he marries," Nuno said quietly, "there is a good chance that he will choose Raya. He is a man who may have his choice, but the woman he marries must be content to live here on the island. Raya, like myself, is part of Janaleza. A woman from the world across the water would not settle down easily to island jungle life— not a woman like your friend Poppy."

As he spoke, he turned Morvenna's hand within his and crushed it gently, urgently. "Why did you not wear my coral?" His hand stole up her arm to her shoulder, to the silver shells. "Why?"

She felt his touch and heard his question, but was lost in thoughts about his sister—the Latin girl the *patrao* had ransomed, lovely as a jungle flower, made for marriage with a dominant man who shared her affinity with the untamed jungle.

"Morvenna, answer me." Suddenly Nuno's warm hand was pressing into the small of her back, gripping so that her dress was drawn up above the backs of her knees. His tough young body was against hers, compelling her awareness of him, and she dragged her gaze from the green fireflies that hung in the sultry air as still as gems in a jewel shop, and met the gleam of his eyes. "Were you afraid to wear my coral?"

"No—"

"Perhaps you did not think it good enough? A piece of coral on a chain is hardly comparable to a necklace of silver."

"Nuno, let me go!"

"No." The exultation of having her at his mercy was in his voice. "Here in this part of the world the men are the masters; when we are angry we give way to it, we don't stifle it like your Englishmen. That is how women learn contempt, when they are given in to all the time."

"Englishmen don't expect women to behave like doormats," she stormed. "Now grow up, Nuno, and stop behaving like. . .like a spoiled little boy—"

"Little boy?" he growled. "I will show you just how grown-up I am—" In an instant his lean, boyish body was full of adult intention, and her backbone nearly cracked as he arched her over his arm and brought his face close to hers.

"*Oh!*" she gasped, partly from pain and partly with dismay as the doors of the living room were swept open and light streamed out onto the veranda.

"My dear," Poppy caroled, "whatever are you doing up there in the corner?"

"*Let me go!*" Morvenna said in a low, fierce voice. The hard young arms released her, and as she brushed past Nuno in a storm of embarrassment she met the *senhor's* gaze above Poppy's tawny head. Poppy was smiling with malicious enjoyment.

"This island of yours, *senhor*," she purred over her shoulder, "is having the most primitive effect on all of us."

"The intangible threat of the jungle is in our air, and sometimes it goes to the head like strong wine. Small

doses of it are advised, especially at night.'' He gave
Morvenna a dismissive bow. "*Bona noite*, Senhorita
Fayr.''

It was the first time he had addressed her in that way.
Always before he had used the term *senhorinha*, which
was more old-fashioned; more appropriate, he had
probably thought, until tonight. "Good night, everyone.'' She hurried away from the small group to the
refuge of her room, so annoyed with Nuno that she
decided not to go fishing with him in the morning.

She had been looking forward to the outing, but if he
was going to be silly and demanding then she would be
wise to keep out of his way until he came to his senses.
He had known her only a week, and was a trifle infatuated with her pale coloring and the fact that she was
British.

At some time, not unreasonably perhaps, the rumor
had got around that British girls were cool-looking and
warmhearted. Morvenna's awareness of her own warm
heart was one of the reasons she protected it so fiercely.
It would be too easy to fall in love while she was far
from home and stranded like a waif on an island that
was both savage and beautiful.

She unfastened the *senhor*'s necklace of silver shells
and studied them by the lamp on her dressing table.
Pretty but dangerous. Nuno would not have pounced
like a young panther if she had not been wearing them.
She let them slide in a shining chain from her hand, and
as she glanced up she met her eyes in the dressing mirror. In that moment they were as intense as violets, shel-
tering within her lashes as that secretive flower shelters
within the coolness of a wood, or in the shade beneath a
wall.

You might well look perplexed, Morvenna Fayr, she
thought. *Life is a puzzle, isn't it? We do things we don't
really reason out, and cross bridges recklessly in the*

*dark and wonder why we fall and get hurt. You crossed
the biggest of your life, my girl, when you bought a
ticket for Brazil and boarded that jet plane in England....*

England, so far away, so out of reach, where she had
not felt threatened by the intangible dangers that hung
in the lush air of Janaleza.

Island of secrets, remote from all the world, the
fragrance of its Virgin's Pagoda filling her room as she
prepared for bed. Arrayed in one of the ankle-length
nightdresses supplied by the store—ruffled at the throat
and quaint—she went over to remove the flowers from
beside her bed. She cupped the brass bowl in her hands,
and the scent from the shy, hanging heads of the
blossoms was intoxicating as she carried the bowl to a
bamboo table near the veranda doors.

Morvenna marveled at the fragile flower, which grew
and flourished in the barbaric soil that also gave life to
strange wild orchids, heavy masses of flowering vine,
and the oleander with its painted petals and poisonous
sap.

She put out a hand to the petals of one of the flowers,
then drew back hastily with a low gasp of horror.
Crawling over the side of the bowl was a slim mottled
shape; it slithered out inch by inch from among the
white pagodas, and Morvenna stood transfixed as the
snake undulated across the bamboo table and would, in
another second or two, be within striking distance of her
bare left arm. The snake quivered and made a queer little sound, which echoed in her dry throat as she unfroze
and fled out blindly onto the veranda.

Hands caught her. She glanced up wildly and in the
light slanting from her room saw the rugged outlines of
a familiar face, and above the questioning eyes a shock
of ruffled hair.

"What is it, honey?" Leird's eyes raked her pale,

upraised face. "You look frightened out of your wits. Is there a spider or something in your room?"

"A s-snake," she stammered. "It crawled out of the f-flower bowl and it might be venomous."

"My dear girl!" He let go of her, took a quick step to the doors of her room and slammed them shut. Then he swung around, and before she could protest that she wasn't going to faint, he swept her up in his arms and carried her along to his own room. He put her on his bed, and now she saw that he was clad in pajamas and a robe.

"Stay here," he ordered. "I'll rouse up the *senhor*, who will know best how to deal with the snake—say, you've gone paler than ever! Are you going to pass out, Venna?"

"Of course not." She was shaky, that was all, and anxious for him to attend to the business of getting that horrible thing out of her room.

"Relax." Leird ruffled her hair as though she were a child. "These things are sent to try us."

His words remained with her after he had loped off to arouse the *senhor*, and she gave a shudder as in her mind's eye that long mottled shape crawled out once again from among the Virgin's Pagoda. Like the serpent in Eden, she thought, and glanced up big-eyed as someone appeared in the doorway of Leird's room. It was Poppy, her hair in a wheat-ripe cloak around the shoulders of her negligee, her eyes avid with curiosity as they took in Morvenna's night-clad figure on Leird's bed.

"I've just seen Roque and a couple of his servants going into your room," she said. "What are they doing in there?"

"Hunting a snake," Morvenna said tensely.

"You don't say? Poppy strolled to the foot of the bed, a glamorous contrast to Morvenna in the Quakerish nightdress, into whose long skirt her feet were tucked. "I wonder how a snake got into your room? I understand that snake repellent is used in the polish they use on the furniture and floors here at the *fazenda*."

"It didn't repel this one." Morvenna felt cold and bleak, the usual aftereffects of a scare. "It was curled up in the flower bowl that stands on the table beside my bed. If I hadn't moved the bowl it might have crawled out in the night and slithered beneath my bed netting—"

"It won't do that now, Miss Fayr." The *senhor* entered, clad in a dark robe over his pajamas. A frown joined his brows in a black bar above his eyes. "I am sorry you have had a fright, but the snake has now been removed and your room has been searched to ensure that it was not accompanied by its mate."

"Was it venomous, *senhor*?" she asked in a low, shaky voice.

He shook his head, his hands deep in the pockets of his robe.

"Well," Poppy drawled, "don't tell me we've all been dragged out of our beds by a harmless little grass snake?"

"Not a grass snake," he said, "but fortunately harmless."

"I—I'm sorry—" Morvenna slid off the bed and flitted past Poppy and the *senhor* like a small white ghost "—for waking everybody up. I don't know anything about snakes, you see—"

"One moment." The *senhor* made a captive of her just as she would have escaped out of the doors. "When in doubt, Miss Fayr, never be brave—or polite. I have told you before! This is a jungle house and our precautions don't always keep out the things of the forest. Those things are not always harmless."

She couldn't look at him. She, who had talked brave-ly about searching the jungle for her father, had flut-

tered and fled from a snake without a sting. He, who
had said that the jungle was no place for an inexperienced girl, had been infuriatingly correct in his judgment of her.

"I would like to go to bed now," she said, like a tired
little girl.

"No one is stopping you." His hands released her
and she had to force herself not to turn and run from
him, from Poppy's smile of condescension, and her own
vulnerable youth.

"Shall I come and tuck you in?" It was Leird who
spoke laughingly, and a small imp of torment made her
say:

"That would be nice, Leird."

But he didn't go as far as tucking her in. He came just
inside her room with her, and when she cast a quick
glance at the flowers she would never trust again, he
said gently, "Don't be nervous, honey. I can vouch for
the fact that the snake was carried off among the trees
by one of the *senhor*'s men, then we made sure its
slinky girl friend wasn't around. You won't be nervous
of sleeping here?"

"No." She gazed up at him, a quaint, barefooted
figure in her long nightdress. "You're a nice person,
Leird. Thank you for being kind to me."

"I can be kind because there's no nonsense of any
sort between us." He heaved a sigh and drew a hand
down over the attractive crags of his face. "Why is it
that we're comfortable with the people we like, and on
the defensive with those we love? Have you the answer,
little witch?"

"Perhaps it's because our hearts hold a strange fear
of happiness," she said quietly. "We all know that the
people we love are the ones who can snatch it from us."

He gazed down at her, somberly. "I'm in love with
Raya," he said. "You guessed, didn't you?"

She nodded.

"Loving Raya frightens me for the first time in my life," he said harshly. "I could never settle down on an island, I'm too much of a wanderer; and if she tore her roots out of this hot, lush soil I know it would do something terrible to her. Morvenna, don't fall in love—it hurts too much!"

With those words he turned and left her standing alone, her bare feet sunk in the tawny pelt that stretched across the floor of her room. Out in the jungly darkness the cicadas chirred. In here the scent of the pagoda flowers was a tormentingly sweet reminder that beauty—especially the beauty of love—held a strain of sadness and bitterness.

CHAPTER SEVEN

MORVENNA'S UNSETTLED FEELING continued for several days. Nuno, his mood a sulky one, had gone off into the jungle to fish in one of the hidden streams for golden dorado. Leird was battling with his private problem in a bout of photography. He went down to the wreck in the lagoon and took a series of photographs that were so vivid and haunting when developed that Morvenna wondered how Poppy could study them with such interest.

The answer was that Poppy was a flower without a heart, and Morvenna found herself avoiding the other girl whenever possible.

In matador denims and a shirt worn outside them for coolness, she roamed the shore beyond the plantations of the *fazenda*, and hunted for shells and branches of coral. The Indians dragged their nets in the surf and captured small fishes that were delicious roasted over a fire on the sands. They gravely offered her some on a big banana leaf and she ate them, crisp and crunchy, in her fingers, and drowsed under a spreading banyan tree with her grass-woven hat tilted over her eyes.

Often a whole lazy morning passed in this way. Bemused by the sun, her bare toes in the warm sand, she would lose that sense of tension, that tightening of nerves somewhere under her ribs, whenever she returned to the *fazenda*.

The fishing craft out beyond the reef were lateen-rigged and flimsy. Riding the blue ripples, misted by the spray from the reef, the Indians were like bronzes as they stood to aim a spear at a large fish, or to haul in a net of struggling silver minnows.

A soft breeze blew over the sun-fired water, bringing with it a tang of coral from the castellated reef. Castles and turrets of subtle colors, guarding this jungle island; the rustle of palm and breadfruit fronds mingling with the shuffling of the surf; the chants of the fishermen far out in their boats all added to Morvenna's sense of the elemental.

She pushed her toes into the warm sand and basked in peace beneath her banyan tree. Here she was undisturbed with her thoughts—until around noon one morning when a long shadow suddenly stretched across her lazy, sand-trapped figure. Her shaded glance stole up the strong, flexible figure in cool drill. Silence spun a web between her and the dark lord of the island.

While watching the colored sails of the boats and listening to the carefree chanting of the fishermen, she had been thinking of the man who ruled over them; of the affection and loyalty that they gave to him. It had not made him a tyrant, she admitted that, yet whenever he came near her she felt a compulsion to run away from him.

"Let me escort you back to the *fazenda*." He extended a brown hand, which she took reluctantly. His fingers closed around hers and as she rose out of the sand she was caught by the blue glint of his eyes, and the gleam of his teeth in a quizzical smile. He knew that she was nervous of him and she felt him pull her closer than was necessary just out of devilment. She pulled free of him and brushed sand from her denims. He was a man who was a little too alarming at close quarters!

"My sandals are around here somewhere." She padded in her bare feet around one side of the wide-buttressed banyan, and he found them at the other side.

They were woven out of grass, with fiber straps that crossed her small feet. After slipping into them she glanced up and saw the dents of amusement at the corners of his mouth.

"You look like an urchin out of a Mark Twain story," he said. "Here are your bits of coral and your conch shell."

"Thank you." Her cheeks grew pink as she took them. "One of the fishermen gave me the shell. It's full of sea talk."

"You like the islanders, don't you, *senhorinha*?"

They mounted the shore that sloped toward the trees, and she gave him a swift, eloquent glance. "How can one help it?" she asked. "They're so kind without question, and they take life so calmly and enjoy small pleasures so much, that I can't help contrasting them with the people in cities, who are so ambitious and uncaring toward each other."

"You live in a city yourself, but your heart does not belong to one, eh?" He was looking serious as he glanced down at her.

"No." She gave a sigh. "My father and I used to talk of having a little house in the Welsh hills. He would find a small pot of gold, he said, and then we would settle down in a green valley—but I mustn't think about that! Some of our hopes must remain dreams."

"Such a resigned statement for one so young." The *senhor*'s accent was more noticeable, as though she might have touched him.

"You've helped to make me resigned, *senhor*." She tilted him a look from beneath the brim of her grass hat. "You've pointed out to me all the things my father was up against. Devilfish, crocodiles, crazy water—Leird suggested that other treasure seekers could have been after his map. *Bandidos*, he called them, who would stop at nothing—"

She broke off, for it was too appalling to think of her carefree, adventurous father falling into the hands of men without mercy, just for a map that was probably as worthless as most treasure maps.

"That could not have happened." The *senhor* spoke with crisp authority. "Such scavengers take everything; they would not leave tinned provisions behind to rot in the bush, nor a canoe that was still useful."

She drew what comfort she could from this and walked quietly at his side as the shadows of the trees enclosed them like cool arms. *Cri-cro-o!* cried a bird, while the kingwoods reared up all around, and monkeys peered and chattered among the branches. A silk-winged jacamin crossed their path, and a fawn fled away on silent feet, a shadow-spotted, fairy-tale creature.

When the *senhor* suddenly left the path that Morvenna usually followed to the *fazenda*, she glanced up at him inquiringly. "I want to show you something that might appeal to your collector's instinct." He gave her a quirk of a smile and gestured at the shell and the coral that she carried. "By the way, I must remember to return the piece of coral that I confiscated—Nuno was hurt, eh? He thinks himself in love, and he will do so several times before he grows up."

"He's the same age as Raya," Morvenna pointed out. "She is certainly not a child."

"Miss Fayr," he said dryly, "most girls grow up more swiftly than boys. There are exceptions, of course—the girls who need a father more than they need a lover."

Protest winged sharp and painful through Morvenna, and died on her lips. Perhaps it was true! She had never sought romance. Her loneliness had always been that of a child who longs for security, the curtains drawn against the night, the flicker of candlelight on the face of a man with protective eyes.

A honey scent filled her nostrils as they passed beneath a tree laden with kapok blossom. He was so tall that he broke some of the blossom in passing and it showered down over both of them—clinging, scented petals, which he brushed from his black hair and his wide shoulders.

They entered the cool coffee groves, full of an amber twilight, and somewhere among the trees one of the Indian workers played a bamboo flute. They passed an Indian woman carrying her baby in a shoulder sling. The *senhor* paused to admire the child and exchange a few words with the mother, who smiled shyly as Morvenna petted the baby, lying naked and glossy in his sling. His eyes were sable dark, set at a slant in the brown face that was sticky from sugarcane. A bee buzzed and clung to his cheek, and Morvenna brushed it off quickly. At once it flew toward her, and as she hopped to one side to avoid a possible sting, she bumped into the *senhor*. "It's these pink pants," she laughed in confusion. "Fly away, bee, I'm not some odd sort of blossom!"

The Indian baby chuckled and sucked his piece of sugarcane, and was still gazing back at Morvenna with big dark eyes as his mother continued on her way with her father's lunch, which was wrapped in a red and white bandana.

"It is the brother of that young woman who becomes a bridegroom tomorrow," Morvenna was informed by her companion. "She hopes that you will attend the ceremony. Visitors bring good luck, you see, and she is a widow and wishes her brother to have better luck in life."

"I'm looking forward to seeing a Janalezan wedding, *senhor*." Their meeting with the Indian girl and her baby had eased the constraint between them. He aroused it almost deliberately, it seemed to Morvenna, as though he had little patience to spare for girls who were not like Raya. Lovely, exotic Raya, without inhibitions or fears for the future. The future that Leird would have no part in—she was to be the *patrao*'s bride.

They were deep in the coffee groves, with the mysterious amber dusk all around them, and the chik-chak of tree lizards. Perhaps it was the intimacy of being alone with a man in a forest of growing things that caused Morvenna to wonder what sort of a husband Roque de Braz Ferro would make.

He was a Latin and bound to be possessive. His lean strength, the texture of his skin, and the dark gleam of his hair denoted a strong virility. In his arms Raya would find all that she probably sought—but what of companionship? Did he attach no importance to that side of marriage?

Raya was pretty beyond description, but her conversation, Morvenna had noticed, was almost dull. She liked to curl like a kitten against a man's knee, and she loved to dance. She never argued with either Leird or the *senhor*.

A wry little smile tugged at Morvenna's lips. *She* had probably had more arguments with him in ten days than Raya had had in ten years!

"Here we are." He paused before one of the giant palm trees at the edge of the grove, and Morvenna saw sprouting from the trunk crevices a cluster of velvety lavender orchids. They were streaked with gold, and as the *senhor* pulled off a couple they clung around his fingers like live things. "Here they grow wild," he smiled. "In the cities men pay luxury prices for them in order to please a lady."

"You must give some to Poppy," Morvenna said. "She'll be crazy about them."

"Don't they appeal to you?" he asked.

"My tastes are simple," she replied. "Anyway, they look rather like lavender spiders. See how they cling!"

"What a child you are!" He laughed low in his throat, the palm frond shadows obscuring the expression in his eyes as he gazed down at her. "I suppose a nosegay of wild violets would be more to your taste?"

"With Welsh valley dew on them," she agreed. "Poppy will love the orchids."

"Then I shall certainly give them to her." He seemed amused rather than annoyed by Morvenna's dislike of the flamboyant orchids. "She will no doubt wear them tomorrow evening, when we attend the wedding festivities."

"Will Nuno be back in time for the wedding?" she asked as they made their way out of the groves and along a path that led to the *fazenda*.

"He should be." Morvenna felt a side-glance. "Remember my warning, *senhorinha*. Nuno is very attractive, but he is yet too young in his ways to make happy a girl like yourself."

"A girl in search of a father?" she flashed. "There's no need to keep reminding me, *senhor*, that you would not approve of me as a possible sister-in-law."

"I beg your pardon?" He stopped in his tracks and stood in front of her so that she could not proceed.

Her eyes lifted to meet his, the color of wood smoke in her fine-boned young face. "Nuno let the cat out of the bag," she said defiantly. "He told me that you will probably marry his sister. Congratulations. She's the prettiest girl I have ever seen."

Silence followed—silence with the pounce of a panther in it. "I don't wish this private information to become public knowledge," he said at last, his voice as chilling as his eyes. "I trust you to keep it to yourself."

"Of course." Her reply came huskily from a dry throat. He had looked angrier than she had known a man could look, as though she trespassed on hallowed ground and was lucky to have escaped with only a vocal whiplash. "I'm sorry, *senhor*. I had no idea that Nuno was revealing a secret to me."

"Which will prove to you how young he is, *senhorinha*, to reveal to a woman something he should have kept to himself. A woman vexed will use any weapon to stab a man, or to defend herself."

"You shouldn't be so keen to vex me." She tried to speak lightly, but it was a shaky effort. "I like Nuno, but it will be a long time before I shall want to. . .to fall in love."

"You expect to choose the time, the place, and the man?" he said dryly. "Attraction is a strange thing. Sometimes it exerts a pull on a person quite against her will."

"I suppose so," she admitted. "But I do assure you, *senhor*, that what I feel for Nuno is quite innocent. I shan't make an ass of him, or myself, because I'm all alone."

"There are no relatives in England?" His glance seemed to sharpen to steel. "You live alone there?"

"Yes, when my father's away—" She bit her lip, for Llew's homecomings had been so welcome and would be so missed. Like a rush of clean air from far places where traffic did not blare; where people did not seek wilder distractions and louder music to tame their discontent.

"I am sorry." The blue gaze grew softer. "Now I understand a little more about you. Why you came along to a strange land, seeking the unknown, which must unnerve you. Why you remind me—do you mind if I speak frankly?"

"Be my guest." Though she smiled she was disconcerted by his sudden change of mood. One moment a panther on the verge of attack, the next almost gentle. She wanted to flee from both sides of this savage, charming, unpredictable Brazilian.

"You remind me," he said, "of a chamois. Always on the verge of flight, as easily lost among people as that little animal is lost among trees and foliage. The chamois is also venturesome, and just as easily startled. She will follow a beckoning hand, but will never come too close in case that hand strikes instead of stroking. The chamois has too much heart. She guards it by flight, and too often runs into a trap laid in another direction."

"She sounds rather foolish," Morvenna quipped. "I think I would sooner be a tigress. No one hurts a tigress. She's too beautiful and clever."

"A chamois has a strange, lost, fablelike attraction," he said deliberately. "Some have eyes to see it, others do not."

What was he saying—that *she* had attraction? Not for him, not here in this lonely place, among trees hung with leaves as long as a man! Her eyes dwelt wide, almost a little stricken, on his Aztec face. Copper-carved, the eyes flame blue beneath the slashing eyebrows and helmet of black hair.

A dart of fear winged through her, released from a tension as old as time and new as the moment. She retreated a step or two, then true to everything he had said about her, she fled from the path that he blocked and the next instant blundered into something that caught at her clothing like barbed wire, raking her arms as she fought to free herself.

"You little fool!" The cotton of her shirt ripped, and his eyes blazed above her frightened face as he tore his own hands in freeing her from the macca bush into which she had run—the wait-a-bit, a bush of the tropics that will entrap a person as a spider web traps the unwary moth.

She felt the stings, and the violence in his hands as he pulled her free. Her eyes raced over his face while her mind darted down her torn shirt. There was a rip that bared her left shoulder, and another lower down, revealing her white skin to the scorching flick of his eyes.

"You are the most impulsive and infuriating young creature it has ever been my misfortune to meet!" His smile was ferocious, showing the edge of his white teeth. A lance of black hair jagged his forehead, and as he shook her, her grass hat fell off and revealed the alarm in her eyes. Near where he held her grew blossoms the same size and pallor of her face.

"You have no sense at all. You just follow your instincts and look where they land you—in the middle of a macca bush." His voice sank down, velvety and dangerous. "Why did you suddenly plunge off the path like that? Do you still think I bite?"

"You aren't the most gentle man I've ever met," she rejoined, feeling the bite of his fingers into her upper arms, and the flush in her cheeks. Suppose he guessed that for a ludicrous moment she had thought he found her attractive!

"That does not answer my question." Very deliberately his eyes roved her face, taking in each feature, each angle, each winged brow above her apprehensive eyes. Her pupils expanded until they were filled with his lean and mocking face. *He knew*. She could tell that he knew why she had run away from him. His lips were quirking as his blue gaze drifted to her lips.

"Answer me," he insisted.

"Y-you know the answer already." Her cheeks and her scratched arms were tingling. "I'm not used to the jungle and the odd effect it has on giddy, green newcomers."

"Tell me, Miss Fayr, just out of curiosity, how far you imagine you would get in the real jungle if you gave way to your nerves. Do you know what would happen if you got entangled in a macca bush in the forest? It would hold you as a web holds a fly, until a puma scented you and came prowling after a tender meal.''

"You've made your point," she said with what dignity she had left. "I'm sufficiently convinced that I'm a nitwit and that you will breathe seven prayers of thankfulness when the steamer arrives from Manaos to take me off your hands!''

"Only seven prayers?" he mocked. Then her left arm was free as he gestured at the orchids he had meant to give to Poppy. They lay on the ground, trampled by him when he had rescued her from the barbed bush. His gesture was eloquent, and a little tremor ran through Morvenna as his fingertips traveled to her bare shoulder, which the wait-a-bit had scratched.

"Come, we must get these attended to. Raya will do it for you in the dispensary."

"M-my conch shell." She broke free of him and ran to pick up the glossy pink shell. Her coral fern was broken and she didn't bother with that. When she turned around, holding the shell, the *senhor* was brushing off the ants that had got onto her grass hat. He jammed it on her head, and she caught a glimpse of his quizzical smile just before the shaggy brim came down over her eyes.

"Come along," he said, and he marched her along as though she were a child, her wrist so firmly fettered by his fingers that she felt the pressure of his ring. It was the seal ring against which Raya had struck a match to light his cheroot—its twining symbol of eternal devotion pressing against Morvenna's wrist bone.

CHAPTER EIGHT

NUNO HAD STILL not returned from his fishing trip when the occupants of the *fazenda* set out on Saturday to attend the wedding in the Indian village.

The orange sun seemed double its size as it went down behind the trees of the forest, and the thudding of feast drums and wailing of bamboo flutes took on a pagan quality as the foursome made their way to Raya's house.

The house of the ransomed one, as she called it, sat in a grove of whispering trees. The pagoda eaves overhung the veranda, and she insisted upon serving drinks and little cakes before they proceeded on their way to the wedding feast. "Now come, you must all sit down and let me be a real hostess." She smiled and fluttered among them, wrapped exquisitely in silk that looked as though it had been woven by silver spiders. There were creamy flowers in her hair and small corals around her throat. She was guileless and charming, lovely as the moonflowers that grew in her garden.

"How are the scratches?" she inquired of Morvenna as she offered her the honey cakes.

"Heaps better," Morvenna said quickly. "Mmm, yes, I will have one of those. They look delicious."

"I am very envious of Morvenna." Raya smiled up seductively at the *senhor*, who declined the honey cakes with an indulgent shake of his head. "Such a pity to scratch such skin on the barbs of the macca bush. It is white like the kernel of coconut."

Morvenna flushed as the others looked at her simultaneously. "How did you come to get tangled up in a macca bush?" asked Leird, while Poppy fussed with the stole that she wore over a dress studded with rose pink bugle beads.

"Miss Fayr was startled by a jungle creature," drawled the *senhor*. "He lurked in her path and she thought he would bite her, but as it turned out his intentions were not quite that fierce."

"You are a nervous little biddy," Poppy laughed. "Look at that snake the other night. Really! It wouldn't do for you to live here permanently."

"I wouldn't want to live here." Then Morvenna bit her lip, for she sounded ungracious. "I'm grateful for the hospitality I've received here, of course, but if there's no chance of finding my father alive, then there's nothing to keep me in Brazil."

"It's a shame the map was lost," said Poppy. "There might have been some buried treasure that we could have shared between us. As it is, you're without a sou, Venna. However will you manage?"

"I shall go to the British Consul at Manaos." Morvenna avoided the quick blue eyes of Roque de Braz Ferro. She didn't want even the offer of her home-going expenses from him. He had been generous enough, and once she left Janaleza she wanted to be independent of him.

"I shall be cabling from Manaos for an advance on my photographs and articles." Leird spoke with an eye on Raya. "You're welcome to whatever you need, Morvenna."

"Thanks, Leird, but I shall manage."

"Independent little cuss, aren't you?" Although Leird spoke to Morvenna, he was gazing at Raya. She was being elusive, and looking so lovely tonight that he had an openly tormented look in his eyes.

"That dress you have on is rather attractive, Venna." The ice whispered in Poppy's drink as she swept a probing glance over Morvenna. "Don't tell me you got that from the island store? If so, then I must inspect Flavio's merchandise."

Flavio was the young Latin Indian who owned the store, slim and handsome, his single gold earring giving him the look of a pirate. He flirted outrageously with the pretty girls of the island, but for all that he was shrewd and responsible, and even owned a *lancha*, which traveled up and down the jungle rivers, carrying food supplies and merchandise to the Brazilians who lived on isolated plantations.

"Raya was kind enough to lend me the dress. She let down the hem because I'm a little taller, and Flavio let me use his iron to press it," Morvenna explained.

"That could have been done for you at the *fazenda*," the *senhor* said crisply.

"Flavio was at the dispensary having a splinter removed, and he's always so gay and obliging. He insisted on bringing over the iron, and somehow he's one of those people you can't resist." Morvenna smiled as she recalled the gaiety, the joy in living that surrounded the young Amerindian. The golden ring in his ear, he had told her, was meant for his bride when he fell in love. Raya had teased him and said that he would never love one girl. His eye was too roving and his fancy too fickle.

Raya wasn't smiling at the moment. She stood rather pensively with her back to the veranda rail, the sunset flames burning out behind her in a sky that was deepening to purple. The wedding drums pounded and the tongues of the feast fires leaped among the trees that shielded this little bamboo house from the rest of the village.

The Latin girl was like a filigree carving; a delicate, mysterious creature with a skin of softest amber, her triangular jade eyes surrounded by lashes dark as jet.

Morvenna was mystified by Raya. Up until yesterday she had not shown much inclination to be friendly, but at the dispensary she had been charming—soft and generous and pert, like a kitten in the sun. "You cannot wear to a wedding one of those cotton dresses from Flavio's store," she had laughed. "I have just the dress for you, and it would please me very much to lend it to you."

The dress was of palest gold, shading to apricot edged by flame, the colors of the island dawn.

"What are the drums saying?" There was an excited catch in Poppy's voice, and her rings glittered as she laid a hand on a sleeve of the _senhor's_ suit. Beneath the tropical tussah he wore a tan silk shirt, which Morvenna noticed was only a shade darker than his skin.

"That man is conquest, and woman submission," he replied. "That is the Indian viewpoint, and the Latin, but perhaps you feel differently about the matter?"

"I wouldn't say no to being conquered by a real man." Her painted eyes flicked his shoulders and dwelt meaningly on his lean, dominant face.

"Latin women are submissive," Raya said quietly, "because the love of a Latin man is adoration—when a woman has been fortunate enough to arouse it."

Morvenna heard Leird catch his breath. A Latin man, Raya had said, excluding the English photographer as surely as though she had shut a door in his face. Big and rough-haired, he climbed to his feet and Morvenna saw the angry pain on his face as he strode to the veranda steps. "Shall we be off to the wedding festivities?" His voice was harsh. "It's a pity I can't take any photographs, but I suppose that's prohibited, _senhor_?"

"I would not advise it, Mr. Challen. A wedding to

jungle people is a festive occasion, but also a magical one. They would not welcome the eye of the camera. To them it might be casting an unlucky spell on the felicity and fertility of the groom and his bride.''

"I wouldn't want to do that," drawled Leird. He ran down the veranda steps and on impulse Morvenna followed him. She tucked her arm in his. "It's me," she said gently.

"Hello, you Welsh witch." He squeezed her arm against his side to let her know that he understood her sympathy and accepted it. They walked ahead of the others through the trees, toward the glow of the fires, and the coppery sheen of the Indian faces. Pig and kid meat was roasting over the flames. Great grass platters were piled high with jungle fruits and reef lobster and fish. Breadfruits, melon-big and knobby, sputtered and sizzled in the smaller fires.

Excitement ran through Morvenna. Never in her life had she seen anything so colorful. The drums beat out a rhythm to which circles of dancers gyrated, fierce and strange in their festive masks and feather crowns, with jaguar fangs strung around their throats and silver jewelry gleaming on their coppery arms. The smoke from the roasting meats and flames added a fearsome touch to the scene.

Over came the bride's father, beaded and befeathered, to welcome the *patrao* and his guests. They were offered palm wine from cups carved out of coconut shells. Felicitations were exchanged and the wine was drunk—strong, sweet, causing tears to sting the corners of Morvenna's eyes.

She caught the gleam of blue eyes upon her, filled with wicked amusement. "You must drink every drop, or the toast to the bridal couple will not be complete."

She obeyed, gasping. "W-where are the bride and groom?" she asked, looking around for the usual shy figure who was the center of interest at a wedding, a newly ringed hand clasped in that of a proud young man. Were Indian girls given a ring as a symbol of the marriage bond?

The bridal couple, she was told, had departed for their honeymoon in the jungle several hours ago. They would live there like Adam and Eve for about ten days, fishing, hunting, and loving in the idyllic way of pagan man and his mate. The drums would go on all night to ward off bad spirits from the nest of fern and flowers that the groom would make for his bride. The wail of the bamboo flutes had in them something of the laughing, sighing, joy and tears of a girl when she becomes a woman.

It was primitive and strangely touching, with a beauty about it all that Morvenna would remember long after she had left this jungle island.

"This is how my parents' marriage was celebrated by the islanders." There was a deep note in the *senhor*'s voice. "My mother loved to talk about it. She had a great affinity with these people, and they adored her."

"Did your mother and father go off into the jungle, just like Indians?" Poppy turned from the spectacle to give him one of her long, flattering glances.

"All lovers like to be alone at the start of their life together." The firelight cast shadows beneath the thrust of his cheekbones and outlined the nose that was as straight as his glance. His eyes caught the gleam of the leaping flames and his skin was as coppery, as tautly stretched as that of the Indians. "Would a honeymoon in the jungle not appeal to you, *senhora*?"

"Are you asking my opinion, *senhor*, or inviting me to find out?" Poppy said outrageously.

He laughed, and Morvenna caught the eloquent look that Raya cast at him. When his marriage took place, it would certainly be celebrated in this pagan fashion.

He would take his bride into the jungle, and the drums would echo the beat of their hearts all through the opulently scented night.

The feast was about to begin, and the *patrao* and his guests were invited to sit among the relatives of the bride and groom. Morvenna found herself beside the groom's sister, whose handsome baby was sound asleep, like most of the younger children, in a palm-wood hut that was thatched with an undulating roof of banana leaves and fiber.

The girl smiled happily and piled choice pieces of meat and roasted jungle vegetables onto the big banana leaf that served Morvenna for a plate. Every crisp bite was smoky and delicious, and the two girls laughed together as they ate, and admired the tireless dancers. The din was ceaseless. The flames of the fires leaped high and sparks flew up to meet the stars that burned in a sky of wine-dark velvet.

IT WAS LATE, and Morvenna was replete. All at once she felt a longing to steal away for a few quiet moments from the smoke and noise and the pungent smell of dancing bodies. The *senhor* was in conversation with several Indians, a flushed-looking Poppy at his elbow. Leird sat on a log drinking palm wine, a look about him of a man who wanted to be alone if he could not be with the girl he loved so hopelessly. Raya was nowhere to be seen, and after watching Leird for a hesitant moment, Morvenna slipped away under the arch of palm leaves and hibiscus that had been erected for the bridal couple. The hibiscus for love, the palm for fertility.

She pushed her way through the jungle denseness. Lianas roped the trees and the big silent bells of the flowering vines swung above her head. At last she reached a small clearing where it was dim and peaceful as a cloister. She breathed deeply of the green and scented night air; it was good to clear her head of the smoke and the smell of food, the noise and the pungency of coconut oil on dark hair.

Stars gleamed through the fronds of the trees like ice-hot gems. A bird screeched. She gave a little jump, and then smiled wryly at her tendency to nerves, which the iron-nerved *senhor* so deplored. He seemed to forget that he had been born to these unexpected, savage sounds in the night.

The lace of a tree fern hung around her like a mantilla, and she felt too languidly depleted by the excitement and the feasting to move away in case it concealed something that crawled. She rested against the fibered trunk of the palm, a slim maenad in her silk dress, dwarfed by the great trees that half concealed her. She would return to the festivities in a little while, she told herself. In the meantime she wanted to enjoy these moments of solitude that she had found.

She sighed quietly, restfully, and thought that the starlight-silvered palm fronds looked like magic wands. They waved with little rustlings, and then above the chirring of cicadas Morvenna heard a thrusting back of the surrounding foliage that made her stiffen against the palm trunk. Her thoughts leaped to a puma on the prowl, or an Indian or two who had drunk too freely of the palm wine. Her instincts wanted her to flee, but her body was held transfixed against the palm as into her solitary glade came two figures, that of a slim young man, and a delicately curved girl clad in what in the starlight looked like the shimmering, metallic wings of a dragonfly.

Morvenna felt herself going rigid, and her fingernails dug into the fibered trunk against which she was pressed. She wanted to step forward, to make herself heard and seen, but as the girl's slim arms stole around the neck of the young man, as she raised her lips to his and had them fiercely taken, Morvenna knew that this was one of those fateful moments from which there is no retreat.

It was as though chains held her by the ankles as the couple clung and kissed. They kissed wildly, and with yearning, his lips against her throat, her eyes, then roughly against the side of her neck so that a creamy blossom became detached from her dark hair and fell to the forest floor. The starlight showered down on them and caught the gleam of a single gold ring in the man's left ear.

It is said that all women possess a secret. This was Raya's—this passion, or this dark enchantment, for Flavio, whose dark eyes were Latin, whose blood was half-Indian.

Raya caressed his hair and his handsome face with her tiny, speaking hands—the age-old gesture of a woman who yearns to be one with a man. Her mouth raised to his, as he gazed down at her, was a flower longing to be crushed.

A night bird broke into song and out of it, and suddenly without words Flavio swept the light and lovely figure up into his arms and carried her away through the trees—but not in the direction of the drummers and the dancers. He carried her in the direction of her little bamboo house.

How long Morvenna stood, almost without breathing, she hardly knew. The pounding of her own heart brought her back to reality, for no matter how hard she tried to believe it, that love scene in the glade had not been a chimera. Passion had flickered there, flaring like a light in the man's eyes, blinding the girl's to all danger, her face against the hard, male shoulder as he carried her off into the darkness.

Raya and Flavio!

A beautiful girl whom nature had fashioned for a

pagan love, who had answered the call in the wrong pair
of arms.

Pain had been growing in Morvenna's throat, and
now she put up her hands as though to ease it. The excitement of the Indian wedding, the feasting, the drums,
the pagan embrace she had just witnessed, had all been a
little too much for her. She found herself crying, curved
sideways against the palm tree, mantled by the lacy fern,
lost to all eyes but those accustomed to the jungle at
night.

"Why do you weep?" The voice seemed to come
from out of nowhere, deep and demanding. "What has
happened, *senhorinha? Tell me*!"

The stars burned above the treetops, revealing her
pallor and her wet, shadowy eyes. A step and he was
closer, the shadows masking his face because he was
looking down at her. "Has something frightened you?"
he said again.

"D-do you think I am frightened all the time?" She
mopped the tears from her cheeks with the back of her
hand. "W-what a timid fool I must seem to you."

"No, not timid. You are overimaginative, Miss Fayr.
I have known you before to paint the shadows with
goblins; what goblins brought these on?" He touched
with his fingertips a tear that spilled from her lashes, the
last of that mysterious little deluge.

"Someone should weep at the wedding—th-thank
you," as he thrust a large silk handkerchief into her
hand. She scrubbed her cheeks with it, rather angrily—
anger as illogical as her tears.

"It occurred to me that your tears might have something to do with Mr. Challen. A woman weeps more
often for other people than for herself, especially a
woman who is more sensitive than is good for her."

"I can't help my nature, *senhor*. If I'm thin-skinned,
then that's my worry." She thrust his handkerchief into

his hand and went to walk away from him. At once he stepped in front of her, and forgetful of the tree behind her she backed into it and within a startled flutter of her lashes and her heart was nailed to it by his hands. He gazed down at her and she saw the glimmer of his teeth in a narrow, dangerous smile, and felt his touch right through the silk of her dress.

"Why waste tears on a man to whom love is but a passing fancy?" he asked. "Mr. Challen finds Raya attractive. Doubtless he thinks himself in love with her—and perhaps you think yourself a little in love with him, eh? He is the hero who saved you from the sharks, and you are still but a girl who must suffer the growing pains of being in love with love."

"Everything I do, and feel, you dismiss as callow!" She wanted to wrench away from him, but knew too well his strength and suspected his ruthlessness. Her heart beat in her throat and made her voice shaky, adding fuel to her fury in having let him trap her like this. "I suppose you came looking for me because you think I'm incapable of looking after myself, even in this part of the forest?"

"Are you?" There was a purr of mockery in his voice. "You seem to me adept only at running into situations from which you find it difficult to escape."

What he said was all too true, and she hated him! He was so unshakeable, every pathway of the island, every danger known to him, his life all planned out. What would he do if she said outright that the girl he planned to make his wife was having a love affair with Flavio? That right now they were together at Raya's bamboo house? That would shake him, and surely hurt him. She wanted to hurt him, but knew she had not the lack of heart for such cruelty.

"I—I want to go back and watch the dancing," she said as coolly as possible. "May I?"

"You cannot bear my touch, eh?" His soft laugh brushed warm against her temple. "It is like being caught again in the macca bush, only worse."

"Yes." She tossed back her head and met his eyes fearlessly. "Y-you enjoy tearing at me because I'm young and I don't know a lot about the world, like Poppy Tyson. But at least I have a heart. She keeps a diamond where hers should be!"

"And what kind of heart have I?" he asked with mocking interest.

He had one! She could feel the deep beat of it against her shoulder, and the fact that he was near enough for her to feel that deep, steady beating was instant robbery of her moment of courage. Her knees went weak and all she wanted was to be back among the noisy merrymakers from whom she had fled.

"I—I've never given your heart much thought," she said. "You seem too armored, too self-controlled for feelings—"

"Be assured that I have them, *pequina mia*, like any other man." Even as she caught the note of danger in his voice, his arm locked her to him, a muscled vise from which there was no escape. He tipped her back, into the cradle of his arm, but whether he intended to kiss her or merely meant to frighten her she never learned, for in that instant a scream rang through the forest.

It rose to a pitch of anguish, and Morvenna's wide, frightened eyes locked with the *senhor*'s an instant before he released her. They turned from each other toward the direction of the scream and saw a tower of flame gush above the treetops. The drums went deadly still, so that the roar of burning thatch and palm wood could be plainly heard.

"The sparks from the feast fires have blown onto one of the houses!" exclaimed the *senhor*. "If the fire spreads to the eucalyptus plantation there will be an inferno!"

The next instant he was gone from Morvenna's side and was thrusting his way through the forest toward the roar of the flames, the hubbub of voices, and the intermittent screaming of a woman in hysterics.

Morvenna raced after him, her heart in her mouth.

CHAPTER NINE

WHEN MORVENNA ARRIVED at the scene of the fire, billows of pungent smoke were arising from a trio of palm-wood huts not far from where she had sat during the feasting. The young Indian girl who had sat beside her, laughing and swaying to the rhythm of the drums, was being held back forcibly by her parents from plunging into one of the burning huts, and Morvenna realized with horror that the young widow's baby son was still inside.

Even as she stood stricken beside Arima, not knowing what to do or say, a figure leaped out from among the flames that were consuming the central hut. A lean figure, cast in copped by the red glare, sparks and burning thatch raining down on him and the bundle he shielded close to him as he raced through the blaze into the clearing, where someone snatched his burden, while other dark hands tore the smoldering jacket from his shoulders and beat out the flickers of flame at the bottoms of his trousers.

Morvenna felt her heart turn over with relief, her eyes fixed on that tall, seared figure, his face glistening with sweat, his hair in disorder, rattling orders about beating out the fires even as the Indians beat out the flames from his clothing.

Arima clutched her baby son to her. She looked him over with frantic, tearful eyes, and then rained kisses all over him. He was crying loudly with fright, but had emerged otherwise unscathed in the sure arms of

the man who had snatched him from the hut that
was now a roaring bonfire. It lit up a fantastic
scene, one that burned its way into Morvenna's memory
as the fire fighters ran to attack the flames that
were running to the edge of the forest, where beyond
the bushes and palms and straggling banyans stood the
eucalyptus trees, fuel for an inferno that would spread
across half the island if it got going, and rage for
days.

Morvenna joined one of the groups and beat away the
flames in the bushes with a branch of green palm someone had thrust into her hand. It was Leird, aroused out
of his melancholy by the danger in the air, a rugged pur-
poseful look about him.

"Where's Poppy?" Smoke tears made channels down
Morvenna's cheeks as she and Leird beat at the burning
bushes side by side.

"I saw her making for the *fazenda*," he coughed. "I
bet she's gone to put her diamonds in a safe place, while
we work like demons to put this fire out."

Morvenna grimaced, for it was just the sort of thing
Poppy would be doing, safeguarding her loot while
others suffered the acute discomfort of smoke-burned
eyes and parched throats. Morvenna sneezed as the
pungent smoke tickled her nostrils, and she saw through
the trees a group of Indians, dominated by a figure in a
scorched tan shirt, beating like maniacs at the fibered
trunks of some palms that had caught fire.

"Are we going to make it, Leird?" she asked huskily.

He flashed a smile at her begrimed and anxious face.
"If the Senhor Patrao keeps us busy all tonight and
tomorrow. *Wow*, I'm hot!" He stripped off his shirt.
"Come on, Venna, we'll head left and have a go at
those bushes before they flare right up."

A few minutes later they had drawn near to Raya's

house, and Morvenna saw outlined by the firelight the figures of Raya and Flavio as they worked side by side to keep the flames from the fencing that surrounded the bamboo house. Sparks were flying like fireflies, and all at once Morvenna heard a cry of pain from Raya. One of the sparks must have caught her near the eye, for when Morvenna glanced up she saw Flavio standing over the slim figure, his arm around her waist as he attended to the mishap.

Morvenna pushed at the hair that was plastered to her forehead, fingers of apprehension gripping her heart as beside her Leird stood staring at Raya and Flavio, the smoke and the noise of the fire beaters a dramatic setting for that intimate scene. "What the devil—" Morvenna caught at Leird's arm as he was about to stride over to Flavio, unable to bear seeing another touching the girl he wanted.

"The fire, Leird!" she said tensely. "Look, it's spreading toward the fence!"

She heard the harsh sound made by Leird's throat as he swallowed, then with a grimly set jaw he was lashing again with his palm branch at the flames that threatened Raya's house.

THE LONG, ARDUOUS, suffocating hours passed away and the flames were finally stifled. As dawn's light filtered into the sky above the eucalyptus trees, Morvenna saw a smoke-grimed figure striding slowly through the forest toward her.

She had become separated from Leird ages ago and at this moment was leaning against one of the trees she had helped to save, working through the night as tirelessly as the men. Her dawn-colored dress was ripped, singed, and smoke-blackened. Near the tree where she rested wisps of smoke curled up here and there, and much of the bush close to the village was burned to stubble. The birds did not sing as daylight approached; they only created a worried sort of activity deep in the forest.

The ashy scrub crunched underfoot as Roque came to stand in front of her tired, sooty figure. *"Madre de Deus!"* he murmured, his teeth flashing white against his smoke-scorched face. "Do I look as dirty as you, *meninazinha*?"

"Worse," she said huskily. "You look like a pirate who has been busy at the cannon, besieging the island."

He laughed, his black hair tousled, his red-rimmed eyes agleam with the triumph of a job well done. They had saved the island from extensive damage, and the huts that had been destroyed could soon be rebuilt.

"I wish you to know how grateful I am, Miss Fayr, for all your assistance last night." His bow was gallant, old-world, and somehow in keeping with his piratical appearance. "I saw you working alongside Mr. Challen, and I knew he would not let you come to any harm. Where is he now?"

"Flaked out on his bed, I expect." Her smile was half a yawn. "Forgive me, *senhor*, I'm ready for my own bed—after a long cool drink and a shower."

"You shall have both, at once!"

In an instant she knew his intention, but it would have been as futile to fight him now as it had been dangerous to provoke him last night. As he swept her up in his arms and carried her in the direction of the *fazenda*, she wondered at the ruthlessness that ran side by side in him with an amazing gallantry. Not many men would have plunged into a blazing hut after an Indian baby, emerging out of the flames like one of the fire gods of the ancient Aztecs.

Morvenna remembered the scene vividly, and as he

carried her, as though she were no more of a burden than Arima's baby had been, she glimpsed through the tatters of his shirt several painful-looking burn marks on the coppery muscles of his chest and arms.

"I hope no one got badly hurt last night," she said, her lashes lowered so he wouldn't see her gaze on his branded shoulders.

"The islanders are tough." He was smiling. "Those who were slightly burned will enjoy the fuss their wives will make of them."

"You appear to have a few minor burns yourself, *senhor*."

"And no wife to make a fuss of me." His smile grew mocking.

Only Raya, Morvenna thought, biting her lip. Who was playing with the most dangerous fire of all—the hearts of three men.

Morvenna thought of the girl in Flavio's arms last night—being carried off as she was now being carried in the *senhor*'s arms! Her pulse gave a disturbing leap while the rest of her lay very still in his arms.

As they neared the *fazenda* they passed under one of those honey-scented trees whose flowers were like pale stars in the dawn light. His tall head disturbed a cluster and they showered down, cool, fragrant, dusting his copper frame with their petals. Morvenna gently brushed the blossoms from his shoulder before she realized the intimacy of the action. He glanced down at her and again she lost a pulse beat as she met the sapphire gleam of his eyes.

A moment later they reached the compound, and the sky overhead was soaked in morning fire. He halted to gaze up at the sun as it rose, and they were bathed together in the warm rosy glow.

"Glorious," he murmured. "Can you wonder, *senhorinha*, that for me the island of Janaleza is all the world? The dawns like a bursting pearl, and sunsets to stop the heart. Tonight the *lua nova* will be born, and when she dies the steamer will be on its way from Manaos."

The new moon, herald of Morvenna's remaining days on the island.

"My stay has certainly been a memorable one." Her gaze was on the sunrise. "When I am home again in England I shall remember all this—the scents of the island, the sounds, and the unexpected that seems as much a part of it as the tall trees and the Indians."

He lowered her to her feet and then for a moment held her face lifted to his. "This quest for your father, you intend to discontinue it when you return to Manaos?"

"I have no map, no money, no more hope in me that he's still alive, somewhere in the jungle." She sighed. "Still, I have grown up on this trip. Now I can face the future without him."

"There is yet the journey into love for you to take." The blue eyes looking down into hers smiled quizzically. "Do you hesitate to take it, after daring alone the hazards of a strange country?"

"Love has to come to one, doesn't it, *senhor*? If it comes, then I shan't be afraid. If it passes me by. . . ." She shrugged and tried not to feel the warm strength of his hand cupping her face, holding her so that she had to meet the flame blue of his eyes. "Does a woman *have* to marry? Is she such a weak reed that she cannot stand alone?"

"Woman is not weak, *senhorinha*, but a woman alone is one without companionship or children."

"Please—" she gave a weary little shiver "—I would like to go indoors. I . . . I'm so tired—"

"Forgive me." His hand dropped away from her face. "Take a shower, and then when you are in bed

I shall send Isidra to you with a pot of delicious coffee."

"Thank you." She gave him a grave, grubby-faced smile. "It was wonderful what you did, saving Arima's baby." Then she was hurrying from him, holding up the torn skirt of her dress as she hastened up the steps of the veranda and sought the haven of her bedroom.

EXCITEMENT ALWAYS BRINGS with it a sense of anticlimax, and the occupants of the *fazenda* (excluding its master) were inclined to laziness for a day or two. Poppy and Leird played cards and quarreled, and then made up again over iced glasses of gin and lemon.

Morvenna shared a bamboo lounger with her pet *coati* and listened idly to her two companions on the veranda as she stroked Ringo's furry coat. Suddenly her lashes stirred and she watched as Poppy tilted back her head and laughed mockingly at Leird. "There, I've beaten you again! Whatever's the matter, my Red Lion? You are all growl and no bite this morning."

"It's this outlandish place!" He eyed his drink, then tossed it back as though it stung him. "I shall be glad to get back to civilization."

"I thought you were having fun here." Poppy gave a flirt of her esparto fan. "You know, Leird, you might have guessed there was a No Trespassing sign around that tropical flower who plays at being nurse of the island. Raya read it out the evening of the fire, didn't she? She said that Latin love is adoration—when a woman has been clever enough to arouse it. She meant the grand *senhor*, of course, and that she had aroused his love."

"You must have got a few scratches yourself, trying

to climb through the barbed wire around him." Leird hit back.

"I'll admit that physique, that accent, and those blue eyes got me going for a while, but just think—" she glanced maliciously at Morvenna "—of being tied to a man who thinks an island is the world, and who is so steeped in feudal ideas that his wife would never be allowed to take little trips on her own. A man like that has got to marry a girl of his own sort, and Raya is the obvious choice. I'm sure Morvenna agrees with me."

Morvenna had a swift mental picture of Raya in the arms of Flavio, and she seemed also to see the flash of the blade that had made the girl the possession of Roque de Braz Ferro. He would not let go of anything he wanted—of that she was very sure.

"Whatever happens here on Janaleza, we shall be gone by this time next week," she replied.

"You sound very cool about it all." Poppy eyed her inquisitively. "Won't you be sorry to say good-bye to Nuno? I mean, there have been those visits of yours to his tree house, and since he's been away you've been looking rather pensive."

"Nuno should have been back by now," Leird put in. "The *senhor* said as much last night, when we were out here having a cigar together. I think he's sending some trackers out after the boy if he isn't back by Wednesday. He told me that no matter how well you know the forest, it can still be a dangerous place—"

"Does he think something has happened to Nuno?" Morvenna was gazing at Leird with troubled eyes. "Please tell me!"

"He's anxious," Leird admitted. "The boy is Raya's brother, and Latin men have this strong feeling of responsibility toward members of their family—I expect he already regards Nuno as such."

"Did he go off into the forest in a huff?" drawled Poppy. "Really, my pet, you shouldn't have upset him—"

"Don't say that!" Morvenna jumped to her feet, disturbing the *coati*, who made a grumbling noise and dug his pointed nose into a cushion. Morvenna walked to the veranda rail and gripped it. "Nuno has got to be all right. I . . . I couldn't bear it if anything happened to him—"

"My, you have got it bad!" Ice tinkled in Poppy's drink as she lifted the glass to her lips. "I've always said that the cool-looking girls are the ones with the warmest feelings when it comes to love."

"You don't understand." Morvenna swung around and let her dislike of the other girl's hardness show in her eyes. "This treasure hunt has been unlucky enough—it's killed two people already. I don't want to see a third added to the list."

"Superstitious, as well?" Poppy quirked a painted eyebrow, and a cold flash of light was caught in her eyes as they dwelt on the slender, silver-haired figure by the veranda rail, where a cluster of Virgin's Pagoda clung and climbed. "Let me tell you that if the treasure map had been recovered, I'd have gone on with the hunt. Gerry had a notion there was something in it. He said that the Indian settlement marked on the map was on the site of an old Aztec sun temple. It was in those temples that the Aztecs buried their gold and their gems."

Morvenna stared at the greedy light in Poppy's eyes. "Is money all you care about?" she asked. "Don't people mean anything to you?"

"Some of them can be fun," drawled Poppy, "but I dislike those who are a little too intense. Life, my pet, is a rich, raw merry-go-round. And love is like tropical fruit, sweet but swiftly perishable."

A pointed fingernail flashed downward and stabbed one of the green gold papayas on the bamboo table, where the playing cards were scattered.

"Any arguments, Leird?" Poppy looked at him and laughed.

He frowned morosely. "Leave Venna alone," he said. "She's nicer than we have ever been, Poppy. She doesn't understand our kind of philosophy."

It was true, and Morvenna wasn't staying to hear any more of it. "I'm going for a walk," she said, and the next moment she had snatched her grass hat from the bamboo lounger and was running down the veranda steps and heading across the compound. The sun burned overhead, a sultry orange sun with something a little stormy about it. Morvenna didn't notice. She was thinking of Nuno, and upon reaching the coolness of the trees she followed the path that led to his tree house.

She hoped he would be home and safe, but upon daring the rope ladder alone she found the thatched turret among the treetops still unoccupied. The monkeys in the nearby trees screeched at the intruder, and the macaw on his perch bade her *ate a vista*.

"All right, I'm going in a minute." She gazed around at the Indian masks and other oddments adorning the walls of the hut, and glanced at the little shelf of books. About half a dozen of them were out of line with the others and she gave them a tidying push. They wouldn't move. Something was thrust behind them, and upon taking an idle look she saw something that made her drop several of the books in astonishment.

She stared at the object they had concealed. It was of brown leather and oblong, with a sea-rusted latch—her writing-case, which had been at the bottom of the sea, and which Nuno must have found.

Her hand shook as she reached for it. The rusty latch

was difficult to open and perspiration broke out on her body as she fought with it. At last the flap fell open, and there among the envelopes and writing paper were her passport, her visitor's visa and her vaccination certificate, all of them stained with the brown dye from the leather.

Her fingers riffled through them, but there was no sign of the treasure map that her father had sent her. It was gone. Nuno had taken it.

She stood in unbelieving silence, staring at the stained contents of the writing case. Nuno must have found it the morning she had refused to go fishing with him, and without telling her, or the *patrao*, he had gone off on a treasure hunt of his own. She swallowed dryly, and gave a jump as with a flutter of bright feathers the macaw flew to the bracket that held Nuno's books. *"Ate a vista!"* he croaked.

Morvenna stared at the bird, who stared back at her. Good-bye for now! Good-bye for now! Suddenly she knew that with crazy Latin gallantry Nuno had gone off alone to find out what had become of her father.

She relatched the writing case and thrust it into the waistband of her matador trousers. Then she descended the swaying rope ladder without giving a thought to the dizzying drop to the ground and the bad fall she would suffer if she lost her balance. All she could think of was to find the *senhor* as quickly as possible. He alone would know how to deal with the problem of finding Nuno.

The trouble was, the *senhor* could be anywhere. The various plantations were under his supervision and he was always busy at one or the other of them. As she stood regaining her breath she decided to continue to the village. Someone there was more likely to know his whereabouts than anyone at the *fazenda*.

Her breath regained, and her grass hat tilted back to

allow what breeze there was to cool her hot young face, she made for the path opposite to the one that led back to the *fazenda*. A calabash tree stood beside the path, hung with pumpkinlike fruits, and in her anxiety Morvenna failed to remember that there was no calabash tree beside the path that led to the village.

Not having been used by Nuno in almost a week, the village path had become overgrown with elephant-ear plants and so Morvenna failed to notice it.

Instead she followed a hunting track, which led away from the village. . .into the forest.

CHAPTER TEN

THE GAME TRAIL twisted and turned, and Morvenna followed where it led, unaware for some time that it led away from the friendly Indian village into the heart of the bush.

She was lost in her thoughts and automatically she brushed aside the immense ferns and big-leafed plants that grew halfway across the track. Insects buzzed in the humid air and she was glad of the repellent she had applied to her face, neck and arms earlier that morning. Wild and roving vines tripped her out of her abstraction now and again, but since she was a novice to the jungle it all looked alike to her and she didn't really notice that she was penetrating the wilder regions, where palms sprouted other trunks, and tiger gold bamboos interlaced with dark-foliaged trees hung with creepers.

In a while she brushed a hand across her eyes, which were smarting with sweat. The atmosphere was plastering her cotton shirt to her body, and when she glanced up she saw the density of the vegetation all around her, the overhead mass of vine-locked branches, and through them the flick of tiny monkey eyes.

A shadow of dismay crossed her face. The cry of a bellbird echoed through the forest, and she could taste the salt on her upper lip.

No wonder everything was steamy and eerie! For over an hour she had been chasing along the wrong trail, into the bush! Her heart gave a thump. She would have to retrace every single step, and crossly she snapped off a big leaf and fanned herself, her hot and tired body slumped against the trunk of a bamboo.

Imperceptibly, as she gathered the will to start trekking back the way she had come, the cool, enticing sound of running water came to her through the forest. For a minute or two she was sure she imagined it, so intense was her longing to dip her lips in water and feel it cooling her hot, dry throat. But as certain as her heartbeats it continued, and wasting not another second she tossed aside her makeshift fan and hastened along the game trail until, suddenly, it stopped at a tangle of fiery red flowers and dense green creepers.

She thrust her way through them and caught her breath as she found herself almost on the edge of a jungle gorge. A cascade of water roared down the other side of it, misted by a spray that was fired into a rainbow by the sun's rays.

Deep down into the gorge flowed that silver coil, bursting into a river that glinted far below, between green banks of teeming vegetation.

Morvenna knelt on a bank of bushy ferns and creepers and peered downward, drinking in all that water with longing eyes. It gurgled, beckoned and mocked her thirst, and with a sigh of sheer frustration she rested her hot face on her forearm and in so doing dislodged her grass hat from her head. The next instant it was tumbling over the edge of the gorge, and she was making a grab for it when the tangle of creepers on which she lay gave a frightening shift. She grabbed wildly at a handful as they unwound like a curtain and carried her with them over the edge of the gorge.

She cried out in fright, clung on for dear life, and felt her arms nearly wrenched from their sockets as the slithering curtain of vines stopped shifting and she found herself dangling among them like a fruit on a branch.

She hung there, catching the breath that had been knocked out of her by the shock of being carried into midair on the back of a moving plant, woody stemmed, thick with leaves, its dank green smell strong in her dilated nostrils.

What a situation! If it weren't so alarming it would be laughable, for she hung there, gripping the vines, like a heroine in one of those silent-movie serials of long ago. Cliff-hangers, they called them. A very apt description!

In a while, when her nerves were a little steadier, she peered upward and saw that she had fallen some yards from the edge of the gorge. Could she pull herself up to that edge? She unlocked the fingers of her right hand and carefully shifted them upward until she found another woody handhold. She gripped and swayed alarmingly on the curtain of vines as she pulled herself an inch or two up the face of the gorge.

Her dry throat was rasping, and her teeth were clamping her lower lip as with each slow, upward pull the pain in her arms grew more intense and cramping.

She paused for breath, her body drenched in sweat as she laid her face for some vestige of coolness against the green leaves of the vine. She wasn't really making much progress, for each painful inch she gained was followed by a slight downward movement of the curtain itself. Her weight, though slight, was pulling on it, and she was desperately afraid that it would suddenly break and send her crashing down the gorge into that roaring river below.

She groaned at the pain in her strained wrists. The will to think and act seemed to be leaving her. "Roque...." Why she said his name she hardly knew, except that he seemed the one person capable of getting her out of the predicament that had befallen her. Roque. She never called him that to his face. It was always *senhor*.

She listened to the roar of the cascade, and the pounding of her heart. In a moment she must make the effort to continue her climb. She shivered, hot and cold at the same time, and listened as the cry of a bellbird rang like a clarion call through the forest. What a good idea! Perhaps she should call out herself and see if some friendly Indian was within hearing.

"Hallo! Hallo!"

It was a poor effort, for her throat was parched, but after a minute she tried again.

"Help! Please, someone, help me!"

She listened, her heart in her throat as the curtain of creepers gave another little shift downward. "Help!" This time panic lent strength to her voice and her cry echoed in the gorge.

"Hallo!" A voice answered clearly, and it wasn't the echo of the cry she had just made. "Hallo, where are you?"

Not an echo, not a bellbird, but the voice of a man!

"I'm here!" She struggled to make herself heard. "I'm hanging on to some vines, j-just below a bank of red flowers n-near the edge of the gorge."

She didn't give it a thought that an Indian would not have answered her plea for help in fluent English. All she could think of was getting out of this gorge and feeling the ground under her feet once more. "Hurry! Please, hurry!" It was a mere sob, though it sounded like a shout in her aching head.

"I am coming—hang on!"

She could hear the man plainly now, thrusting his way through the bushes and creepers above her on the bank of the gorge.

"Be careful," she cried out hoarsely. "Th-these creepers move—*they move*!"

She was gazing upward, a small, dangling figure, her hair in silvery spikes along her damp forehead, her eyes like great lilac bruises in her pale face, when her rescuer thrust his head over the edge of the gorge.

"Oh...." She went so dangerously weak for a moment that she almost let go of the vines to which she was clinging. The face above hers could belong to only one man in the world; only his eyes could blaze that blue and consuming light.

"Good afternoon," he said. "I refuse to be surprised at finding you in yet another predicament that other people would be sensible enough to avoid."

"Please, save the lecture for another time," she gasped. "And do mind those creepers—they move!"

He examined them and muttered a Latin name. Then once again he was gazing down at her with that look of fierce exasperation. "Hold on with all your might," he ordered. "I am going to pull you up."

He withdrew from her sight and for a moment she wanted to call out to him in panic, then her heart came into her mouth as she felt a sudden movement that sent her swaying on the vine. She held on grimly, knowing that the strong arms up there were hauling on the vine as though it were a net, with a fish inside! Knowing, too, that if the "net" were suddenly to break she would plunge into the river below.

Up and up, inch by careful inch, the longest minutes of her life, then a sweet gush of relief as she was drawn over the edge and safely landed. "Jump clear!" he ordered. She did so clumsily, and fell among the fiery red flowers as he let go of the vine and it went slithering and tumbling back over the edge of the gorge, a dark green snake of leaves.

There was silence, then a sound of brush and blossoms being crushed as the *senhor* knelt beside Morvenna and drew her into those strong arms. He pressed her head to his shoulder and held her to him until she stopped trembling with reaction. He stroked her hair while she clung to him, her face buried against his chest. She could feel a quick, hard beating near her cheek and knew that the effort of hauling her to safety caused his heart to pound like that.

"Y-you seem fated to be my paladin." She drew away from him and managed a shaky smile. "Thank you for coming to my rescue. I couldn't have hung on much longer. Each time I tried to climb upward, that thing slipped downward."

He accepted her thanks with a frown and turned her hands within his so that he could examine the palms of them. They were red and lacerated from clutching the vine, whose woody stems had gradually cut into the flesh as she had grown more tired and heavier. He ran his thumb over the lacerations and she winced.

"The skin is broken in one or two places," he grunted, "and it is a good thing for you that *I* don't travel around in the jungle as though it were an English wood. Come!" He helped her to her feet and marched her out of the sultry sunshine into the shade of the trees. There, hanging on a branch, was a machete and a water flask.

"May I have a drink of water?" Morvenna asked eagerly.

Still frowning, his blue eyes fixed on her face, he unscrewed the cap and filled it with water. She drank thirstily, her eyes half-closed like those of a young cat lapping cream. "Mmm, I was dying for that—it was the sound of water that drew me to the gorge. I—I nearly died of fright when that vine pulled me over the edge."

"Hold out your hands." He had taken a pouch from one of the pockets of his bush shirt and, floppy bush hat pushed to the back of his head, was ready to doctor her scratched palms with some ointment that looked as though it would sting. Her lip clamped between her teeth, she obeyed his injunction, her eyes fully open now and fixed on his dark, unsmiling face as he applied the antiseptic ointment.

"Ooh!" she said, and at that he did smile, grimly.

"So you were looking for Nuno," he said, handing her another cap of water and a salt tablet.

She swallowed the tablet without demur and chased it with the water. "No, I was looking for you—" She touched a hand to her waist. "*Oh no*! It's gone—my writing case is gone!"

"What are you talking about?" He took a drink of water himself. "When I returned to the *fazenda* after inspecting some infected coffee bushes, Senhora Tyson told me that you were upset about Nuno, and Mr. Challen thought you were at the tree house—"

"Yes," she broke in. "I climbed up to the tree house and I found my writing case there. Nuno must have found it out on the reef. My passport and other papers were still in it, but the treasure map was gone. I...I think Nuno has gone off on his own to find out—*senhor*, I had the writing case with me, and I was looking for you, but I took the wrong trail...."

"Calm down." He took her by the shoulders. "You say you found your writing case at the tree house?"

She nodded. "When I saw that the map was missing, I wanted to tell you at once, so that you could send out trackers to look for Nuno. That map's unlucky. I...I don't want anything to happen to Nuno."

"Of course not." His tone was crisp. "So you decided to look for me, eh?"

"Yes, in the village, but I took the wrong trail."

"I know that. Your tracks were near the tree house and I saw at once that you had taken a game trail that would lead you into the bush. I took a water flask and a machete from the tree house and followed your tracks."

"How could you tell they were my tracks?" she asked. "I'm wearing Indian sandals."

"Quite." He quirked an eyebrow as he glanced down at her feet. "But you do not walk like an Indian. They are rather flat-footed, but your tracks are those of a lightly built girl with small, high-arched feet. You have also the novice's habit of plucking bits of grass and chewing them, and blundering into the wild vines that an Indian would automatically avoid."

"There's no need to sound so scornful." She bit her lip. "I can't help it if I do everything all wrong. If I'd known you were returning to the *fazenda*, I'd have gone back there instead of chasing off on a wild goose chase. Now I've lost my writing case down the gorge, and all my papers."

"Don't worry about them." He was glancing at the sky, which seemed to reflect his frown. "We should be starting back at once from the look of that sky, but I think you need to rest for a short while. Are you hungry?"

"A little," she admitted. "It's a sort of dry hunger that a juicy pineapple would satisfy."

"Well, sit down here and rest—" he gave some bushy ferns a good shake "—and I will go and have a look for something resembling a pineapple. If you hear a few rumbles of thunder, don't worry. And for heaven's sake don't wander away again. Stay just here and be a good child."

"Yes, *senhor*," she said, giving him a demure smile as she sat down on the springy ferns. They clustered around her slight young figure, and as he reached for his machete he glanced down at her and a smile flashed across his dark face.

"You look like a babe in the wood," he said. "Don't be nervous. I shall be within call if you want me."

"I'm going to have a catnap." She clasped her arms about her updrawn knees and rested her cheek on them. She closed her eyes and listened to his receding footfalls.

This was a wild and lonely place, and ominous clouds were gathering above the trees and thickening the shadows, but Morvenna felt too drowsy and spent, too drugged by the lush jungle scents all around, to care that a storm might be brewing.

She drowsed while bees buzzed in the tangle of red flowers and the waters cascaded down the nearby gorge. She awoke with one of those falling starts that make the heart beat fast, and saw a tall figure looming out of the shadows of the trees. As the *senhor* came toward her she saw the outline of his muscles under the fawn drill of his shirt, the width of his shoulders tapering to lean hips, the knee boots that added to his look of strong, assured, almost flagrant masculinity. She realized that she was alone with him in the heart of the forest!

"I found a thicket of mangoes." He showed her some round, hairy-looking fruits. "They are not as attractive-looking as pineapples, but full of juice. Did you have your catnap?"

She nodded and watched him slice open the mangoes with his machete—a handy weapon. With one of those a man of the jungle need never go without food, shelter, or a bride!

He pared the mangoes and laid the quarters on a couple of big leaves, which he plucked from a tree. Then he sat down beside Morvenna, relaxing his long body and nodding at her to eat her fruit. "We must be on our way as soon as we have eaten," he said.

"Is there going to be a storm?" She nibbled the refreshing fruit and put out her tongue to catch some precious drops of juice.

"Are you afraid of storms?" he asked.

"I've never seen a jungle storm." She took another piece of mango and bit into it, and watched him do the same. These glimpses of his humanity were oddly disturbing. He could, she realized, be as tender as he could be tough—a most shattering combination in a man.

"How mysterious everything begins to look." She avoided his eyes, which shone steel blue through the shadows. "Those trees over there look like a meeting of dryads."

"It is the senses that make a mystery of the natural." He struck a match and lit a cheroot, and her nostrils tautened as the smoke stole from his lips and brushed her cheek. "Listen to the silence, *senhorinha*. The birds and animals sense that a storm is coming and they have crept into hiding."

The silence and the false twilight were uncanny. The sultriness was increasing, and through the silence there stole a growl of thunder like that of a leashed animal.

"A jungle storm can be fierce and unpredictable." The *senhor's* eyes caught and held Morvenna, blue as the flame on the edge of lightning. "There is every chance that we will be caught in this one—will you be afraid, with me?"

She sat there, slim and silver-haired against the dense greenery, her eyes quite huge in her pointed face, eyes whose hidden sorcery seemed revealed in this strange setting and atmosphere. "I don't know," she said honestly. "I'm not the hysterical type, anyway. Perhaps my witch-ancestor implanted in me a feeling that the elements are less to be feared than people. People are far more unpredictable."

"That is very true." A little smile clung to his lips as he regarded the tip of his cheroot. "But there would be no drama, no comedy, no love without at least two people in any place together, preferably a man and a woman. And if they always knew the thoughts of the other, and how they were going to react to everything, it would surely make life less exciting."

"Don't you mind that I have caused you to lose an

afternoon's work?'' she asked. "My unpredictability
must surely irritate you? You said the other day that I
do things from instinct rather than from common
sense.''

"That is because you are a woman.'' His amused eyes
flicked her face and her throat. "I don't pretend to
understand women, Miss Fayr, nor my own fury at their
antics at times, but I would not wish them to react to
situations in the same way as men. How dull life would
be without women to enliven it with their delectable
comedy—ah, do I surprise you? Did you think me a
misogynist because I am over thirty and still unmarried?''

She shook her head, for she knew that he had waited
for Raya to grow up. He would want a woman, not a
half-grown girl. A woman of feeling and temperament,
who would be able to excite him and amuse him. It did
not do to remember that Raya had broken his trust in
her, and that inevitably he would find out.

"Love makes people very vulnerable,'' he said, his
eyes narrowed and darkened by his lashes. "It is the
revelation of our secret selves, so it is no wonder we
treat the emotion as though it were a weapon aimed at
our own hearts. No one enjoys pain, or pity—'' There
he broke off as lightning flickered above the treetops. In
one lithe movement he was on his feet and killing the
end of his cheroot against the trunk of a tree.

"Come, we must be making a move.'' He assisted
Morvenna to her feet and brushed pieces of fern from
her shirt. She felt his touch right through the thin cotton
and she looked up at him as though magnetized, at his
mouth that was so self-controlled and at the same time
so passionate. She went curiously weak and couldn't
stop herself from swaying against him. His arm came
around her, steel-strong and warm, crushing her for a
moment.

"What is a little storm?" he murmured. "There are worse things to fear."

"I know." She was breathing quickly, his hard lean body against hers, here in the forest where the shadows were stabbed by that noiseless lighting. The atmosphere was electrical, menacing, curiously exciting, and suddenly Morvenna was rent apart from the *senhor* as thunder crashed and a blade of violet steel cleft a nearby palm tree from its crown to its roots.

Fingers of iron gripped Morvenna's wrist and she was borne away swiftly as the tree flamed like a torch and a sheet of rain came down, blindingly. Fighting the abrupt fury of the storm, he thrust a way through the trees and drew her in under the primitive shelter of huge cabbage-palm leaves. "This is what we call a storm of the devil," he shouted above the roar of the rain. They would have to take a chance on the lightning, he added. Rain like this was even more dangerous, because it could batter a person to the ground and drown him in mud.

A giant wave of the rain threw her against him. He gripped her and she huddled against him for shelter. In the extremity of the moment a girl could not feel shyness toward a man, and any reluctant feeling of fascination was forgotten with rain pouring down her neck.

"A little storm, did you say?" she gasped.

She heard him laugh and a flash of lightning lit up his dark face and made her burrow close to him again.

The tumult went on and on, and all the time there was the fear that at any moment the claws of lightning would find them and strike them. The trees all around thrashed in the wind, and the rain was frightening in its intensity. It lashed and blotted out everything, made of the jungle a misty green blur.

At some time in the timeless moments of danger and discomfort her arms locked themselves around his neck and her face buried itself in the warm hollow of his shoulder. It wasn't until the storm grew quiet at last that Morvenna realized what had been going through her mind all the time. That if the lightning struck it would strike them as one person and they would die together like lovers in a legend.

The storm slowly died away and a hushed, dripping twilight was upon them. They stepped out from under their sopping shelter of leaves, and mud splashed their ankles as they made their way back to where they had dined on mangoes. Mud, petals, butterfly wings and feathers littered their path. The air was drenched with damp green smells and the spilled sap from torn lianas. Everything dripped, including Morvenna and her companion. The rain had turned her hair to a metal cap. His shirt clung and dried in the steamy heat. The wet skin of his face and throat was burnished copper.

"Well—" he gazed down at Morvenna when they reached the rain-battered bank of flowers where they had eaten slices of mango "—we cannot follow the homeward track in the dark. There will be a moon later on, but it will be overclouded and we cannot take a chance on going astray in the forest...."

He paused, and the smile in his eyes was a grimly humorous one. "We are going to have to spend the night together in the jungle, Miss Fayr," he said. "It will not be exactly comfortable, but I have a machete and the palm tree that was struck by lightning will provide fuel for a fire. Even a smoky fire will be better than nothing, eh?"

She gave a shiver and tried to smile. "Don't you feel like shaking me, *senhor*, for all the trouble I'm causing you?"

"Of course." He put out a hand and ruffled the damp hair at her temples. "But I shall save what I feel like saying to you for another time."

"Thank goodness for that!" Her smile was shaky. "Are you going to give me a job to do in the meantime?"

"I certainly am." His teeth glinted in a brief smile as he picked up the machete, which lay in the wet fern. "You can hold the pieces of wood as I chop them. The lightning will have charred the wood, so it should make good fuel for a fire."

"I feel hot and close at the moment," she said as she followed him to the stricken tree.

"Soon it will grow cool," he told her. "We are going to need enough fuel to see us through the night—not only because it will soon grow cold, but to keep off the animals that roam in the jungle at night."

CHAPTER ELEVEN

AFTER THE RAINFALL the forest seethed with small sounds and a wild bouquet of scents. Their camp fire leaped smokily, and the breadfruits baking at its edge spat and split with little hisses of steam. The *senhor* had noticed the round loaves earlier on, tucked high among the hand-shaped leaves of the tree. The storm had blown down several and he had collected them and set them to bake. Slices of hot breadfruit were not exactly tasty, he said, but they were filling.

He was alarmingly resourceful, Morvenna thought. Armed with a machete he could live as comfortably in the jungle as any Indian. As he tended their supper, his profile was outlined against the flames—the well-defined cheekbones, the high-bridged nose and fleshless angle under his chin. The face of a strong and subtle man, with a sureness to all his movements.

"Our supper is almost ready." His eyes were upon her before she could pretend to be looking elsewhere. "What a pity we have no coffee to go with it, eh? I must remember in future to carry coffee beans and a billy-can when I go searching for you."

"I must try in future not to go astray." She sat on the tree stump that he had dragged to the fireside, holding her bare feet to the warmth. She wriggled her toes and absently scratched a mosquito bite on her left ankle. At once her ankle was pinioned by his fingers.

"Don't do that," he said. "You will break the skin and cause a fester."

"But it itches." A tremor ran through her, for his touch made her very aware of their aloneness. Like a current it seemed to leap from his fingertips into her bones.

"I will give you something to apply to the bite." As he bent over her, she caught the glint of his teeth and his eyes. "Suddenly you seem nervous. You have never been alone like this with a man, have you? Are you afraid of me?"

"Have I cause to be?" she fenced.

His fingers pressed against the fine bones of her ankle, then let go. In silence he withdrew from his pocket the square oilskin pouch in which he carried about a week's supply of the medicaments that were so necessary in the jungle. "Here you are—" he handed her a small tube "—squeeze some of that onto the bite and smooth it in. It will stop the irritation."

He stressed the word as though she irritated him. She supposed she did get on his nerves, what with blundering into the jungle with a storm coming on, and saying things that made his nostrils flare and his eyes look narrow and dangerous.

Half a moon floated in and out of the clouds left behind by the storm; it peered through the branches of the trees like an inquisitive golden eye as Morvenna applied the salve to the welt on her ankle. At once the irritation began to go. "Hang on to the stuff." The *senhor* was stabbing the breadfruits with a pronged stick and lifting them out of the fire. "That tender skin of yours is going to invite a few more bites before the night is over."

"Th-thank you." She stuffed the tube into the pocket of her trousers. "It certainly works like magic."

"Many of these remedies were discovered in the jungle long ago by the Indians and used by them in a cruder form." He built up the fire now their supper was cooked; the smoke rose up in a tangy column and the hovering insects and moths buzzed off for the moment. "Nuno may have gone searching for a new medicine. He does this for a pharmaceutical company in Brazil."

"But he took the map with him," she said tensely, "and I'm afraid that it may bring him bad luck. It seems to have done that for my father and for Poppy's husband. Aztec gold that the old gods guard! Isn't there a superstition to that effect, *senhor*?"

"A tribe of Aztecs was said to have fled to this region long ago, and superstitions are always rife in the jungle, but the Spanish invaders of the Aztec kingdoms were too greedy for gold to have let much of it slip through their fingers. The Aztecs may have escaped with a few golden idols, but a boy who has lived among the Indians would know that such things are best left alone."

"I don't think Nuno is looking for treasure," she said. "He—well, he's at the gallant age and he may be trying to find out if my father is still alive."

"Miss Fayr—" suddenly his blue eyes were as keen as steel "—I hope you are not letting any more false hopes take hold of you?"

She shook her head, but for searching moments his eyes were upon her face in the firelight. Suddenly all her taut nerves jumped as the *mae da lua* cried through the forest.

"It is only a bird, known as the mother of the moon." He lifted his face to the jungle moon, and Morvenna's arms tightened around her knees at the look he had with the moonlight shining down on him. "We think of the jungle as a woman, *senhorinha*, for all plants and flowers are female, and also the rivers that run through it."

"You love the wildness and the mystery of it all, don't you?" Never had she felt so strongly that love of this jungle island was in his blood, at the very core of his heart. Was that why he loved Raya, because she was as lovely and secretive as the jungle?

"I belong here," he said simply. "For generations my family has lived here, and the pulse of the place beats in me."

He haunched down, supple as only a man of the open air could be, and sliced the breadfruits that had now cooled to a breadlike firmness. He piled the slices onto the big leaves that made such handy plates, and handed Morvenna her supper. They enjoyed it sitting side by side on the tree trunk, and then they each had half a cap of water.

The creeper-veiled trees shook now and again, as if with the nighttime cold after the heat of the day. Strange sounds stole to Morvenna's ears, a mingling of chirps, drones and treetop chortles. There were slithering noises in the undergrowth, and she was informed that giant lizards prowled at night for food. They were harmless, the *senhor* added, his eyes agleam in the firelight—like a panther's.

Their eyes met as he carried a small burning brand to the tip of the cheroot he had just slipped between his lips. He tossed the brand back into the fire and puffed smoke at the flitting insects. "Are you too shy to sing me one of your folk songs?" he asked. "After all, I cooked the supper and deserve some reward."

"I...I never sing without a guitar," she said in some confusion.

"I shall make allowances," he grinned.

"I couldn't." Her cheeks flamed. "Y-you make me feel shy enough as it is."

"Do I?" He quirked an eyebrow. "I am only a man, *senhorinha*. Why then should I make you feel more shy than Mr. Challen does, or Nuno? You sing for them."

"They're different from you," she said bravely. "Leird is English and I understand him. Nuno is only a boy, and not nearly as complex as you are, *senhor*."

"So I am complex?" His cheroot smoke brushed her cheek. "What you really mean is that because I am not British, I look and behave differently from your own countrymen. Do I take it that you would sooner be spending a night alone in the jungle with Mr. Challen than with a Brazilian? Are you still afraid that my Latin passions will erupt at finding themselves alone with a lilac-eyed, white-skinned little witch who has never been kissed properly?"

"Oh—" The breath was shocked out of her. "I've never thought such a thing!"

"What, about being kissed properly?"

"About being kissed—by you."

"That is just as well." Firelit shadows played over his face and revealed the shade of wickedness in his smile. "At this moment I have no intention of testing your reaction to a kiss of mine. If by requesting a song I make you shy, then I hate to think what would happen if I took a kiss. Tell me, has Mr. Challen ever kissed you?"

"Of course not." She dragged her eyes from the demanding, fire-etched mouth. "Leird is only a friend, whatever Poppy may have implied. I've known him only a little longer than I've known...you."

"Love strikes quickly, *senhorinha*, in some cases. But I do not think your heart will be stolen by a man who has loved many other women."

"One expects a man to be experienced." She rose in defense of Leird, who had been kind and big-brotherly toward her.

"Experience is not the same as a restless searching that leads in the end to nowhere. Mr. Challen finds Raya attractive, but she will never marry him."

No, because the flash of a blade had cut Raya out from the rest, and she only played at friendship with

Leird. But what of Flavio? She was more than friendly with him. She had kissed him with the passion of a girl reckless of the consequences. . . .

The fire flared as the *senhor* tossed on some of the branches he had set to dry, and Morvenna saw the profile of a man who could be many things. A master and a friend. . . and a formidable enemy.

She rubbed her eyes, which felt gritty from tiredness and the smoke of the fire. She wanted to sleep, but the forest ferns were still damp from the storm and the *senhor* would not allow her to curl down among them. She yawned, and at once his blue eyes were quizzing her sleepy face.

"No—" he shook his head as he saw her casting a wistful look at the ferns "—you will catch cold, and a cold can lead to fever in the jungle."

"But I'm desperately tired." She yawned again, knuckling her eyes like a child. "Please, *senhor*—"

"You will sleep against my shoulder, here by the warmth of the fire." He spoke decisively. "But first let me pile up some fuel so that I will not disturb you too much when I replenish the fire."

She watched him, her heart pounding, as he shifted the woodpile to the side of the tree trunk on which he intended to sit. He glanced at her. "Do you need to go into the bush?" he asked casually.

"Yes, but I can manage." She hastened away before he took it into his head to come and stand guard over her. When she returned to the fireside she was shivering a little from the cold. Some animal had coughed gruffly in the dark and that had helped to raise goose bumps on her arms.

"Do. . .do the jaguars prowl around in the vicinity of a fire?" she asked nervously. "I thought I heard one."

"One may sniff around," he said, "but the jaguar is too cunning to come face to face with a man. He prefers to attack from the limb of a tree, while someone is walking below.''

Morvenna caught the sudden note of hardness in his voice, and saw the somberness of his face as he pulled some ferns and used them to wipe his hands. She knew that he was remembering his mother and the way she had died.

"Don't be nervous," he said. "I know the jaguar and I am also quite handy with the machete."

He picked it up and the firelight glinted on the blade as he placed it beside the tree trunk, within easy reach of his hand. "Are you thirsty?" he asked. "I think I can spare you a small drink."

"No, I'm all right, just tired." She put a hand to her throat, as though to ease that strangling sense of intimacy in being alone with him in the dim, moist, mysterious jungle. He was so tall in the firelight, so dark and vital. Still such a stranger in many respects, in whose arms she was about to sleep.

Shyness raged through her when he placed an arm around her and drew her head to his shoulder. "Are you warm, *pequina*?" His breath was smoky from his cheroot as it brushed her temple, and he drew her closer, so that she felt again that deep, strong pounding of his heart. She had clung to him in the storm, but this was different. Now she was aware of him as a man rather than a refuge, and that the arm that enclosed her was both gentle and strong.

"Yes, I'm warm, thank you." She closed her eyes, for the only escape from this acute awareness of him was in sleep. And then her eyes opened again as a thought stabbed her. "You must be tired yourself, *senhor*."

"You little worrier, go to sleep at once and don't give that prowling cat another thought." He gave a gruff laugh. "I promise not to doze off in the night."

She knew he would not doze off and that was what worried her—the thought that he must stay vigilant and not get any rest. "If you wake me up in a couple of hours, I could keep the fire going while you have a nap," she said.

A taut little silence followed her offer, then her heart nearly stopped as warm lips touched a kiss to her temple. "Go to sleep, little one," he said. "It will not cause me any hardship to stay awake, whereas you are little more than a child and unused to the enervations of the jungle. Sleep deep, Morvenna. Soon it will be dawn."

Her name on his lips had an exotic sound, and she fell asleep with a tiny smile of wonderment on her lips.

THE MIST BEGAN to clear as morning light crept through the forest, and Morvenna awoke in alarm to a sound like the raging of surf. "Oh—" she blinked, and felt pins and needles tingling in her legs "—whatever's that?"

The *senhor*, rough haired and dark jawed, flashed a smile down at her. "Howler monkeys, greeting the dawn."

Still cradled in his left arm she stared up at him, her hair tousled and damp from the dew that was glittering on the jungle foliage all around, gleaming like diamonds on the huge spider webs that the darkness had concealed. The air was moist and loamy with jungle vegetation, and for Morvenna this was the strangest awakening of her life.

"Up with you, my jungle waif." He swung her to her feet and steadied her while she stamped the cramp out of her legs. Then he exercised his arms and his legs. "I want to start our homeward trek before the sun gets high," he said. "But first we must have something to eat."

"I'd like a wash." She gazed in consternation at her

grubby hands and knew her face must be in a similar
state.

"Follow me to the bathroom." He strode over to a
bush of red flowers, brushing aside a big web whose
occupant bobbed on the broken strands and then fell
into the long wet grass. Morvenna gave her clammy
grass sandals a shake before putting them on to join the
senhor, who was plucking the red flowers and squeezing
them between the palms of his hands. They exuded an
oil, to which he added the moisture from the trumpets
of wild convolvulus. The oil mixed with the water made
a passable, pungent-scented lather. "Don't be afraid to
use it on your face," he said, and Morvenna heard the
rasp of his strong dark beard as he rubbed the soap
vigorously over his own face. She followed suit, and
found that a flower-and-dew wash was about the most
refreshing she had ever had. There were pools of dew in
the cups of the flowers, and she washed face, neck and
arms with it.

"I feel as primitive as Eve," she laughed.

"And I am as hungry as Adam." The blue eyes
flashed in the lean piratical face as he took a look at the
surrounding trees. "A coconut palm would provide us
with milk, but it looks as though we will have to make
do with mangoes. I shall be but a few minutes fetching
them—you will stay right here?"

"Of course." She glanced up at him and felt stunned
by the look of him with that dark jaw, those vivid eyes,
and his throat brown and bared at the opening of his
shirt.

He swung his machete, studied her for a moment, and
then as silently as an Indian he disappeared among the
trees.

Morvenna did what she could to tidy her tousled hair
and felt hungry for one of those peachy mangoes they
had enjoyed yesterday. The howler monkeys had

quietened down and birds were waking up with the sun, which was beginning to fire the tops of the trees. Irridescent birds flitted to the flower cups and as they drank the moisture they cocked a look at the stranger in their grove.

She sat down on the log by the fire, which still smoldered, and thought of the strange night that she had shared with Roque de Braz Ferro. She had slept securely in his arms, unafraid of the jungle all around them and the many dangers that it held.

Now, as she looked around her at the wall of trees and curtains of floral liana, she felt a stirring of nervousness. The *senhor* was within call, she knew that, but the dense foliage seemed to cut him off from her, and she was suddenly aware that an uncanny silence prevailed. She listened and heard only the beating of her heart. The birds had flown off again to their treetop perches and were curiously silent.

Morvenna stood up, dry lipped and tense. Then a twig cracked, as though under a stealthy tread. "Is that you, *senhor*?" An alarmed note jarred in her voice as she called out.

There was no answer and she gave a sudden shiver of apprehension. She knew with all her nerves that someone—something—lurked among the foliage where that twig had cracked. Then she clamped a hand to her mouth as the foliage stirred and, silent and sinewy, four Indians appeared one by one from the bush. They carried bows and quivers of arrows. They wore breechclouts and their black hair was cut in fringes above dark, impenetrable eyes.

Morvenna strove not to betray her intense alarm, but sweat broke through her pores and her heart hammered as those four pairs of black brown brooding eyes took her in from head to toe. A beam of sunlight broke through the trees and struck her hair to a halo. The

Indians muttered among themselves, and Morvenna was getting ready to yell blue murder when the *senhor*'s tall figure emerged out of the bush.

She knew at once from the way he walked, and the way his eyes were a flamy blue, that he was as tensed as a panther. He came with his swift stride to her side and clamped a hand on her shoulder. "*Kurumi,*" he said, and added some other Indian words she did not understand. *Kurumi* was a word she knew. It meant woman.

At once the leader of the group stopped glowering at Morvenna as though he had never seen a woman before. He replied to the *senhor* in a soft guttural tongue, and instantly Morvenna felt a reassuring pressure of the hand on her shoulder. Then the warm hand withdrew, and he approached the Indian, who immediately greeted him with a hand on his shoulder. They spoke together for several minutes while Morvenna watched and wondered. Were they friendly Indians? Somehow the strokes of red paint across their brown cheeks gave her the feeling that they were less acculturated than the Indians who lived near the *fazenda*.

They looked like warriors, she thought, her nerves tingling as the three silent members of the group stared at the machete in the *senhor*'s hand. If he had been carrying mangoes, he had discarded them, and this told Morvenna that upon seeing the Indians he had prepared himself for possible trouble.

Suddenly he turned to Morvenna. "These men are Incalas," he said. "Nuno is at their camp and very sick with fever. They want me to go with them to the camp. Their *brujo* has tried to help Nuno, but he needs white man's medicine."

"Are they speaking the truth?" she asked anxiously.

"We shall have to trust that they are. They inform me that they were on their way to the *fazenda* to fetch me." He beckoned her to his side and she went to him, an obedient movement that evidently impressed the In-calas, for they suddenly grinned, showing teeth stained by the strong tobacco the *senhor*'s own Indians were fond of chewing.

"I am carrying quinine ampuls and a syringe," he told her. "Nuno sounds as though he might have malaria, and the sooner I get to him the better his chance of recovery. Now listen, Morvenna! I am going to show you the track that you followed yesterday, and I want you to follow it all the way home to the *fazenda*—"

"But I'm coming with you," she broke in. "I wouldn't dream of doing anything else."

"You will do as you are told," he said crisply. "You will only hinder me by coming to the Incala camp. We have to cross the gorge and then travel by dugout upriver—"

"Please, I must come with you!" She caught at his arm and felt the muscles tauten under her grip.

"Why must you come?" He stared down at her, scanning her face with its look of wild appeal. "Does Nuno mean so much to you?"

"Yes," she spoke recklessly—anything to make him take her with him. "He's sick because he wanted to do something to help me, and I want to help nurse him. I have the right, and you can't send me back to the *fazenda* like—like a child. I'm not a child!"

"No—" his eyes were a fierce blue as they raked her upraised face "—it would seem that you are desperate to get to Nuno, and it may be to his advantage, in the circumstances, to let you have your way. Very well! But let me warn you that the trip will take several hours, and it will be a hard one."

He turned to the Indians, and again the word *kurumi* was used as he spoke to them. They frowned, then gestured at the sun, which was climbing higher all the time and spilling its raw gold down through the branches of the towering trees. The *senhor* spread his hands in a very Latin gesture, and after some more talk was exchanged one of the Indians unslung a calabash container from his shoulder and handed it to the *senhor*, whom he addressed as Tushaua Braz. A leaf flap was also handed over, and Morvenna was relieved to see that it did not contain fish roe, or a mess of rice and meat.

The *senhor* handed her a couple of the mandioca cakes, along with his own water flask. "I have insisted that we need food, so you had better eat every bit," he said in that crisp tone of voice that meant they were back on the old footing, and that his guardianship was no longer the gentle, rather shattering thing it had been last night.

"Thank you." She bit into one of the cakes, too hungry to care that an Indian had supplied it, and washed it down with a gulp of water. The *senhor* drank from the calabash, which probably contained river water, and made short work of his own cakes.

The Indians watched, and this sharing of their food seemed to make them more amiable. One of them, young and handsomely broad featured, was busily plaiting some leaves together with a length of vine. He handed the result to Morvenna—a hat, no less, the leaves tied together in a pagoda shape.

"How kind of you." Morvenna gave him a dazzling smile. "I needed a hat."

The *senhor* translated her thanks, and the young Indian gave her a bashful smile in return.

"Be careful." The *senhor* gave her hand a rather painful tap as he slipped a salt tablet into her palm. "The Incala braves fancy their luck with the ladies."

"Must I take this?" It was an Incala he had fought for possession of Raya, and now he was returning to their encampment for Nuno's sake. She knew she looked distressed and hoped he would associate it with the salt tablet.

"Yes, you must." He looked firm and stern. "Loss of body moisture and salt enervates the system, and we have a trying journey ahead of us. Put the tablet at the back of your tongue and chase it down with some water."

She obeyed, grimacing. Then she screwed up the courage to say to him, "Don't be angry because I want to come with you to the encampment."

"I am angry with myself for letting you come." His face was teak-hard, his eyes a vivid, snapping blue. "I suppose it is useless to ask you to change your mind?"

She nodded, and her chin had a determined tilt to it. "You would have to tie me to a tree to stop me," she replied.

"You foolish child—" he ground out the words "—you are thinking with your heart, as usual."

"Yes." She gave a shaken laugh and twisted her pagoda hat around in her fingers. "I have a crazy heart, *senhor*."

"*Kehami*," said the leader of the Indians, and Morvenna was told to make ready for the trek that would take them across the gorge and down to the riverbank, where the canoe was tied up. She larded her face, neck, arms and ankles with insect repellent, and the *senhor* took a look at her sandals to make sure the soles were not worn through.

"You don't have to keep considering me." She strove to speak lightly. "I shall keep up all right."

"Now the other sandal," he said firmly, and she had to let him have it while she stood on one leg like a crane. He dug his finger into a small hole that had worn into the sole of her left sandal, and repaired it by cutting a piece of oilskin from the pouch that held his first aid kit and shaping it with his knife to fit the sandal.

"You needn't have done that." She pushed her foot into the sandal. "You've spoiled your pouch."

"You have small feet, so I have not had to use too much of the oilskin. Does the sandal feel comfortable?"

"Yes, thank you." She gave him a grateful smile but he didn't see it, for he had turned away to speak to the Indians. She bit her lip as she donned her pagoda hat, but was glad in a way that he was brusque in his attentions this morning. That dangerous intimacy of last night had been a little too shattering. She still seemed to feel the warmth of his lips against her temple—his good night kiss for someone he thought of as little more than a child.

He swung his water flask over his shoulder, patted the pocket of his bush shirt to make sure his first aid kit was in place, and clasped his other hand firmly around the handle of his machete. "Come, *senhorinha*," he said. "It is time to go."

CHAPTER TWELVE

A PROFUSION OF CREEPERS and vines lay across the path they followed Indian file. Great mossy ropes hung from trees hundreds of feet high, falling in loops and knots. Wicked-looking orchids clung to the trees, and small birds flashed like gems among the branches of orange blossoms.

They were making their way around the gorge, to where a rope bridge was slung across to the bank of the river. The *senhor* threw this information over his shoulder, for he was walking ahead of Morvenna, treading down the knotty vine and thorny bamboo growth to make her path easier. The Indian who padded behind her was as silent and dark as a big cat.

A dew of sweat shone on her face, for it grew hotter all the time, and tendrils of hair clung to her temples and the nape of her neck. She threw self-defensive slaps at herself to keep off the gnats and noticed that the Indians seemed impervious to the tormenting insects. Their bare, leathery feet trod the path as though it were overgrown with moss instead of trip-wire vines and thorns that cracked underfoot, and she wondered whether their women were as tough and enigmatic.

The vegetation seemed impenetrable at either side of the track. Lianas curled around the tree trunks like giant snakes, and there was a murmurous hum from the wild bees plundering the deep-hearted flowers.

Suddenly there was another sound, a sharp creak,

almost a groan, and one of the giant trees was toppling out of the bush toward them. The Indians leaped out of the way with the agility of cats, and an arm of iron swept Morvenna off the path into the bush. The air was rent with noise and the panicky screech of animals and birds as the tree came crashing down.

Tree lizards leaped and the bush seethed with flight and activity as Morvenna lay crushed against the *senhor*. Her face was against his throat; she was held roughly close to him as the echoes died away. His half-painful grip on her finally relaxed and he released his breath with savage audibility. Morvenna felt her frantic heartbeats and suddenly pulled away from him. His eyes blazed into hers, then he was on his feet and thrusting through the bushes to the path, now blocked by that enormous tree.

The Indians jabbered together, and one of them touched the corded fang that hung around his neck and cast a rather belligerent look at Morvenna.

"What are they saying?" she asked as she scrambled over the great trunk of the tree. A hand gripped hers and she jumped down onto the other side of the path.

"The tree has been strangled by matador creeper," he said, "but Indians are superstitious devils and inclined to blame sudden mishaps and alarms on... women."

"On me?" Her eyes widened with indignation. "What a cheek! As if I can help a tree falling down. They leaped out of the way quick enough—I'd be underneath if you hadn't grabbed hold of me."

"Put your hat straight." His smile was mocking. "You look like a tipsy gnome."

The trek continued, and all at once the path broadened and they had arrived at the rope bridge that spanned the gorge. It looked a frightening catwalk of a bridge, and the great foaming arc of the cascade would splash them with its foam as they traversed the gorge.

Morvenna cast a nervous glance at the *senhor*. "Don't look down as you cross over," he said. "I shall be right behind you."

"One needs to be a tightrope walker," she said, and her hands clenched the rope handles as she stepped on to the flimsy, swaying catwalk. She took a step and panic gripped her as remembrance of yesterday's ordeal swept into her mind. The bridge spanned the wide-torn gorge at its narrowest end, which was not so narrow when viewed from this bridge that seemed alive under her feet.

Three of the Indians were almost across and she envied their equilibrium. The rather nice one, who had made her the pagoda hat, was in front of her, guiding her, and it also helped a lot to know that the *senhor* was right behind her.

At last, with a deep gasp of relief, she stepped off the bridge. Her legs felt boneless for a moment, and the *senhor* told her to take a rest before they clambered down the bank to where the long Indian dugout was secured. They stood looking at the cascade, a scene of roaring splendor, and were splashed with cool drops of moisture. And then he said they had better be moving, for the Indians were getting into the canoe.

The sun on the river was dazzling. The air hummed with insects and it was a relief when the canoe, long and dug out from a great tree of the forest, was pushed off from the bank and with hefty thrusts of the paddles was propelled into the middle of the river, where the gnats were less troublesome.

The air was cooler on the water, for as the dugout skimmed along it made a breeze that fanned Morvenna's face and neck. This was her first trip on a jungle river, and she had eyes for everything—the clumsy flight of yellow-billed toucans across the water, and at one bend in the river a black and tawny jaguar sunning himself on a sandbank, stretched out like a cat on a hearth and blinking his green eyes as though he wouldn't hurt a fly.

The forest smoked with heat, and the mass of green vegetation was aflame here and there with flamboyant flowers. The river dwindled in places to shallow creeks, and petals wafted down from the mats of blossom as the dugout was paddled through the green tunnels.

Without thinking Morvenna reached for a chain of mauve flowers that floated on the water, and at once a voice rapped out from the other side of the canoe: "Don't feed your fingers to the *piranha*. These shallow waters harbor them by the thousand."

Like a child with rapped knuckles, she withdrew her hand and turned her gaze in the other direction, hurt by the lash in the voice whose deep, warm gentleness had lulled her into sleep last night. She watched the wildfowl feeding on the crabs that scuttled in the reeds, and then the river widened out again into a stretch of sun-shot water. Logs floated on it and had to be deftly avoided, and sometimes they skimmed past dark shapes that were not logs but scaly brutes who drowsed just below the surface.

The rhythmic swish of the paddles through the water was sometimes the only sound to be heard, and then all at once the monkeys in the forest would set up a clamor, and birds would fly up into the gauzy sky.

Around noon the Indians edged the canoe onto a sandbank and shared out their food and water. Morvenna's admirer handed her a pickled hog's trotter, and from sheer hunger she battled with the tough meat, and a thin piece of bread that was rather like a slimming biscuit.

The people who slimmed, and went to work by bus and car, seemed a million miles away from these green deeps and stranger to her than the Indians of the forest; and the tall Tushaua Braz whose eyes were bluer than the sea that had stranded her on the shores of this faraway island.

"There is still a little water in my flask." He handed it to her. "You are not used to drinking river water, though it is quite unpolluted by industrial chemicals."

"I was just thinking how far away civilization seems." She took a thirsty gulp of water. "All this is like another world, another time. Look at those birds! They look painted."

"Jewels of the forest, and the sun its gold." He smiled quizzically as she chewed away gallantly at the trotter in her hand. "Are you enjoying that?" he asked.

"I'm as hungry as a hunter." She gave a laugh. "I can't imagine Poppy enjoying this trip, her hair in damp tangles, her face as shiny as a mirror—oh, I've just had a thought! Leird must be feeling rather anxious about us."

"But not Poppy, eh? She thinks only of herself." The *senhor* quizzed his cigarette case and gave a sigh that indicated he had run out of the slim, dark cheroots he was fond of.

"Nuno must have been taken ill in the forest and then found by the Incalas," she said thoughtfully. "*Senhor*, do you think my father was looking for their encampment? Is it at all possible that the treasure is connected with them?"

"The Incalas are an ancient and mysterious tribe," he said quietly, "but you must not entertain the idea that they had anything to do with your father's death."

"You say it so definitely." Her eyes locked with his,

the lashes dark and sweat-clustered around her violet
eyes. "Why are you so certain, *senhor*? What do you
know, and why do you keep it from me?"

"Perhaps I had to wait to judge how much maturity
hides behind your young face." His own face was as if
sculptured out of teak and shadows. "I knew weeks ago
that a white man had died while following the Rio
Rona, which leads to this island and the Incala camp.
His canoe and supplies were found on the north bank of
the Rio Rona. The news reached me by bush telegraph—the drums—and I went with a tracking party to
find out if this man could still be alive, somewhere in the
bush. . . ."

The proud nostrils contracted, and a tiny stream of
sweat coursed down the broad forehead into the black
arch of an eyebrow. "The *piranha*, the cannibal fish,
swarm in the still waters of the shallow creeks. Your
father must have become grounded in one of these
creeks—perhaps some underwater weeds entrapped the
prow of his canoe—and I would say he went over the
side with the intention of freeing his boat. . . and the
devil fish attacked him."

"Oh no!" Morvenna buried her face in her hands.
"H-how can you be so sure that. . . that it was the
piranha?"

"Because of the location of your father's canoe—a
heavy downpour of rain had filled up the creek and
washed the boat onto the bank, where it overturned. A
creek swarming with *piranha*, as I discovered for
myself. Though cannibalistic, they will not always attack unless a man has an open wound on his person. I
think it must be assumed that your father might have
cut his hand while opening a tin of the supplies he was
carrying. Also," he added gently, "I made a conclusive
discovery while I was investigating the nearby woods to
make sure he was not lying injured, or ill with fever."

"What...sort of discovery?" Her knuckles were pressed white against her lips, her eyes were pools of pain, and fear of his next revelation.

"I met some forest Indians," he said quietly, gravely, "and I noticed that one of them was wearing an identity-disk on a chain around his neck. I asked to see it and very reluctantly he handed it to me. After taking a look at the name inscribed upon the disk, I asked how he came by it and he told me that he had been dragging a crab net in one of the creeks near where your father's canoe was found. When he hauled in his catch, he found the disk and chain entangled in the pincers of the crabs. He gave it a polish and hung it around his neck, regarding it as *icaro*—a talisman."

But for Llew Fayr it had not been a talisman, and the *senhor*'s lean face was somber as he added, "After some haggling, I persuaded the man to exchange his find for the watch I was wearing."

"Tell me the name that was on the disk," Morvenna said huskily.

"Llew Gwilym Fayr. His date of birth was inscribed, also his blood group and nationality."

"Welsh," she sighed. "He was proud of being born in Wales, and he wanted to settle there, one day."

"Perhaps he is there in spirit, *senhorihna*."

"I wonder." She glanced around at the jungle forest that was so green and wild; a paradise where danger walked hand in hand with beauty. "I sometimes think he loved these jungles more than anything else. They appealed to the tiger in him that was part of his Tiger Bay heritage. No, *senhor*, I feel that in spirit he is here. I think I have been feeling this ever since I came so strangely to Janaleza—as though I was meant to come here."

"Fate plays strange games with us." Lean fingers enclosed hers, steely and warm. "I dispatched the disk and a letter to the authorities in Manaos, but when you said that you had come to Brazil to search for your father, I guessed that the package had somehow gone astray, that no one in Manaos could have told you that a search would be in vain.''

"Did you tell Nuno about finding my father's identity disk?"

"Yes, he knew. But I asked him not to speak of it to you, but to leave the time of telling to me. Have I hurt you very much in the telling?''

She gazed down at his brown hand and felt the vitality in his finger tips stealing into her like an infusion of strength that made the pain easier to bear, somehow.

"It had to be told, *senhor*. I . . . I only hope that it was quick—would it be quick?"

"Quicker than snakebite, or the fangs of a jaguar.''

"Your mother. . . .'' Her eyes lifted to his face. His mother had been a victim of the jungle, so it was no wonder he was being so understanding about her own loss.

"Yes.'' He spoke abruptly, and as the Indians pushed out from the sandbank he took a paddle and Morvenna sat and watched the darkening of the back of his shirt as he wielded the diamond-bladed paddle as deftly as any of the Indians. There had been something else to ask, but he had evaded the question. He knew, as she now guessed, that Nuno had gone looking for the treasure marked on that fatalistic map.

A GOLDEN RED HAZE was stealing over the sky as they turned an arm of the river and came in sight of a sloping beach and the Incala settlement. Drums began to boom among the trees, signaling their approach. Indians began to appear out of the big stilt houses; they scrambled down the bamboo ladders, men and their wives, naked urchins and barking dogs. They came running down the beach as the dugout nosed its way between the inverted V of a natural landing place. The four Indians leaped ashore, but Morvenna was so stiff from sitting still that she had to be lifted over the side by the *senhor*.

Her nerves tingled as she glanced around at the throng of Incalas. They had fallen silent for a moment and were staring at her, so pale, slim and youthful, such a contrast to the brown-skinned women with painted faces, wearing short aprons fringed with beads, and little else.

A tank of wood smoke from the evening cook fires hung over the settlement, and the setting sun cast a weird pink light over the scene.

"Come." A lean hand gripped her elbow, and with tall, calm assurance, the *senhor* made a way for them through the throng. Small hands reached out to touch Morvenna, and she smiled down at the children, black fringed, big eyed, with teeth like polished rice. She was among people of the wilds, a tribe of lithe, black brown people who had a look of savage innocence. A disarming, deceptive innocence, she knew, for these were the people who had kidnapped a white woman and reared her twins; their chief was brother to the man who had fought a machete duel with the *senhor*—and been beaten.

The chief was coming forward to greet his male visitor—he did not bother to notice Morvenna—and the two men clapped each other on the shoulder and exchanged greetings in the jungle tongue. While these formalities went on, Morvenna took stock of her surroundings and wondered in which house poor Nuno was suffering. The thatched houses were on stilts, she guessed, because of their nearness to the river, and children clung to the bamboo ladders that hung from the open doorways with all the agility of the forest monkeys, who were setting up their usual clamor as the tropical twilight approached.

All of a sudden the *senhor* turned to her, and she noticed in an instant that he was grimly amused about something. "A woman of the chief's household is going to show us to a *choza*," he said deliberately. "Our hut."

As they crossed the compound, where the cook fires gleamed and smoked, Morvenna glanced up wildly at the coppery profile of her companion. "Our hut?" she echoed.

"Yes." The smile he slanted down at her was tenderly cruel. "To these people you are my woman—my she-thing."

She caught her breath, shocked.

"It is for your own good that you are my woman while we are here." There was a hint of a sting in his voice, and a flare of firelight showed that his eyes went hard. "Perhaps you would sooner we slept in a communal hut? It can be arranged."

"There's no need to be sarcastic," Morvenna said stiffly.

"Last night you were alone with me in the forest," he said through his teeth. "Don't you trust me yet?"

"Of course." It wasn't the sharing of a hut with him that shook her—or was it? "Was there any real need to tell these people that I... belong to you?" she said with a rush. "They saw you fight for Raya...."

"So they did," he drawled. "They also think it quite in order for a chief to have more than one woman, so don't worry that our being together at night will shock them. Don't let it shock you, *pequina*. I shall be with Nuno most of the time. Come, we will have a look at our *choza* because these people take their hospitality very seriously, then we will go to the boy. I am told he is extremely sick, and not responding to the treatment he has been given by their witch doctor."

He spoke to the elderly woman who had guided them to a thatched abode set among the trees, then he mounted the ladder to the rough-hewn doorway, and when Morvenna joined him he was applying a lighted match to the oil-burning lamp hanging from the cross beam that supported the roof.

The floor was of clay, and hammocks were secured to the roof supports. The wick of the lamp burned suddenly bright and Morvenna saw the ant holes in the woodwork, and the shaggy thatch that overhung the outside of the hut. It was the kind of roof in which long-legged creeping things could be hiding, and she gave a shiver.

"You need some food and some coffee," the *senhor* said briskly. "The old woman is going to bring it to Nuno's hut."

This hut was next to their own, and they found him in the care of another of the elderly crones who always did a good share of the work around any Indian settlement. Nuno's young face was colorless and streaming with sweat; every now and again a harsh tremor shook him.

"Poor boy." Morvenna stroked the damp hair from his closed eyes, and another fever tremor shook the hammock in which he lay. He seemed unaware of their presence, and the *senhor*'s eyes were narrowed as he took Nuno's pulse and then pulled up the lids of his eyes to examine the color of the whites. They were yellowish, his skin clammy, his pulse rapid.

"Is it malaria?" Morvenna asked anxiously.

"I am not sure." The *senhor*'s lean fingers gently probed the glands in the boyish neck. "He has picked up something—anyway, a strong dose of quinine won't hurt, and he may react to it if it is given in the vein."

The needle of the syringe gleamed in the lamplight as

it was plunged into an ampul of quinine. The quinine was carefully injected, and the old Indian woman leaned over the hammock and studied the proceedings with eyes as dark as the shadows in the corners of the hut.

She muttered something and Morvenna glanced at the *senhor* in the hope that he would translate. He frowned as he tucked in the blankets around Nuno, carefully fixing them beneath the sides of his body and under his feet. "The old one knew him when he was a boy," he said. "She says he will not get well because I stab him with a needle—she thinks he is bewitched."

Morvenna's eyes widened in the smoky lamplight, and she thought of the map and the ill luck that it seemed to bring to those who tried to find treasure with it. "He looks so ill," she whispered, "and those tremors seem to shake him to the bone."

"He certainly has a very high fever." The *senhor* spoke somberly. "We must keep him covered up and try to induce as much sweating as possible. Are you nervous of illness?"

"I don't think so." She wiped away the sweat that coursed down Nuno's face and then glanced at the calabash of water on the floor beside the hammock. She picked it up and looked around for a cup of some sort, but there wasn't one. The old woman must have held the calabash for Nuno to drink from, but now he was too weak for that, and half-unconscious, and the moisture he was losing had to be replaced or he would grow even more exhausted.

"If I had a cup and a spoon," she said, "I could get a little moisture into him. If his lips were wetted frequently, he would gradually absorb the water." Then, gazing at the calabash she commented, "There isn't much left, and I bet it's stale."

"Give it to me." The *senhor* took the calabash and turned to the old woman. He spoke to her in the dialect of the tribe, a succession of guttural sounds that seemed to add to the strange atmosphere of the hut. Smoke from the lamp hung in the air, and its wavering light cast shadows over faces that might have been depicted in a tapestry of long ago. There were broken places in the walls of the hut, and Morvenna heard movements outside and felt that Indian eyes were looking in at them.

The old woman shuffled away to get fresh water and the other things the *senhor* had asked for, and Morvenna looked at him across Nuno's bunk. Their eyes met in the lamplight and she knew this moment to be the strangest they had yet shared.

"Don't look so anxious," he said. "Between us we will make Nuno well again."

"*Senhor*—" she could feel her heart beating fast with what she had to put into words "—I think we should find that map...and burn it."

His eyes narrowed as he looked at her. He didn't speak for fully a minute, while Nuno's dry, feverish gasping filled the silence between them.

"Please," she begged, "let's find it and burn it!"

They found it among the things Nuno had brought with him in a rolled groundsheet—a square of tracing paper, glued to a square of brown paper, much folded, the tracings beginning to fade from the handling the map had received. Morvenna watched as the *senhor* flicked his eyes over it, then, his face as though carved from teak, he held the map to the wick of the lamp. It caught fire at once, flared, and was ground to ash beneath the heel of his boot.

Neither of them said anything, and Morvenna felt an easing of the tension as Indians came into the hut, bringing bowls of strong coffee and larger bowls of stewed meat and rice. The aromas blended, and Morvenna realized how hungry she was.

She fortified herself with the hot, tangy coffee, sweetened with the brown sugar the Indians made from wild sugarcane, and then ate hungrily the chunks of meat—wild deer or tapir—and the spicy clumps of rice. Her spoon was of hand-carved wood, and throughout most of the night that followed, she and the *senhor* took turns in moistening Nuno's lips from one of these spoons dipped in water.

CHAPTER THIRTEEN

TOWARD DAWN Nuno began to lick at the drops of water like a feeble puppy, and when Morvenna saw this, she smiled. The long, tedious task had been worth every bone-aching minute spent on this hard, backless stool beside his hammock, and when she glanced across to say as much to the *senhor*, she saw that he had dozed off to sleep, his dark head pillowed against the bamboo wall, his long legs stretched out from his backless wooden stool.

She gave Nuno a little more water, then set aside the cup and spoon and rose, stiffly, to change his blankets again. He had sweated profusely, and several times in the night the *senhor* had massaged his limbs in order to ease his fever cramps. Now, with the dawn light filtering into the hut, he felt much cooler to Morvenna's touch.

As she tucked him in, a little breeze stirred through the hut, and she glanced at the floor and saw some pieces of ash scattered into a dust indistinguishable from the clay dust. Then that errant breeze died down, and with it a rustling of leaves from outside, and everything was still again.

Morvenna came around the other side of the hammock and was careful not to arouse the *senhor* as she finished tucking in her patient. She stood looking down at the man who had not slept a wink for two nights running—such a complex man, so seemingly tough and self-contained, and yet so ready to spend himself for those he cared for....

Those he cared for? A tremor of a smile touched her lips. In her case he felt obligated to see that she came to no harm, but he cared for Nuno as though he were a young brother—indeed, in the near future they would be brothers.

Morvenna walked quietly to the doorway of the hut and gazed out at the Indian encampment, where the river mist twined among the trees, and lean hunting dogs were curled asleep near the embers of the fires. In a while the women would awake and come from the thatched houses to relight the fires. Coffee would be set to brew, and *farina* pancakes rolled out ready for breakfast. Children and dogs would race to the river and the men would roll out of their hammocks and yawn at their women that they wanted food and drink before they went hunting for the day, or fishing.

But for now, for about half an hour more, the camp was wrapped in mist and sleep, and Morvenna decided to go down to the river for a wash. She had noticed a bar of soap among Nuno's things, and a hand towel.

She found them and with eager stealth made her way down to the riverbank. Everything was dewed, faintly pink from the flickers of dawn sunlight, and so fresh and loamy that it was like drinking a cup of wine to stand and take deep gulps of the air. It was then that Morvenna noticed the slab of rock that jutted out over the river, a natural diving board for the Indians, and irresistible to someone who was sweaty, grubby, and almost desperate to feel cool, clean water all over her.

There was absolutely no one around. She was alone on the shore, and within seconds she had stripped off her shirt and trousers and had climbed to the top of the rock. From there she dived into the cool, tea-colored water, and after swimming around for a few minutes she scrubbed herself briskly with Nuno's bar of soap.

How good it felt to be clean again! Treading water,

she rubbed the soap through her hair, then swam again until the soap was rinsed off and floating away on the water, iridescent bubbles in the pink and gold sunlight that was spreading across the river.

The birds were setting up their morning chorus and arrowing brightly from one green bank to the other. Morvenna swam in lazy circles and felt her heart respond to the pagan loveliness of the jungle morning. No wonder her father had loved these faraway places. No wonder Roque de Braz Ferro called the island his world. She thought of him asleep, curiously vulnerable, his lashes curtaining those vital blue eyes, his black hair rumpled, giving him a boyish air until you looked at his dark-stubbled chin.

She smiled a little to herself, for she couldn't imagine him in a city. He would look as out of place and uncivilized as a jaguar walking the city streets.

She came out of the water, wishing she had fresh clothing to put on... and there on the sands, as if put there by magic, was a length of gaily patterned material such as Raya sometimes wore as a wraparound, the end being fixed just above the bosom. Morvenna snatched up the towel and held it against her as she took a swift look at the surrounding bushes and trees. She couldn't see anyone, but upon seeing the wraparound her thoughts had leaped at once to the *senhor*. He was curiously perceptive where she was concerned. If he had woken and not found her, he would have guessed at once that the water had drawn her like a magnet. If he had brought the wraparound to the river, he would have seen her in the water, arms raised as she washed her hair, naked as a naiad.

Her cheeks crimsoned as she hastily rubbed herself down. The Indians bathed in the jungle rivers without inhibitions, so perhaps he had not noticed her nudity. Consoling herself with that thought, she picked up the length of material and wound herself into it, not without a certain natural grace that was part of her Celtic heritage. Already the sun was climbing up through the trees, and its warmth touched her damp tousled hair and bare white shoulders. Soon her hair would dry, and she laid the towel across the drooping limb of a tree to catch the sun.

In her *itipi*, as the Indians called the wraparound, she rested against a palm tree, which inclined gently and bore great fans of green leaves and clusters of fibered nuts. She would return to the hut in a few more minutes, but it was peaceful here and she wanted to savor the feeling of freshness imparted by her swim and her pagan mode of dress.

It came to her, like a touch that thrilled her every nerve, that she had grown to love all this, the sense of freedom, the unutterable beauty, the scents and sounds. They had penetrated her pores, and she knew that a part of herself would be left behind when she left the island of Janaleza.

She wasn't proof against the sudden feeling of desolation that swept through her, and she reached out blindly to a nearby bush of pointed, fragrant-scented leaves. She plucked a handful in her rush of pain and crushed them in her fingers.

"Heart's desire," said a voice.

She glanced around wildly and there was the *senhor*, standing tall and looking at her. He had used Nuno's razor and was clean shaven again; his hair was combed back and agleam with moisture. He had been in the river, farther along, where it curved like an arm, where he must have gone after leaving her the *itipi*. He wore no shirt. He must have washed it out and left it to dry. He looked brown and hard, hewn out of jungle teak, and right through her being Morvenna was aware of the refreshed and wonderful look of him.

"The leaves of that bush are called heart's desire," he said again.

"It's a wonderful scent." She bent her head and breathed the scent of the crushed leaves, feeling almost strangled by emotion as he drew nearer to her and she felt his gaze flick her bare white shoulders. It was this pagan place that aroused this awareness of him. She had noticed before that he was more vital than other men, that he had raven glints in his hair, and a lean grace of body. Why then this sudden breathlessness, this acute shyness, this female urge to know whether she looked attractive or absurd in the flamboyant native garment?

She felt his eyes upon her like a touch and didn't dare to look at him. He must be comparing her to Raya, who looked as exotic as a jungle flower in one of these garments, and Morvenna turned from him to look at the river, glowing bright as agate as the sun chased away the mist.

"I couldn't resist taking a dip," she said. "Did you leave me the wraparound?"

"Yes. The old woman who cooked for us last night left it for you in the other hut."

He didn't say "our hut" this morning, with a wicked glint in his eye.

"She is sitting with Nuno," he added. "He will now get well, thanks to you."

"No." She faced him, protest in her eyes. "I did no more than you, *senhor*. We broke his fever together."

"He sensed that you were by his side, for when you left the hut this morning he became restless and spoke your name aloud—"

"I...I left you both asleep," she broke in.

"I awoke as you slipped from the hut with Nuno's towel over your shoulder." A smile touched his lips. "It was all right to let you come to the river to bathe. The water runs fast and is always fresh."

And free of piranha, she added to herself.

"I enjoyed my dip very much, with everything looking so green, and Nuno out of danger." She ran a shy
hand down the folds of the gaily patterned wraparound.
"Thank you for bringing me this to wear. I was longing
for something nice and fresh to put on—I didn't hear
you bring it to the riverbank."

"You were singing—" he quirked a black eyebrow
"—as you washed your hair. I left the *itipi* and stole
quietly away to take a dip of my own."

So he had seen her in the water! She blushed. In fact it
felt like a flame licking over her, and she couldn't control her instinctive retreat from his tall, dark maleness.
She picked up her shirt and trousers. "I'll give these a
rub through."

She knelt by the water and as she proceeded to wash
out her things, she felt a curious constriction in her
throat, and a stinging at the back of her eyes. Whatever
was the matter with her? A little while ago she had felt
so happy, now all at once she felt like crying. She knead-
ed the soapy trousers between her hands and was aware
of the barking dogs and sound of voices from the encampment. Wood smoke drifted tangily through the
trees.

The soap bubbles floated away as she rinsed her
things. She gave them a shake, then walked to a nearby
tree where she intended to hang them to dry.

"No—" the sands crunched behind her and as she
reached the tree a pair of hands took hold of her, rather
roughly "—not the Palo Santo tree!"

"Let me go!" The warm, hard touch on her bare
shoulders sent panic winging through her, and she instinctively fought with him. "Y-you're hurting me...
and I'm fed up with your bossy ways!"

"That is too bad." He spoke crisply above her head.
"But I am afraid you are going to have to put up with

my bossy ways for a while longer. You child!'' He gave
her a shake. "Whatever I do is for your own good, and
you should know that by now!''

"Such as bruising my shoulders?'' she flashed.
"Y-you're a jungle savage!''

"Of course.'' He laughed low down in his throat.
"The jungle is bound to bring out the primitive in man,
and I have naturally taken hold of you in order to pacify
all that you arouse in a flimsy wraparound that shows
off your white skin. Such fine skin, soft as a baby's, and
hair of silver that curls in tiny tendrils at the nape of
your neck.

"Yes—'' his fingers deliberately caressed her shoulders "—you are very beguiling in the garment, and I
shall be quite sorry to see you again in a shirt and a pair
of trousers.''

"Please take your hands off me!'' A moment more of
this and she would drop the dripping trousers and shirt
and turn without restraint to the touch that only
taunted. It was unbearable, and her heart knew why!

"I shall be happy to oblige—'' his tone was suddenly
cruel "—for as it happens I am not holding you because
I find you irresistible—but the fire ants will, if you go
too close to that Palo Santo tree. They make their nests
in such trees and their bite is vicious!''

His teeth snapped whitely on that final word, and
Morvenna went meekly to the dwarf palm at which he
gestured and hung her things on its branches to dry in
the sun. It was firing the tops of the jungle trees—the
tropical sun that gave birth to the ardent foliage, and to
emotions such as Morvenna had never felt in her life
before.

The *senhor* strolled up the beach to the encampment
and she followed him. When she caught the glances and
smiles of the Indian women, she knew that they were
thinking of her as the woman of Tushaua Braz.

Morvenna's eyes dwelt on the broad, coppery back that she followed. She took note of the dark peak of hair that stabbed the nape of his neck; the pagan freedom and assurance with which he held himself.

His woman would be totally his. His love would be a commanding one, but there would also be a world of comfort and humor and security in it. Morvenna watched him mount the ladder into Nuno's hut, and she paused among the trees and leaned a moment against one of them. She was shaking and weak. She told herself she was tired after her sleepless night at Nuno's bedside, but she knew that it was not quite true. She knew that she was building a defense against the invasion of her heart by a man whose plans for the future did not include her.

They would leave this place tomorrow. They would return to the *fazenda*, and on Friday the steamer would arrive and she would say good-bye to Roque de Braz Ferro, feudal chief of Janaleza, master of her fate for a few short weeks out of a lifetime.

She pulled herself together and a minute later had joined the *senhor* and their patient.

Nuno's frightening rigors and mind wandering had given place to quiet sleep, and the *senhor* said with a quiet smile that he would awake without fever in a few hours and would be ready for a bowl of soup.

"Why did he take the map, I wonder?" Morvenna watched the boyish, sleeping face, with its long lashes and slender nose that reminded her of Raya. Like this, fragile after his fever, Nuno was very much like his twin to look at.

She glanced across at the *senhor* and saw him studying Nuno with eyes that were suddenly fiercely blue. "Hidden treasure is like love," he said quietly. "A man has to find one or the other, and Nuno may have thought that if he found treasure he would be able to take you wherever you wished to go.''

A quick little flame of denial licked through Morvenna. She was fond of Nuno, but love was something else. Love was being aware of a man with every vein and nerve, as she had become aware of Roque. Love was knowing she would die a little when the steamer drew away from Janaleza, and the tall figure on the shore waved once more before striding off into the shadow of the jungle trees.

She forced a smile, which etched tautly her cheek-, bones and her lips. ''I am glad we burned the map. It can't hurt anyone else, or lead them astray.''

''Has Nuno been led astray?'' The blue eyes looked directly across at her; there was no evading them.

''Not deliberately,'' she said. ''I've never learned how to pretend anything I never really felt. I like Nuno, but I've never led him to think that when the time came for me to leave Janaleza, I would want him to go with me. He belongs on the island, as you do, *senhor*. As Raya does—as I, or Leird or Poppy, could never belong.''

She turned then and went from the hut. The old Indian cook had built a fire and was cooking a breakfast of fish and coffee. Morvenna ate hers sitting on a tree stump. The dark smoky coffee tasted good, and from here she could watch the activity of the Indian camp. The men had eaten their fill of *farina* and fish and were setting off with their brazilwood bows and quivers of arrows for a day's hunting in the forest.

There was a look of ageless vigor about these people, and in daylight Morvenna noticed the latticed designs on their upper bodies and limbs. Gourds of water were slung over their brown shoulders, and when they had disappeared like shadows into the bush, their women got down to their various tasks of grinding corn and spinning wild cotton on hand looms.

The younger children were free as the monkeys and birds to enjoy this strange Eden, but the older girls were given household tasks to perform, while the boys carved bows, or worked around the canoes.

The lively infants hid in the bush and peeped at Morvenna, but when she smiled and spoke to them, they scampered off in wild shyness. Their bare skins were as glossy as silk, and the wild sugarcane they sucked accounted for their polished teeth. She snapped off a piece herself and chewed it to clean her own teeth, as the *senhor* had advised her.

All at once she noticed that he was in conversation with a rather haughty-looking Incala, and her heartbeats quickened as he turned and came striding over to where she sat. The Incala watched, and Morvenna remembered seeing him last night, with the chief. In the dusk she had not noticed any specific details about him, but now she saw the scar running down his left cheek, a deep slash, long healed, slightly twisting the edge of his mouth.

She listened, all on edge, as the *senhor* told her that he had been asked to attend a palaver in the chief's hut.

"That Indian over there—" she caught at his arm and felt at once the tensing of his muscles "—is he the one— you know?" Her eyes met and were held by eyes so vividly blue they melted her bones and made her want to put her arms tightly around the bare, coppery shoulders. She wanted to jump up, to stand and shield him, to hold and never let go.

She died inside in case he guessed her feelings, for his glance had shifted to her fingers holding his arm, slim and white against his tanned skin.

"Cuchillo and I buried the lance long ago," he reassured her. "We are friends now."

"H-he doesn't look all that friendly—"

"I assure you he is." Warm fingers pressed hers.

"You are tired, *pequina*. Nervy and on edge from lack of sleep. The palaver will be a lengthy one, so why don't you go to the *choza* and rest in your hammock? Nuno will be all right. The old woman is keeping an eye on him."

"I . . . I don't think I could sleep," she protested.

"Have a try." He drew her to her feet, and she was exquisitely aware of his arm across her shoulders as he walked with her to the bamboo ladder of the hut they had been given to share. "Go along." He watched her climb the ladder to the doorway, then he swung around and walked away with the Incala he had scarred in the machete duel over Raya.

Morvenna kicked off her grass sandals and climbed into her hammock. She pillowed her head on her arms and rocked the hammock to try to ease the aching tension that gripped her. So this at last was love? This loss of self, this longing to be close, and closer still to just one man.

The rocking motion lulled her nerves and in a while she drifted off to sleep.

A RAIN SQUALL awoke her. The hut was almost dark and the rain was pounding against the roof, big drops bouncing through rents in the thatch. Something larger than a raindrop plopped onto Morvenna's hammock and she sat up with a drowsy cry of alarm. It scampered and leaped away into the shadows, a black lizard, almost the size of a frog.

Unnerved by the lizard, the fury of the rain, and the dimness that told her she had been asleep for a long time, Morvenna scrambled out of her hammock and made for the doorway of the hut. It was barred by rods of rain. It drove down out of the sky, steel-cold, lashing the trees and turning the ground to mud.

All the same, Morvenna didn't feel like staying here

alone. She sought her sandals and put them on. It wouldn't take her a minute to run through the rain to Nuno's hut—anything to escape being alone just now.

Tightening her *itipi* around her, she caught at the rungs of the wet ladder and made her way to the ground. The mud splashed coldly as she dived through the rain toward Nuno's hut. The rain was so blinding that she didn't see a tall figure emerge out of the trees; she ran full tilt into him. She gasped as hard arms closed around her. Her head went back and she blinked her rain-wet lashes as she met eyes dangerously blue in a face burnished to copper by the streaming rain.

"I was coming to you," he shouted through the noise of the squall.

"I was on my way to Nuno," she gasped.

"My faith—" she had never heard that tone from him before "—you must be anxious to be with him to chance a squall like this one!"

"No—" she shook her head "—it was awful being alone, the hut was dark, a-and I was worried about you—"

He stared down at her as the rain pelted them. "Why should you worry about me?" he demanded.

"We're getting wet to the skin." She tried to pull out of his arms, scared, confused, and excited by the blaze in this eyes. "Please, Roque—"

As she spoke his name, he said something that was half-strangled in his throat, then he swung her up into his arms and raced with her back to the hut she had just left. He pushed her up the ladder and she staggered inside, rain-wet, yet laughing. No man—surely no man treated a woman so roughly unless he cared for her as crazily as she cared for him!

He lit the lamp and they faced each other in its smoky light. He looked rather grim and dangerous, his black hair plastered to his forehead above eyes that burned.

Her eyes were as intense as the violets they resembled, and no longer laughing.

"Why should you worry about me?" he said again.

"Y-you know why...." She drew a step away from his tall, dark maleness; his look of being tried to the edge of something she didn't dare to put a name to.

"I don't know, but I would like to." He advanced on her retreat, and suddenly it was quiet outside and all around them. The rain had stopped as suddenly as it had started, and in the silence Morvenna heard the pounding of her heart.

"You've been good to me, *senhor*," she said breathlessly. "In your way...."

"My bossy way, eh?"

She nodded, and her smile came, and then went again. "He looked so fierce, the Incala you fought with—for Raya."

"Raya was a child, you realize. Both children were Brazilian and I wished them to be brought up at the *fazenda*." He was close now, and she could see every detail of his face, lean, proud, with something added that took her breath away. Her breath that seemed to die as his hands touched her waist, holding lightly, holding with intention.

"Let me tell you something." He spoke with a fleeting smile. "Raya came to see me the day after the fire at the Indian village. She told me that she loved Flavio, and that she wished for my consent to their marriage. She had been a little afraid of my reaction because of Flavio's mixed blood, but as it happens I like the young man. He is a hard worker and full of initiative, and most sensible men settle down once they become family men. I gave my consent, and their marriage will take place at Manaos in a few weeks, then they will return to Janaleza for a cermony that will please the islanders."

"But I thought...." Morvenna couldn't go on; his closeness was too much, added to what he had just said.

"I know what you thought." He stroked the damp hair out of her eyes. "It was at times convenient to let you think that I wanted Raya. It would not have done, *carestia*, to let you guess in the heart of the rain forest that I wanted you."

The incredible words in the silence of the hut, and then his warm hands were cupping her face. *"Minha querida?"* It was a question, a doubt, and she had never seen him doubtful before. She touched his hair, the strong neck, his shoulders.... It was as though touch had to tell her that he really had called her his darling.

She felt him go tense at her touch, and then his lips were on hers without mercy. The fierceness of his embrace and his kisses was a pain she reveled in. In a timeless void her lips and her arms clung to him.

Then he held her with more quietness, there against his shoulder, and her heart sang.

"We, too, will be married at Manaos," he murmured, "but the islanders will expect to celebrate our marriage as my parents' was celebrated. We will walk under the hibiscus arch together, *cara*, into the jungle, then in their eyes we will be husband and wife."

She couldn't speak. It was too wonderful that a dream could come true, and she might find she only dreamed if she spoke.

"Lift your lashes." The old command was in his voice. "Look at me."

She did so, shyly, and for a long moment he read in her eyes what she couldn't speak of—not yet. "For a terrible moment—" he gave a shaken laugh "—I thought my plans for the future did not appeal to you."

"I love them," she said huskily. "I love you—Roque."

"Rock?" He mocked her mispronunciation. "Do you think me a hard man?"

"I am not going to tell you what I think, *senhor*." Laughter came into her eyes. "I don't want a conceited husband!"

His arms tightened again when she used the word husband.

"Roque, is it true?" she whispered. "Do you really love me?"

"From the moment I found you on the shore, my beloved castaway." He kissed her hair. "But it was something I could not speak of because my home is on a jungle island, my life is here, and I could not tell if you could settle here, or even if you could love a man of a different nationality and culture from your own. Then came these days alone in the jungle, and I knew that you had the courage to live here. I could only hope that you had the love to live here with me."

"I have the love." She smiled. "The thought of going away on Friday was unbearable. I think I would have got lost again in the jungle rather than board that steamer."

"Don't worry." He quirked a black eyebrow. "Having found that you had courage as well as everything else I desired, I intended to bribe the Incala paddlers to get us lost on the return journey to the *fazenda*. One way or another I was keeping you here, my Senhorinha Fayr."

THE CASTLE OF THE SEVEN LILACS

The Castle
of the
Seven Lilacs

Siran was a dancer, entranced by beauty and music—and the ghost of an old love. Kurt was an Austrian aristocrat, as ruthless and dangerous as the mountains he strove to conquer.

They were as different as fire and ice. Siran couldn't make herself like Kurt, yet she couldn't be indifferent to him.

But when fate inevitably brought them together, love took hold of their lives....

CHAPTER ONE

A BUSY MORNING at the Danube Coffee House had just tapered off, and the young English waitress was taking a well-earned rest in the kitchen when Rudi, one of the musicians, came to tell her that a Baron von Linden was asking for her by name. The Herr Baron requested an interview with her right away.

Siran stared at Rudi in amazement. "Whatever can an Austrian baron want with me?" she exclaimed. "Do you think he's anything to do with the opera house?"

Rudi shrugged. "He could be. Now off with your cap and apron, and go at once to speak with this man." Rudi broke into a smile. "He looks very important and rather impatient."

"Oh dear." Her hands fumbled nervously with the sash of her apron and her cap. "There, do I look all right?"

"For a girl who has been busy all morning you look amazing to me."

She smiled. Rudi was her kind friend, and having worked at one time in London he could speak to her in her own tongue. He always said the encouraging thing, but before entering the dining room of the café she took a quick look at herself in the wall mirror. Her glossy red brown hair was bobbed smoothly to the line of her cheekbones, and her face had a delicate kind of strength and independence. A small cross on a chain filled the hollow of her throat, where a pulse beat nervously as she left the kitchen and made for the large dining room, now empty except for a couple of waiters clearing the tables and a tall figure standing near the door.

Siran hesitated to approach him, for he looked intimidating in a gray overcoat with an astrakhan collar. He beat impatient time with a pair of driving gloves, and the cool sunlight through the window shone on his crest of silvery hair. Siran thought he must be middle-aged. Then he met her eyes and she quickly changed her mind. There was a piercing quality to his looks, a gleam of lake-gray beneath his heavy eyelids.

He was a man in complete command of himself and a total stranger to her.

"You are Miss Siran Winters." His English was faultless, his accent slightly grating. "The young woman who was among those saved from a hotel fire about five weeks ago, in a courtyard just off the Ringstrasse?"

She stared at his firm features, tanned no doubt by the mountain sports indulged in by men of his virile stamp. "Yes." She spoke clearly, though he made her heart thump with a certain alarm. "I was staying at the hotel that caught fire, and my name is Winters."

"*Guten Tag.*" His look of autocracy gave way to something more human. With a click of his heels he gave her a formal bow. "I have had some trouble finding you, Miss Winters. Why are you working in a *Kaffeehaus* when I am informed that you are a dancer? I understand that you were to dance in the corps de ballet at the opera house."

His gray eyes took in her black silk dress with its frilly white cuffs, the copper shine of her hair and the wand slimness of a girl trained for ballet.

"I hurt my ankle at the time of the fire and another girl took my place in the company. I am working here until there is another vacancy for a dancer.... I thought, Herr Baron, that you might be connected with the opera house. Aren't you?"

"Not in any capacity." A trace of a smile touched his lips as if the idea amused him. "My business with you has nothing at all to do with your career, except that it might be said that it was extremely fortunate your career brought you to Vienna. Why was that?"

"The ballet company I was dancing with in England had the sad misfortune to lose it director, and there were debts to pay off. All of us, apart from the principals, found ourselves out of a job. My teacher, who is Austrian, arranged that I dance here in Vienna. Then the night I arrived the fire broke out." Siran gave a rueful little shrug. "I twisted my ankle climbing out on to a windowsill with a baby in my arms...anyway, you don't want to hear about that."

"On the contrary." His gazed seemed to pierce her. "I am here because of the child you saved from the flames that night."

Even as she looked astonished by what he said, he was glancing around the café at the bare tables and frowning at the lingering aroma of food. "Can you get away for an hour?" he asked abruptly. "We cannot talk here, and I have something to say to you that requires a calm, unhurried answer."

Siran hesitated, then remembering the child with whom she had crouched on a windowsill that night, she became curious about this tall stranger whose white gold hair was in such contrast to his sun-weathered features. Her eyes flicked across his mouth and she felt that it expressed a man of deep, controlled passions. He looked like a man who could be kind to those he cared for, but merciless toward those who made an enemy of him. This she felt keenly. It was all there in his strong face with its thrusting cheekbones.

"Yes, I can get away for a while, but I must be back by teatime, when trade picks up again." Her brown eyes met his, shy and intrigued and aware of him as a haughty baron. "Will you excuse me while I get my coat?"

He inclined his head, "I will await you in my car, which is parked just around the corner."

She hastened to the cloakroom, where Rudi was smoking a cigarette and awaiting her with a friendly smile. "Well, is he a patron of the arts who has offered you a fabulous contract?"

"Nothing so good." She smiled regretfully as she slipped into her tweed coat and buttoned the collar high about her slender neck. "I think the Baron von Linden has some connection with the child I snatched out of his crib the night of the fire. I expect he has traced me in order to offer me some sort of a reward...he's very formal and serious about it all. I couldn't refuse to take a short drive in his car."

"Be careful, *Liebchen*." Rudi's smile faded. "A certain arrogance lingers still in these men of the old Austrian nobility. That *savoir rein* is not assumed, and young women are impressed by it. It's part of the privilege of being born with a crested spoon in your mouth."

She laughed, for Rudi disarmed her rather than alarmed her. He made her feel the security of having a good friend to turn to in a strange city. "I'll be careful," she promised. "I don't really think the baron has a roving eye, but I will admit that a girl can't always be sure of a man's motives. Anyway, I'm probably too slim to appeal to an Austrian. Don't you like your women to be blond and buxom?"

"I am Viennese." Rudi took her hand and kissed her wrist. "We admire a pretty face and a fine-boned ankle."

"Which is all very nice, Rudi, but I haven't time to stay and be flirted with. The baron is waiting for me."

She ran through the café and out of the door into the

cool sunshine of Vienna in the autumn. As always she was aware of a magic and charm in the air, memories of the waltz kings and the Imperial guardsmen. As she passed by, there still hung about an old courtyard an air of having seen exciting times. Here the handsome *kavaliers* had leaped upon their black horses, resplendent in their scarlet and blue. *Der Rosenkavalier* had been alive in all its gaiety...and yet Vienna still whispered of romance. Of lovers who met in the woods of Wienerwald in the springtime, when the lilacs and lindens were out in bloom.

She paused beside a black Mercedes and the occupant opened the door for her. She slid inside and was at once aware of the things Rudi had warned her about. She cast a faintly nervous glance at the baron's aloof profile and was reassured. He was not interested in her as a young ballet dancer, a stranger to his country. He had something else on his mind.

He drove along the Ringstrasse in silence, leaving her to her thoughts...and suddenly they were filled again by the clamor of fire alarms, the cries of people in distress and the frightened sobs of a child left abandoned in a hotel room. She kept her eyes averted from the courtyard where the burned hotel was boarded up; silent now, empty and forlorn, its scorched signpost still hanging above the door.

It still seemed a sad omen to Siran that a thing so terrible should have happened on her first visit to Vienna. She had arrived with such high hopes, but they had tumbled down, and her single consolation was that she had awoken to the smell of smoke and saved the life of a child.

"What impression have you formed of Vienna?"

She gave a start as the baron spoke and saw the Burggarten looming ahead of them, a rambling place of lawns and birds and half-hidden steps leading to secret places. "Vienna has an old-world charm about it," she murmured. "I love it."

"You young people find the word 'love' very easy to say." There was a sardonic note in his voice, as if he thought her naïve and unaware of what love really meant. Her heart felt that familiar ache. She had been privileged to know Cassian, the great *premier danseur*, and in her young and unawakened way she had loved him. He had been so wise and so kind at times and had predicted that one day she would be a real ballerina. It was still her cherished dream; she would not let go of it for anyone, not in any circumstances.

"I'm not a child, Herr Baron." She spoke stiffly. "You asked my opinion of Vienna."

"You appear from your reply to fall in love very easily."

"It's in the nature of a dancer to have lots of imagination." She defended herself. "I can feel the magic in the atmosphere of Vienna. I can see it in the lovely old buildings and in the faces of the people."

"What do you see in my face, *Fräulein*?"

His question startled her, and she had no way of answering him frankly. She saw strength in his face, a controlled passion and a certain relentless irony, as if at some time someone had made it hard for him to forgive a broken dream. Siran knew about dreams. As a mere girl of fifteen, straight from ballet school to the Cassian Company, she had looked at the lean, dark, gifted director and dreamed of growing up to become his partner... perhaps his girl. She had known there were other women, ballerinas with striking looks and graceful talents, but always when he spoke to her there had seemed a waiting look in his dark eyes.

Jewish on his mother's side, he had given her a special name. Feigileh, little bird.

"I see a question in your eyes, Herr Baron. You want to ask me about the fire."

"Can you bear to talk of it?"

"I think so, although it was very terrible. Some people died."

"I know." His tone was somber, and he was driving steadily toward the outskirts of the city, to where the Vienna Woods loomed in their autumn colors against the distant mountains. There was snow on the peaks, and soon it would mantle the sides of the hills and the long ski trails would gleam darkly against the white.

Her bobbed hair swung against her cheek as she glanced at the baron. "Are you a relative of the little boy?" She recalled the very fair hair, the large blue eyes filled with tears, the expensive shawl in which she had wrapped the child in order to carry him to safety.

"Yes." There was a long pause, and the car went faster, as if he needed to feel in control of the life and force of the powerful engine. Soon they were on the edge of the woods, driving in the shadow of the slender trees of Wienerwald, where masses of tinted foliage etched itself against the autumn sky, gilded like the sun before sinking to the ground.

All at once the car came to a grinding halt, and as the engine throbbed, the baron turned to look at Siran, the gray eyes piercing her, a deep groove between his brows. Then he patted his pockets and took out a cigarette case. "Will you smoke, Miss Winters?"

"No, thanks. It's bad for a dancer, who needs all her wind."

"You will permit me the indulgence?" Again his smile was saturnine, as if her youthful seriousness amused him. As if to be a dancer was a flighty thing.

He applied the flame of his lighter to his cigarette and smoke jetted from the nostrils of his dominant nose. He wasn't exactly a handsome man, but he was distinguished, well built, and well dressed. A man to be obeyed rather than liked at first glance. Well, she had come this far with him, but if he meant to offer her some reward for a humane act, then she would have to refuse him. It would be hard enough to talk about that night.

"So you have had bad luck since arriving in Vienna?" He leaned back in his seat so he could study her. "And now you are working as a waitress. Such work cannot be too congenial for a ballet dancer. Did you not think of returning to England?"

"Yes, I thought about it." Suddenly her heart was aching again; she lowered her gaze and her lashes made shadows on her cheeks. "But my reason for leaving was to get away from a personal sadness, and there seemed little chance of finding a place in a ballet company. There are only a few good ones and they are filled to capacity. It was a choice between dancing in pantomime, or coming to Vienna. I chose to come here and I'll stay if there is a chance of dancing at the opera house. If not, I'll work at the coffee house until I have saved enough money to go on to Paris. I am ambitious, you see. I have made up my mind to become a dancer with a good company."

"There is no one in England to raise objections?"

"I was brought up by a couple of kind, elderly aunts, who have since died. I have no one, Herr Baron."

"Then the girl who falls in love with cities is not so vulnerable when it comes to young men, eh?" Blue gray smoke drifted about the gray eyes etched by lines of authority. "You have never let love for a person overrule your desire for a career?"

Siran thought this conversation had taken a very personal turn, and it faintly annoyed her that he should talk about love, that gift you gave without asking that it be returned. It couldn't be, not always, and this man looked the demanding sort. He would see love in a different light from her.

"So you intend to stay in Austria for the next few months, working as a waitress, carrying trays from table to table and too tired at the end of the day to keep up with what I believe is a strict training."

"I—I have to live," she said defensively. "I have to pay the rent of my apartment. I am untrained for anything but being quick on my feet."

"Quite so." He stubbed his cigarette and was not looking at her as he said quietly, "Tell me about that night at the hotel. I wish to know exactly what occurred."

"You speak as if you have a right to know."

"Believe me, Miss Winters, I have every right."

Again that somber note grated in his voice, and when she looked at him she saw a profile hard with tension, except for the movement of a muscle in his jaw.

"You said you could speak of it...it is equally hard for me to listen."

Her hands clenched together on her lap and she fixed her gaze on the Vienna Woods, as if it helped to look at living things when she had to speak of fire and the terrible death it had brought to three people.

She heard the sound of her own voice, speaking to this man who was a stranger, yet who was strangely linked to what had happened after she had awoken that night to the choking fumes and smoke. She had scrambled into her dressing gown and dashed out into the corridor, where the smoke was even worse, catching in her throat, smarting her eyes and alerting her to the fear of fire in every human being. She had run toward the staircase in the hope of escaping that way, and it was then she heard a child crying in a room with its door flung wide open.

By the time she had snatched the child out of its

crib—there had been no one else in the room—the flames had reached the stairs and she had returned to her room, closed the door and climbed out on to a fairly wide windowsill where she and the baby could at least breathe freely.

It had seemed like hours, crouching there on the sill, in pain from a twisted ankle, trying her best to comfort the child. Then out of the smoky darkness, shot with flame and filled with cries, had loomed a ladder and the reassuring face of a fireman.

"You are a brave young woman," they said to her. "But who is the child? Is he yours?"

She could only shake her head. She knew nothing about him, beyond that he was well cared for and about a year old. He was also a handsome youngster, with a pair of deep blue eyes and hair so fair it was silvery.

Had she noticed the number of the room in which she had found him?

No, but she could tell them it had been about four doors away from her own room. And later, after checking the duplicate register found undamaged in the safe, it had been found that the room was part of a suite booked by a Frau Kristy. Whoever she was, whoever she had been, was uncertain. She had not been among the people rescued, and when later a woman's body was found in the wreckage, it was assumed that she had abandoned the child and been caught in her flight by the flames.

Siran gave a shiver. What sort of a woman could leave her child all alone like that, to perhaps die from suffocation?

Silence followed her story, and when she glanced at the baron she found him looking rather drawn. In his hand he was holding a blackened chain and pendant, and with some difficulty, for the catch was damaged, he opened it and showed Siran a pair of painted miniatures inside. Though somewhat blurred they were recognizable. A young woman with a pretty oval-shaped face framed by soft gold hair and a young man with a rather dreamy dark face, handsome in a Byronic way.

Siran gave the baron a questioning look.

"This was found on the body of the dead woman," he said huskily. "It belonged to my young sister Kristy and was traced to our family about a week after the fire."

"How terrible!" Siran touched his hand with involuntary sympathy. "I am so sorry for you. Then the child...?"

"Unquestionably the child was hers." He snapped the locket shut and plunged it into his pocket. "Kristy was not happy at home. She ran away from Mayholtzen about twenty months ago. Mayholtzen is in the mountains and something occurred around that time that made her hate the place. She may have known that she was to have a child...we certainly didn't."

He drew a deep sigh. "It was not until I saw the boy that I realized the truth. The boy's likeness to his mother, combined with the locket found on the dead girl, confirmed my own and official opinion that she had been my sister. The name she used was Frau Kristy, and I now believe that she may have been on her way home to Mayholtzen. She had stayed away from us long enough and decided to bring her son home."

He gazed somberly from the window of the car. "Then came the fire, and it was typical of Kristy to run away again. Always she has run away in a crisis, thinking of no one but herself. This time—" he shrugged his broad shoulders "—she ran into something from which there was no escape."

"Did you never try to find her?" Siran asked.

"Of course I did. I am not quite a man of stone." He looked angrily at Siran, and she drew away from him, seeing the power in his body and sensing something of the fear and uncertainty that must have been felt by his young sister when she found herself in trouble.

"I found her soon after she left us," he went on. "She was living with a friend at Interlaken. I told her she could come home any time she wished, but she refused. She said the castle and the surroundings had grown hateful to her. She would do as she pleased, and I could return to Mayholtzen and tell the rest of the family that she was now living her own life. My mother was extremely upset, of course. And later on Kristy told us nothing of the child we had some right to know about. You see, Miss Winters, she had a sweetheart, and he died from a mountain fall. He was the father of the boy. I am sure of it. If only she had let me know she was in Vienna I could have come for her and the tragedy need never have happened."

His eyes dwelt broodingly on Siran's face. "She was so impulsive, and it worries me that she may have been a little frightened of me. Do I look such a bear? No, she kept everything to herself and chose to conduct her life as if it were an operetta. She kept me from knowing my nephew for a whole year . . . he is a fine child. I think she must have been proud of him, in her way."

Siran supposed so and tried not to think of the baby crying all alone in that smoke-filled room.

"You could not have run and left your child in that way, eh?" Suddenly he reached for Siran's hand and enfolded it in his own. "We have you to thank for the boy. You saved his life, Miss Winters, and you must be rewarded—"

"No—" she broke in "—it's reward enough that he's with you, safe and sound."

"I have to insist." He smiled, but she saw the look of command in his eyes. "I came looking for you so I could express my own gratitude and my mother's. She invites you to come to Mayholtzen to meet her, and to perhaps stay for a holiday."

"That's so kind of her, but I couldn't—"

"You are full of refusals." His smile became slightly dangerous. "It is hardly good for a dancer to work as a waitress. Not only is the occupation a tiring one but you will find no time to keep up with your training." He paused as if to let these words sink in. "You are aware that your talent could become impaired. Then what will happen to you?"

"I am young, Herr Baron, and only as yet a dancer in a corps de ballet."

"But all the same you value your talent? You have talked of being ambitious for the future."

"Yes."

"Therefore would it not be better for you to enjoy the freedom of our mountains for a few weeks, where you will not be rushed off your feet in a coffee house?"

"I need the money I earn. It's kind of you to invite me to your home at Mayholtzen, and I'm sure I would have enjoyed such a change of scenery, but it just isn't possible."

"I see no impossibility," he said suavely. "If you are concerned about money, then it is no effort for me to write a check."

"I'm sure it isn't!" Color stormed into her cheeks. "But I happen to be an independent person and I wouldn't dream of accepting money from you."

"The boy's life is worth every penny I have, Miss Winters. It would give me pleasure to make you financially secure for a year, let us say, until you are established with a good ballet company."

"No." She shook her head firmly, and her pewter hair bobbed against her cheeks. "I like to stand on my own two feet, and I don't wish to be known as a dancer who was kept by an Austrian baron—"

He laughed sardonically. "I would not advertise it, *Fräulein*. It would be our secret."

"When a thing is kept secretive it always seems worse when someone else stumbles on to it. You're generous, Herr Baron, but my answer is no, thank you. I like to work for my living. I like the feeling of self-respect."

"You are very British," he said, and his grip tightened on her wrist. "You won't give in without a fight."

"I won't give in if we sit here till the moon rises!" She tried to pull her hand free of his and found steel in his fingers. "Nor will I beg, Baron. But I will remind you that I am a visitor to Austria, and so far I have found only courtesy and gaiety, and respect for the ways of a stranger."

"Obstinate as well as fearless, eh?" He smiled down into her eyes, and she was abruptly aware of being alone with him in his car, on the edge of the Vienna Woods.

"I—I must be getting back to the coffee house," she said. "Herr Wilder will sack me if I'm not there to serve the teatime customers. I had trouble finding work, being English, and I can't afford to lose this job."

"What if I offered you another...at Seven Lilacs?"

Her eyes looked into his, large and startled. Brown eyes with little gold lights in them and a faun slant to their corners. Rather unusual eyes for an English girl, but then her mother had been a rather wild young Cornish girl who had liked to wander the beaches and the moors and who had pined away the winter her young husband Tor did not return from a fishing trip to Arctic waters. He and all his crew had died at sea in a fearful storm, but Siran had been but a baby and all she remembered of her childhood was being reared by a pair of kind, elderly aunts. Without spoiling her they had not stopped her from following her dream of becoming a dancer. She had a natural, willowy grace inherited from her mother, who had climbed the cliffs and roamed the moorlands up until the day Siran was born. The aunts said always that she had her mother's eyes and her agility, but from her seaman father she had the heritage of independence and the will to face up to life fearlessly.

She looked at the Baron von Linden and thought of the strange twist of fate that had brought about their meeting. She saw that he had the strength of will to get what he wanted and equally the pride to turn his back if he found himself unwanted. He had done so in the case of his young sister, Kristy.

He was an intriguing man, Siran had to admit, and though capitulation would be easier than argument with him, why should she give in to him? What possible sort of a job could he offer her? And what sort of a place was Seven Lilacs? It was a romantic name, but she mustn't be carried away by that.

He must have read the questions in her eyes, for he replied to them without being asked. "Our castle in the mountains is known as Seven Lilacs. The trees were planted by an ancestress of mine, and in the springtime they bloom all shades of mauve, violet and pink. There is a legend that while the lilacs bloom at Mayholtzen there will always be Lindens at the castle. You have made the legend come true for young Lorenz. Now he will grow up at the castle, and I find it hard to put into words the gratitude I feel. Miss Winters, I offer you a position in my household if you will not stay as my guest."

"What sort of a position?" Though interested she forced herself to look and speak coolly. As she had admitted to Rudi...a girl could never be really sure of a man's motives.

"As dancing teacher at the local school in the valley. It's a rather delightful place, and I am sure the young girls would enjoy being taught ballet. What do you say, Miss Winters?"

"I don't know what to say, Herr Baron. Surely the staff at the school is chosen by the local authorities, and it would be for them to add a dancing teacher to the payroll."

A trace of a smile quirked his lip. "Mayholtzen and its valley belong to my family. I am part of the local authority, and if I put forward the idea that it would be educational for the schoolgirls to learn the art of ballet, then very few objections will be raised."

"You mean you hold a rather feudal position at Mayholtzen?" Siran said dryly. "Your word is law?"

"My suggestions are not enforced, nor do the people lick my boots, but as the head of an old established family I have a voice in what goes on. Though the old titles mean less in this modern age, the people of the mountains like the idea of a baron to whom they can bring their troubles. My brother Kurt is always a little amused, or he pretends to be. You may have heard of Kurt von Linden? He risks his neck bobsledding and winning ski trophies when he isn't climbing mountains."

"I know the name of every renowned dancer," Siran said with a smile, "but I'm afraid I don't know much about sportsmen."

"Then it will make a change for Kurt to meet a young woman who has not fallen in love with his picture in the magazines."

"I haven't said I'll come to the castle."

"But you will come."

"You don't ask, you command."

"It is only my way. Does it stiffen your resistance?"

"Yes, a little. Do you intend to pay my wage yourself?"

"Would you object to that?"

"Only if you offer me a ridiculously high sum."

"I promise not to." He smiled sardonically. "I dare not corrupt that shining independence of yours."

"I suppose I'll be expected to live at the castle?"

"My mother the baroness will expect you to do so."

"Your brother Kurt is also staying there?"

"At present. He plans to climb a mountain we call the Glass Turret. Some time ago he attempted it with a party that included that young man of Kristy's. Helmut fell, and Kristy blamed Kurt for the accident. He feels he must conquer the mountain, and I won't persuade him to abandon the climb. He must make up his own mind."

"You are not allowing me to make up mine," Siran protested. "You want me to say right away that I'll come to Mayholtzen. You feel you owe me something, but you don't owe me a thing."

"Perhaps I owe the world a dancer. With us you would have the freedom and the atmosphere in which to keep trim, so that when the time comes for you to join a corps de ballet you will be ready for it. You will not be run down and tired from a tedious job. Come, your dancing instincts must respond to what I offer you."

"They do," she admitted. "I'd be foolish to turn down such a chance, but I can't come right away. The proprietor of the coffee house was good enough to give me a job, so I must give in my notice and work there another fortnight."

Baron von Linden frowned. "If I spoke to him he would release you from the necessity to work off your notice. Won't you permit me to do so?"

Siran shook her head. "You must play fair, *mein Herr*. You are a little too ready to take control of people and events, and that may have been why Kristy was afraid of you."

"Are you afraid of me?" His eyes challenged her. "Do I seem a hard, demanding man to you, one who has no understanding of the fears and affections of a young woman?"

"You are one of the strong people," she replied. "The world can't frighten you, so you are yourself a little frightening. People sense your impatience with their weaknesses."

"What a brute I am," he drawled. "Dare you come after all to Seven Lilacs?"

"If you dare me, Herr Baron, how can I resist?" She smiled, but meeting his lake-gray eyes beneath those brooding lids she felt her heartbeats quicken with the alarm he engendered. "Is your brother Kurt like you?"

"Does it worry you in case you find yourself in the mountains with a pair of tyrants instead of one?" A smile of irony gleamed in his eyes. "Well, Miss Winters, I am going to leave you to decide for yourself about Kurt. I am but a man, so what would I know about the reactions of the female heart."

"You are too modest, Baron. I am sure you are rarely at a loss to understand women. You struck at my weak spot right away; you knew I couldn't resist anything to do with ballet, so you contrived this job for me. What if I am a bad dancer?"

"I am certain you are a good one." His eyes flicked her slender body in the tweed coat and dwelt on her face with its faun-brown eyes above the delicate definition of her cheekbones. An elusively attractive face, lighting up in a smile, a little sad in repose. A dancer's face, just as her legs and ankles were fine to look at and yet supple and sure in performance.

"I imagine if your ballet company had not come to grief you would soon have danced solo?"

"I hoped for that. Our director had confidence in me." She bit her lip, for it hurt to talk about the lean, dark man who had told no one that he was suffering heart pains the night of the *Sleeping Beauty* ballet. Dear Cassian, exciting and terrific, who had died after dancing the Blue Bird *pas de deux*. Still with a flying movement he had entered the wings, and there he had dropped like a shot bird. They had been stunned, all of them, and then had come the pain, the cruel realization, that never again would Cassian, the kind tyrant, dance or direct, or look at a girl with a waiting smile deep in his dark eyes.

"There will never be another Cassian," she said quietly.

"You cared for him?"

"Yes." She met with a frank directness the gray eyes of Baron von Linden. "To know him was to love him."

"Such people are rare, *Fräulein*. One usually needs to adjust to an attraction, to assess its meaning, to feel the magic deepen or decline. Perhaps your feeling for this man was a form of hero worship...you are but a girl even yet."

"Girls grow up fast in a ballet environment. Ballet is an art in which the body has to be understood if it is to express correctly all the emotions."

The baron stared at her, the glint of his eyes under the heavy eyelids a disturbing combination. Then with a startlingly quick movement he caught her by the shoulders and pulled her to him. Her swift reaction was to fight his touch. Her entire being was shocked into protecting itself...and then he started to laugh.

"You are as innocent as the day you were weaned," he mocked. "Do you need this pretense because I invite you to my castle? The wicked baron and the ballerina!" He laughed dryly. "You are a nervy young thing. Not at all the controlled, efficient heroine I expected to find."

"I'm sorry to disappoint you." She felt his hands still holding her and wanted to wriggle out of them, to retreat into a corner of the car, away from the power of his body. To be close to him was to be aware of the primitive things between a woman and a man. Dusk was falling in the woods, and he was a masterful stranger.

Then he did the most prosaic thing. He glanced at the watch on his wrist. "It grows late and I have to attend to my business. Could you travel to Mayholtzen on your own, in two weeks' time?"

"I traveled to Vienna on my own." She could smile now, with the relief of being released. "I'm really a very efficient person and perfectly able to take care of myself."

"You make me wonder if you will change your mind about coming to the castle."

"If I promise, then I won't break my word."

"The baroness would be most disappointed. You saved her grandchild and it was at her insistence I came to Vienna to find you."

"Your mother may not find me a very dramatic heroine."

"She will find you a very human one, Miss Winters."

After that he drove her back through the falling dusk to the coffee house, and there by the car he bent over her hand and clicked his heels in that imperious way, making her think of operettas about princes who fell in love with poor girls they were forbidden to marry.

"Until we meet again, *Fräulein*. You will hear from the baroness. She will send instructions for your journey to Mayholtzen."

"*Auf Wiedersehn*." She half smiled at him.

He looked into her eyes. "*Ja*, in two weeks I will see you again, Miss Winters. *Auf Wiedersehn*."

She watched the Mercedes drive away, the street lamps glimmering on the dark shape of it until it was lost to sight. She had a feeling of having made a promise she was half afraid to keep. Yet she should feel excited by the prospect of staying at a castle in the mountains and of being able to practice her beloved ballet at this village school in a valley.

She had struck it lucky. Yet when she thought of that

strong, formidable Austrian face she was unsure as never before in her life. There were elements of tragedy to meet with at his castle home. A girl had fled from it, her sweetheart lost to her in a fall while climbing with Kurt von Linden. Kristy had blamed her brother Kurt for that fall, and in her unhappiness she had run away to Switzerland to bear her child alone.

As Siran entered the *Kaffeehaus* to begin her evening's work, she heard the voice of Frau Wilder ordering her to put on her cap and apron. There were trays to carry, customers to serve, a busy time ahead of them.

Siran realized that she need tolerate this kind of work for only two more weeks, and suddenly she smiled. Whatever awaited her at Seven Lilacs, it could not be as tedious as carrying trays of cakes and coffee back and forth. Herr Wilder was a jovial man, but his wife had a sharp voice, and right now she was hustling Siran into the kitchen, scolding and clucking like an agitated hen with a truant chicken.

"Frau Wilder," Siran faced her with a flash of her brown eyes. "I wish to give in my notice. I will be returning to my ballet dancing and leaving the coffee house in two weeks' time."

CHAPTER TWO

SIRAN TRAVELED by train to the mountain village of Mayholtzen, and from the window she watched the scenery flash by. It was fascinating to pass vineyards at the outset of her journey and then to come in sight of the snowy peaks with a spread of forest around them, deepening into valleys where farmsteads clung to the hillsides.

Even as the train sped beneath the shadow of the mountains snow began to fall, drifting down past the windows like little white feathers. It was like traveling into a wintry picture of blue white crags and chalets set among pine trees.

Siran began to feel excited and a trifle apprehensive. She had left behind her the security of a job in Vienna to come and teach the schoolgirls of a valley school the intricate art of ballet. The end result could be wholly charming, like a fairytale come to life, but it was hard work and she was glad she was taking on girls who were used to skating and skiing. Their young bodies would be supple and they would have a sense of rhythm and timing. She had started training when she was nine, and at the age of twelve she had started her *pointe* work. She had learned stillness and poise, lightness and grace, and all this she had to teach these children, with the hope in mind that they would enjoy it, and their parents would approve of the lessons.

Wisely or not she had chosen to come to Mayholtzen,

and she could feel her senses responding to the pic-
turesque views glimpsed through a ballet of snowflakes.
The train thundered through a tunnel cut into the mountains, and when it broke out on the other side it slackened speed as a small station came into sight.

Siran jerked her Robin Hood cap down over one eye
and looked rakishly attractive in a tan suede jacket, a
short skirt and green jester boots. Reaching for her suitcase and the smaller case which held the things she
would need as a ballet mistress she waited for the train
to come to a standstill before alighting onto the platform. She breathed the tang of pine and fir trees and
saw the smallness of the station set against a tapestry of
wooded hills and snowbound peaks.

She had arrived at Mayholtzen, and she stood a moment, feeling tiny and overawed, as the train whistle
echoed up the slopes and the train slowly gathered speed
and left her alone on this wayside platform. Everything
was very quiet, and as Siran stood and felt the snowflakes on the wind she had the lonely feeling of having
been dropped off in the mountains with no one to care,
after all, that she was here.

No one had come to meet her, as the baroness had
promised in her letter, unless the man awaited her outside the station. She picked up her suitcase and walked
to the barrier. There was no one to take her ticket, so
she left it on the ledge and passed through the turnstile.
On the narrow road fronting the station, not a soul was
in sight. No man, no black Mercedes, nothing but hills
all around and already a thick furring of snow on the
road that sloped into the mountains. She felt her heart
sink a little...and then give a bound as a figure
appeared suddenly from among the trees and the crunch
of his footfalls on the snowy road drew nearer and
nearer.

He was tall and broad in the shoulder, and Siran

braced herself for her second meeting with the Baron von Linden. His long strides had brought him within a couple of yards of her tensed young figure when she realize that this man was a stranger to her. . .a stranger who was yet familiar.

He had a mane of tawny hair sweeping back from a pair of arresting blue eyes. He wore a chunky sweater over ski trousers tucked into leather boots, and Siran knew in an instant that he was no manservant sent to meet her.

His gaze passed over her from eyes that were as brilliantly blue as the tip of an iceberg and about as friendly.

"*Guten Tag, Fräulein.*" His voice was deep and crisp and cool as snow. "I take it you are the ballet teacher, though for a moment I thought you had come out of the woods."

A flush stung her cheeks at the way he looked her over, taking in her rakish cap of green and her slim legs beneath the short hem of her skirt. She was about to answer him when he introduced himself as Kurt von Linden. . .the trophy-winning brother whose manner matched his name.

"The baroness planned to come and meet you, Miss Winters, but then it started to snow again. She is like a cat who prefers the warmth of a fire to the feel of the wind." A smile quirked the arrogant lines of his mouth. "We are having an early winter this year, or have you brought it with you?"

Siran put a hand to the flying bird brooch on her lapel, a quiet fire in her eyes as they dwelt upon this man's unfriendly face. He was mahogany brown from the mountain sports, and this made his eyes glint even more above a set of rugged features. This was the man from whom Kristy had fled; it was he who had invited her dark-eyed young man to join a climb from which he had not returned. In a flash all Siran's doubts came rushing back, and if the train had been standing in the station at this moment she would have snatched up her suitcase and dashed away from a man who seemed as hard as the rock and ice and danger of this mountain country.

He looked down into her wide brown eyes and seemed to read them. "Have you been warned about me?" he drawled. "Have you heard that I am dangerous to know?"

"I know about your sister Kristy. I have been told her story," Siran admitted.

He picked up her suitcase with a deliberate movement and glanced toward the station. "I don't think you have had much to do with people like us, Miss Winters. You are a city girl, a dancer who is used to the bustle and gaiety of a theater. You might find a winter at Mayholtzen not much to your liking. When the snows fall hard we at the castle are sometimes cut off from civilization, and then the things that have happened to us begin to play on our nerves. You as a stranger might be caught like a moth in our web of drama. The castle is like that. One has to love its isolation, or it can seem like a place of captivity."

His eyes were narrowed against the snow glare as he turned to gaze up the mountainside. "You would be wise, I think, to await the four-thirty train that will carry you back to Vienna."

Siran's fingers clenched the brooch that was her talisman. It had been a gift from Cassian on her birthday last year, and now to feel the little gemmed wings was to regain a measure of her composure. "I have come to take up a job at Mayholtzen," she said. "I can't walk out on it...because you don't happen to want me at the castle. Your brother the baron offered me the position, and your mother wrote me a charming letter endorsing his offer.''

"Have you taught in a school before?"

"I don't think that is any of your affair, *mein Herr*." Annoyance tautened her slender figure, and yet she still felt tiny and somehow insignificant beside this man. There was an arrogant strength about him, vital and un-tamed as the mountains he set out to conquer. There was a devil in him that no woman had conquered.

"I like children," she said stiffly, "so I am confident I'll get along with the pupils of the valley school."

"Do you speak German?" he demanded.

"You really are the limit!" she gasped. "You ask more questions and make more demands than the baron himself. I—I can speak a little of your language. My own teacher in England was from Austria, and it was through her that I came to Vienna in the first place. I am sure I'll manage quite adequately, Herr von Lin-den, and having spent my early childhood in the country I think I shall manage to enjoy some aspects of May-holtzen."

The wind blew his tawny hair as he looked down at her. "I don't think I will be among them, from the tone of your voice," he drawled.

Siran met the steely zircon blue of his eyes and once again she felt like running back to Vienna and the friendly smile of Rudi. Yet why should she allow this man to frighten her away? She had come at the invita-tion of his brother and would be under his protection. She need fear no one if she had the friendship and grati-tude of Baron von Linden; he was the master of the cas-tle and the suzerain of this remote, craggy, almost mythical place.

"So you want me to take you to Seven Lilacs?" he said.

"I would be grateful if you would drive me there."

For the first time he really smiled, the sun lines deepening in his face, his teeth glimmering white against his brown skin. "Then let us be on our way, Miss Winters. I see you are wearing boots, so I gather you expected snow?"

"A friend warned me that the snow starts early in the mountains."

"Do you ski?"

"No. I think I'd be afraid of injuring a leg."

"Are you a coward?"

"No," she said indignantly. "I'm a dancer, and a badly broken bone has been known to end a career in ballet. If that happened. . . it would seem like the end of my life."

He glanced at her. "I note that you have the dramatic temperament. Would it really be that bad? I am sure you aren't unaware that some men find you attractive."

She flushed and gave his tall figure a look of dislike. He could say such a thing because he obviously didn't find her his type. It would have satisfied him if he could have scared her away with his talk about a snowbound castle and web of drama. He didn't want her there. . . perhaps because his brother did.

They reached a bend in the road, and parked in the snow stood a sleigh, painted scarlet and with bells attached to the harness of a black horse with snowflakes on his windblown mane. At the approach of people he tossed his head and the bells jingled.

Siran was surprised and delighted by the prospect of a sleigh ride to the castle, but Kurt von Linden put a check on her pleased comment, and in silence she took her seat in the sleigh and wrapped about her knees the fur laprobe he handed her. He put her suitcase down by her feet, making it a barrier between them, and took the leather reins in his hands. He called out something to the horse, who gave a skittish leap and then started off at a tinkling trot.

The sleigh was open to the mountain winds, but with a rug of warm fur tucked around her Siran didn't feel the cold. The wind flushed her cheekbones and made her eyes sparkle. There was pleasure in the airy touch of the snowflakes, and she tried not to feel the hostility of the man beside her.

She let herself imagine that she was a ballerina of the old imperial times, who was being taken in a *troyka* to the castle of her benefactor by a wild, blond Cossack. She smiled to herself, and in that instant he looked at her. The snowy wind had tousled his hair, and his eyes were startling...blue like the sky pierced by those icy peaks.

"When in England I have never seen a horse-drawn sleigh, so I take it this is a novel ride for you, Miss Winters?"

"Yes," she admitted. "It's a colorful way to get around. One can enjoy the countryside, breathe the fresh air and listen to the music of the sleigh bells."

"Quite romantic, eh?"

"That aspect depends on your companion," she rejoined. "Why, look at that! How charming!"

They passed a wayside shrine with a tiny bell in its tower and her eyes shone in her slender face; the green of her hat was a foil for her red brown hair. She noticed the wide, deep gables of the mountain chalets and saw shaggy-maned ponies racing about on a hillside. She felt a thrill at the awesome beauty of the towering crags and glaciers etched against the sky. They were fascinating and at the same time fearful. A man who dared to climb those could have little fear of anything else.

There was an air of drama about the place, and the spicy scent of the pines tingled in her nostrils as this narrow road curved around the rim of the valley, in which lay half hidden the slanting roof of houses and the colorful steeple of the village church.

"That is the Chapel of the Little Nun," she was told, and the bells were ringing as they passed, a silvery sound in the pure air. She felt a sense of enchantment. Here in such a place she might adjust to the loss of Cassian, who had befriended her and believed in her dancing ability. She had wanted so much to be a great dancer, but fate with its ironic touch had made her a teacher of the dance instead.

"The mountains look superb from here, as if made of crystal, but believe me, they are full of dangers. There are glassy walls of ice, chasms that are bottomless, great waves of snow that engulf climbers before they can beat an eyelash. There are snow bridges that crumble beneath one's feet, ropes that give way, howling tempests that keep you stranded for days in a freezing tent."

"Then why do you climb, *mein Herr*?" she asked. "It all sounds very risky and uncomfortable."

"Why do you dance, *Fräulein*?" His long whip sang through the flying snow without touching the horse, whose dark mane was spattered with flakes of crisp white snow.

"You mean. . .you enjoy it?"

He gave a laugh that came deeply from his throat. "I am, as Breck says, a crazy fool who will one day break his neck or plunge down a crevasse. Yes, I enjoy the challenge of the climb."

"Who is Breck?" She gave him an inquiring look.

"My brother, *Fräulein*." His smile was faintly mocking. "The Baron von Linden."

"Oh, I see." Her fingers clenched the laprobe. "I didn't know his first name."

"But you were curious about it."

"Not unduly so. He's my employer and one isn't usually on a first-name footing with the man at the top. You speak to me as if I'm a gold digger who has come here with the intention of making a play for the baron. It was he who found me, he who tendered the invitation to Seven Lilacs. I was quite willing to work as a waitress until the chance of returning to ballet came along."

"I daresay Breck is grateful to you for saving the child."

"Yet you asked me if I were a coward."

"People are sometimes driven to do a thing that deeply frightens them. Often we act on impulse."

"How could I leave a child who was crying bitterly in a smoke-filled room? I admit I was frightened, but I didn't think about that, and if that is acting on impulse then I am glad I can, because I should hate to be a person who thinks only about herself."

"If looks could kill," mocked the tawny Austrian, "I might have been struck from the sleigh by the flash of your eyes. You have quite a temper, Miss Winters. Frosty and biting like your name."

"You have a provoking way of saying things."

"I want you to have no illusions about us. Mayholtzen is no place for pets."

"Is that what you think I am?" She looked at him with indignation firing the gold flecks in her brown eyes. "A chorus girl who charmed your brother into offering me free lodging at the castle for the winter?"

"Confession is said to be good for the soul, so I confess I did think something of the sort." He spoke with an unrepentant note in his voice, and when Siran glanced at him she saw a deep groove of amusement beside his mouth.

"You can't have much of an opinion of your

brother's good sense with regard to women," she said tartly.

"No," he agreed.

He didn't bother to elucidate, but slackened the pace of the sleigh as they came in sight of a cascade that tumbled down the mountainside. She hadn't realized how high into the mountains the train had climbed so that she and Kurt von Linden seemed alone above the world. They gazed together at the cascade, misty and color-shot as the sun touched the spray. The snowflakes danced into it and were gone forever.

It was a lovely, unforgettable thing, and then Siran felt again the skimming movement of the sleigh on its runners. Siran half closed her eyes. She had just shared beauty with this man who was so much a part of these mountains, and it had made her feel curiously defenseless, aware of him as a person who had his hurts and his dreams and his reasons for not wanting her at the castle.

She came as the stranger who knew all about Kristy. Kurt resented her because in a way she had the right to know everything and the right to come to Mayholtzen. She felt him to be her enemy and was glad that Breck von Linden would be her protector.

The mountains formed a high, awesome chain around Mayholtzen. Their great shadows loomed over the sleigh as it sped scarlet through the snow. Their lower flanks were clad in evergreens, and their peaks were glacial blue, stabbing at the small clouds that sailed over them.

"You have gone as pale as the snow."

She gave a start at the sound of his voice. Did he guess something of her thoughts? Did he sense that she was rather afraid of him, a girl seeing for the first time his world of glaciers and storm gods? He was like one himself, with that thick tawny hair sweeping back like a mane from his broad forehead and those blue, smoldering eyes.

"I suppose I'm feeling strange and rather apprehensive about meeting your mother. Although the baroness sounded kind in her letter."

"Don't worry, my mother is kind and still very much the charming Viennese woman who gave up her light-hearted life in Vienna to come and live among the mountains. Things have happened that might have broken her spirit, but they never did."

"Please, won't you tell me about her?"

"Breck has not talked about her to you?"

"There wasn't the time. I snatched an hour from the coffee house the day he came to Vienna to see me."

"It took but an hour for you to decide about him as an employer?" A rather cynical smile slashed a line down the brown cheek. "Some people find him intimidating. He takes very much after our father."

"He is now called the baron, so your father—?"

"My father has been dead for many years. I was small, but I remember him. A tall, fair man, both stern and kind. A man of deep principles who rose from barrister to judge. It was on a winter's day that he was ordered to go to Germany. The next my mother heard was that he had been judged himself as a political offender against the regime then in power. It made no difference that he was an Austrian...he was imprisoned. We heard no more of him for a long time, and even powerful friends of my mother's could do nothing to get my father released. We as his sons, she as his wife, were made virtual prisoners at the castle. The good people of Mayholtzen brought food to us and news of the war and how it was going. Not that they heard much, but rumors of the English and Allied victories did filter through sometimes."

He paused as if living it all again, the guards daringly

eluded by the villagers, the daily concern for the father who had been stern but greatly loved, the longing to be as free as the other children, the awareness that they lived in danger as the sons of a man who had spoken out against a regime that made its own terrible laws.

"About two years after my father's imprisonment my mother was sent a small parcel by the authorities." Kurt von Linden drew a harsh breath. "It contained ashes...they said he had died of heart failure. The baroness knew otherwise, and she grew even more fearful for Breck and myself. At last she found someone to conduct us over the mountains into a neutral country, while she remained behind at the castle and pretended we were still there. When they found we were gone, she could have suffered imprisonment herself, but her family was important in Vienna. She was bullied for days despite this. They tried to extract from her the identity of the man who had helped her to get her sons out of Austria. She still bears upon her cheek the scar made by the heavy ring of the officer who slapped her face."

Siran gave a cry of distress. "How could they!"

"Easily, *Fräulein*. They were men without souls. But how good it was after the war to return to the castle and to find it was our home again and not a prison. Much of the furniture had been stolen—the chandeliers, the paintings, the carpets and the Buhl cabinets—but they had not managed to get my mother's jewelry. All the time it remained hidden in the belfry of the Little Nun chapel, and piece by piece it was sold to help rebuild what those brutes had destroyed. It was only a year or so ago that Breck was able to trace and buy back the pieces best loved by Trinka. That is our name for her."

"Trinka," Siran murmured, and a picture began to form in her mind of a small, indomitable, still lovely woman, who with true Viennese spirit had lived by the principle of "*biegen, nicht brecken*." Bend but do not break.

"*Mein Herr*, I don't quite understand about your sister...Kristy."

"Our young adopted sister," he explained. "Trinka always wanted a daughter, and Kristy was orphaned as a baby. A small golden imp whom Trinka adored and adopted."

"It must have been so sad for your mother when she heard...about Kristy?"

"Yes, it was a great shock. But she has the boy, thanks to you."

"You really mean those kind words, Herr von Linden?"

"But of course." His glance was piercingly blue. "Though if I were Breck I would have used my influence to find you a place in ballet. It's where you belong, is it not?"

His frankness had about it the shock of a blow, as if nothing could make him like her, or want her at the castle. The story of his childhood had not been a play for her sympathy. He wanted her to know that it wasn't only the memory of Kristy that haunted Seven Lilacs.

But if he had shocked her, he had also stirred her imagination and she was eager to meet the baroness.

It was only moments later that she glimpsed the castle turrets rising above a forest of trees. The sleigh entered the forest and the path ran on for about half a mile, the evergreens and the pines scattering their shadows and their needles beneath the runners. The sleigh bells made an enchanting sound among the trees, and to Siran's delight they emerged beside a lake with the castle situated on the rocky verge of it, the wooded slopes of the mountains towering above its turrets. It was built of stone as carved and weathered by the winds as the icebound crags. Two round towers guarded the front of the castle, rising to conical roofs white with snow. A place so dangerously romantic that Siran caught her breath.

"It's wonderful... like a fable!"

"As old as heaven, as we say, *Fräulein*."

The sleigh made a curve around the lake, a broad expanse of cold blue water set with small islands. The runners skimmed over the cobbles to the front door under a stone hood... and there around the base of the towers stood the seven lilac trees, bearing snow on their branches instead of blossom. They were old, strong trees and when in bloom they would curtain the weathered stone with color and send their tangy scent wafting in through the latticed windows of the castle.

It would be a sight to behold, and Siran wondered if she would be here in the spring to see flowers breaking open on the boughs that were today laden with snow. Kurt von Linden gave her a hand from the sleigh, and her sudden nearness to him made her aware of how defenseless certain men could make women feel. There was about this man a vitality akin to the mountains, a tang of the piney air, a hardiness that made him impatient of a girl who danced for her living.

She drew away from him and assumed an air of coolness.

"*Danke schön, mein Herr*," she said, with a touch of humor.

"For the sleigh ride, but certainly not the advice I gave you, eh?" His hands gripped her elbows and she was forced to meet his gaze and to see in his eyes a promise of more opposition in the future. They antagonized each other... a glance, a word was enough to set them off.

"Surely you can see for yourself that I prefer to work for my own dish of herbs," she said. "I worked hard at the coffee house, and I shall work equally hard at the school.''

"I think you would prefer to work at dancing instead of teaching it. Will it satisfy your ambitions to be in charge of schoolgirls who in the main will be as graceful as a pot of turnips?''

"It will be my job to set those turnips hopping and spinning, *mein Herr*, and I'll do it, despite your doubts. I happen to like children . . . don't you?''

"I am not sentimental about them, *Fräulein*.''

"I doubt whether you are sentimental about anything, even your beloved and challenging mountains. You seem very self-controlled to me, and such people are usually cool in their feelings.''

"You sound as if you are challenging me, Miss Winters.''

"I am making a statement about you, Herr von Linden.''

"On such short acquaintance?''

"You dared to assess my character, let me remind you. You summed me up as useless and decided I should return to Vienna.''

"For your own good.''

"What can possibly happen to me here . . . and what harm can I do, even if I don't produce a classroom of young Pavlovas?''

"You aren't a child yourself. You must know that you could disrupt our lives just as one of us could cause havoc to yours.''

"Why on earth?'' Her brown eyes widened. "I fail to understand you. What possible havoc could be caused because a dancing teacher comes to Mayholtzen?''

"Miss Winters, I refuse to believe you as innocent as you sound.'' He quirked a blond eyebrow, and with deliberation his blue eyes roved her face, taking in the shape of it, the winged look of her brows, the flush over her cheekbones, the delicate cleft in the center of her chin. "You are not exactly retiring and dowdy."

"I have heard that you aren't exactly retiring yourself!" She stood taut between the iron grip of his climber's hands. "Do you imagine that like other girls I am going to throw myself at your head...when I have the time from dancing lessons, and aiming myself at your brother the baron? Even if I felt so inclined, I've only to look at you to see I'd be wasting my time. You don't like me, and I don't like you, so let us call a truce on the understanding that we'll stay out of each other's way as much as possible."

"But we will be polite in front of Trinka, eh?"

"Of course. I wouldn't want to upset your mother. I imagine she is fond of you."

His lip quirked. "As a climber I make this rule. When the mountain is quiet, listen for the slightest disturbance...the avalanche comes when one is least expecting it."

"And what do I surmise from that remark, *mein Herr*?"

"A climber can't afford to be impulsive, therefore he suspects impulse in other people. You are a stranger who gives me the same feeling I have sometimes when I am climbing...that tingle of the unexpected just around the corner...that suspicion of having one foot on a snow bridge that will send me hurtling into space. If only you were the sensible, solid type, Miss Winters!"

"I must apologize for being the flighty type instead," she said tartly. "But despite it I don't need a keeper."

"Don't you? It isn't so long ago since you lost the one who used to be your director."

"He didn't regard me as a nuisance and a danger."

"How did he regard you?" A glint of curiosity came into Kurt von Linden's eyes. "Was he in love with you?"

"How dare you ask me that?" Siran felt deeply shocked by this stranger who pried behind the curtain of her secret dreams and sorrows. He had no right to speak as if he would have the bother of her while she was here. She came at his brother's request!

"Shall we go in before we really start to fight?"

He laughed in that lazily mocking way of his. "Perhaps it would be a prudent move, and I daresay my mother is eager to meet you."

"It will be nice to see a friendly face." Finding herself free of his touch, she turned to the hooded door, but he motioned her to precede him to the left-hand tower while he followed with her suitcase. She paused in front of the latticed glass doors that framed the ruddy glimmer of a firelit room and noticed also that among the lilac trees had been planted a linden tree. It had heart-shaped leaves and she touched them with a sense of delight. She wouldn't allow the youngest son of the baroness to blight her pleasure in this rare old place beside an Austrian lake. She would ignore him...but even as she resolved to do this, his hand brushed snow onto hers.

"The linden tree...do you know the superstition attached to it?"

"Is there one, *mein Herr*?"

"Yes. They are planted beside a doorway to keep witches away."

Her eyes clashed with his, and she could have hit the smile from his sardonic mouth as he opened the glass doors. "Please go in, *Fräulein*."

"You would really like to shut me out, wouldn't you?" Her voice shook. She told herself it was from temper.

"Perhaps so. I think, little witch, that you bring more trouble to Seven Lilacs, and in all conscience we have had our share of that!"

And to these words that held no tinge of welcome, Siran stepped past the linden tree and entered the castle. It had a stove that glowed warmly in the center of the room, and Siran was aware of snow bear skins covering the floor and of books covering the walls. A black piano stood at an angle to catch the light, and a marquetry music cabinet stood nearby. Assorted chairs and sofas gave the room a cozy look, while a carved old side table supported a small keg and some painted tankards.

It was a room with a lived-in air about it, as if here in the leisure hours the family gathered to read, to smoke, to take a drink and to listen to music. Apart from the piano there was a radiogram with a spacious rack of records, and Siran knew already from her stay in the capital that Viennese people loved their music.

She looked about her for the baroness, but the room was empty of an occupant. There was, however, a chair drawn close to the stove, with its cushions disarranged and a book face down on the arm of it, as if someone had been reading there and had left the room for a few minutes.

Siran glanced at Kurt. "It's a charming room," she said.

"Yes. Trinka said to bring you here. This is her favorite room, where she has her books and her music about her. I daresay she has gone to take yet another look at the child. I think she imagines that a being from the forest will fly in to carry him off."

"Love makes people anxious," Siran pointed out.

"Of course." He seemed to be mocking her again as he strolled to a table and bent to a carved box. "Dancers don't smoke, eh, or do you relax the rules now and then, as I do?"

"Never, when it comes to smoking."

"Your dedication is complete, eh?"

"Isn't yours? I imagine that it takes a lot of fitness to climb a mountain, or to win a skiing championship."

"I manage, and my self-indulgences are really very few, despite the opinion you have formed of me as a playboy sportsman."

"I couldn't be bothered to form an opinion of you, Herr von Linden."

"Really?" He smiled through the smoke of his cigarette, and his face took on a saturnine look in the growing dusk of the room. "You have decided that I am opposite in all ways to Breck, and as it happens you are not far wrong. He takes his responsibilities to heart and will sacrifice himself to the traditions of this old Austrian house. I see you look at me askance, Miss Winters, as if I speak a sort of treason. *Ja*, the castle is an enchanting place and I am fond of it. Mayholtzen draws me to her mountains each year, and I am proud to be the son of a brave man. But in my philosophy each man has his own path to tread, his own life to live, and I see beyond Seven Lilacs to other horizons. My brother works and plans and lives for this place."

Kurt von Linden flicked ash into the stove in a significant way. "He is bound by tradition and it will rule all his decisions. I am different and I will decide my life as I decide which part of a mountain to climb...or which woman to love."

He gave a sardonic smile. "You have large eyes, Miss Winters, and they speak for you. You think me a terrible egotist."

"You speak as if a sense of duty is a tedious thing. What if you had been the eldest son?"

He quirked a rough blond brow. "I would no doubt have turned the castle into a hotel for skiers and developed Mayholtzen into a sporting center. There, does that shock profoundly your sense of what is proper...and improper?"

"Really, Kurt, have you managed to shock our young guest so soon?" The voice held the lilt and charm of Vienna, and Siran turned eagerly toward the door. A woman had quietly entered and she carried a tray to a sofa table. "My dear, you must be feeling in need of a cup of coffee after that long train journey. It is a slow train, I know, crawling as it does through the mountains. Kurt, will you please light the lamps so I can see if this child is as attractive as Breck told me."

Siran's heart seemed to miss a beat. To be thought attractive by the baron was as unexpected as it was pleasant. More than that...it made up for being thought an interloper by his brother.

Tall in the shadows of the room Kurt went from lamp to lamp, and as they bloomed alight Siran met his mother's eyes and was startled to find them almost as blue as his and set like jewels in a face with elements of tragedy in it as well as charm. It was a face that stirred the onlooker, like a painting of depth and true beauty.

Such wonderful bone structure, and there against the black velvet of her dress gleamed a large uncut topaz in a claw of silver, an almost barbaric stone that must be part of the baronial jewels once sold and then redeemed by Breck von Linden.

"So at last we meet." The baroness came forward and held out both hands to Siran, slender hands with a musician's grip. "My dear, you can't know how I have waited for this moment. To be able to tell you in words how deeply in your debt I feel. *Mein Liebe* Lorenz would have been lost to us if you had not been courageous enough to save his young life. Siran—you must allow me to call you so—you are welcome to stay at the castle for as long as you wish, and I hope we will be such friends. Indeed I am sure of it. You are a dancer of the ballet, and there was a time when I could have become a concert pianist."

The blue eyes smiled, but a little sadness lurked in them. "I chose love instead. *Liebesleid*. You know what it means?"

"Yes...I think so." And as she spoke Siran was aware of the glance that came swiftly from the tall son of this petite and charming woman. At once she felt gripped by shyness and wished she had pretended not to know the meaning of the word.

"Say it for us," drawled Kurt, "in your nice English way."

Siran gave him a look his mother could not have missed, a flash of the eyes that spoke their own language.

"It means love's agony, Baroness. A lovely word but a little cruel."

"As there is some sadness to real beauty there is also a certain pain connected with love...but this is not the time for us to be talking of such profound things." The baroness smiled and indicated the sofa near the stove. "You must sit here by the warmth and we will drink coffee, enjoy apple cake and discuss the matters that will be of little interest to my son. Tell me, did he give you a pleasant welcome at the station?"

Siran had to smile, for the mother was looking at the son with every indication that she knew him well, and when he bent over the maternal hand his blue eyes met hers in quizzical affection.

"As I am not welcome here, Trinka, I will take myself off to my workshop. I can see you are delighted to have Miss Winters here to talk to."

"Are you jealous, Kurt?" With the audacious hand of a mother she ruffled his tawny mane, and Siran watched amazed. It was as if someone stroked a proud young lion, putting a hand through the bars of his cage, daring him to snarl or bite. Siran could imagine no one but his mother having the love to approach him so closely.

"You have always been a heart stealer, Trinka." He carried her hand to his lips and smiled as he kissed it, and with a lithe stride he was at the door, where he turned for a moment to give Siran an enigmatic half bow.

"I hope you enjoy your stay at the castle, Miss Winters. When the snows come early this usually means that our winter will be a long one. I hope you won't find our mountain life too monotonous, but you must say so if you do, before we become snowbound and the railway tracks freeze over. It will happen this year...mountain climbers sense these things."

"And yet you will climb...that mountain?" Trinka put out a hand to him, as if in appeal, but he looked unmoved, and gone was his smile. His jaw was hard like stone, and Siran looked into eyes that were ice-blue and strangely impenetrable. He was a man who was so used to facing hazards that he had become curiously aloof from other aspects of life. He seemed quite sure that a dancer like herself would come apart at the seams of her *tutu* when the mountain winds howled and spread the snow in thick layers over the countryside.

"I'm looking forward to my stay at Seven Lilacs." Her eyes dwelt on his chin above the rolled neck of his jersey and then lifted quickly to meet his gaze. "I'm not an unworldly child, you know, though I must admit I enjoyed the sleigh ride."

"Did you indeed?" A devil danced in his eyes as he took in the slightly defiant tilt to her chin. "I'm gratified, *Fräulein*."

"Being shown some of the scenery was most enjoyable," she emphasized.

His sardonic laugh seemed to linger after he closed

the door behind him and left her alone with the baroness.

"You mustn't allow Kurt to ruffle your feathers," she said with a smile, pouring coffee into the cups and indicating that Siran help herself to cream and sugar and one of the delicious-looking apple cakes still warm from the oven.

"My sons are very Austrian, and for a while they will overwhelm you. Their creed is that if you climb, climb to the very peak. If you love, love the night through."

The silver gleamed in the firelight, spoons tinkled against china and the baroness laughed softly. "We are a little feudal, Siran, here in our mountain *schloss*, but I think in time you will grow used to our ways. I don't think it will be necessaary for Kurt to take you away when the snows begin to close our roads. I can see you have a lot of spirit, and I know it because today, tomorrow, and in the time ahead I can hold my grandson in my arms."

The fine blue eyes filled slowly with tears. "Kristy was so foolish to run away from home. You know that her young man was killed while climbing with Kurt?"

"Yes, I was told. It has all been very sad and tragic for you."

"Sadder for Kristy, and perhaps for Kurt. The girl blamed him hysterically for what happened...did Breck tell you about it? Helmut died on the Glass Turret, a notorious climb which our young men seem driven to attempt. A snow bridge gave way and Helmut plunged down a chasm while tied by a rope to Kurt. It dragged Kurt to the very edge, where suddenly it was severed by the sharp rock, saving his life. He came home after long hours of searching for the boy, dazed, soaked to the skin in a thunderstorm that broke over the mountains, to be met by his sister's accusations."

The baroness paused and her gaze dwelt somberly

upon the warm glow of the stove. "Kristy accused him of cutting the rope so he wouldn't be swept down the chasm with Helmut. Wolfgang, his guide, was lower down the ice wall when the accident occurred. He examined the rope and testified that it had been torn by the rock. . .and Kurt still carries about his body the mark of it. It cut through his clothing and scarred him. But Kristy would not believe Wolfgang or anyone else. She ran away as she did to punish Kurt. . .and because of her he will climb that awful mountain again. Like her he will not listen to reason, and I have to let him do it. Until he risks his life again where Helmut died, he will not be at peace."

There was a dramatic little silence, and then Siran gave a shiver as a cold draft seemed to brush the nape of her neck. She recalled the look on Kurt von Linden's face when he had warned her that like a moth she might be caught in a web of drama if she stayed at the castle of the seven lilacs.

Yet how could she leave when the baroness made her so welcome? How could she go when she longed once more to meet Breck von Linden? It would be foolish to run away because the younger son reminded her of the icy crags that towered over the castle.

"A little more coffee, my dear?"

"Yes, please." Siran smiled, her mind made up. She would stay and let this sad, romantic place weave her into its web.

CHAPTER THREE

THE SUN WAS SETTING over the castle when Siran followed a young maid to her room. From the window she could see the lake, fired by the final red blaze of the sun, and she heard the sigh of the wind through the reeds and the willow trees at the edge of the water. Gazing from the partly open casement, she caught a whiff of cigar smoke and wondered if Breck von Linden had arrived home and was smoking alone in the falling dusk. She pictured him with his astrakhan collar turned up about his strong-boned face to shield it from the snow. He seemed to her more worldly than his brother Kurt, less fond of the elements and doing battle with them.

With a smile she glanced around her room and saw the big goose-feather bed, looking like an illustration for the tale of the princess and the pea. Its tall bedposts reached almost to the ceiling and the great puff of the eiderdown was embroidered with berries and pine trees. The walls of the room were smoothly white, with shadows thrown by the china lamps. The furniture was of polished pine, with rugs of thick colored wool and shelves filled with books and small wooden animals... the sort of oddments a young person would collect.

Siran put a hand to her throat, where her pulse beat rapidly. Had Kristy slept here? Had this room been that of the girl who had run away, unable to forgive Kurt for returning alive from the climb that had killed her lover? Siran glanced slowly around the room. No, the baroness was too kind to have put her in a room haunted by a ghost. The books and the little animals had belonged to one of the boys. Here in this room overlooking the blue lake, a child had curled up in the windowseat and gazed at the mountain peaks.

A yearning child who couldn't go out to play unless watched by dark-uniformed guards; who had felt so much a captive that as he grew into a man the mountains had seemed to offer the ultimate freedom of spirit and body.

This room had once belonged to Kurt von Linden!

As the realization swept over Siran she had the feeling of being an intruder. Though this room was now too small for that towering Austrian, it had once been his youthful sanctuary and he might resent her presence here.

Well, it couldn't be helped, and with a little shrug Siran took her kit along to the bathroom, which the maid had shown her, and found it old-fashioned but well supplied with hot and cold water from a grumbling geyser. She found pine-scented bath crystals in a jar and added them to the water, and later when she emerged she felt invigorated by the alpine smell. Her skin tingled pleasantly, reminding her of the touch of snow, and as she toweled down she caught a glimpse of a smile on her lips, reflected in a rather steamy mirror on the wall. Tendrils of hair clung in coppery brightness against her white neck...and in that moment she thought of Kurt von Linden's remark about some men finding her attractive.

Was he afraid that his brother might become attracted to her? Yet why should that matter to him? Unless he thought that a dancer was not quite good enough for the Baron of Mayholtzen!

Her cheeks stung. What thoughts to be having, draped only in a towel, but like other girls she was curious about love, and the love she might have found with Cassian had not been fulfilled. Her eyes grew a little sad as she tied the cord of her long green robe and remembered those times alone with him.

Those lessons in ballet when the rest of the company had left for the day, their walks along the Embankment, and the warm, tight holding of his hand when they crossed a busy road.

He had been waiting for her to become a really fine dancer. He had wanted that for her, holding back the words that had lain slumbering in his dark, faintly slanting eyes. The eyes of a faun, people had said, and one of his best dancing roles had been *L'Après-Midi d'un Faune*.

She recalled something he had once said to her at that little coffee place in the Strand, not far from their studio near the Covent Garden theater. "If a person is to be great in music, song or ballet, then she must be detached. Human attachments fray the bond between the artist and her work. Loyalties change. Ambitions are lost in the love for another human being."

He had been warning her that love would demand first place in her heart, but with Cassian it would have been like loving one and the same thing. He had been a part of ballet. From now on she could never form an attachment that would steal her away from the dream of becoming a perfect dancer. She would make that dream come true, come what may.

She met her own reflection in the mirror and saw a young and rather lonely girl, far from all that was familiar to her, with no one to turn to for guidance any more. On her way back to her room she collided with someone and gave a startled gasp as a pair of hands caught hold of her in her silky robe.

"Miss Winters!"

"*Mein Herr*!"

She was terribly confused, for in the shadowy light of the corridor she had once again mistaken Kurt for his brother, the baron. They were of a similar height, and she had caught that whiff of good cigar smoke clinging to his jacket.

She looked up into his blue eyes, felt the crush of rock-calloused hands and knew from the sardonic face that he would filch not only his brother's cigars but his girls as well. . . if he felt so inclined.

"You smell of the pinewoods," he drawled, "early in the morning when a man sets out on a climb and the air is pure."

"Please." She struggled to escape from him, and she noticed even in her panic how the black of his dinner jacket offset the tawny mane of his hair. His shirt was very white against the tan of his throat. He was hard of nerve, keen of eye, physically splendid as young men are who have skied the mountain slopes all their lives and dared the highest peaks.

He looked down into her eyes, and there was in his look a sudden disturbing intensity. "You have been given the room that used to be mine," he said, and his grip on her waist seemed to tighten. "Though I no longer sleep there, I keep some of my things in a chest I had as a boy. I wanted something."

"Then you had better come and sort out what you want." She was alarmed not only by his touch, but she knew how vulnerable her thoughts of Cassian had left her. "I—I hope you don't mind that I have your boyhood room?"

"It's a nice room and it overlooks the lake. I hope you will like sleeping there."

A lazily deliberate look came into his eyes as he spoke, and she forced herself to be composed. "Shall we go and look for what you want?" she asked.

"It had better wait. The dinner bell will ring very

shortly. . .and catch you still not dressed.'' His fingers pressed her waist, a subtle hint that he could feel how little she had on. She pulled away from him and he let her go, but still his touch lingered as she hastened from his tall figure in the corridor. Never had she felt so unsure of anyone. His moods were like those of his mountains; the ice might break suddenly, or the avalanche wait but a breathless moment away, to sweep a person off her feet.

She closed behind her the door of her bedroom, in which he had once slept, a boy, then a youth and eventually a man who had to bend his head to avoid the slant of the ceiling beams. She leaned thoughtfully against the door that shut him out and then aroused herself as in the distance she heard the sound of the dinner bell. She must dress at once, or be late downstairs, and luckily she was a girl who had been trained in ballet to dress swiftly, to have her hair neat and glossy in seconds, her face a picture of composure as she sped on stage to the opening bars of the ballet music.

With equal lightness she sped down the stairs without appearing to touch them with her feet, the skirt of her dress fanning out to show her legs. She had bought the dress in Vienna, after she had lost everything in the hotel fire, all but her purse which she had snatched from the bedside table as she fled to safety with the abandoned baby. It had a full skirt of many-colored stitchings, with pockets in which a pair of kittens could have nestled. The neckline was embroidered and the sleeves were puffed to just below the elbows. It had about it something of the goose girl and the woods, and suited her mood as a guest at a castle.

As she reached the foot of the stairs, a great dog stirred and rose to its feet. A mountain dog, all white and big as a bear. Siran stood hesitant and then someone spoke. "There is no need to bristle, Bruno. This is our visitor from the world of ballet."

It was Kurt again, appearing to find her at a disadvantage. She wasn't afraid of normal-sized dogs, or men, but the castle seemed a place of giants. There was about it a tang of mountain winds and mystery. Of wine among candles, of music and tears. Cruelty had left its shadow, and love was now a whisper, a muted waltz that wouldn't swing into gaiety.

"May I touch him?" she asked. "Or will he bite my head off?"

"Not while I am here." A smile flickered on Kurt's mouth, as if he took the point of her remark.

"I thought for a moment that a bear had got into the castle." She smiled and ran a brave hand over the dog's handsome head. He growled deep in his throat and accepted the caress of the stranger with something of his master's suspicion. Then he retreated and stretched out again like a bearskin against the dark polished wood of the floor.

Siran glanced about her and noticed the lamps held by bronze figures, the paneling with its gothic tracery, the arched windows of colored shield glass and the high ceiling braced by carved beams. She and Kurt were reflected together in a great mirror surmounted by a worn eagle, and she was startled by the way she reached only to his heart, the embroidery of her dress bright against the darkness of his jacket.

Suddenly there came the chiming of bells and she looked at him with inquiring eyes.

He studied her image in the mirror, and his blue eyes glinted as if amused by her smallness beside him. "The bells are rung each evening in the bell turret. They guide home a climber, or someone lost in the forest."

"It's a nice thing to do." The luminous brown of her large eyes dwelt on him. "Like the bells at sea. The cottage I lived in as a child was close to the seashore and on foggy nights I used to lie in bed and listen to the bells and be glad they were there to guide to safety the little ships. My father and his crew were lost at sea...the ice floes caught them in Arctic waters, but I was too young at the time to realize that he wouldn't come home again.''

Then, as if she regretted saying too much to a man who was curiously ice bound himself, she glanced away from him. ''Shouldn't we go in to dinner...your mother will be waiting for us.''

There was in her voice a note of eagerness she couldn't quite restrain, and Kurt was looking sardonic as he strode to a door and held it open for her. ''Yes, only my mother awaits us, Miss Winters. My brother is still detained in Bavaria...on business, he writes to say, but I suspect that some other interest holds him there.''

Siran felt her cheeks grow warm at his mocking tone of voice, and she hated him for being right. She had been looking forward to seeing the baron again, that man of command and presence, with his crest of silvery hair and his lake-gray eyes. It was disappointing to hear that he was absent from the castle.

She swept past Kurt, bunching her full skirt in her hand so she wouldn't be in contact with him. He might resemble his brother in looks, but in ways they couldn't be more different. The baron was courteous and kind, but Kurt treated life and women as if they were a challenge, to be conquered but never loved.

''Ah, there you are.'' The baroness turned with a smile from the window and the curtain fell into place, shutting out the darkness that had fallen over the mountains. ''What an attractive dress, my dear, and how well it suits you. You look like Giselle, poised on the threshold with Prince Albrecht.''

Kurt gave a sardonic laugh. "I have hardly the build or the temperament for ballet...take a look at Miss Winters. She doesn't know whether to laugh or weep at the idea."

He drew out his mother's chair, and Siran sat down quickly on the other side of the table, hiding a reluctant smile as she unfolded her napkin with its little silk coronet. She was amazed that a woman so gracious and willowy could have a son like Kurt. He made his mother seem breakable, and yet Siran couldn't help but notice his gentleness with her...the one person he loved, perhaps.

"In this room we used to have Bohemian chandeliers, but they were stolen away from us, like other things." A shadow darkened Trinka's blue eyes. "They were such a delight to my boys, with their blown-glass flowers and leaves. Their crystals used to chime very softly if the door was closed too hard."

"Don't let us talk of days that can mean nothing to our young guest," said Kurt. "She could not have been born."

"Yes, how young you are." Trinka shifted a table vase so she could gaze across at Siran. "It amused Breck to find you such an independent young thing. He said you refused to come here unless he found you a job, and you are to start school next Monday, which gives you time to settle in at the castle. Is this your first visit to a place like Mayholtzen?"

"My very first." Siran tasted her soup, in which tiny fluffy dumplings bobbed about. A dumpling melted in her mouth with a delicious taste.

"Are you afraid that our Austrian fare will spoil your dancer's figure?" drawled Kurt.

"Luckily I never put on weight," she returned. "I seem to burn it off and remain as light as when I was sixteen."

"You have a cool name but an ardent disposition, eh?" Mockery seemed to glint in his eyes as he studied her. "I have in my mind a picture of some of those solid schoolgirls in the valley who have been brought up on dumplings and strudel. Miss Winters, I hope you have patience and will be able to control your red-haired temper."

"My hair is not red," she protested.

"No, Kurt." His mother gave a laugh. "If you had an ounce of artistic temperament you would notice that Siran's hair is the color of that copper coffeepot of mine, which gleams when I make coffee beside the fire. Really, you have eyes for nothing but your snowy crags and your cool cascades. You are a man of ice, Kurt!"

"You are saying I have no feelings, Trinka?"

"I sometimes wonder."

He shrugged his broad shoulders with a look of unconcern and helped himself to a veal steak and cabbage salad, adding a liberal spoonful of cream sauce.

Temper, indeed! Siran was more than ever certain that she and Kurt von Linden had best keep out of each other's way if the fireworks were not to explode. Her eyes smouldered as she caught him looking at her. She felt like a cat in a room with a large teasing dog and knew it would have soothed her nerves to scratch him. Her thoughts shocked her. She had never wanted to hurt anyone and was by nature a kind girl.

She was glad when Trinka began to ask her questions about the ballet. Kurt did not join in. It was as if the subject were beneath his notice.

"We are taught to express the emotions," she said. "We are not puppets going through a series of postures."

"There are many emotions...have you felt them all at your age?"

Siran gave a little start when Kurt spoke and then replaced her wineglass on the table in case he made her drop it. "We have to portray character, also pain, pleasure, joy and fear. One doesn't have to be a dodo to have experienced those, *mein Herr*."

"I thought ballet had to do with love, *Fräulein*."

"It does," she said, concentrating on her apple baked in pastry with cream. "Love is not always a happy emotion, is it? Very often it causes heartache."

"And you are taught to dance this, eh?"

"A good dancer can express a whole range of feelings without saying a word."

"Are you a good dancer?" He was leaning back in his carved chair, a wineglass held casually in his hand, the lamplight reflecting in the shield glass of the window behind him. Overhead the ceiling was honeycombed in dark wood, and the upright chairs and circular table were of the same darkness. The walls were smooth and white, giving way to a few modern paintings, bought to replace the old masters that had been stolen. It was a severe yet beautiful room, as if monks might appear through the paneled door and chant a prayer.

It was strange, somehow, that she should think of monks as she looked at Kurt, and Siran almost laughed at the vision. "I'm not a bad dancer," she replied. "I hope to be a better one, and I live and work for that."

"Only for that?" he mocked.

"Now, now," the baroness reproved. "Why so quarrelsome, you two?"

"Your son thinks that Mayholtzen is no place for a girl who dances for her living." Siran met Trinka's blue eyes and was reassured by their warmth, so in contrast to Kurt's coolness. So lovely a woman should be painted on canvas so that in future years other eyes could look at her and respond to her looks with the admiration she deserved. Her plaits were still a thick dark gold about the small crown of her head; her skin was fine and only faintly lined, with the tiny mark of a scar on her left cheekbone. To look at her was to know without being told that she came from one of the ancient and noble families of Austria.

Siran, who had lost her own mother while still a baby, was deeply disturbed, even confused, to find herself so swiftly fond of Kurt von Linden's mother. This was a woman with whom one could share secrets, and Siran had never known that kind of a relationship. Her two old aunts, her girlhood guardians, had been kind but a trifle eccentric. More often than not she had found herself looking after them.

She smiled, and there was a grave charm about her smile. And then she saw Trinka press a hand against the pearls at her throat, as if a young girl at her table reminded her poignantly of Kristy, who had not found herself able to share her secret with the woman who was Kurt's mother.

"Kurt is full of opinions, *Liebling*. You must not allow his opinion of your profession to annoy you. Some would say that mountain climbing is only for him who has his head in the clouds."

"Perhaps it makes him feel lordly to climb a mountain," Siran said daringly, taking a sip at the wine that was sweet and old.

The baroness laughed and glanced at Kurt for his reaction to this remark. Without speaking he raised his wineglass in mocking acceptance of it, but there glinted in his eyes a promise of retaliation. He and Siran had become opponents in a duel that would demand surrender and flight on her part...if he should win. She was determined not to let him in, but dared not look at the firm chin that brooked no sort of defeat.

He would climb again the Glass Turret in order to

prove to a pair of dead lovers that he was no coward who had saved his own life at the cost of another's. Such a climb would take nerves of steel, for in the wind he might hear again a cry of agony; in the lonely snows he might see a shape that beckoned.

He was strangely unapproachable in Siran's eyes, like the high mountains themselves; yet she hoped that when the baron returned to the castle he would find a way to persuade Kurt not to make the climb. It would surely break Trinka's heart to lose for the third time someone she loved. Kurt was her son, and a mother remembered the little things, the childhood things, which were too deeply embedded to be torn out by even the cry of Kristy that he had killed her sweetheart.

At the end of the meal they retired to the music room to drink their coffee. The room curved to the shape of the tower, with the linden tree at its entrance, with branches still and heavy with snow tonight. It had ceased to fall for a while, and everything was hushed but for the warm crackling of the pine branches on the stove. A lovely old brass coffee maker bubbled over a flame, with a tap at the side, and a decoration of imps and berries around the handles and the lid.

"I've never seen a more charming room than this one." Siran explored it with her eyes and hoped the baroness would play some Schubert on the mellow-looking piano. Had she played to herself in the evenings long ago, after her boys had escaped with a guide from the castle, or had the music room been locked against her as a punishment?

"Good, I am pleased you like my den." The baroness smiled and poured coffee into small cups, and Siran concealed a smile at the toylike look of such a cup and saucer in Kurt's hand. He seemed to threaten everything in his mother's room, towering there in the glow of the stove, restless, Siran felt, for the clasp of skis on his feet, or the feel of an ice axe in his fist.

"Why do I climb?" Abruptly he took up the subject again, as if her thought communicated itself to him. "Because most things out of reach are fascinating, and to reach the snowy summits is to possess them for only as long as a man can withstand the biting winds. Sunset over the Himalayas gives the peaks a look of warmth, like diamonds and gold, yet take off a fur mitten and the hand will freeze within minutes."

Siran shivered. "How can you dare?" she asked.

He gave her a deliberate look. "They attract with all the dangerous forces of love, and I am sure, *Mädchen*, that you think of love in terms of danger and thrill."

"You always seem sure of my reactions," she said. "Am I naïve, or are you a clairvoyant?"

He quirked an eyebrow at his mother. "Whoever started the rumor that British girls are shy?"

"We might be shy of some things," Siran murmured, "but not of a challenger."

"You think you are being challenged by me?"

"I know I am." She met his eyes, and told herself she would not be daunted by him. He was but a man even though he looked more elemental than other men. More capable of being ruthless to women, whom it amused him to taunt but never to love. Siran looked at him and knew with all her instincts that he had chosen to give his love to the high crags that burned in the sun like diamonds and froze the hand if you dared to touch them.

To what lengths would his ruthlessness carry him if ever she found herself alone with him? Even as she wondered she was pinned like a moth on the blue steel of his glance and dared not pursue the thought. He mustn't guess that she felt alarmed by the thought of being alone with him.

And then as if he had prowled enough he lay back in a large winged chair, and to Siran's delight the baroness went to the piano and sat down in front of it, spreading the skirt of her pearl-gray dress over the red silk of the cushioned stool.

"What will tame you tonight, Kurt?" she asked. "Take a look at him, Siran. The tiger who sprawls in his cage with every muscle alert for action. Take a tip from me, my child. Never attempt to stroke him or he will take a bite at you. He's quite untamed."

"A little more of such talk, Trinka, and Miss Winters will depart so hastily that she'll melt the frost under her feet as she runs away."

"No, Kurt, this child does not run away from a challenge... you heard her say so."

His gaze drifted from the logs that had fallen into a kissing cross as they burned, red with flames like the ruby-glassed lamps, and his lashes concealed his eyes so she could only guess at the smile they held. She was shaken again by the flagrant strength and carelessness of this man who might be capable of many things... everything but the one thing Kristy had accused him of. Kristy had been hysterical with misery or she would not have said it, or believed it. To look at Kurt was to know deep inside that he feared nothing—that he would have died with Helmut if that rope had not broken.

"The rope marked him," his mother had said.

Siran's eyes were hidden by her lashes as she let her gaze pass over those wide shoulders under the dark broadcloth, over the throat that was brown against the crisp white shirt, and she had a mental picture of that scar like a snake across his chest, biting deep, leaving in him the venom of Kristy's accusation.

"Play some Schubert," he said casually. "Somehow it seems appropriate in the firelight, with a ballerina for a guest at the castle."

The music was tender and lovely, like the echo of a lost love, and Siran relaxed to listen to it, her skirt of many-colored stitchings spread around her like a fan. The music made her think of Cassian, and her sadness gave her the strength, somehow, to stay here and be a teacher of ballet until she could become the ballerina whom Kurt von Linden so softly, so deliberately mocked.

Then all at once the baroness broke the mood she had created with music and began to play a lively Viennese waltz. She laughed as she played. "Our moods change like the rhythm of the waltz, did you know that, Siran? Come, you two, dance and pretend we are in gay Vienna. Kurt, I command you to dance with Siran. I won't have altogether a social disgrace for a son."

Siran was startled, and then she smiled and told herself he would not be commanded by anyone and would go on lounging there by the stove like a big cat who liked the feel of the warmth.

Her heart gave a jerk when instead he rose to his feet and came to her with a look of deliberate intent.

"No." She shrank away from him as he reached for her. "I don't want to."

"You said you weren't shy." He caught hold of her hands and drew her to her feet with remorseless ease. "Come, you aren't trembling, are you? I do this to please Trinka, not myself. She's the only woman I ever bother to obey."

"You just want to embarrass me," Siran whispered fiercely, and then he put his arms around her and she felt how easily he could have crushed her. Hateful man! He didn't have to try to make her tremble. She had never trembled like this in her life before, not even that first time she had danced for Cassian. She wanted to thrust Kurt away from her, and in a second he had drawn her so close and hard to him that all she was conscious of was the thudding of her heart and the warm pressure of his hand through the material of her dress.

"For Trinka," he breathed. "Only for her, not for you. . . or me."

Why the insistence that he waltzed with her only to please Trinka? He whirled her around and she found him supple and sure and far from clumsy. She was amazed, and when she glanced up at him he gave her an impudent look. How naïve of her to be amazed by this man! Being a sportsman he would be coordinated in all things; and being a man he had danced before tonight with a girl.

"Does this very natural and ordinary accomplishment bring me down to earth?" he asked, sardonically.

"I thought you were contemptuous of the dance," she said and felt the swing of her skirt and the rhythm of the music and the longing that always came to dance on and on.

Out of the door they whirled and the music became an echo behind them as she became aware of a smoother floor underfoot. Moonlight was streaming through long windows, and a pair of dancing ghosts flitted in and out of mirrors lining the walls. It seemed like a dream, but his touch was too real for dreaming. The Strauss music belonged to another time, and yet it was as vital as it had ever been.

"We dance in the empty grandeur of the ballroom," said Kurt, and his voice was deep above her head. "There were lovely things in this room long ago— cherubs and sofas in the alcoves. Breck has had exact copies made of the chandeliers and they will be sent here soon from Vienna. Everything will look the same, but the old magic will be gone. No copy can be the same as the original. The silk drapes at the windows will smell of newness, not of the musty scents a boy remembers from hiding among them to watch the dancing. I was six years old and it was the last time a ball was held here, so perhaps I remember the occasion so clearly because of that. One of my mother's friends discovered me behind the curtain. He was a conductor of music and very famous in Vienna; he sat me on the piano and gave me chocolate cake to eat.''

Kurt gave a nostalgic laugh. "The next day when Breck found out he was wild with me and he pelted snowballs at me...until I fell in the lake.''

Siran gasped and stumbled. Of course, in those days Breck would have been the bigger of the two boys, but right now the hard feel of Kurt's arms made it seem impossible that anyone could have got the better of him.

"Breck pulled me out, so don't die of shock," he drawled, mocking her. "Already you have put him on a pedestal, eh? The handsome baron who marched into your life and saved you from being a waitress. It's quite a romantic story, isn't it?''

"Why do you spoil everything?'' she asked.

"Perhaps it is in my nature...to be destructive.''

The music of the waltz died away and they came to a standstill beside a window. In the moonlight the snow was drifting down again, and the lawn lay under a silvery mantle to the edge of the lake. She pictured Kurt falling into the lake and told herself Breck had not meant to hurt him. He had made it sound a little cruel in order to disillusion her...he would use any weapon to make her run away, and again she wondered why he was so opposed to her staying here.

She didn't take up too much room, being quite a small thing. She had saved his nephew's life, and his mother seemed lonely for feminine company since the loss of Kristy.

Was he afraid that like Kirsty she might hurt his mother in some unforeseen way?

She glanced up at him, but his face by moonlight was

a mask of mystery and his eyes could not be read because he chose to watch the falling snow. "You have never been sleigh riding by the light of the moon, have you?" He spoke abruptly. "It's quite an experience, and you would look more than ever like a *barishnaya* in a Cossack fable. I wonder if you would dare to take such a ride with me?"

She shook her head, for she must never be so alone with him, out there in the snows where she would be at the mercy of his unpredictable nature. "I think it might be wise of me to forgo the pleasure of such a ride... with you."

"Are you hoping my brother might invite you to ride with him?"

"If he did so, then I certainly wouldn't refuse him." She turned away from Kurt, saw the direction of the door and made for it. She heard him laughing to himself, there by the window where the soft shadows of the snow fell one after the other. Siran met his mother in the hall and they went upstairs together.

"I am going to the nursery to take a look at Lorenz," she said. "Will you come with me? He looks so pretty when he's asleep."

Siran smiled and followed the baroness into the baby's room; it was softly lit by a tiny lamp and there he lay fast asleep in his antique cot, a curl adrift on his forehead, cared for and safe in this castle of the seven lilacs. Siran stole a look at Trinka and saw on her face a pensive look of love. Of which son was she thinking as she gazed at Kristy's baby?

"He is a darling, is he not?" Trinka spoke softly, and her fingers stole over the carving of the cradle, as if they knew intimately each small detail. "Siran, how do I really thank you? What do I give you in return?"

"You don't have to give me anything," Siran assured her with a smile. "There isn't anything I want."

The baroness glanced up and caught Siran's gaze. "There is always something...I'd give you one of my sons...could you love Kurt?"

"No!" Siran backed away as if from a blow. No, she couldn't have been invited here for that! If Kurt knew what lay in his mother's mind, then no wonder he had told her to return to Vienna. No wonder he had warned her that she'd be glad to run away if she stayed.

"Forgive me." Trinka held out her hands in appeal. "I talk like a foolish mother who worries too much about her son. I see that he is not the kind of man you could ever care for. He seems like the mountains themselves, and you prefer the music of life, the joy and the beauty of warm things. Forget what I said. Please."

"It is forgotten," Siran assured her, and she let Trinka clasp her cold hands and kiss her burning cheek.

"I have upset you, *Liebchen? Nicht?*"

"Not too much, but I hope Kurt...?"

"Kurt will always go his own way, despite his mother's wishes."

"Does he know your wishes, Baroness?"

"Perhaps, but don't be frightened of him, *Liebchen.*"

"I'm not," Siran said, with more spirit than conviction.

She bade Trinka good-night and went to her room and as she entered she felt uneasy about sleeping in a room of Kurt's, disturbed by the things the baroness had said. Her nightdress lay on the bed where his pajamas had once lain. He had slept in that bed with its puff of an eiderdown and its goose-down pillows. He had listened to the wind across the lake and dreamed of the mountains.

She hummed to herself as she prepared for bed, opening the cupboards with the wild flowers painted on them, doing her best to keep her thoughts at bay.

Each nerve in her body seemed to give a jump when there was a sudden tapping on her door. Her hand went nervously to her throat, pulling together the lapels of her wrap as she opened the door and found Kurt standing there. "What do you want?" She spoke with panic in her voice, like a girl in a Victorian novel.

"Don't look so alarmed." That sardonic smile pulled at his lip. "All I want is something I keep in that wooden chest under the window. May I fetch it?"

"No. I'll get it for you. What is it?"

"Only a book in a blue cover."

She went and opened the chest and found the book in a corner. It had a leather clasp around it and the letter K was stamped into the cover. It had the look of a private journal, and Siran didn't dare meet his eyes as she handed him the book. He had been afraid that she would look inside and see written there his private thoughts and feelings. As if she cared what they were!

"It's a journal I take with me on my climbs," he said. "I am sorry to have troubled you."

"You don't trouble me," she said. "And you needn't have worried that I'd read anything private. I'm not that sort of a girl; nor am I that curious about you."

"I never supposed that you were, *Fräulein*. I need the diary so I can refer back to my notations on a certain climb. I write for the *Alpine Journal* and I wish to check over an article so it can be posted tomorrow morning. *Gute Nacht*, Miss Winters. I hope you sleep well in the room I slept in."

With almost a click of the heels he was gone, striding away from her until his tall figure was lost among the shadows. She heard the echo of a closing door, and as she closed her own door she could still see that sardonic face with lines carved into it from the mountain winds, the eyes as cool as blue ice. She was convinced that he had come for the book tonight in order to confuse her.

He had known that to find him on her threshold as she was about to go to bed would shake her coolness.

She took up her hairbrush, then put it down again and stared at her own face in the mirror. The lamplight was in her hair, and her eyes were wide and dark, and there lingered in them a look of angry confusion.

Kurt von Linden had come to her room tonight with the deliberate intention of seeing her like this... and it was as if something intimate had happened between them. As if he had touched her when he had looked at her... this man who desired only what challenged him!

CHAPTER FOUR

SIRAN AWOKE and felt as small as an egg lost among feathers. The light that streamed into her room was bright and snowy, and for a few moments she couldn't remember where she was. She heard no city sounds, only a curious stillness. She sat up and saw from the clock that it was eight-fifteen and for a moment she was in a panic. She had to get to the coffee house...and then in a flash she remembered that she had left her city job and was many miles from Vienna.

At once she slipped out of bed, tied her wrap and went to look out the window. She caught her breath at the sheer majesty of the mountains, diamond-hard and sparkling in the morning sun, their lower slopes furred by snow and the evergreen of pine and fir trees. So near did they seem in the clear light that she felt she could have stretched out a hand to touch them. The lake below was blue and icy, with water birds skimming across it.

Siran's brown eyes glowed in her slender face. This was a wonderful place, and this morning her courage had returned in full force, so she felt able to cope with the people she had come to live among...these people of the snows with their burning secrets.

"*Guten Morgen, Fräulein*." It was the young maid with her breakfast tray, blond and smiling and bringing with her the fragrant smell of fresh-baked bread and steaming coffee in a blue pot. There was butter and plum jam and a pastry filled with fruit.

It was a delightful breakfast, and Gerda hummed a song as she moved about the room opening cupboards and laying out Siran's clothes. The cream sweater and pleated skirt, *ja*? The woollen stockings instead of the nylon ones if the *Fräulein* was going out.

"Yes I'm going as far as the village to see the school. I will be starting work there in a few days."

Gerda understood a little English and she replied that everyone was eager to meet the English young woman who was to teach dancing to the pupils at the school.

Siran had expected some curiosity from the villagers, and now it occurred to her that she must be quite a talking point among them. The baron had arranged for her to come here and there must be speculation as to his interest in her. She was young, single and not unattractive, and she saw Gerda looking at her as if already there had been some talk at the castle. It made her feel confused, and it also made her wonder if during that brief meeting with Breck von Linden he had become interested in her in a personal way.

Her pulses quickened. He was an attractive, compelling man, but she was a girl dedicated to a dream a man must not interfere with.

Siran quickly finished her breakfast and prepared to face the day ahead. In a wool cap to match her sporty attire she made her way downstairs and glanced in a couple of the rooms. They were unoccupied and she guessed that that baroness was with her grandson, giving him his breakfast and his bath.

She stepped through some glass doors and found herself in the courtyard, where she took a deep breath of the pure mountain air. It was a real autumn morning, with the sun shining mistily through the snow-boughed trees. The grass by the lake was frozen and it shattered like glass when she trod upon it. Soon the water would be turned to solid ice and she imagined skating parties at the castle and the merry sound of laughter winging across the lake. There had surely been such parties before Kristy had run away... and then Siran tensed as she caught the sound of someone crunching through the snow toward her. At once she was on the alert, the wind at play with a strand of her red brown hair, a chain of small footprints leading to where she stood.

Kurt came, obliterating her footprints beneath his own, his eyes intensely blue against his wind-tanned face. The cool sunlight made his hair seem very light, a chunky white sweater was high about his throat and his legs were long in dark fitted trousers. Shafts of sunlight fell across his tall figure and he looked superbly fit and craggy as the mountains that loomed over the castle.

He loomed over Siran and she had to tilt her head in order to meet his eyes. Never before had anyone made her feel so slight and unworldly and at the same time so ready for a battle.

"I saw you gazing across the lake at the mountains," he said. "Does the look of them unnerve you, Miss Winters?"

"They make me feel rather tiny," she admitted. "Even someone as tall as you, *mein Herr*, must feel dwarfed by their majesty."

"I do indeed." A smile flickered on his firm lips. "My arrogance—as you no doubt think of it—is as nothing compared to all that strength and danger. But I have the advantage of having known them all my life and I am used to the way they crown the sky... it takes time for a stranger to look and not feel a small clutch of fear and uncertainty."

He gazed fearlessly at the ice-bound peaks. "In cities things are man-made, but here at Mayholtzen one is aware of natural forces at work, of the things beyond our complete control. That is why you lose your breath when you look at the mountains... they are out of this world, and yet if one is prepared for the hazard they can be conquered.''

He looked at Siran as he spoke and his eyes were intensely alive, so that it came as a shock to meet them, no longer icy but flame-blue. How he loved the lonely grandeur of the glaciers! They moved him, stirred him as love for a woman might stir another man. Siran took a step away from him, in retreat from his eyes and from the memory of what the baroness had said last night.

''. . . could you love Kurt?'' she had said.

She might as well have asked Siran to go and climb those high and lonely crags that could not be warmed even by the stroke of the sun. He seemed to Siran so aloof from loving a woman that her heart shrank from him. . . even from the strange attraction of his face and his proud strong body.

''I wonder if you have heard of the Nanda Devi?'' he said.

''No.'' She felt the crackle of ice at her heels, for her nervous step away from him had taken her a little too close to the ice that was not yet ready to bear even her slight weight. She stood on the edge of the ice rather than take a step forward and find herself close to Kurt von Linden. . . he seemed to her more perilous.

''It was an inaccessible peak on which the Princess Nanda took refuge in order to escape a would-be ravisher. Now she is called the Goddess Nanda and for many years no climber could reach the peak of the Goddess because of the guardian chain of sheer rock all around her. It seemed as if no man would find a way up those jagged cliffs and over the deep gorges and torrents of icy water, but climbers are persistent and in the end Nanda Devi was conquered.''

''From the way you speak, *mein Herr*, I think you prefer your lonely goddess to a living woman.''

''She can only give a man frostbite, or lure him down

a crevasse." A cool little smile glinted in his eyes. "A woman of this world can be cruel in ways more subtle."

"If some women are like that it's usually because some man has hurt them in the first place."

"As I hurt Kristy, eh? So that she ran away and left me accused of cutting a rope in order to save my own neck."

"It was at your suggestion that Helmut attempted the climb, and she loved him and expected to marry him."

"I thought to climb a mountain would make a man of him."

"Not every girl wants a superman." Siran stood tensely between the ice at her heels and the flame that glimmered suddenly in Kurt's eyes. "Women have loved poets and shoe-menders, as well as those who dare the unknown and those who fly higher than your mountains to the moon itself. Women love for unknown reasons."

"You speak like a romantic, Miss Winters."

"I wouldn't want to be a goddess with ice in my veins."

"No, you want to be a famous ballerina with men at your feet."

"That isn't true at all . . . how dare you say that?"

"It's in my nature to be daring, and you told me yourself that your greatest hope is to be a great dancer. You want that above all."

"Yes, I wished to dance when I was quite young, and every dancer hopes to be a ballerina. Just as you always hoped to conquer the Nanda Devi."

"What if you fail to achieve your ambition? Will you remain in the corps de ballet and be content?"

"I—I shall be dancing."

"You have given your heart to a ghost, and for him you will always dance, eh?"

"That is none of your affair!" In her sudden flash of temper Siran forgot that she was so near to the ice and her left heel was through it before she realized. Even as she gave a gasp of alarm and felt the ice giving beneath her a pair of strong arms swept her clear of danger. With relief and yet with exasperation, she felt the crisp snow under her feet and the hardness of Kurt's hands holding her about the waist. He had saved her from a ducking in the icy water of the lake, but he had provoked her in the first place and she wasn't grateful to him.

"Don't I get a word of thanks for saving you from a plunge in the lake?" he asked mockingly. "You would have enjoyed that even less than you are enjoying the feel of my arms around you. When we danced in the ballroom last night I noticed how tense you were... is it that when we are together we are like electric wires that should not come into contact with each other?"

"I—I am sure we both feel our dislike of each other." She pressed away from him, feeling beneath her hand the muscular chest and the chunky wool, the warmth and the masculine danger. "Your reflexes are admirably quick, *mein Herr*. I would not have enjoyed a swim in icy water, but now may I go to the village?"

"You intend to walk?" He looked down at her with a smile that set her nerves tingling. How different he was from Cassian, with his wind-browned, daring face and his touch that held no tenderness. He was unknown behind his smile and not to be known.

"It's several miles to the village, Miss Winters, and you could go astray."

"Is there someone who could drive me?" she asked, standing slim and tense between the hands that were more used to the feel of rock than the fine bones and soft skin of a girl. She had a panicky image of being held closer still to him and being kissed against her will. He had such hard lips... they would surely bruise rather than caress.

"You may remember that I have a parcel to mail in the village," he said with a drawl. "Permit me to drive you there in the sleigh."

"No—yes." She had to submit, for there seemed no one else available to take her. "I wish to see the school where I'll be working. I wondered if it might be possible to meet the principal?

"I am sure Franz Donner will be delighted." Kurt took his hands from her waist and added that he would fetch the sleigh if she would wait a few minutes. He strode off, and with a sigh of relief she adjusted her woolly cap, smoothed her skirt and took a look at her face in the small mirror of her powder compact. Her eyes were huge and doelike from the shock of being held captive by him. For a moment she was tempted to run while she could, and then common sense returned. They were going only as far as the village school, not in the direction of the mountains, and if he touched her again she would slap his face and be done with it. He was only a man, after all. It was absurd to behave as if he could do just what he liked with her!

THERE WAS A JINGLE of bells, the whisper of the sleigh runners over the snow and the steady beat of the horse's hooves as they sped along.

Siran saw pine trees jeweled by the frost, and she snuggled closer into the fur rug. Smoke rose against the sky, spiraling from the chimneys of the chalets tucked into the hillsides, and she couldn't help but feel pleasure in this land of fable and drama, cradled forever by the blue white peaks of the mountains.

A wanton curl of hair danced on her forehead and the wind took her breath away, carrying with it the sound of a train on its way to Vienna, reminding her of what Kurt had said about the cold winter cutting them off from civilization. She felt his glance and knew he was thinking the same. There would be no running away when Mayholtzen became snowbound...but by then the baron would have returned. There would be no need to be nervous of Kurt when his brother came home to Seven Lilacs. Breck must like her. He had told his mother she was an attractive girl.

Siran stared at the taut leather reins in Kurt's hands and at the dancing black mane of the horse. Breck had said he found her attractive...yet why had the baroness asked if she could ever fall in love with Kurt?

Siran felt a strange little lurch of apprehension which she tried to ignore as they came in sight of the village and she glimpsed a cluster of rooftops and gables and the pink steeple of the church, set in a valley with the mountains all around, great stern guardians of the place.

"We leave the sleigh here at the top of the hill and walk the rest of the way."

He brought it to a standstill, tethered the horse to a tree and offered a hand to Siran. She would have liked to ignore his proffered hand, but that would have underlined her awareness of him. As it was she saw a faintly sardonic smile edging his lips as he assisted her from among the furs, gripping her hand in his until it seemed lost.

"Here we are, *Liebchen*, upon the path that leads down to the village."

People had been walking it, and there were ski trails in the snow as well, and a snapping of frosty twigs as Kurt brushed past them with a swing of his arm. He carried a large sealed envelope addressed in a bold handwriting...his article for the *Alpine Journal*. Siran would not have thought of him as a writing man, but there could be many aspects to a character so complex, and she didn't want to think about that.

They came to the village and she saw a cluster of old-world shops around the market square, the baker's loaf and the butcher's lamb chop carved in wood and painted and hung above the doorways. There was a charming old inn with woodcarving all over it and a wrought-iron sign, and it was as if Kurt von Linden had brought her by sleigh into the heart of a Grimm fairytale.

The school itself was fronted by a rambling garden of graceful old trees bent under burdens of snow, and there was a silent fountain framed by an arched doorway leading into the hall. As they stepped through the doorway Siran could hear young voices singing a hymn, and there was an unforgotten smell of chalk dust, floor polish and the binding of books.

"I could close my eyes and imagine myself back at school," she murmured. "One is so carefree as a child, so unaware of the decisions one has to make as an adult. Schooldays are the smiling days."

There she broke off and glanced at Kurt. He stood tall and silent beside her, gazing at the framed photographs of students on the paneled walls, and she wished belatedly that she had not mentioned the days of childhood to him. . . for how could he forget, ever, that he and his brother had been imprisoned in their own home, the sons of a brave man who had spoken out against tyranny and suffered for it?

It came as a relief to hear the approach of footsteps, and a few moments later she was being introduced to the headmaster of the school. Even as they shook hands Kurt bade them goodbye for a while. He had business to attend to in the village and would return for her in about an hour.

A pair of shrewd eyes studied Siran through the lenses of glasses that sat halfway down the bridge of Franz Donner's nose. He looked like a brown owl of a man, she thought. His moleskin jacket and bushy moustache gave him a look of wisdom and curiosity.

"So you come to teach my girls how to pirouette, eh?"

"You make my job sound trivial, Herr Donner." Her chin took a tilt. "Did you agree with reluctance to take me on as a teacher at your school?"

"The baron's suggestion did come as a surprise, but now I must admit that it will be interesting for the girls to have lessons of such an artistic nature. It will take off their baby fat, *hein*, as well as introduce them to classical music and stories."

"I'm sure they will love everything to do with ballet," Siran said, still with a touch of defensiveness. "I was unsure about taking on this job. I felt that anything so unusual would meet with a certain amount of opposition. If you are opposed to having me on your staff, Herr Donner, I should like to be told so before I begin work."

"Now we have met, Miss Winters, I can see for myself that you will be a tonic for my girls. My other teachers are older than yourself, more set in their ideas, and you bring a breath of spring air into our old school building. And now if you will come to my study we will discuss the matter more fully and take a cup of coffee together."

"I'd like that." She smiled and walked with him to his private sanctum, a cluttered, leathery, book-lined room, where she sat down in a deep chair and heard a bird chirping in a tree outside the window. She was reminded again of her own schooldays, of being sent for by the Head because she wouldn't concentrate on her sums and had her mind filled with dreams of the ballet.

She hoped Franz Donner would not regret his decision to let his girl pupils learn an art form so far removed from the more studious subjects.

Coffee was brought to them by one of the pupils, who

stared at Siran's red brown hair and slender figure. The girl's eyes widened with amazement as if she and the others had been expecting a martinet with a long stick to tap on the floor to keep the dancers in order. Siran smiled at the girl, but in shyness she fled.

"I think I've come as something of a surprise." Siran stirred cream into her coffee, while the headmaster chuckled.

"I am going to tell you now, *Fräulein*, that the baron is usually a down-to-earth man, so you must have bewitched him."

"Herr Donner!" She was shocked that he should put into words what everyone seemed to be thinking, that she was a young witch who had gone to the baron's head. "He wished to find me a form of employment I would enjoy. I was of service to his family in a certain matter."

"The matter of the child, *ja*? I was told the story by the baron himself. You were brave, Miss Winters. Cool in a crisis as the English always are."

"I just happened to be there. It was like fate."

"You believe in fate, *Fräulein*?" Franz Donner gave her a shrewd look that did not deride her belief. "Strange things happen to us when we are young, eh? They are part of the excitement of living. What of the baron's brother? What opinion have you formed of that stormy young man of the mountains?"

"His opinion of me is that I should have stayed in Vienna."

Herr Donner met her eyes and a little twitch of amusement moved his moustache. "I can see that you are perplexed by Kurt von Linden. Well, you are not alone in that. Like a young lion he is born free and in the way of such creatures he is hunted and blamed when a tragedy occurs. Quite naturally it is now in his nature to be on the defensive, and strangers are especially aware of this. They never know if he will pounce or purr, and a girl like yourself would feel that he is best left alone.''

"The trouble is—'' she clasped her hands together in almost a prayerful attitude "—I don't know if he'll leave me alone. I—I'm not being vain. I don't mean to imply that he finds me attractive or anything like that, but he enjoys teasing me. I think to him I'm like a dancing doll on a musical box. If he were not at the castle then everything would be perfect.''

"The poor young man!'' Herr Donner blinked owlishly at her through his glasses.

She flushed. "I know it's wrong of me to dislike someone I've known only a short time, but his mother is such a kind and charming woman, and the baron was courtesy itself when I met him in Vienna. With Kurt I fight and wrangle all the time and it spoils what would otherwise be a marvelous visit.''

"All castles, *mein Kindl*, have a spell cast upon them that must be broken before happiness can come to its occupants. Perhaps fate intended you to come here for more reasons than one. Perhaps you will break the spell of sadness that has lain over Seven Lilacs for many years now.''

"How?'' Siran's wide-apart eyes were filled with wonder and something of fright. What happiness could she bring? The castle was to be her home until she returned to Vienna, but even so she had her own life to live, her own ambitions to fulfill, her own sad loss to overcome. Kurt had said of Cassian that he was the ghost for whom she danced, but in her thoughts he was so alive still, lean and dark and with a magic of his own.

"It isn't my wish to become involved in the von Linden drama,'' she said. "I hope to remain only a visitor with a job to do.''

"A pretty girl in the house of two bachelors?" Franz Donner looked quizzical and cast an eye over her hair with its burnished tint of red. "Already your arrival has set the folk of this village talking. Here we are far from the city and tucked among the mountains, where every marriage and every birth is a matter of lively interest. The people are bound to wonder if it will be Kurt or the baron who will win your heart."

"My heart is given to my career, Herr Donner."

"You don't say so?" He polished his glasses and the twinkle in his eye could be seen more clearly. "I warn you that a career and perhaps some trout fishing are not very exciting substitutes for love, and I speak from experience. When you are my age, *Mädchen*, will you look at your ballet shoes, your trophies and your press-cuttings and be as sure as you are right now that stage triumphs are warmer bedfellows than a man of your own? Stars are remote and lonely things, shining at night but forgotten during the day."

"I am sure that could be said of many wives," Siran retorted. "Why is there so much discontent among women if their lot is so satisfying?"

"Because they will ask questions of life instead of allowing it to carry them along as the Danube carries the cargo and the flotsam. Life and love are mysterious things. To try to understand them is to break down a lovely piece of music into black and white notes, or to take a flower apart in order to find its secret scent. Women should revel in the mystery of things and remain themselves the deepest mystery of all."

"So you don't advocate careers for women?" Siran spoke with a smile, for she liked this man and the way they were speaking together like old friends. "I think you are a little old-fashioned, Herr Donner."

"I am proud of it, Miss Winters. I left Vienna many

years ago and I return only to visit my relatives now and again. I have become a part of Mayholtzen, a familiar figure coming from my chalet each morning puffing a pipe on my way to school. I love this place. The vista of mountains, the clear air, the bells, the beauty of the snows are followed by the loveliness of our springtime and our summer. You will fall under its spell, *Mädchen*. I can tell just by looking at you."

"Already I feel the spell of the place," she admitted. "But places can't hold on to one as people can. I have taken a vow not to become deeply involved with anyone. I want friends, but not lovers."

"You may be loved against your will, Miss Winters."

"You smile when you say my name...just as Kurt von Linden smiles."

"Your name is such a cool contrast to the warmth of your hair."

"Men always assume that auburn hair means...passion." She fingered an ornament on his desk, a curious plaything of crystal with a thousand colors trapped inside it. A rainbow in the hand.

"How else could you be a dancer without some fire in your veins? How else could I be the principal of a school if I were not a shrewd old fellow with a fondness for mathematics?"

"I was always being scolded for not doing my sums right." She smiled. "Are you sure you want me to teach your girls the dance? It can be most distracting."

"I consider that grace in a girl comes before scholarship, and that is a secret between you and me. My other teachers would be rather shocked."

"How did they react to the idea of a ballet dancer on the staff?"

"My fellow men were rather intrigued, but my lady teachers were a trifle disapproving. All will be well when they get to know you."

"I suppose they think of me as the baron's protégée?"

"A certain amount of gossip is to be expected when a handsome man like the baron takes under his wing a young English ballet dancer."

"But I'm not his baronial pet," Siran said in exasperation. "I'm not an operetta girl who needs a titled protector because I have no talent."

Franz Donner looked amused by her outburst. "You are on the defensive, maybe because you find him attractive and a possible danger to your independence?"

Her fingers clenched the crystal ornament. "I've already loved someone, Herr Donner, and I don't intend to let it happen again. It hurts too much to lose someone special, and he died so suddenly that I still can't believe that I'll never see him again. He was a great dancer. A man who was all heart and talent, a flame that burned out at the height of its brilliance. I can't imagine how I could care for anyone else."

"Yes, it is sad to lose someone very much loved, especially when one is young. It seems a cruel blow, because to the young to die is the greatest cruelty; yet your very youth will be the enemy of your grief. It will make you smile again and enjoy the things you don't want to enjoy because he is no longer with you. He filled a great part of your life, but now he is gone and you mustn't let him haunt you."

"I don't want to forget Cassian," she said ardently. "He was truly like a flame and you felt warm and alive just to be in the same room with him. It was cruel that someone so alive should be suddenly so ill...it was like seeing a wonderful bird shot down in flight...none of us could believe it. It was as if our particular world came to an end, and in a way it did. The company disbanded, most of us went in different directions and I'm still bewildered to find myself in a mountain village. I keep asking myself if I've done the right thing in coming here.''

"I think you have.'' Franz Donner gave her a long, wise look. ''It is good to come to the mountains when one is feeling lost and uncertain. Each day you will see them, eternal and symbolic of forces greater than ourselves. You will learn from them that for each cruelty there is a joy. For each loss a discovery. For each shadow a ray of sunlight.''

Even as he spoke a shadow darkened the glass doors that led into his study. Siran glanced over and saw Kurt von Linden standing there. He had a remote, very still look, almost like that of a tree or a statue standing alone in a garden. He was looking in upon them, but with the same air of remoteness, as if they were strangers to him and he was indifferent to their talk. His eyes were unsmiling in the face that wind and sun and snow had beaten so relentlessly, carving deep the lines from cheekbone to jaw, squaring off the chin until it seemed like rock.

Siran gave a little shiver, as if a chilliness had crept into the study and touched her. She took hold of her scarf and wrapped it around her neck, and she gave Franz Donner a slightly nervous smile. ''My escort awaits me, I see.''

"Yes, looking as if he was carved from the rock itself, eh?'' The headmaster's smile was quizzical as he rose to his feet and went over to the glass doors. Siran followed, bracing herself for the cool shaft of air as they were opened.

"Hello, Kurt. We have discussed Miss Winters' appointment at length and I look forward to having her on my staff. I suppose now you have come to return her to the castle?''

"I am on my way home.'' The deep crisp words were like a snowball thrown into the warm atmosphere of the study. "I wish to put in some ski practice, but Miss Winters tells me she dare not ski for fear of damaging a leg."

"Perhaps she will enjoy watching you?" Franz Donner slanted a rather wicked look at Siran. "She may not be aware of how expert you are on the snow slopes, as one of Austria's leading exponents of the sport and the daring leader of our local tradition of skiing down the slopes with flaming brands on the night of the baron's birthday. That is really something to see, Miss Winters. All the young men are clad entirely in black so that only the torches seem to stand out against the snow. Like dark angels they seem to drop from the sky with their emblems of flame."

"It sounds a very dramatic occasion," she said. "But my visit might be over before the baron's birthday comes round."

"My brother celebrates his birthday in three weeks' time," Kurt drawled. "I daresay you will still be here, won't you? Herr Donner would not employ a teacher who did not intend to stay for the winter term, at least."

"You're so clever, Herr von Linden, that you must have been a star pupil here at the school when you were a boy." She spoke quickly, not pausing to choose her words, forgetful in the heat of the moment that Kurt and his brother had been kept from attending the school by order of a dictator. They had not been allowed to mix with the other children. They had not run laughing down the valley to the sound of the morning bell. Not a single photograph of a classroom group included them. Their father had been judged a traitor for speaking in defence of freedom and justice.

Shock registered in Siran's eyes. She hated to hurt anyone with an unthinking remark, but the next instant she saw a sardonic smile flit across his face and realized that his armor was proof against anything she might say or do.

"Shall we be on our way, Miss Winters? The horse stands in the cold waiting for us."

She winced a little, for he was well aware of her own vulnerable nature. He knew just by looking at her that she could be hurt more easily that she could inflict it. It was to his advantage that from a boy he had been hardened against pain, and it was a hardness that made her want no contact with him as they walked to the sleigh. She gave the horse a pat on the neck and his harness bells jingled as he arched his head. She then hopped into the sleigh and tucked the robe around her knees. The wind blew snow from the boughs of the trees as they started on their way to the castle.

"You seemed to enjoy meeting Franz Donner," said Kurt.

"I found him a very pleasant person," she replied, "and I think I'll like working at the school. No doubt you were hoping for the reverse, *mein Herr*. I know you don't like having me at the castle, and I've a good mind to rent a chalet."

"My mother wouldn't like you to do that." He gave her an intent look. "Nor, perhaps, would my brother."

"But in a chalet I would be nearer the village and I wouldn't have to bother anyone to take me there in the sleigh."

"If you learned to ski you could use the slopes and travel there like the children do." The smile he gave her was faintly mocking. "Or are you still afraid to trust yourself to my skill? I really have no wish to see you break a leg, and as a ballet dancer you know that it's far less risky to take lessons from an expert than from a...friend."

"I—I would have to think about it." Her gaze was on the snow slopes, steep and burningly white in the cool glow of the sun. Her glance traveled higher and she caught her breath at the perfection of the peaks and the certain disdain of cold, untouchable beauty. One could admire that chaste loveliness, but how could anyone love what was so distant and so without warmth?

"You will miss a lot of fun if you don't learn how to ski," Kurt added. "We often go out in the moonlight and ski over slopes that seem made of silver...you catch your breath at the idea, eh? Think about it... there is something of the chamois about you that should make you an agile pupil."

She shot him a startled look. His mane of hair was ruffled by the wind and she was reminded again of a young lion. Even Franz Donner had applied the term to him...did the lion hope to chase the chamois over the snow slopes? Did he see further sport in teaching her a sport he excelled in?

"You are giving me a strange look." He gave a laugh. "Do you imagine I'll lure you away to the Siebengbirge?"

"I've never heard of the place." Her fingers gripped the robe, which was made of the soft furs of hunted creatures.

"It is the Seven Mountains of the Grimm tales, where lovely maidens are held captive in black castles."

"You are talking about fables," she said with a laugh. "I have noticed that Austria has quite an effect on the imagination...when we arrived yesterday at Seven Lilacs it reminded me of a rhyme I used to know."

"Won't you recite it, *Fräulein*? I might also know it."

"I—I'm not good at recitation, *mein Herr*."

"Perhaps you are shy of me?"

"One is always a little shy of new acquaintances."

"You seemed to get along with Franz Donner without a trace of it. I watched you laughing with him as if you had known each other much longer than an hour."

She bit her lip, for how could she retort that Herr Donner was a kindly man old enough to be her father? Kurt himself was a vigorous young man, who had in his eyes a look that made a girl feel as if she would be helpless to fight back if he ever took hold of her . . . a blue flame of a look that ravished the breath . . . let alone the body!

"We seemed to find ourselves in accord," she said. "He's a kind and tolerant man."

"You think I am neither of those things . . . now don't bother to deny it. I can read your eyes."

"I wasn't going to deny it." She glanced away from him and gazed at the pinewoods, through which the turrets and walls of the castle could be glimpsed as they approached at a fairly rapid rate. The sun was not warm enough to melt the snow and it was hard-packed beneath the runners of the sleigh and the little balls of it were thrown up by the hooves of the horse.

Siran couldn't help smiling a little. The scene touched her heart, and it couldn't be denied that Kurt was exciting to fight with. He said whatever he pleased and so made it possible for her to retaliate. While their battles stayed verbal all was well, but she intended never to find herself at the mercy of his lips in any other way. Though they were held in a firm line, there was a dangerous curve to the lower lip . . . a promise of passion that Siran didn't wish to put to the test.

As they drew nearer to the castle there ran through her mind the lines she couldn't speak aloud to Kurt. Was it shyness, or the fear that he might laugh at her? She couldn't tell what he would do . . . he was too unpredictable.

The rhyme seemed to take on the rhythm of the sleigh as it raced through the snow. . . .

> *Rare are these six things,*
> *A nun who never sings,*
> *A maid without a man,*
> *A lake without a swan,*
> *A fair without a tune,*
> *A day without a boon,*
> *A castle without a secret.*

Seven Lilacs was a place of mystery and sadness...
and there her thoughts broke off as something dashed
from the pinewoods and startled the horse. He flung up
in the shafts, the dappled thing of the woods sped on,
but the sleigh swiveled on a patch of ice, hovered as on a
knife edge, and then plunged over on its side, burying
Siran in furs and snow.

"Oh...really!" Hands caught at her and pulled her
free, and with her woolly cap askew she met blue eyes
that laughed openly and wickedly at her predicament.

"Let go of me!" She fought with him, but couldn't
break free of his lean hands, as wind-whipped of surplus
flesh as the rest of him. His strength panicked Siran as
something had panicked that fawn, and her only weapon was words and she used them without measuring
their truth or their falsity.

"I can't bear to be touched by you," she cried out.
"Your hands make me shudder!"

"Why?" His face and his voice were harsh. "Do you
believe what Kristy said about me? Do you think these
hands cut the rope that sent her young man plunging to
his death? Look at me!" He forced her to do so. "Yes,
it's there in your eyes...the same accusing look...the
same wish to hate me. Go ahead and hate me, *Liebchen*,
but first let me give you a reason!"

He bent his head swiftly and Siran's cry of protest
was trapped between his lips and hers. The black horse
whinnied, impatient of the overturned sleigh. There was

a flurry of snow as the wind shook the pine branches, and a strand of Siran's hair was bright against the whiteness of Kurt's sweater.

She had been kissed before...but not like this. Cassian's kiss had been a warm flick of the lips across her cheekbone...this angry kiss from Kurt found its way to the bottom of her spine, and when he let her go she stood nerveless, his face a blur against a background of trees and turrets. It wasn't until she started to run from him that she stumbled and felt the tears on her cheeks. His loveless kiss had brought back achingly the loss of Cassian and his affection for her. Little bird. His dancer and his dream perhaps, never to be realized.

She ran on until she came to the outer court of the castle. A sleek black car was standing there between the twin towers, the snow-laden lilacs bowing over it. It was a Mercedes, and as she came to a breathless halt she remembered that she had driven in such a car to the Vienna Woods, and there in its comfortable gloom the Baron von Linden had invited her to stay at Seven Lilacs.

The baron was home again...Breck had returned, and the castle beckoned.

CHAPTER FIVE

THEY MET AGAIN at *Mittagessen*, when he was polite but distant. He asked her how she was and they exchanged a few formal remarks. Then he devoted his attention to his mother and Siran ate her lunch and listened to Kurt on her left, in conversation with the surprise guest the baron had brought home with him.

The girl was called Marla Landl and she had been introduced to Siran as the daughter of the business associate Breck had been staying with at their lodge in Bavaria.

She was quite lovely, with the fragility about her of a Meissen figure. She wore a dirndl and a blouse embroidered with snow flowers, baring her throat and her shoulders. A raven braid of hair encircled her small and beautiful head, her face was a vivid oval and her eyes were dark, sparkling, and faintly slanting.

"*Meine Liebe,*" she said softly, each time she addressed the baroness, and whenever she said it her almond eyes seemed to look sideways at Breck. She seemed not to notice Siran's presence at the table. It was as if she knew already that she had charmed the baron and could do the same to Kurt whenever she chose. She was poised and amusing and she knew all about winter sports...not once did Kurt bother to glance at Siran, or to say a word.

An hour before he had punished her with a kiss, and now between them at the lunch table there was an arctic barrier.

"I would be pleased to show you my workroom, Marla," she heard him say, and never with her had there been that friendly note in his voice. "I make some of my own climbing gear, and I have also been working on skis that are both light and strong on a steep run. You may like to try a pair? They can be adjusted to the female height and weight."

"How can I resist your invitation, Kurt?" She spoke seductively and just loud enough for everyone to hear her reply. "It will be a thrill to ski with the man who made that daring jump two years ago and gave me his golden medal to wear on a chain. I still have your gift to the schoolgirl I then was. It's my talisman... to bring me luck and the things I wish for."

"Does a beautiful girl need luck?" he drawled. "Surely you have only to look at a man and he becomes your devoted slave?"

"It's easy enough to enslave boys, Kurt. The men I like are no woman's vassal." She laughed and looked at the baroness. "These men of yours are proud because no woman has them beneath her slipper."

Trinka quirked an eyebrow, more delicately yet with something of Kurt's irony. "How right you are, *Mädchen*. My sons are like the mountains of Mayholtzen... not easily conquered."

"They are a challenge," Marla said softly. "Each in his own way."

Breck glanced up from his lake trout with spicy butter and Siran noticed how he studied the girl from Bavaria... as if she were a lovely portrait upon which the eyes could be feasted. Siran had never wished for beauty, but when he flicked his gray eyes over her face she felt the pain of being compared to Marla Landl, whose features were so perfect, whose poise was so finished. She was not from a village in a remote corner of Cornwall, where the fisher folk were superstitious and still believed in witches.

"You visit us at the right time of year, Marla. You and our little English guest. In late autumn, if the snow is not too cruel, our lilacs sometimes bloom with a sort of Indian madness." The baroness put her hand upon Breck's sleeve, as if the reality of him, home safe again at Seven Lilacs, was a blessing she had to cling to. "They say in the valley—though I have known Kurt to laugh at the idea—that when the lilacs bloom at the castle there is a wedding in the air."

"There is wishful thinking in the air," Kurt said mockingly. "Trinka sees a satin slipper pressed lightly upon your neck or mine, Breck."

"Most mothers are matchmakers." The baron smiled in his thoughtful way, and in his iron-gray suit he looked attractively severe. "I think, Kurt, that when Trinka watches you set off on a climb, cowled like a monk against the icy winds, she fears in her heart that you will never fall in love with a woman as you have fallen for those cold monarchs...the Monte Rose, the Nadehorn, the Glass Turret."

"Breck!" His name broke on a note of pain from his mother's lips. "Please don't mention that awful place!"

"Not to mention it, my dear, is to make it all the more sinister."

"It is sinister." Her fingers gripped the sleeve of her older son, even as her blue eyes dwelt entreatingly on her younger son. "Kurt, must you torment me by climbing there again? Can't you forget and accept that it was an accident, what happened there?"

"I know it was an accident," he said grimly. "Everyone else knows only what Kristy called it. For my own sake I must return to the Turret, to climb again and prove myself no murderer. I did not cut the rope, but I did take Helmut up that mountain and for that I must answer."

"No!" Trinka shook her head emphatically. "Breck, speak to your brother, make him understand that the gods can be greedy. They have taken from this house before and they may do so again...Kurt, don't you care at all that I am afraid? Is your own pride all that concerns you?"

"I am a son of Karel von Linden and I need to remind other people of the fact. Trinka—" he smiled and spoke her name gently "—I have climbed the Nanda Devi, a devil of a mountain. Why should I be afraid of the Turret?"

"Because it took Helmut, and in a way it took Kristy as well. You are my son and I don't want anything to happen to you."

"I will live to be a hundred, *Liebchen*." He laughed and changed the subject, but an atmosphere of drama had entered the room and it was with relief that Siran escaped when the meal ended.

"I wish to write a letter to a friend in Vienna," she explained, and she left the family and their Bavarian guest to drink coffee in the music room. Halfway up the stairs she turned, feeling a pair of eyes upon her. A little tremor ran all through her. Breck stood lighting a cigar and he was watching her intently, his thick fair hair crisping above eyes with a steely glint to them. His white teeth gripped the cigar, and his stance was one of authority, there in the hall with its great oriel window, dark oak floor, and white walls.

Abruptly he came to the foot of the stairs and beckoned her down to him. She approached cautiously, one hand gripping the stair rail, pausing about five steps above him. His eyes held hers, a smile waited on his mouth...as if he had been waiting this moment when they would really meet again and greet each other.

"*Grüss Gott!*" he murmured. "You are exactly as I remembered, a slim young thing, with a quiet fire in your eyes. Are you a little angry because we did not speak much at *Mittagessen*? A little hurt, perhaps?''

"No, why should I be, Herr Baron?"

"Because you are a woman." His gaze passed over her, the smile traveled to his eyes. "We cannot speak right now, but I wish to see you later on. Meet me beside the lake as the sun goes down."

"Is it an order?" She hoped the nervous quiver in her voice went unnoticed and felt an eager leaping of her heart, a response to the look of him. His was arrogance combined with charm no girl could resist when he chose to exert it.

"Yes, an order." He bowed slightly, turned on his heel and strode to the arched door of the music room. As he entered the sound of Marla's laughter drifted out to the hall. Unlike Siran she was without shyness. The Baron von Linden would not have sent her in flight up the stairs, heart pounding because he made a secret rendezvous with her.

Siran closed her door behind her and sank down breathlessly on the feather puff that covered her bed. How ridiculous of her to feel so shaken! A dozen pirouettes in succession couldn't do this to her when she was dancing!

She lay back on her bed with her head pillowed upon her arms and wondered what he meant to say to her. Behind the smoke of his cigar his eyes had smiled, and it no longer seemed to matter that she wasn't beautiful like Marla, or clever enough to say always the right and charming thing. He seemed to remind her of Cassian though they were so unalike to look at. If she closed her eyes she could almost hear again the wise and whimsical voice of the man she had loved, talking about the abiding attraction of certain dancers.

"There is a type of beauty that turns the head," he had said. "And another kind that touches the heart.

Pavlova wasn't all that lovely to look at, but when she danced she was beauty as a man dreams of it. She was eternal youth and innocence. Woman in flight, untouched and uncaptured. The butterfly that kisses in the air and dies in a net. The most striking of women cannot compete with this kind of magic. You have it, Siran... you are fey."

Siran cooled her face in a pillow and wondered if she dared meet the baron by the lake. An attraction between them could not lead to anything permanent. His mother and the people of Mayholtzen would expect him soon to marry, and he could hardly marry a dancer. Nor could she give up her dream of being a ballerina.

Her cheeks tingled with the shock of a sudden thought. Perhaps he wanted an affair with her. A romance here in the snowlands, amid the strange unreal beauty of it all. Something for him to remember when she went away. Something to replace for her the aching loss of her dearest Cassian.

Tears stung the back of her eyes. She was so far away from all she had cared about. Morning exercises at the *barre*, eating her lunch perched on a costume basket, wrapped in a dream of dancing the role of Juliet, for which Cassian had been training her.

Perhaps it would be a long time before she heard again the ring of the bells, summoning the corps de ballet on stage, costumed and eager to dance.

She stared at the window that framed the cold blue peaks of the mountains. Could she ever feel for all this the same warm fondness she felt for those shabby yet lively rooms in London where she had lodged with other girls of the ballet? Could she ever care for another man with the ghost of Cassian between them?

There was a compelling charm about Breck von Linden, and each evening when the sun drowned itself in the lake there was no lovelier place than Seven Lilacs.

The turrets and towers against the skyline took on a dramatic look, as if the place had been fashioned for tragedy and love and it would not be wrong to let the heart be swayed, as the willow trees by the lake were swayed by the wind.

If she met him there he might only talk about her job at the school. . .if she didn't meet him he might assume she was afraid of him.

She was drawn to the window that framed the mountains, as if some kind of magnetism drew her. She couldn't look at them without a tiny shiver of fear, and she knew she could not have kept that rendezvous if Kurt had been the one to ask her.

It was he who made her feel afraid.

He lived with danger and would cause his mother great anxiety while he climbed again that fateful mountain she hated so much. Breck had not tried to dissuade him. . .he knew it was a waste of breath to argue with his brother. He had described him as cowled like a monk against the icy winds, and it was curious, the feeling Siran had that the high peaks had made him theirs and closed his heart to the warm love of a woman.

Breck wasn't like him. Only in looks did they resemble each other; in ways they were as apart as those towering crags, one so cool and dangerous, the other tipped by gold as the sun touched it.

When the sun set she would meet Breck by the lake. It was exciting to think of seeing him alone. . .of being the one he wished to be alone with this evening of his homecoming.

To settle her thoughts she sat down to write to Rudi in Vienna. He had insisted that she let him know that all was well with her, that she found the baroness kind and the brothers congenial. She smiled and nibbled her pen. He had said that Austrians who lived in castles had a certain arrogance, a swagger that might turn her head and make her forget that she was a girl of integrity. Dear Rudi—he was afraid she might fall a victim to the baron's charm, and she dared not admit, even to herself, that the danger existed.

"I think I'll like it here," she wrote. "These people have known very sad times and Trinka von Linden is a rather lonely person, who plays Schubert as you would love to hear it played. I seem to have stepped into a family tapestry with certain of its threads sadly torn, and I hope to help in some way, to bring a little joy if I can."

She signed and sealed her letter, then ran downstairs to place it on the hall table for mailing. The baroness had told her to do this. Gerda and one of the other maids went home each evening—skiing down the slopes of the valley—and they took any letters or parcels that needed mailing.

As Siran placed her letter with others on the pewter tray, she thought of Kurt making the excuse that he must mail his article in the village himself...he had done so in order to drive her there in the sleigh, so that he might impress on her not his desire for friendship but his warning that he would make her stay a difficult one. To him she was the outsider, the girl who didn't ski or attend the winter sports as Marla Landl did. She was a ballet dancer from London, who would, he believed, pine for the bright lights, the applause of an audience, the attentions of a *premier danseur.*

Yet she missed them even as she wandered into the room where the long mirrors had once reflected the dancing couples invited here in the old days, when the chandeliers had sparkled overhead, and a small boy had heard the music and stolen in to watch and listen.

She missed the life she was used to with a deep ache, but she wouldn't pine. She wouldn't show it. Siran had a dash of spirit that was reflected in her red brown hair and her quick, slender limbs. She would prove Kurt wrong in everything he thought about her.

She paused in front of a mirror and saw reflected the long empty length of the room, and the scars of the many dancing feet showing against the marble. She saw the archways crowned by stuccowork in white against the blue. Windows reached almost to the ceiling, with a long sweep of blue silk curtains, worn in places so the daylight showed through. There was a pair of antique tables and one of them was deeply scarred about the legs, as if someone had sat there and swung a black leather boot, marking the carved wood, leaving a momento of those unhappy days. One of the wall panels was damaged, as if a brutal hand had flung a glass and left the stain of wine on the wall. The covering of a stool was ripped...and it was strange, somehow, that the baroness had left this room to harbor memories that must be painful to her.

Was it here that she had said a last goodbye to her husband? Was it at one of the long windows that she had stood alone, after a guide had smuggled her boys across the mountains to safety? Was it here she had been interrogated?

Siran could only imagine all these things...for her the ballroom was a place of bruised loveliness, where she had been forced to dance with Kurt. He imbued everything with a sense of drama. He left her wondering each time he spoke a name, mentioned the past, insistent that she be under no illusions about the beauty of Seven Lilacs. It was a house in which people had suffered, and he seemed to imagine that Siran had lived in a ballet costume all her life and had not been touched by realities of living.

She stared at herself in one of the long mirrors and it was true that she looked young and untouched...a girl who found it easy to respond to music and who lost herself when she danced. But that didn't mean she was the dancing figure of Kurt's imagining. She was as real as anyone else at the castle...more real, perhaps, than Marla Landl, who didn't work for her living, or have any ambition beyond looking lovely in the clothes provided by her wealthy father. Siran wasn't envious, but it did rankle that she should be treated by Kurt as the useless creature.

She knew how hard a girl had to work to succeed in ballet; at the beginning there were the long hours of training, then if you had the luck to be selected for the corps de ballet you earned far less than a good secretary. The ambition had to be there, the inborn awareness that you were born to dance...the best of dancers had something unique about them, an extra dimension of personality, a gift for creating beauty in movement.

As Siran stood there in the empty ballroom she became aware of the sound of music drifting across the hall from the music room. It was *La Captive* by Berlioz, and as if compelled she began to dance to the music, her slim feet as light as thistles on the black and white marble. She felt no sense of shyness. She was in her element when dancing, as a bird is when it takes to the air.

The shyness gripped her when she caught suddenly a glimpse of another figure in one of the mirrors. She became as still as a chameleon when it sees an enemy, her eyes large and startled as they dwelt on the reflected tallness of the one observer who could make her feel foolish. He walked toward her with deliberation and she knew from his ruffled hair and the brilliance of his eyes that he had been out on the slopes with Marla.

"I was passing," he smiled slowly, "and it seemed a pity not to provide such a charming performance with an audience."

"You—you think me foolish," she gasped.

"Not at all," he drawled. "I too have been young,

and a ballroom is the place for dancing. Please continue. I will watch and perhaps learn why men go mad for ballet dancers."

At once she went to pass him, but he put out a hand and caught at her arm. It had made her happy to dance; now he came and spoiled it. "Let go of me!" she said tensely, and her eyes flashed to meet his, full of those not-so-quiet fires that Breck had spoken about. "I don't want to be tormented by you."

"I was paying you a compliment."

"I—I don't ask for flattery from any man."

"All the same it's pleasant to get it, eh?"

"If sincere."

"And you doubt my sincerity?"

"How can I help it, when you've shown me that you think me useless, when you've said frankly that I should return to Vienna? You made up your mind at the station that I had little to contribute to this household. I suppose you expected me to be carrying a pair of skis over one shoulder and a pair of skates in the other hand. Well, I'm not the sporting type. I'm a ballet dancer and I expect I've worked as hard at the *barre* as you have ever worked at winning a gold medal."

"You think me a mere playboy," he drawled.

She shrugged. "You've said yourself that your brother is the one who works to maintain Seven Lilacs. You only please yourself. You won't be tied down by a sense of duty and responsibility. You have to be free to climb mountains."

"Yes." His smile was sardonic. "I have to feel free, and because of it I gave up training to be a surgeon. I believed I wanted that. I felt an inclination to mend people, but after three years of study I felt closed in, desperate for air that did not smell of drugs and pain. I broke away from medicine. I turned to the mountains and found I was more at home among them than in the laboratory and the lecture room.''

"A—surgeon?'' She looked at him in frank amazement, and he laughed outright at the expression on her face.

"Don't be so incredulous,'' he mocked. "I could return to it and become qualified in a couple of years. As it is I'm handy to take on a climb. Several times I have saved a man from losing his fingers through frostbite, and my hands are adept at setting broken limbs.''

"You would sooner waste your life on the mountains than do good with your knowledge?'' He seemed to her more reckless than ever, as if some devil drove him to those greedy monsters of ice, where one day he might lose his own fingers and not be able to be a surgeon. She looked at his strong, firm-jawed face. She remembered that as a child he had been locked up in this castle. It had happened then, the trauma that made him break free of every bond. It might now be too late for him to give himself to a career.

"Oh, what a waste!'' she protested.

"He who becomes a surgeon must be totally dedicated. Miss Winters—'' his smile was half mocking "—are you actually sorry that I have this divided nature, wanting one thing and driven to seek something else? Are you giving me a little pity?''

"Yes,'' she admitted, "even though you don't deserve it. You have at your fingertips the chance to be of real use to people, yet you gamble with your life up there on those cruel peaks. You torment those who love you.''

"You mean my mother?'' His eyes had narrowed and seemed to hold the flicker of a tiny blue flame.

"Of course. . . and Breck.''

"What do you know of Breck?'' He spoke curtly. "I should warn you that he is very different from me.''

"I can see that for myself." She gave a faintly scornful laugh. "Warn me, indeed! What about? That he's no playboy but a man who works hard to keep Seven Lilacs in your family? The castle must be expensive to run in this day and age, when staff won't work for low wages. There are many rooms, the lake and the woods, and you said yourself that he is gradually restoring the place to its old beauty."

"Yes, out of pride. Look close at my brother, *Fräulein*, the next time you are alone with him, and you will see how proud he is. In his library he has books relating to our history and the connections the von Lindens have with the old Austrian nobility. There are midnights when he pores over the old bound documents, which during the war were secreted with Trinka's jewels in the Chapel of the Little Nun."

"I think it's fascinating," she said, a glow in her eyes. "Aren't you interested in the history of your family?"

"Our distant connections with the Mayerling affair?" he drawled. "And the fact that one of our ancestors was a Prussian general...his portrait hangs in Breck's sanctum. The likeness is startling."

Siran stared at Kurt, and forgotten for the moment was the fact that she stood so close to him that she could feel the pulsing strength in the fingers holding her wrist. All she was aware of was the implication in his words...that in Breck ran the blood of arrogant men who had ruled the lives of other people, who had been involved in court scandals and cruel wars.

She let her mind and her senses absorb what he said...and then she thought of Breck at the foot of the stairs, the light through the windows silvering his hair as he asked her, in a voice deep and demanding, to meet him beside the lake.

Her eyes met Kurt's, and at once they were as cool as ice in his craggy face, as distant and mocking as the

peaks he preferred to people. He said these things to unnerve her! If she listened to him she would be a little
fool. She must let her own instincts be her guide, and all
at once she felt that blind instinct to run away from him
to the farthest corner of the castle.

There was in Breck—admittedly—a blend of iron and
autocracy, but they weren't things to be afraid of. It was
Kurt who was wild in his ways, restless and ruled by
what was past.

"I see." His lip took a sardonic twist. "I am the one
you disapprove of. I have no sense of duty, no down-to-
earth ambitions, no ties strong enough to hold me from
going my own way. I believe you think I have no affections."

"You love your mother. . .in your way. You respond
to a pretty face."

"Yours?" he mocked.

"No." She flushed and felt that swift, primitive urge
to fight him until she hurt him in some way. But how
did you hurt the invulnerable? How did you make a
block of ice bleed?

"You mean Marla?" His eyes smoldered blue again.
"She has been a friend of the family since childhood. I
taught her to ski and to skate. Breck and I have watched
her grow from a leggy schoolgirl into the Bavarian beauty she now is. Are you jealous she is here? Afraid she
will steal some of Breck's attention?"

"Oh, you!" Siran's hand twisted in his grip in an effort to reach his face. With no effort at all he controlled
the impulse, and he laughed at her lack of strength when
it came to fighting him.

"I bring out the temper in you, Siran. It suits you. You
become a rival to Marla when your eyes flash and your
cheeks burn. You need not worry about other women,
Miss Winters. You have a wild sort of grace, like a young
fern tree, or an evergreen at the turn of the year."

"Stop it!" she gasped. "It was enough before lunch...what you did. I told you then that I didn't like to be touched by you. You make me shiver."

"You think I am made of ice, Miss Winters?" He emphasized her name and his mouth mocked, taking on that smile that held no humor, only a little twist of irony. "If I can only make you feel cold, then be sure that nothing ever happens to put you in my hands for a night. Remember your history books. The Prussians marched across Europe and they took whatever pleased them. It was pleasing a while ago to watch you dancing. Perhaps I could become mad for a ballet dancer."

Braced for the pain, she wrenched free of him. "You mock everything. I don't understand you, or like you very much. The things you say about Breck are the things you are yourself. You belong to your ice goddess out there in the Himalayas!"

"Don't stop there," he taunted. "Go on and say what I see in your eyes...I belong to the Glass Turret as well."

"Y-you seem to think so yourself. Your mother has asked you not to climb there, yet you intend to...what are you waiting for? The heavier snows and ice all the way. A chance to break your neck so you can prove you didn't break Helmut's? That will be easier, I suppose, than knuckling down to your studies again and becoming a person of usefulness and worth."

"You think me worthless, eh?" He shrugged. "You may be right, but there is something in each of us which drives us to heaven or the devil. We have within us hopes and longings that oppose each other, a pull in a certain direction that we follow blindly. It could be likened to love, or hate. Very often we fall in love against all our instincts, or we dislike someone for no basic good reason. We are human beings, Miss Winters. We are disciplined or stormy. Right or wrong. We have to work out our own destinies, despite all the talk about being controlled by the stars. We are, I believe, at the mercy of what is in our blood, and what happens to us when we are young. You were left an orphan, so you seek the strength and protection of the father you hardly knew. I venture to say that your director of the ballet was a man much older than yourself.''

"Cassian was eternally young," she retorted. "He could dance with all the drama and grace that couldn't be attained by younger men. He was a superb human being and I loved him, as a man and as a dancer. I—I'm not ashamed to say so—even to you.''

"Even to me?'' Kurt raised an eyebrow, corn-light above his eyes and thick and tousled as his hair. "You think I know nothing of love and care even less? You really think I have ice in my veins and a frozen block of it for a heart? You believe I don't know how it can hurt to lose someone very much loved? I loved my father, Miss Winters. I was six, but old enough to sense the kind of man he was, and I have hated ever since the injustice in the world, the ambition and power that exists. I go to the mountains because they are natural in their beauty and their cruelty. I climb with men who are simple in their lives, who have the peace in their hearts of the Tibetan bells, or the shrines one finds on the hillsides of the Alps.''

Slowly he looked away from Siran and fixed his eyes upon the antique table scarred by a jackboot. There was a whiteness about his nostrils, showing clearly against the deep tan of his face. "I make no apologies for the kind of man I may appear to be. I have never found my fellow climbers to be anything but gallant, helpful and enduring. Some of the medical students with whom I trained were merely ambitious. They wished only for self-promotion, the big car of the professional man, the gold plate on the door, the big fees of the rich, bored women seeking a doctor to worship.''

He shrugged again the wide, strong shoulders that even yet carried the burden of sadness and bewilderment from his boyhood. He had seen more cruelty than kindness in those days and he couldn't forget...not here, only in the mountains where the wind sang among the crags.

Siran looked at him and knew an impulse to say something sympathetic. He was too complex for her complete understanding, but all at once she knew that Kurt von Linden was drawn to the mountains to seek the person he really was, and when he found himself— her heart gave a curious little lurch as the truth struck home—when he came face to face with what he truly wanted, those monastery bells might call to him with more insistence than the voice of a woman ever could.

But before she could speak, to say at least that she had been wrong to think him heartless, he swung on his heel and strode the length of the ballroom, the mirrors reflecting his tallness one after the other. Then his footfalls were gone; the room was still as snow and curiously empty.

He had so imposed his presence on the room that its worn beauty and its furnishings now gave her the feeling of being unreal. She glanced at herself in a mirror and her face looked ghostly...and suddenly she ran from the ballroom. The music, *La Captive*, was being played again. It followed her upstairs, an instant melody with an evocative title.

Was she a captive at the castle...made so by this unusual family with its charm and its tragedy?

She closed her door on the distant music and felt the quick beating of her heart. Not since knowing Cassian had she felt so disturbed, so aware of herself as a woman rather than a dancer. In her present mood of awareness she wondered if it would be wise of her to keep that rendezvous with Breck.

The lake at sunset was almost too lovely, and Kurt had stirred into life tiny fears and doubts. He had hinted that Breck liked his own way where women were concerned...dared she meet him, to look again into his lake-gray eyes, to feel herself at the command of his smile?

In the Vienna Woods he had compelled her to give up a job that kept her in touch with the opera house. There had been something about him even then she had been unable to resist or deny. An attraction that had drawn her to his castle in the mountains, where sometimes in the autumn the lilacs bloomed again, a mad little rebellion against the dictates of nature, a purple cloak against the whiteness of the snow.

It was a sign, said the people of the valley, that a wedding would soon take place at Seven Lilacs.

CHAPTER SIX

THE EVENING LIGHT had cast a spell over the lake, which reflected the dying of the sun. Birds called to each other across the water, and the reeds whispered...a lonely sound.

The air was cold, filled with the scent of pine trees, and Siran wore her lamb's wool coat with the hood attached. The hood warmed her and also gave her the feeling of being half concealed as she approached the lake and saw the baron standing there, waiting for her. He turned as he heard her footsteps in the snow and he held out a hand to her. The sunset was on his face and it was as if there were little flames in his eyes. She felt a heart leap at the sight of him, and then his hand was holding hers, pressing her slender fingers until she felt the bite of his crested ring.

"We touch hands again and smile, eh?"

But she couldn't smile. He made her feel too shy. He was so tall, so in command of himself, and her. Slowly he raised her hand to his lips and kissed her wrist. It was an imperial gesture and yet at the same time so natural.

"I could not be sure you would be here," he said. "I hoped, but girls have a habit of changing their mino and Mayholtzen is far from the gay distraction of Vienna."

"I—I'm not a gay person, Herr Baron," she protested.

"But you would not have come if I had not provided

an occupation for you. You are not the type to enjoy being idle and ornamental, though in that hood you look charming. Charming but a trifle apprehensive, as if I might be a wolf." He smiled and his teeth glimmered in the quickening dusk. "Or are you shy of me? This is only the second time we have really talked together and you are not quite sure of the kind of man I am. But you like my mother, eh? You find her charming."

"Oh yes." His brief kiss had made her feel unbearably shy; he looked so attractive in his dark plush jacket with a scarf at his throat and the wind off the lake tugging at his hair.

"And what do you think of the castle? Do you find it romantic...like a setting for a ballet? Which ballet, I wonder? *The Snow Maiden*?"

She smiled, for it was as if he knew her mind... though he mustn't know her heart and how turbulently it beat when he put back the hood from her face and studied her in the reflected glow of the lake. The dusk light had grown mysterious, darkening the mountains and leaving for several still moments the castle in silhouette there beyond the baron's head and shoulders.

"I thought in Vienna that you would suit this place we call Seven Lilacs. There is something symbolic and haunting about it, *ja*? My mountain kingdom."

He said it with humor, and yet beneath his words rang a note of pride and possession. The things that belonged to him, the things he cared about would always be kept safe by him and treasured. So would it be when he took a wife; she would be protected by his sense of pride in what he loved...and owned.

Siran wasn't shocked that unlike Kurt his possessions were important to him. He needed more than a roll of camping gear on his shoulders, and an axe to make icesteps. How different they were, these two brothers with the same background, almost the same looks and build, and the same lovely mother! It was strange to Siran, who had no sister or brother, no family anymore, that those akin could have personalities so unalike.

The wind blew cold off the lake and she gave a little shiver. The baron suggested at once that they go to his study and talk there. "I don't much like the cold myself." His hands seemed to caress as he replaced the warm hood about her face. "The mountains rarely tempt me. I find there are distractions enough here on the ground to keep me intrigued. When I go to the peaks I go by cable car."

"I'd love to do that," she said eagerly. "Could it be arranged?"

"Whenever you wish. There is a restaurant inn at the summit and the scenery is quite spectacular, viewed from the comfort of the lounge. If Kurt joins the party he will probably ski down from there. Have you seen him in action yet?"

"No. I hear he's very accomplished at the sport."

"There are few to equal him." They crossed the lovely old courtyard with carved balconies looming over them, lit here and there by lanterns now it was dark. "You seem not too friendly with my brother. Has he said anything to upset you? I know he can be a devil when the mood takes him."

"Oh, I just don't take any notice." She tried to speak lightly and hoped she convinced him that there was nothing he need smooth out between herself and Kurt. It wouldn't break her heart if she and the storm god couldn't be friends...it was enough of a thrill to be well thought of by Breck. He did like her. She could sense it, feel it in his touch as he guided her through an entrance into his own sanctum. There was a big desk, carved and important-looking, and leather chairs big enough to get lost in. There were timbered recesses filled with books and an antique carpet of a strange design glowing against the polished wood of the floor. There were wall lamps set to reveal good paintings, and the curtains were rather sumptuous, drawn against the night and the mountains.

"It's a nice room." she looked about her. "I like the carpet in particular. Is it oriental?"

"It's a Transylvanian carpet." He leaned against the desk and took a finger-slim cigar from the engraved silver box that matched the ink set. "I am a man who likes unusual things...please drop your coat and sit down. There in that chair with the wings." He studied her, frankly, as he lit the cigar and a small plume of smoke issued with a subtle fragrance from his well-defined nostrils. "I brought you a small gift from Bavaria...in the hope that you would be here when I returned. Would you like to see it?"

He seemed to be faintly teasing her as he flicked his eyes over her white wool dress with a trim of ruby. She sat neatly in the large chair and felt like a small girl undergoing the inspection of someone very adult. He strolled to a corner table and lifted from it a box carved into the form of a chalet. He touched a tiny spring at the side and at once the music of *The Snow Maiden* tinkled out of the box. He brought it to Siran and placed it on the arm of her chair. "I hope you like it, *Mädchen*. Anything else would perhaps have been too personal, and somehow the music reminded me of you."

"How delightful!" She took the box into her hands and saw how intricate was the carving, with minute figures upon the veranda and tiny tubs of flowers; the eaves were speckled as if with snow, and a glow as of a fire could be seen through a window made of real glass.

"I love it, Herr Baron. How kind of you to think of me."

She glanced up, and the lingering look he gave her made her cheeks grow warm.

"I have not ceased thinking about you since that evening in the Vienna Woods," he said. "It's my pleasure to give you the musical box. I am pleased you like it."

"It's so beautifully detailed." Her glance wavered from his so direct one. "It looks expensive."

"With money one cay buy many things...happiness is not always among them, and it makes me happy to see you at Seven Lilacs."

"You're kind to say so." She let her fingertips wander over the musical chalet and the music made her remember a night at Covent Garden when with Cassian she had watched the ballet performed by a famous ballerina. She had a rare and spirited magic, so that when she danced in her partner's arms she inspired in the audience a feeling of wanting to protect her against the bruises of life, the sensuality of the love that might melt her. Each touch of the male dancer had seemed a strange outrage.

When Siran met the baron's gray eyes she saw in them a smile and a question. He knew her to be innocent, and his own masculinity might outrage her. Would she weep, shudder, attempt to flee from him if he should reveal his feelings? She just looked at him, and then his face drew near and she felt his lips for the first time, hard yet gentle, smoky from his cigar and very male.

"I wanted to kiss you that first evening in my car, but the time was too soon, the place too evocative. You might have taken me for the sort of man who fought duels long ago in the woods and kept a hunting lodge for his weekend *amours*. Men in my position are still looked upon as being rather wicked where women are concerned. Siran—'' he spoke her name in a deep voice ''—do you find me very wicked?''

A smile trembled on the lips he had kissed but a moment ago. ''I like your castle, Herr Baron. I like your kindness and your gift. I am glad I came to Mayholtzen.''

''Well said!'' His smile cleft a line in his tanned cheek. ''We shall drink to that, I think. I have a monastery wine Kurt brought back from one of his trips to the Himalayas. I believe I must have been keeping it for a special occasion such as this one.''

He approached a cabinet of somber dark wood, and when he opened it there was a gleam of fine glass, twisted stems and bottles long and squat. The bottle he took from the interior had a long neck and a strange label, and when his thumb dislodged the cork there was a hiss as if he released a hidden spirit. He glanced up and shot her a smile, then deep red ran the wine in the bowls of matching glasses.

''What shall be our pledge?'' He handed Siran a glass, and the monastery wine glimmered. It was strange that Kurt should have provided the wine for this moment. ''No, perhaps no promises. All I shall say is that I am charmed by you...a young companion and an old wine.''

The wine held a subtle flavor and strength, and it seemed to go to her head...or was it Breck who did that? He had such a worldly, polished charm, so that she couldn't help but feel flattered by his attentions. It seemed a long time since a man had shown her that she stirred his imagination and his senses. It was nice—it melted her heart—to be cosseted by a warm fire in a deep chair, a man like Breck giving her this hour of comfort and kindness.

"Yes." He leaned an elbow upon the carved mantel and gazed down at her. "We must arrange an outing for you by cable car. You must see everything that Mayholtzen has to offer...not only because we are grateful to you for saving Lorenz, but because you are the sort of girl to appreciate and enjoy the things that are new to you. You aren't spoiled by having too much. You see everything with fresh and wondering eyes. Your eyes, by the way, are the color of a tawny wine. They could, I think, intoxicate a man."

She glanced away from him in confusion, and it was then that she saw the portrait of his Prussian ancestor. It filled an entire alcove, but she had been so held by Breck that it came as a little shock to meet the eyes of the canvas and find them equally penetrating beneath heavy lids, to see features that so closely resembled those of the warm, living man. The man in the portrait wore full dress uniform and the top of his helmet was tipped by steel. The color of the steel matched the glint of his eyes...Breck's eyes without the smile in them, but reminding her all the same of what Kurt had said.

He had warned her that Breck was dominated by family pride. His roots went deep in the soil of Seven Lilacs, and the springs of the past were in his blood.

She glanced from the portrait to the living man, and there was an expectant look about him, as if he awaited her comments about his likeness to the General.

"If you were dressed like that," she said, "I think I would be a little nervous of you."

"Aren't you nervous of me at all, in modern dress?" Behind a drift of cigar smoke she caught the glint of amusement in his eyes, and suddenly she was unsure of him. Was he playing with her, intrigued by her response to his charm, and by the shyness a year in the corps de ballet had not tarnished? She had been too wrapped up in the magic of the dance; too well guarded by Cassian to have fallen from grace...though there had been girls she knew who had succumbed to the bribe of champagne and flattery.

"I suppose you think me a little naïve," she said. "I imagine it shows that I have never been a guest of distinguished people before. My own people were quite humble, though in their way they had pride. My home was a cottage in sound and sight of the sea, and then later on I lived in lodgings in London, a shabby house divided into flats and hardly genteel. I'm bound to be a little overawed by your castle, Herr Baron. And by your title and your attention...but I don't intend to be made a little fool of."

"My dear child—" he quirked a blond eyebrow "—I would not dream of taking you for a little fool. Did you think I invited you to Seven Lilacs in order to seduce you? Surely it would have been easier to do that in Vienna, where there are softly lit restaurants and theaters."

"It wouldn't be easy anywhere for a girl to be seduced against her will, Baron."

"Perhaps not." His gray eyes held hers and she was made aware of the power he could exert, the command he had over those who liked him. "In days gone by, my little ballerina, I would have had it in my power to make of you what I pleased...a famous dancer, or my close companion. Both, perhaps. You once spoke of a man you much admired. I begin to wonder if you mistook veneration for love. Love is not an easily controlled emotion. It's more a passionate flame than a compassionate warmth. It can burn away the protective veils, as the foliage is burned away to uncover the sugarcane, the wild sweetness at the heart of life. You are very young yet, Siran. Magic has touched you through the ballet, but not the full magic of love. The tawny wine of your eyes holds the promise of intoxication, not the fulfillment of it.''

He paused as the bells far up in the tower began their pealing, a sound that had to carry far across the snow-bound countryside, beckoning the person who might go astray, promising shelter at the castle.

''We must join the others for dinner.'' Breck extended a hand and after a momentary pause she took it and was drawn to her feet, to find herself close to the dark plush of his jacket, the firm pride of his features, the silvery sweep of his hair. She had felt his attraction in Vienna...here at the castle she felt it with increased force. She felt a compulsion to touch his face, to smooth away that deep line beside his mouth. Then he moved his head slightly and the line had been only a shadow after all.

''What is it?'' he asked. ''Just then you looked at me as if I had become a stranger. I thought after this hour alone that we had become—friends.''

That deliberate pause between his words made her pulses quicken, and then in the small tense silence between them the study door opened and a voice sang out: ''Breck, we are waiting for you—oh, you are delayed by Miss Winters!''

Siran pulled her hand free of his and turned to see Marla Landl in the doorway. Marla slowly raised an eyebrow, then catching hold of her full skirt she whirled about and went across the hall to the dining room. ''Breck is about to join us,'' she said gaily. ''Miss Winters had something she wished to discuss with him.''

''Come, Miss Winters.'' The baron was laughing softly, close to her ear. ''We will start a scandal if we are caught alone too often.''

Kurt didn't join them for dinner; he had gone to dine with a friend, Eric Gerhardt, a guide and sportsman who lived at the other side of the valley.

"Trinka, you worry yourself to no avail." Breck accepted a cup of *mokka*, the dark, after-dinner coffee with deep cream added to make it really delicious.

"But right now Kurt is making plans for that climb of his." She looked anxious. "How I wish he would return to his studies, or do anything but what he does with his life. Breck, can't you persuade him to go into business with you and Herr Landl?"

Breck set his jaw. "He would be more of a hindrance than a help, and you know I'm right. Kurt was not cut out for business...it would be like caging a lion. Trinka, let him be. You have me, you have Lorenz, and you know that I care about Seven Lilacs and the future. Accept that Kurt has the *wanderlust*. There is nothing to be done about it...not now."

"I sometimes think of him as a baby, like Lorenz. He was so fair, and not at all the independent person he became as he grew older. If we had a party—do you remember, Breck—he would come creeping downstairs to see me."

Breck gave a laugh. "I think I was sometimes jealous of him because he was younger than I and could still be treated like a baby. Now—now he's as unapproachable as his mountains."

"He has changed since the last time I saw him." Marla was curled up on a sofa, with an orchid-gold lamp burning beside her on a low table, filtering its soft light on to the thick silk of her dress and her dark hair. Her faintly slanting eyes dwelt on Breck, who lounged on the piano stool. Trinka sat near the stove as if she felt a little cold. Siran sat in the shadows of the windowseat, watching, listening, taking sips at her cream-topped coffee. These people were so striking, and it gave her pleasure to be an onlooker. She could hug to herself the secret of being kissed by Breck. When he looked at her with a cool smile, she had no need to wonder why. He wanted it that way. For them to be polite in the company of others rendered it all the more exciting when they were alone.

Marla sang for them, and her voice was curiously rich in so petite a person:

> "Still is the Nacht, Mein Schatz.
> Still is the night, my love."

"Bravo!" The baron looked pleased and admiring as he took the singer's hand and kissed it. Siran felt a swift stab of jealousy and told herself not to be foolish. Breck had known the lovely Marla for years; he was bound to be fond of her.

Suddenly he swung to face Siran. "Marla has given us a song; now you will dance for us."

"Oh no." At once she was embarrassed. "I'm not wearing the proper shoes."

"That is easily remedied. Run upstairs and fetch them."

"No, I—"

He strode across the room to her, took hold of her hands and pulled her to her feet. "I won't be denied, *Liebling*. Not tonight when like a pasha I have three pretty women at my sole command. Run, run upstairs this instant." He hurried her to the door and his mood was so gay that it was hard to resist him.

"Please, I'm shy," she whispered.

"We are just another audience," he said indulgently. "You have danced often in front of a much larger one."

"It's different on a stage in a group of other dancers."

"Breck, don't insist if Miss Winters feels she cannot perform for us." Marla spoke with tart sweetness. "We will get out the Tarot cards and I will tell everyone's fortune. It will be much more fun."

"Yes," said Trinka, and for a brief moment her eyes met Siran's in a look of understanding. "Let Marla amuse us with the fortune cards. Do you remember the last time we had them out? Aunt Bertha was here from Vienna and oh, the things that wickedly amusing old lady predicted for us all!"

He smiled and gave in, but he insisted that Siran sit within the family circle. "You are not getting out of this," he said. "Your fortune is going to be told as well."

Marla looked deliberately at the girl who was almost her own age, who could also be expected to want the romantic love of an attractive man. "There are secrets in every heart," she said. "Do you wish me to reveal your secrets, Miss Winters?"

"Are you that good with the Tarot cards, Miss Landl?"

Marla laughed softly. "I think I'll be very good at reading the cards for you. When a girl leaves her own country to come abroad she is either running away from something, or searching for someone. You came not as a tourist, eh? I am told you were working in Vienna."

"Yes, as a waitress."

"How disagreeable for you, to have to wait on other people. I would not like that at all."

"Well, you will never have to do it, will you, Miss Landl? In some respects the work was quite interesting. Some of the customers were very amusing."

"Were any of them handsome? I fear I'm terribly spoiled, Miss Winters, and I do enjoy having handsome men around me. When Breck invited me to Seven Lilacs I couldn't resist coming. Was it the appeal of two good-looking bachelors that brought you to the castle?"

"Stop your teasing, Marla." The baroness had taken a rosewood box from a side cabinet and now she placed it on the sofa table beside the Bavarian girl. The box caught the lamplight and gleamed the color of dark red roses, and when it was opened a velvet lining was disclosed and yet another box, card-sized, of silver to match the silver key.

"Have you ever seen a pack of Tarot cards, Siran?" The baroness sat down beside her on the twin sofa, while Breck poured wine into four stemmed glasses and handed them around. He then sat down himself in a large winged chair, a relaxed air about him.

"No, but I've heard they're very interesting." Siran cupped her wineglass like an acolyte at a mysterious ceremony. "Weren't they used by the ancient Hebrews to predict fame, fortune, or calamity?"

"Yes," murmured the baron, "so beware. You may be in for some intriguing revelations."

Siran glanced at him and smiled. She was struck by the nobility of his head at rest against the dark blue wings of his chair. He looked so at home in his castle, so much the master, yet those firm lips had touched her own. As she looked at him they touched the rim of his wineglass, and there was something deliberate in the way he did it, as if he imparted to her his secret wish to feel again the shyness of her kiss.

A flush came into her cheeks and she looked away from him and watched the ceremony of the Tarot cards. Trinka shuffled them first and handed them to Marla. With a little low laugh, almost a purr, the Bavarian girl began to lay them out one by one on the table. They were quite beautiful, with pictures upon them that looked almost as if they were painted with the blade-fine brush of an oriental artist.

"Ah, here we have the Sun, *meine Liebe*. Burning bright above a pair of children. It stands in conjunction with Justice—look, the sword and scales. And—how strange, the Pendulum! The man suspended over a chasm...."

The baroness caught her breath sharply. "I hate that card!"

"It means only duty," said Breck. "The cards look very dramatic, but each one holds a hidden meaning rather than an obvious conclusion. Each one of us is tied by the feet to his duty as opposed to his desires. The two can't always meet, and so we feel tormented and the card expresses this."

"The Sun means joy," smiled Marla. "There is joy in store for one of your children."

"One?" The baroness gave a little shudder—Siran felt it, for she was sitting close to Trinka. "That is enough hidden destiny for me, Marla. Play now with Siran."

"Very well." Marla gathered the cards together and handed them to Siran. "Please shuffle them and we will see what is in store for you, Miss Winters."

Siran did as she was bid. "I do wish you'd call me by my first name," she said. "You make me feel like one of those schoolmarms in a Victorian novel."

Marla stroked a dark eyebrow and stared at Siran, as if she thought the English girl looked a schoolmarm. "*Danke schön.*" She took the shuffled cards and began to spread them out. "You have a most unusual name. I thought all English girls were called Grace, Alice or Jane."

"Only in Victorian novels," Siran said, tartly sweet herself.

The baron gave a little chuckle. "You asked for that, *Liebling*," he said to Marla. "There is a hint of titian in Siran's hair, a sign of temper."

"You like women to have a temper, Breck?" Marla looked at him with a flutter of her long lashes, a slight pout to her red mouth, the sheen of little pearls bobbing her ears.

"Angels are for the wayside shrine," he said teasingly. "I have known you too long to be fooled by that limpid look. I was at the lodge, remember, when your own grapevine was raided by thieves in the night and every grape was plucked. Will I ever forget, *Liebling*, the storm you created? Your father bought a riding horse and a string of pearls to pacify you."

"I meant to make my own wine," she pouted. "It would have been delicious. The grapes were so big and so dark. I was going to tread them myself."

"Poor *Liebling*," he laughed. "To be denied for once."

"I hate you, Breck, when you laugh at me." She tossed her head and gave her attention to the cards. But a tiny dent was showing in her cheek. A hint that his teasing was to be preferred to his indifference. Siran wondered in that moment if Marla was in love with Breck von Linden.

"These are interesting cards," she murmured. "*L'Etoile*, the card of hope. Are you hoping for something nice to happen to you, Siran?"

"Certainly. It's human nature."

"Ah, and Isis the Priestess! You are involved in a mystery, my dear. This card is very significant and means that something strange is likely to happen to you." A slightly malicious twinkle danced in Marla's dark eyes. "I hope I am not making you nervous?"

"Not in the least." Siran spoke gaily, but all the same she wondered why Seven Lilacs seemed a place of destiny, as if each step away from Cornwall had been leading her to the castle. Being of Celtic parentage she couldn't dismiss lightly the tiny signs and portents. She had the feeling of a secret waiting to be revealed—a feel-

ing almost like that of being poised on her toes for a surprising cue.

"Continue with the card reading," Breck ordered.
"It's amusing if nothing else."

"Don't you believe in the cards, Herr Baron?" Siran
turned to look at him and saw a smile quirk on his
lips. He looked like Kurt then, sardonic and a trifle
mocking.

"I would hate to believe that I am not my own
master," he replied. "People aren't puppets on strings.
They make their own decisions, their own disasters,
their own destiny."

"You seem very sure of that, Baron."

"Yes, *Fräulein*. It's for a man to be sure and a
woman to be charming."

His answer confused her, for it held the kind of arrogance she would have expected from his brother. Were
they, after all, more alike in character than she had
thought them?

The rest of the evening was passed amusingly, and
when Trinka played for them Siran pushed to the back
of her mind the card of Isis with its prediction of a
strange occurrence. She had already enough to occupy
her mind, and when at last they all said, "*Gute Nacht*,"
to each other the midnight bells were ringing.

"*Stille Nacht*," Trinka murmured, as she and Siran
paused at a bend of the stairs to gaze from a window at the snow that was falling again. It lay from wall
to wall of the courtyard and gave the trees a tranced
look.

"The lilacs won't bloom if the snow keeps falling,
and it would have been so nice to have a wedding at
the castle. It seems such ages since we had a real cele-
bration here, with lots of food and wine, musicians and
people dancing, the lights blazing out from the long
windows."

"You could have a party," Siran smiled. "Why not, if it would give you pleasure?"

"Kristy has been gone so short a time, and there must be a real reason for a party."

"Won't it be Breck's birthday in a matter of weeks?" A little color stole into Siran's cheeks as she spoke his name. "You can't go on being sad because of what happened to Kristy...perhaps it was meant to be. Perhaps she could never have been happy without her young man."

"She was so impetuous, poor girl. Helmut was a student of art, you know, and he used to come to Mayholtzen for his vacations. Neither Breck nor Kurt approved of him very much. He was so unlike both of them, dreamy and full of flights of fancy, and there were arguments over Kristy's friendship with him here at the castle. Kurt wished her to like his friend Eric, but no one can force a woman to love against her will, and it was her student she loved." Trinka fingered her rings. "I begin to wonder if Breck has brought Marla home for a more serious purpose than the winter sports to be enjoyed here. She doesn't get along too well with her stepmother—Herr Landl was made a widower when Marla was twelve years old, and he remarried about two years ago. Marla was accustomed to being the little mistress of the lodge, and as you can see she has been rather indulged. An exquisite young thing, of course, but fond of her own way. Breck, however, would soon remedy that if—"

The baroness paused significantly, and Siran felt as if a little pit opened beneath her feet. Could it be true that he had marital plans with regard to Marla...and plans quite the opposite when it came to herself?

"We will cause a scandal if we are caught alone too often," he had said. But he had kissed Marla's hand openly. There had been nothing clandestine about his admiration for the other girl.

"Would it please you, Baroness, to have Marla for a daughter-in-law?" Siran asked. "She is very lovely, and very entertaining."

"And accustomed to our traditions," Trinka said thoughtfully. "I do believe that at last Breck has made a decision with regard to the future. He knows Marla very well, and they appear to have tastes in common. I must watch those two. I would like to be certain that Breck is much in love with the girl he chooses to marry. Marriage can be a joy, or merely a partnership, according to the amount of love each partner contributes. I was very much in love with my husband, and Breck has some of his ways. That air of sternness is deceptive."

Siran knew it was, but she had to pretend to be disinterested. She was merely the young English guest who would work in the valley a while and then return to Vienna. For her this was an interlude...the solo dance in the middle of the ballet.

Trinka looked at her and seemed to notice how her eyes dominated her face. "You must be tired, my dear." Trinka leaned forward and kissed her cheek, and then she gave it a light stroke. "English girls have such nice skin, so clear and smooth. Tell me, Siran, what do you intend to do with your life? Ah, I know you are a dancer, but you can't give all your devotion to it. When the curtain falls everyone goes home to someone...who will you go home to?"

"Probably a cat or two." Siran gave a laugh. "A full-time dancing career can be very demanding, and unless a dancer marries a man who is connected with ballet, who understands the various demands and difficulties, it is best if she stays single."

"But, *Liebling*." Trinka looked shocked by Siran's

reply. "An attractive girl can't deny herself the nicest thing in life, the loving kindness and the passion of a nice man."

"Perhaps later on I'll meet someone in ballet, but right now I can see no further than my ambitions."

"You don't look the ambitious sort to me." The baroness looked at Siran from her head to her heels. "You are five-foot-nothing of youth, dreams and a slender shape. You need someone to take care of you."

"I'm really very independent, so you mustn't worry about me, Baroness. I know what I want."

"I wonder, my child." They continued on their way upstairs and parted at the door of Siran's bedroom. "Sleep tight and happy dreams, *Liebling*."

"Goodnight, Baroness, and thank you for all your kindness."

The baroness went on her way along the corridor to her suite which included the nursery. She opened the door and disappeared inside, to insure that all was well with her grandson.

Siran closed the door of her own room and lit the lamp beside the bed, which diffused a muted glow over the room, with its big goose-feather bed, glass animals and castles, and beaver-skin rug. Siran walked to the shelf that held the little ornaments and she picked up one of the castles and fingered the glass turrets. It seemed strange to think of Kurt collecting these as a child. As a man he seemed so strong and defiant and above the trivialities of glass castles and the need to make a home of his own for a woman of his own.

A shadow stirred on the white wall and with a tiny gasp of alarm Siran turned to see the white dog Bruno slithering out from beneath her bed. He gave a wide yawn, cocked an eye at her and then ambled to the door. She followed him and opened the door. He was used to

this room and often she came in to find him looking out
of the window, or sprawled out in front of the stove that
was always kept burning with small logs.

Tail aloft, he went on his way along the corridor, and
Siran gave a sudden little laugh. Bruno was so like his
master, so unperturbed when he startled a girl and so independent. It didn't do to stroke him very often; he
didn't bite, but he did growl if she touched him.

She placed the little glass castle on the table beside her
bed, where it caught the light of the lamp and glistened
with that fairy-tale magic so dear to the hearts of the
young and sensitive. Siran tried to imagine Kurt here as
a child as she prepared her bed. The invasion of Seven
Lilacs by men in jackboots had left an indelible impression on his mind, for he and Breck had been spirited
away from their mother for the remainder of the war,
and when they had returned the castle had been scarred
and marked by those men, stripped of its treasures, and
their mother had greeted them with silver in her hair and
suffering in her eyes.

Breck had been older, more able to understand the
reasons for their banishment, but Kurt had never forgotten, or forgiven. The experience had marked him as
surely as a visible wound and left scar tissue which had
hardened over as he grew to be a man. He was now a
man who was afraid to give of his heart because as a boy
he had seen jackboots march over his mother's heart.

Siran discovered herself by the dressing chest, staring
into her own eyes reflected in the mirror. They were
wide with their discovery, for no one since that time, not
even Trinka, had found a way to show him that love and
pain were twin beings. To shut yourself off from love
was to become one of those who hurt other people. He
had hurt Helmut and Kristy, and he saw only one way
of reparation.

She shivered and went to the stove, where she knelt

down and warmed her hands, her blue robe in a silky pool about her slimness. She looked almost a child, the tiny flickers of flame gilding the soft pewter of her hair. She knew that the ghost of a boy haunted this room, that in the silence he had spoken to her, knowing her to be young herself and rather lost.

"I know what I want," she said again. "I want to dance."

In an instant she remembered the music box Breck had given her; she had left it in his study, and she had a sudden longing to hear again the music of *The Snow Maiden*. On impulse she left her room and ran swiftly downstairs in her robe, a ghost in blue on each different landing until she reached the hall and made quietly for the door of Breck's study. She turned the handle and opened the door, and at once she saw the lamp burning on his desk, and the tall figure over by the cabinet in which the baron kept a collection of antiques.

"Breck!" She stood there, startled and confused, and then he swung around and she was looking at his brother...and in his hands he held one of the black and silver military pistols that were part of the baron's collection.

At once the obvious conclusion leapt to her mind... he was so unhappy that he was about to end things with a bullet.

"Kurt—you can't do it!" She dashed across to him and grabbed at the pistol. "Think of Trinka—it would break her heart!"

For a moment a tussle ensued, and then quite shockingly came the sound of his laughter above her head; she looked up swiftly and met his wickedly amused eyes.

"You came at me like Hildebrund trying to snatch the sword. My dear girl, I am not about to end it all with one of the general's pistols. It would be much easier, on

me and the carpet, to leap off a mountain if I felt like
it.''

"But—"

"Eric and I were arguing about these things—he
maintained that duelling pistols have sights the same as
officer's pistols, but as I pointed out to him, duellists
hardly had time to take steady aim at each other. They
were out to wing, not to kill.''

"Oh dear!" Siran had never felt so foolish... but she
had been thinking about him as a boy, and seeing him
with the pistol had triggered off the wild thought that he
was about to take his life. "I must have seemed like a
crazy woman, hurling myself at you like that. I do
apologize.''

"Not at all. The pistol wasn't loaded anyway. It's
past midnight, Siran. Were you sleepwalking?''

"No, I—I came down for something I'd forgotten.''

"And you heard me in here.''

She hesitated in her reply, reluctant to admit that she
had come down to the study for the music box his
brother had given her. She could see it on the mantel-
piece, where Breck had placed it when Marla had appeared to find them alone together. Oh, it wouldn't do
at all, not if Marla was meant for Breck, for anyone at
Seven Lilacs to get the idea that Siran meant anything to
him.

Kurt was the last person who must know!

"It is very late... the little thing I wanted can wait till
the morning.'' She went to move away from him and
swiftly he stood in her way. He looked down at her intently and made her at once aware that she was wearing
only her robe over her nightdress.

"Please—let me go.''

"I'm not touching you... you might scream and
wake the castle," he said sardonically. "What was so
important that it brought you down here at this late

hour? You see, you give a little jump. You are nervous, yet a short while ago you thought only of wresting this pistol from me."

"I assure you it can wait until the morning."

"Is it something you left in this room?"

"No."

"You are not good at telling untruths. Your lashes flutter madly and your cheeks are red. Shall we play a game of hunt the treasure?"

"Don't be absurd—at this time of night? Someone will hear and—"

"And maybe find us alone like this, beneath the portrait of our fierce ancestor. What do you think of him, Miss Winters? He's very handsome, eh? Can't you see the likeness to my brother?"

"I'm going to bed." She tried to step past him, but with an adroit movement he trapped her in the alcove, the general gazing down sternly upon the scene while his great-grandson smiled and enjoyed Siran's alarm.

"Why can't you leave me alone?" she asked. "You don't torment Marla in this way."

"Marla would merely laugh, but you become angry and alarmed, as if I threatened your innocence. What vanity, Miss Winters! Do you think I find you as attractive as my brother does?"

"I—I really do hate you," she gasped. "Never in my life have I met anyone so infuriating. You do it on purpose...as if you don't want people to like you. If they liked you they might dent your suit of armor. You're armored to the heart, Herr von Linden. It's only your pride that can be hurt."

"Do you want me to like you?" he drawled, close to her, tall and rugged and broad-shouldered, the tie pulled open at his throat so that his dress shirt was a shock of white against his brown skin. He had the vital, untamed looks of a man some women would want to be liked by, but Siran was crushing herself against the paneled wall, widening as much as possible the gap between her and Kurt.

"I—I prefer things the way they are, thank you."

"I think I do as well." He was gazing down at her, studying the bright disorder of her hair, the blue of her robe, the pale creaminess of her throat, the tawny temper of her eyes. "I can see why my brother invited you here. There is more to you than the girl heroine who leaps to save a baby and a man she doesn't even like. If this pistol had been loaded it might have gone off and hurt you. I would hate to be responsible for marking a thing so pretty."

"Don't. . . look at me like that. Do you think because I've been on the stage that I like to be flirted with? I didn't come to Seven Lilacs for that."

"Why did you come, Miss Winters?"

"To see your mother. . . and to work. Why must you assume that I'm running after your brother? And if I were, what business would it be of yours?"

"You could get hurt. . . I warn you. People are not always what they seem, and you are not as sophisticated as I thought you would be when I heard you were coming to stay with us. If you had emerged from the station looking poised and sure of yourself I would not have bothered to warn you of anything."

"Why would I need a warning?" She looked at him with wide and puzzled eyes. "I'm not a child to take people at face value. I know they aren't books to be selected from a shelf and read in a few hours. What are you getting at?"

"What did you come down here looking for? This is Breck's study, so I presume you came looking for something he gave you."

"How dare you ask me that! It's none of your business!"

"I'm curious, when a girl leaves her room after midnight and comes stealing downstairs for some trinket she has forgotten. It has to mean something to her. It has to be a token of affection."

"And what are you, *mein Herr*?" Her eyes were ablazing, topaz, jeweled, in her slender face. "Your brother's keeper?"

"No, not my brother's." His voice went rough. "No, you little fool! I don't want to see you in the predicament Kristy found herself in. You're impulsive like she was, carried away by a bit of magic and poetry. You're vulnerable and a long way from home." He tossed the pistol aside, took hold of her and gave her a shake. Then his hands suddenly crushed her shoulders and she was swept against the hardiness of him, held so strongly that she couldn't beat at him, or break away from him. She saw the blue and angry sparkle of his eyes, and then when she thought he would kiss her, he lifted her as if she were a child, marched from the room with her, carried her all the way up the stairs and dropped her to her feet in front of her door.

"Now go to bed," he said sternly. "You aren't a child to run around the castle in your night clothes. You behave like one, *ja*. But you don't look like one."

At the sweep of his eyes, gone a dark blue in the shadows of the corridor, Siran grabbed at the handle of her door and pushed it open. "I knew it when we met." The words came from her with a rush. "I knew we could never be friends."

"I knew it also, *Liebchen*." He gazed down deliberately into her eyes. "We could never be friends. Good night, and no more wandering."

He swung on his heel and marched off, treading silently like a jungle creature, his tawny head set arrogantly on that strong neck branching into wide shoulders. Siran retreated into her room and closed the door tightly.

She was sure she had shut him out. . .until she saw the glint of the little glass castle. It had been his and in those far-off days he had believed in the magic of it and spun a tale, perhaps, of a princess locked in one of its turrets. She would have liked him as a boy, but try as she might she couldn't feel anything but antagonism for the man.

She climbed into bed and reached out to switch off the lamp, and in doing so she knocked over the glass castle. Her heart seemed to stop, then beat again. If it had fallen to the floor it would have broken. . .tomorrow she would replace it on the shelf for safety.

Most things high on a shelf were safe, if a little neglected, and Kurt had more than intimated that she had better stay out of harm's way.

Out of his brother's way, he had meant!

CHAPTER SEVEN

SIRAN STARTED her dancing lessons at the school. The girls were equipped with dark blue tunics and crepe-soled shoes for their gymnastics class, so these had to suffice for the present, until they became more proficient as ballet students. Siran had no illusions about producing a group of Markovas, but it was amusing and interesting taking this class of older pupils and putting them through a routine so well remembered.

Herr Brandt had arranged for several *barres* to be installed in the gymnasium and Siran found to her delight that the girls were supple and free in their movements owing to the amount of skiing they did, not to mention skating when the ice became thick enough and riding toboggans down the snowy slopes.

They were a nice lot of girls, pleasant and sociable in the way of most Austrians, intent on hearing all about England and the ballet. They enjoyed watching Siran, clad in her sleeveless leotard, going through a series of steps and movements new to them as yet. They had to learn *baloon*, and she showed them how light and bouncy they must be on their feet. Then there was *batterie*, leaping steps in which the feet came together in little beats. There was the *fouetté*, a whipping movement of the leg, and the full turn on one foot called the *pirouette*.

They watched fascinated, and unbeknown to Siran as she danced and explained, the headmaster was watching as well from one of the alcoves, a little smile of enchantment quirking his moustache. This young woman might not teach the girls of this valley school to balance so gracefully on one leg, but she was an acquisition. Someone fresh and talented for his pupils to emulate. He nodded to himself and went on his way, humming a Viennese tune low in his throat, to take the older boys in math.

The days passed, and one morning the gymnasium girls acquired a record player and a pile of records. They were dumped on the doorstep by someone who came by in a yellow sports car. One of the girls saw him driving rapidly away, too modest to stay and be thanked.

"Well, who is this Santa Claus who owns a yellow sports car?" Siran wanted to know.

A couple of the girls spoke English and they interpreted for Siran, often producing gales of laughter as their English and her bit of German got mixed up.

"It's Herr Gerhardt," the girl said. "He comes to Mayholtzen for the climbing, and everyone knows that he was very much in love with the stepdaughter of the baroness. She would never look at him, but he would have married her despite all the talk after the accident on the Glass Turret."

Siran changed the subject, for she didn't wish to encourage gossip about the inmates of the castle. . .fascinating though it might be. They started the record player and she got the girls miming to the music of *Swan Lake*. She would thank Herr Gerhardt somehow for a present so useful and so unexpected. She had heard he was a man of independent means, but not everyone was so generous.

Her meeting with Eric Gerhardt came about as unexpectedly as his gift to the school. A cable-car trip had been arranged for the coming weekend, and rooms for an overnight stay had been booked at the Hotel Blue Rose at the summit of the mountain ride.

It was the baroness who told her that Kurt's friend would be joining them. "He's a lonely man," she said. "It will be good for him to be in our company for the weekend."

"Did Kurt persuade him?" Siran added cream to her coffee, for she and Trinka were enjoying a feminine interlude before the two brothers arrived home from their various activities. Marla always spent about two hours getting ready for the evening. Her long hair could be arranged in all sorts of styles, and she possessed a large and varied wardrobe. Siran, who owned but a few dresses, had grown used to being put in the shade by the other girl. Now she only smiled, for like the others she was entertained by Marla's dramatic appearances. One evening she donned dark red silk that made her look like an orchid. Another time it was sapphire blue velvet. She lit up the castle like some fairy princess, and Siran was quite sure in her heart that the baron would eventually marry her. In the meantime he flirted with Siran and took her for walks through the woods. Sometimes they met there, not by arrangement but by instinct, as if their thoughts had flown together during the day and they found each other in the woods when dusk was falling.

She looked forward to the weekend, when she would stand with him above the world, making polite conversation in front of the others, but speaking with her eyes.

It wasn't a sinful friendship. She was flattered that a man of such distinction should like her, but it would go no further than that. She would not prove to Kurt that she needed a keeper.

"Yes, Kurt thought it would be a good idea if his friend came on this expedition with us." Trinka smiled. "The pair of them never get tired of the mountains, and Eric has no family. He's a slim, shy man, but charming in his quiet way."

"He sounds the very opposite to your son." Siran hid the quick amusement in her eyes by leaning forward to select a pastry bursting with cream and jam. Being one of those lucky people who didn't have to watch the calories she could enjoy these Austrian cakes that tasted so heavenly.

"Don't you find Kurt at all attractive?" Trinka asked quizzically.

"I didn't mean that, exactly." Siran licked peach jam from the corner of her lip. "I mean he isn't exactly the retiring sort. He speaks his mind so boldly, and his personality is so definite. His friend was too shy to bring his present into the school, and he left it with a little note attached and drove off in his car. The note said that he hoped the music would help the girls with their ballet lessons. He thought the idea so excellent, for he himself liked to go to the opera house when he was in Vienna. I thought it was so nice of him and I'm pleased to be meeting him soon."

"You two will find much in common." Trinka ran her fingers over her rings, a habit she had when a thought disturbed her. "As you say, my son Kurt has a very definite personality and those who don't really know him are inclined to find him a little too overwhelming. Would you believe me if I told you he was more lovable as a child than his brother Breck? Then he needed me. Then he would come to me with his small troubles and his scraped knees. Then he belonged to me...now he belongs only to himself. A woman's sons grow up and must live their own lives, but Kurt withholds his heart from people. He has instead become an acolyte of the mountain gods...if that doesn't sound too fanciful to the ears of a young English girl?"

"No." Siran gave the baroness a look of complete understanding. "People in ballet are often like that. David Cassian was completely devoted to the dance and though there were women in his life they touched only the fringe of it, only the part that needed their laughter and their company occasionally. I loved him—I couldn't help myself—but I always knew that if he loved me in return it would be partly because of what he made of me as a dancer, and that he would love me best when I danced for him. I think if you love someone you have to be prepared to be hurt by them. I think if love was all roses and no thorns it would be less exciting."

"You would want it to be exciting?"

"Yes...if I had not made up my mind to be an acolyte of the dance."

The baroness smiled. "I think that at the weekend the cable car will be carrying a group of lost souls to the mountains."

"Even Marla?" A dent appeared beneath Siran's left cheekbone.

"The child is acting all the time. There is something she wants very much, but that other devilish son of mine is eluding her. He walks in the woods more often than he used to, and I have heard him humming a certain piece of ballet music."

"Baroness—"

"Hush, *Liebling*. I too have been young, and Breck is a handsome man. Who knows if Marla will get her wish, or any one of us? The threads of fate are twisted into strange patterns."

As the baroness spoke a wind stirred across the court-yard and a branch of the linden tree tapped against the window of the music room. Siran's nerves tightened at the sound. "I hope the weather keeps all right for the weekend," she said. "I'm told the cable cars travel up and down in the snow, but not in a high wind."

"No. A few years ago a cable snapped and some people were killed, but I think the weather will hold for us.

It will be cold up there, so I hope you have a warm coat?''

"I have my lamb's wool."

"Child, it is little more than a jacket! I would like to lend you a fur coat of mine, if you will accept it. We could go upstairs to my room to look at it now... would you like to?''

"I'd love to, if you're sure."

"Come, let me show you." Trinka was looking eager, as if not for a long time had she been able to share something of hers with someone like Siran. As they approached her suite, which was situated in a curving flank of the castle, the baby cried and Trinka ran in and fetched him from the nursery. He sat on her bed, playing with a scent bottle, while she swept open the doors of her wardrobe and disclosed a line of dresses and coats.

"Here at Mayholtzen it isn't worth putting one's furs in storage, and I am one of those spoiled women who likes to wear a fur coat even to collect fallen branches for the stoves. Viennese women are like cats for comfort—ah, here is the coat I mentioned. Snow leopard. Very attractive, but when my son bought it for me I believe he was thinking of me when I was a much younger woman. You see, the style is too young for a middle-aged widow. There is a muff to go with it and a hat.''

"But the baron might not like me to wear a coat he bought for you." Siran hesitantly stroked the soft pale fur.

"It was not Breck who bought me the coat." Trinka's smile was quizzical again. "I have two sons, remember.''

"Kurt? Oh, then I couldn't possible wear it! He wouldn't like me to—he would think I was imposing on your generosity."

"Then you must tell him smartly that it was my idea to let you wear the snow leopard. Come, try it on. I have an idea it will suit you."

"I'll try it on, but—"

"When you see yourself in it, *Liebling*, you won't be able to resist wearing it. And when Kurt sees you he won't dare say a word."

"I think he'd dare the devil." Siran gave a nervous laugh as she slipped her arms into the sleeves of the coat and let Trinka settle the collar and button it for her.

"There, take a look at yourself in the mirror."

Siran gazed wide-eyed at the glamorous stranger she looked in the sleek, beautifully tailored coat, the collar framing her face and the color of the fur a contrast to her red brown hair. She gave a quick smile of delight, for every girl loves to look nice, and she did look unusually decorative in the snow leopard coat.

"You are charming," Trinka said warmly. "Try the hat. . . you see how young the style is, with that fur bob on top, but it suits you. I knew it would, and you must wear the outfit for our trip to the mountains."

"I'm tempted, Baroness."

"But still a little afraid of Kurt, eh?"

Siran stroked the soft ball of a muff, softly scented with the perfume Trinka used, and there came irresistibly into her mind a picture of Kurt striding tall and sunburned into a smart Viennese shop to look at furs and to find himself captivated by the muff that went with this coat, and the hat with its gay bobble. But even as she smiled, there followed another image in her mind. . . the flash of anger in his eyes to see her dressed for the cable ride in the outfit he had chosen for his mother. . . remembered by him as young and gay as the city of Vienna, when there had been music in the air and laughter without a sigh.

"He wouldn't be pleased, Baroness. He chose these

things for you, and quite frankly I have a vision of him snatching the hat from my head and the muff from my hands." Siran gave a breathless laugh. "He might even toss me from the cable car for my audacity."

"Be audacious, *Liebling*, and take a chance." Trinka broke into laughter as well, until there came a sudden yell from Lorenz and they both hastened to the bed to find he had pulled the stopper off the scent bottle and had drenched himself from head to toe. There was scent in his curls, over his jumper suit and down his legs. He smelled like a flower garden, but he behaved like a young bear until they got him into a bath and washed off the smell which even at so young an age he resented. Siran knelt on the rubber mat beside the bath and played boats with him, and soon he was grinning all over his face and aiming soapy water all over her.

"Pussinka," his grandmother appealed, "do have some regard for the floor!"

"What about me?" Siran was reduced to helpless giggles as Lorenz blithely filled a boat with water and tipped the lot in her lap. She had put on a nursery apron, but it did little to save her, from the water, and there she was, damp, tousled and helplessly laughing as the door opened and the baron came striding into the bathroom.

"Well, what have we here?" Suddenly the room seemed a couple of sizes too small as he stood there in a light gray suit, gazing down at the wet, nude, soapy child in the bath, the girl with a duck in one hand and a sponge in the other, and his mother who was trying vainly to keep back the flow of water with a mop.

"We are a helpless pair," Trinka laughed. "We attempt to give one child a bath and just look at us! Lorenz, you really are a little monster. He tipped scent all over himself, you see. We had to wash off the overpowering smell of it."

"Well, my lad, you seem very much in control of the chaos." Breck grinned down at the boy, who showed his small white teeth, gapped in the front, and promptly flung a boatful of water at his uncle.

"Oh, your suit!" Siran was at once dismayed, for he looked so smart and nice in his impeccable gray.

"The water will dry, and it's good that the child feels so at home with us that he plays without inhibition." Breck's smile held a dignified raffishness. "He grows to look like Kristy, *meine Liebe*."

His mother nodded. "When I see him like this, so happy and trustful, I wonder how we can ever repay Siran for the brave thing she did. I would suggest, Breck, that we offer her the castle as her second home. She may come here whenever she chooses, for she tells me she intends to make dancing her career."

His glance found Siran and held her. He searched her eyes and she had to look away after a moment in case she betrayed to him her divided feelings. He drew her. He gave of his charm and his worldliness, and she could not face as yet what had to be. He was attracted to her, but they both knew that he was destined to marry the girl who would not want anything else but to be his wife. There was no other dream for Marla. When she heard music she sang to it, but she didn't feel the wings spreading themselves on her heels. She knew her heart, but Siran was so unsure of hers.

"Siran knows that our door is always open to her," he said quietly. "We can't hold on to her for ever, Trinka. She has wings, this one. She is not clinging or submissive, and I believe she must dance or die...not physically, perhaps, but in some enchanting part of herself."

So he had read her eyes, too swiftly for her to conceal what they held. "Come, my lad." She swung Lorenz out of the bath and into a big warm towel. He loved this part, being tickled all over and kissed in places he was not yet old enough to think undignified. Soon his happy giggles had burst like bubbles those few serious words, that clash of desires. Siran could not take Kristy's place at the castle, but for now it was enough to laugh with this delightful child of a tragic love; to kiss his warm skin and feel the baron's eyes gone from gray to the mercury of that desire he felt for her.

"I will go and find Marla," he said abruptly. He left them, and Siran gave a gasp as Lorenz tugged her hair.

"Let me take him." Trinka lifted him into her arms. "Little tyrant, you have given Siran a bath as well. My dear, you had better run along and change your dress. But it has been fun, eh? This hour with the child?"

"I've loved it, but before I go I'll help tidy up."

Ten minutes later she was on her way to her room, looking, she knew, as if she had fallen in a puddle and been pulled out. She was near her door when someone stepped out from the shadows and a pair of arms swiftly encircled her. She was pulled back into the shadows and lips found hers, hard and demanding. Her hands bit into the strong shoulders, feeling the power beneath the smooth gray suiting. Alarm shifted to response, a wanting to be secure in these powerful arms, if only for now.

"Breck."

"I had to wait for you like this...I wanted to hold you, like a warm, damp infant. Siran...I want you."

"Breck...please." She pulled away from him. "I couldn't stay here, or face your mother, if we allowed our feelings to get out of hand. It isn't love. It's attraction, and a bit of loneliness."

"Your loneliness?" He held her shoulders with his hands and looked down at her. "I suppose you could be grateful for my friendship...if you want to call it that. You are a long way from home, and I don't insult your intelligence by treating you like a child."

"There are...barriers," she said. "We both know it, and I don't want to be just an affair you had with a ballet dancer."

"What do you want, *Liebchen*?"

"Oh, Breck, it's too soon for me to know what I want."

"You knew that day in Vienna that we felt an instant response to each other. I liked your face; you liked mine. That is the way it usually begins. You came to Seven Lilacs wishing to see me again, as much as I wished to see you. We can't shut our feelings on and off like a lamp in the dark." He took her chin in his fingers and made her look into his eyes. "When we are together, and when I hold you like this, I can feel how much you want to be close to me. Why deny it? When your hands touch my shoulders, when you catch your breath, when you search my face...don't you think I'd be a fool if I thought these the prosaic responses of friendship alone?"

"What of Marla?" Siran, desperate for a defense, had to bring the other girl into it. "She cares for you."

"Yes, I know."

"Then aren't you being rather cruel, and just a bit dishonest, in talking to me like this? Everyone has always known that you might marry her...and she's lovely. She knows your world. She speaks your language. She had no ghost to haunt her."

"And your ghost is this man you knew in England. He died during a ballet—which is very dramatic—and so you can't forget him."

"No. He was part of my life for almost four years. I—I might turn to anyone to ease the pain of losing him. People do."

"You are asking that we keep this—" his hands tightened on her shoulders "—on a friendship level?"

"Please, Breck."

"Despite the fact that it grows dangerous for me to be alone with you?" He gave her a sudden kiss on her brow, pressing his lips hard against her temple. "Are you so modest that you don't know yourself? Yes, Marla is lovely. She has a warm, gay heart, and she speaks my language...but it isn't the language of the senses!"

A tremor ran through Siran, a shock reaction from the sudden passion of his voice. In a second, an instant, she wanted to reach up and smooth from his face that line that grooved his cheek. She couldn't resist the impulse, but when her hand touched his face the deep line was gone again, like a shadow, and she looked at him with a certain bewilderment. She was only an ardent gleam in the gray eyes, and because she had touched him he wanted to kiss her again.

"Breck, we must dress for dinner!"

"In a moment." He was bending his head, and like a moth she was mesmerized by the flame in his eyes, when footfalls broke the silence. They came nearer, and she turned her head just in time to see Kurt. He had come from one of the upper rooms, a turret room where he had a small observatory, and he was brushing at his sleeve, and looking directly at his brother and the girl in his brother's arms.

"*Guten Abend.*" He gave them a faintly mocking bow as he passed by, and Siran felt as if she blushed all over as she met for a brief, electrical moment the mockery of his eyes. Feeling embarrassed and caught out, she broke free of Breck's embrace and made a dash for her room.

Once she had closed the door on the brothers she sank down on the thick woolly rug and clenched it with her fists. It had to happen some time, that Kurt would see her like that with Breck, and now he would think her a little fool who had lost her head over his handsome brother. He would believe his own accusation, that she had come to Seven Lilacs with the intention of captivating the baron.

But it wasn't true, and the rug suffered the bite of her fingernails as she thought of that look in Kurt's eyes. A look half mocking, half contemptuous. Who was he to set himself up in judgment on others? He had no warm, human feelings and regarded love as a weakness.

It had been secret and exciting meeting Breck in the snowy woods, but now all that was spoiled. Each time he looked at her, Kurt would know why. Each time they spoke, Kurt would be listening for the note of hidden meaning in their voices.

She felt as if she hated Kurt, and jumping to her feet she found her toilet bag and went along to the bathroom to cool down under the shower. That evening in a mood of defiance she put on her second-best dress of smoky-blue wool with a pair of cherry red shoes. She had bought the shoes in London and they always gave her courage and made her remember vividly the first time she had worn them. Cassian had been rehearsing onstage, his black hair in damp disorder, a black sweater slashed open to his waist. She had stood in the shadows at the side of the stage and watched him enthralled, a slender stag of the forest, the lean angles of his face and the disciplined litheness of his body giving an illusion of youth that wasn't in his eyes. It was only now, looking back, that she understood that look of sadness in his eyes. It was as if he had some forewarning that he wouldn't dance for very much longer.

But he had that day been entranced by her red shoes. "Come and eat with me," he said, and they had walked along the Strand hand in hand, and every few minutes he had slanted a smile down at her. "I like you in red shoes," he had said. "They're gay and young like you, Feigileh. Whatever happens never lose your youth, and always wear those shoes when life throws shadows, or a few stones in your path.''

There had been no shadows that day, eating whitebait with him at the fish bar they both liked, spearing the little fish one at a time on a fork and talking as they ate about what they loved most. . .the art of ballet.

She stopped on the stairs and her hand gripped the post as a feeling of insecurity swept over her. *Every bird dwells with its own kind,* she thought, *and I'm lonely for what I've lost.*

She gazed around her and suddenly the castle was an alien place. Its scent and its sounds were strange to her, and she longed in this moment for the smell of resin, the laughter and bickering of a group of dancers, the first notes of the orchestra before the curtain arose with a velvety swish.

"Oh, is it you?" She swung around eagerly as hands clasped her waist in a well-remembered grip, the sort made by a male dancer when he and his partner were about to launch into a *pas de deux*.

"Were you waiting for my brother?" The voice spoke above her head, deep and deliberate.

.She found herself gazing at Kurt in wordless confusion. So wrapped in her thoughts had she been that when the lean hands touched her, sure and strong, she had been almost on the verge of melting to them, of yielding to the romance of the dance and feeling that lift into the air that was almost like flying.

"I—I was daydreaming," she said, not choosing her words and leaving him room to think she had been dreaming about his brother.

"I have heard that it's part of the delirium of falling in love," he drawled.

"Have you never fallen, *mein Herr*?" She could feel her composure taken and broken in his fingers like a moth. She could feel how easy it would be for him to break her in his hands, and with inward rebellion she stood there and let him clasp her waist, and she let him taunt her...as if, somehow, she had earned his punishment.

"I have fallen halfway down a mountain," he replied. "Is that how it feels, breathless, bruised and shaken up?"

"Be mocking about it," she said. "But I hope when it happens to you it will be hard and painful...it nearly always is for people who profess not to believe in it."

"So the mysterious emotion called love is going to hit me hard, eh?" His lip quirked and his eyebrow followed suit. "For someone young you seem quite an authority on the oldest dilemma that attacks men and women. Who taught you so young...was it Cassian?"

"He wasn't my lover!" The urge to break away from him was swift as the words on her lips, but instantly her movement was checked by the tightening of his hands, holding her there beneath the brilliant blue gaze that mocked and would know all her secrets. Her red brown head came to his shoulder, her eyes defied him, every inch of her denied him a fraction of friendship. He was too hard, too cynical. He bruised with tongue and touch.

"I never implied that your director was also your lover." He paused and made of the word a mocking caress. "The making of love, and the feeling of love, are surely two separate things. Lots of men make love without feeling anything but desire. Cassian was wiser than that. He made you his without destroying your innocence. That was all I meant, little quick-to-catch-fire!"

Her cheeks took fire, and suddenly she was terribly conscious of his maleness and the desires that lay smoldering in his soul. The outer man was so cool and strong and contained, but whenever she was close to him she sensed the hidden flame, the ice-hot intensity that burned deep in the man. There were things he never spoke of. Passions he kept to himself. Unlike Breck he would take. . . he would never ask, or try to charm.

"Yes. . . David Cassian was a wise person." Her voice shook a little, and she could feel her eyes widening as they dwelt on Kurt's craggy, unconquered face. He was like a mountain that presented several sides to the world and dared the onlooker to try and tame him. His was the kind of danger that set an avalanche thundering down on anyone who tried to know him. The touch of his hands made her feel unsure. . . with David she had always felt safe.

"Cassian had his own philosophy," she said, and to speak of him was to find again a measure of confidence. " 'But pleasures are like poppies spread. You seize the flower, the bloom is dead.' "

"Burns, who wrote these lines, was not a man to leave the flower unseized."

"Do you read poetry, *mein Herr*?"

"Most mountain climbers do. It relaxes and inspires. I have myself written pieces for the *Alpine Journal*."

"Poetry?"

"Yes, among other things. Is it so amazing?"

"Incredible."

"That I should notice the shape of a snowflake, or the snap of frost and the small silences? Do I seem so inhuman? Is my touch so terrible?"

As if to add point to his question he made her feel the grip of his hands, and he smiled in a sardonic way, reminding her that he had seen her in his brother's arms, a willing captive there, not a girl who was tensed all through her being and couldn't wait to be released from the hands made powerful by rock climbing.

She looked at him with uncertain eyes. Was he arrogant? Or was he a proud, haunted man who could only be himself when alone in the mountains?

"Have you fallen in love with my brother?" he asked bluntly.

"How dare you ask me that?" His directness was like a whiplash, leaving a sting behind. She had to sting him in return. "It would be foolish of me to deny that I like him. . . unlike you, *mein Herr*, he doesn't regard me as a child who must be censured every so often. He's charming and friendly."

"So I have noticed."

"And never sarcastic."

"I do beg your pardon. I forget that women prefer the roundabout way to the direct. They like to be misled and then cry when they are lost."

"Are you warning me about something?"

"If you are not a child then you must know what you are doing. . . meeting my brother alone in the forest, allowing yourself to become the plaything of an hour."

Again she felt stung by him. Plaything! He called her that. . . how dared he? Her hand swung of its own accord and there was the sound of a slap, followed by the gasp she gave as he gripped her, lifted her off her feet and swung her to meet the threat in his eyes. A look that left her in no doubt of what it would be like to be *his* plaything.

"You brute!" She could think of nothing more original as he gripped her like a rag doll.

"You little fool!" He let her go and strode on down the stairs, where at the foot of them he turned and waited for her, his eyes shimmering blue in his audacious face. "Come along," he mocked. "I promise not to touch you again."

She hesitated, and then hating to see how he unnerved her she sped past him in her red shoes, hastening into the twilight of the hall, where the lamps on their long chains were not yet lighted.

"Tomorrow night we'll be in the mountains." Kurt

lounged against the newel post, a glint of anticipation in his eyes. "Do you look forward to it, Miss Winters? Or are you afraid of my world also?"

"Your world of snow castles and ice turrets, *mein Herr*?" The way he had worded his question was not lost on her. He knew that he inspired fear and uncertainty in her. "I expect to find them rather cold and awesome."

"You may find them more fascinating than castles on the ground." He strolled to a long window that overlooked the lake, and there a young moon sidled out from a cloud, lighting softly the scene and leaving the hall in denser shadow. Drawn by the moon, Siran walked to the other side of the window and saw how the moonlight wedded itself to the snow, veiling the frosty boughs of the trees in a shifting silver.

"Can your peaks match a moonlit lake for beauty?" she asked.

"Yes, but in a different way. A more overwhelming way. The scene before us is like a piece by Chaminade, but up there in the mountains it is the *Siegfried Idyll*."

"Perhaps I am too English to appreciate what appeals to you," she said. "I'm very fond of Chaminade."

"Fond, eh?" His smile was a gleam of white in the dusk. "The term can't be applied to Wagner. With his music it's a matter of love or hate. It always is with anything strong and complex. Tolstoy put it into words as only he could."

Siran gazed at the moonlight on the snow, feeling again that flick of surprise that he should be so well read, so in touch with things that seemed on the surface to have no place in his life. She looked at his profile in the black and silver glimmer that came from the lake, and it reminded her of the formidable features stamped on old imperial coins; the power of the brow, the jut of the nose, the squareness of the chin were as if carved in bronze. Her palm had stung when she slapped him!

He turned his head and looked directly at her. Even in the dimness she felt the brilliance of his eyes. "You are very English, and you might think the words extravagant."

"I might, but I'm willing to learn."

"I believe you are, when you are not handing out a lesson of your own," he laughed quietly and fingered the jaw she had slapped. "Tolstoy understood passionate people and he applied his words to them. 'When you love,' he said, 'love unto madness. When you threaten, do it fiercely. When you smite, aim well and truly. When you fight, fight to the finish.' "

There was a significant pause, broken by a manservant who entered to light the lamps. As they came alight one after the other Siran felt herself held and dominated by Kurt's blue eyes. The words he had quoted applied to all his actions. . . when he loved there would surely be no tenderness, only a passion to conquer, as he had conquered the Nanda Devi, the mountain goddess.

The others arrived from their various parts of the castle and after dinner they enjoyed some music and then made an early night of it. They were setting out soon after breakfast for their trip up the mountains and their good-nights to each other were tinged with a note of gaiety.

"We are like conspirators," Marla laughed. "One would think that up in the mountains we each hope to find our heart's desire. Or am I being a superstitious Bavarian?"

She looked at the baron, who returned her look with a lazy smile. "You are too warm-hearted not to be romantic, Marla. Each trip to an unknown place seems to offer the prospect of an exciting encounter. . . do you not think so, Siran?"

He pronounced her name with a foreign attractiveness, making it seem alluring. She smiled and was vividly aware of this moment in the hall, poised as they all were on the brink of parting for the night. Outside in the night the snow was softly falling, hiding the moon. Here the stove crackled and it was warm. The memory of good music lingered, and the lamplight shone softly on the blue brocaded skirts of Trinka's old-world dress.

"It's always exciting to have something to anticipate," she replied. "Sometimes that is the best part."

"Do you expect to be disappointed in the mountains?" Breck's eyes were faintly quizzical as they dwelt on her face, large-eyed, framed by her brown hair with its hint of red.

"She expects to be overwhelmed," drawled Kurt. "I have warned her that she will be. . .at first."

"Kurt is always warning me about something." She gave a laugh and avoided his eyes. "I've never traveled before in a cable car, so I really can't wait for the morning to come."

"You will enjoy it." The baron spoke with assurance. "But remember to wrap up warm. Unlike Kurt we are not hardened against the cold winds of the higher regions."

"Your mother is kindly lending me a coat to wear." Siran glanced a trifle nervously at Trinka. "I hope it's all right with Kurt if I wear your snow leopard, Baroness?"

Kurt slanted her a look but said nothing. Trinka laughed, as if she alone knew the secret of handling her unpredictable son. "He will not see you freeze, *Liebling*, and it's such a shame for such a charming outfit to hang in my cupboard and not be worn. Kurt, please assure Siran that she may wear the coat."

"Wear it with my blessing," he drawled. "I never had the knack of choosing the exact gift for a woman, or of paying the correct compliments, but now and again I mean well.''

He confused Siran when he spoke like that, and all she could do was to murmur her thanks. Marla gave her a faintly pitying look, as if it were a small tragedy that a girl should have to borrow a fur coat. Kurt smiled as he caught that look, a groove springing deep in his cheek, near his mouth.

"You will be taking your skis?" he said to Marla.

"But of course," she replied, and Siran could hear them talking together as they made their way to bed, leaving the baron to lock up the castle...mantled in a thick white blanket of snow.

CHAPTER EIGHT

SIRAN WAS DRESSED and ready and waiting by the lake, which in the night had become frozen over, when she was joined by Marla. The two girls presented quite a contrast to each other. Beneath the smart fur coat that was draped around her slender shoulders Marla wore an elegant suede two-piece, velvety green, giving her the look of a young huntress of the forest. Her rakish hat shaded a dancing dark eye.

"The men are putting the baggage in the car," she said. "Eric will probably arrive in that yellow monster of his. You have not yet met him, eh?"

Siran shook her head, feeling strange and exotic in the pale furs that were so lovely and warm. Her hands were clasped in the muff, and the touch of frost in the air made her cheeks tingle.

Marla gave her a considering look. "I thought you a fresh and fairly ordinary English girl when I first saw you," she said. "Now I begin to understand why men are so fascinated by the women of your country. You have a secretive quality, in your looks and your ways. You don't reveal yourself at a first glance. You really are very attractive, Siran, and I am sure now that you are my rival."

"Your rival, Marla?" Siran knew what was implied, but she pretended to be innocent. "Even in my borrowed plumes I'm not as pretty as you are."

"Come, you know what I mean." Marla gave a little laugh that wasn't quite sure of itself. "See that lake, a great frozen mirror, reflecting all, revealing nothing, not even who is the fairest of us in the eyes of the baron.''

Marla looked into Siran's eyes, as if she wanted to know her thoughts. ''You aren't so innocent.'' A sharper note came into her voice. ''You know as I do, as everyone does, that the time has come when Breck must marry. I wonder which of us he will choose? There is only one he can marry...only one he can reject. Are you afraid that it might be you?''

''It would be crazy of me to be afraid of something so out of the question. I didn't come to Seven Lilacs as a prospective candidate for marriage. I came to visit the baroness, and to work at the school until I can dance again in ballet. You know, as everyone does, that the baron cares for you.''

''He cared more before you came to the castle. Now he talks to you, and his eyes follow you. I know he likes you...but you are crazy if you think he will marry you! The men of the von Linden family marry women of position. Both Breck and Kurt. You are to both of them just an amusement.''

''I'm well aware of that.'' Siran felt a stab of pain and was sharply reminded of what Kurt had called her...the plaything of an hour. ''It's silly of you to be jealous, isn't it, when you know that both brothers are merely amused by a ballet dancer. It's an old tradition. Novels and plays have been written about it.''

''But you are poor,'' Marla exclaimed. ''It would be to your advantage to entice Breck to marry you. You would never have to work again. I believe it is hard work, dancing in the corps de ballet.''

''I find it enjoyable, and naturally I hope to dance my way out of the chorus.''

''But every girl wishes to love and marry. You can't pretend to me—even if you pretend to Breck—that you are dedicated heart and soul to your dancing. That would be like being a nun. . .almost.''

Siran smiled at the extravagance of the remark. . .and yet was it so far fetched? Nearly all great dancers led lives curiously sheltered from the world outside the theater. If they loved at all, then it was a curiously impersonal sort of love, their passion given to the dance itself. To the magic and romance of it, things that women sought in a relationship with a man without always finding them.

''We wear lovely costumes in ballet and dance to exciting music,'' she said. ''There is little of the cloister in our lives.''

''You are fond of nice clothes?'' Marla's eyes flicked over the snow leopard coat and hat and dwelt on the plump little muff that concealed the tension of Siran's hands. ''The baroness must be fond of you if she permits you to wear something of hers, and then of course you saved the life of Kristy's baby. The baroness adored her. Breck kept saying that she was being spoiled, but Trinka had suffered so much in the war that she wanted Kristy never to know a sad moment. It was ironical that the girl should come to such a tragic end. . .quite fateful that you should be there, *nicht*?''

''Life has an odd way of introducing us to people,'' Siran agreed. ''I'm glad to have met the von Linden family, but I do intend to return to my own world.''

''I wonder if fate intends you to return?'' Having said this Marla turned with a gay smile as Kurt approached to tell them the car was ready and they were keeping the expedition waiting.

Siran was aware of Kurt's side glance as the three of them walked to the forecourt, where the Mercedes awaited them, its trunk stacked with weekend luggage and its bodywork gleaming in the morning sunlight. A small thrill of half fear ran up and down her spine. She wanted him to say something about the coat and wondered if she wanted him to be flattering.

"A real leopard once wore that coat," he drawled.

"Are you trying to put me off?" She glanced up at him and the sunlight was full on his face and his thatch of lion-colored hair. "I find the coat so lovely and warm that I'm not going to take it off to please you."

He smiled enigmatically. "And now I hand both of you over to my brother," he said. "I'll be driving to the cable station with Eric. . . by the way, Siran, I would like you to meet my friend."

Eric Gerhardt was standing beside his sports car of a vintage like that of old and cherished wine. Somehow in his suit of velour beneath a camel overcoat, with his fine-boned face and fair receding hair, he had the same air of old-fashioned distinction. He bowed over her hand and though his look was a searching one it was entirely courteous.

"I've wanted to thank you for giving my ballet class a record player and all those classical records. It was so kind of you, Herr Gerhardt."

"I was charmed by the innovation of having a ballet teacher in the valley. I wished to make a donation that would be useful."

"It's more than useful, it's a pleasure, and I thank you."

"Come, we must be off!" The baron beckoned imperiously and Siran smiled at Eric and went to take her place in the big car. Marla had settled herself in the front seat, and Trinka sat at the back with Lorenz on her lap. The child's big blue eyes were roving from one adult to another and when Siran slid into the car beside Trinka he let out a crow of recognition.

"Hello, mischief." She stroked his cheek with her muff and right away he wanted to play with it.

"It will keep him amused." Trinka's eyes were content and unclouded this morning, and it was touching the way she looked at Breck as he joined them in the car and closed the door. Then she glanced out of the rear window and her smile wavered as the vintage sports car flashed past them with its two occupants, turning out of the gateway like a leopard on the run.

"Kurt is driving," she said tensely. "Oh, I do hope he will be careful!"

"Has Kurt ever known the meaning of the word?" Breck started the car and they swept out on to the road in the snowy wake of the sports car. "Relax, my dear. You will wear yourself to a shadow worrying about him."

"It's as if a devil drives him, Breck. He hides his feelings behind a cynical smile, but I know how much it hurt him to have to come home that terrible night with such shocking news. He has never been quite the same and seems these days to live so recklessly."

"You think of him still as a blue-eyed innocent like Lorenz." Breck gave a chuckle. "My dear, his baby curls have long vanished, to be replaced by the tawny pelt of a young lion. Ask Marla...or Siran. They will tell you what a barbarian he can be when he gets a girl alone in a corner!"

Trinka looked quickly at Siran and there was a bright curiosity in her blue eyes. Siran quickly changed the subject, for it seemed unfair to discuss Kurt behind his back. It made her feel like defending him, and it would be absurd for her to leap to the defense of a man who was her avowed opponent.

They were admiring the passing scenery, so like a greeting card with the frosted fir trees set against the slopes and the chalets wearing caps of snow, when all at once the baron braked sharply on a turn in the road. There in front of them was the yellow sports car, stalled at the roadside, ice shattered under its wheels, and Kurt in his belted sheepskin coat smoking a cheroot while Eric peered at the engine.

Breck drove around them and halted. He rolled down the window beside him and spoke explicitly in the Austrian tongue. Kurt took the cheroot from his mouth with a deliberate air. "I can hardly be blamed for ice on the road," he said in English.

"It wasn't Kurt's fault." Eric raised his head from the engine. "If he had not been quick to swing the wheel then we would have gone right off the road and plunged down the embankment. Anyway, something has cracked and my car is out for the count."

"Well, I can't give both of you a lift. There isn't the room. You might just squeeze in, Eric." Breck gazed at his brother with cool gray eyes. "It's several more miles to the cable station. Will you ski the rest of the way?"

Kurt inclined his head and went out of sight behind the Mercedes. Siran heard the click of the trunk and a quick glance out of the rear window showed her a glimpse of his tawny head and broad shoulders as he bent over the trunk and took from it his skis and poles.

Eric, with a lazy smile, climbed into the back of the Mercedes beside Siran. "Good luck, old man!" he called out before closing the door.

Kurt stood alone out there and quirked a tawny eyebrow. "Shall we make it a race?" he asked.

"No, Kurt!" Trinka rapped on the window. "Please take care."

He shrugged and smiled, and for a brief instant he looked at Siran through the car window. In that instant he looked almost sorry for himself, then his face hardened and he moved out of sight.

"Will your car be all right?" Siran looked at Eric.

"Yes, I will telephone from the cable station for a mechanic to pick it up. Poor old girl, she breaks down often these days, but I hate to give her up for a modern miss.''

The engine of the Mercedes purred into action again, and Siran told herself that it was mere coincidence that she happened to be gazing out of the window when a supple figure swooped down the snowbound slopes of the embankment and dived out of sight in strong, accomplished leaps and bounds. Only the dark ski trails remained. Kurt went on alone to where they would take the cable car to the top of the mountain.

The cable-car trip was an unforgettable experience for Siran. Her senses leaped at the beauty of the alps... here was destiny, a glimpse of heaven itself. The cable car swooped over the valleys and the peaks. They hung suspended in the air, the high winds singing in the cables, and the baron stood beside Siran and pointed out the wild gorges beneath them that had no bottom, the glaciers that seemed to pierce the sky itself.

They swung in the car above a frozen cascade, misty and color-shot as the sun fired the great sprays of ice. Such views were breathtaking, almost fearful, and Kurt stood a few paces away, cool and assured in their presence, no stranger to their wonder and their danger.

He began to whistle softly to himself, and with a catch of her breath Siran recognized the music as the *Siegfried Idyll*, reminding her of what he had said, that she might at first be overwhelmed by his castles of snow and turrets of ice and then find them fascinating.

The cable car hung deliberately among the wild white glaciers, and then it began to descend, swooping down like some strange toy on a string. It landed them among the peaks, and the men collected the luggage. In a gay group, the cold air stinging their faces, they made for the inn that stood among the crags—a welcome sight with its red peaked roof, double verandas, and alpine shrubs planted against the pine-log walls.

Inside a huge open fireplace burned resinous pine logs, and plum brandy was poured by the innkeeper to warm them after their journey, and warm milk with fingers of buttery bread were soon provided for the baby.

Siran stood clasping her brandy glass in both hands, as enchanted as a child herself by the old-fashioned charm of the inn. The beams overhead were carved and painted, and quaint brass lamps hung suspended in triangles of wrought brass. There were inglenooks, and the ticking of a grandfather clock, great tufted rugs and old polished furniture.

It was the kind of tucked away place where long ago Austrian princes and officers might have dined, plotting their rebellions and love affairs.

She breathed the tangy smoke of the logs in the great stone fireplace and saw the flames reflected in the copper bowls of winter flowers.

The clock chimed, and a girl in a dirndl said smilingly that a goose was roasting for their dinner, and she would show them to their rooms. They trooped upstairs, the deep voices of the men mingling together and making the atmosphere seem vital and somehow conspiratorial, as it must have been in those old feudal days. The tramp of their feet and Marla's excited laughter made echoes along the rambling passages. Siran's room was tucked away under a snowcapped gable of its own, warmed by a porcelain stove; white, gold-flowered porcelain that matched the cover of the goose-feather puff that lay over the bed with its figured bedposts. There was a little saint in a wall niche, a chest of drawers and a washstand. It was a room that reminded Siran of Cornwall, but when she stood at the window she saw the changing colors of the mountains as dusk began to fall, a merging of violet and purple, a slow deepening in the hollows, a burning flush where the sun was going down. Often Siran had watched as the sun sank away into Cornish waters, but this evening she was far away from the sea and high above the world, among the crags and glaciers of the alps.

Her fingers gripped the wooden frame of the window and for a moment she felt a thrill of fear. It made her go cold and she went to the stove to warm herself. It was a relief when fingers tapped upon her door and Trinka came in to find out if she was comfortable and quite happy.

"You look a little pale," Trinka touched her cheek and looked concerned. "The altitude sometimes affects the newcomer... I am going to close the shutters of your window. If you keep looking at the closeness of the peaks you will have the feeling that you are going to fall. In the morning you will have grown used to that feeling... there, with the shutters closed and the lamp lit you are secure again."

"You're very understanding, Baroness."

"You must call me Trinka. It makes me feel younger, and we are good friends by now. Real friends, *Liebling*, who can talk together. Tell me, you are glad you came to Mayholtzen? You have no regrets?"

"No regrets at all... Trinka."

"No one has hurt you?"

"No."

"I ask because I have two sons who are attractive to women in different ways. Breck is worldly and has great charm. Kurt is complex and women are attracted to a mystery. But I think—" Trinka paused and stared at the little saint in his niche "—that you like Breck more than you like Kurt. It is probably he who will cause you to leave Seven Lilacs sooner than I would wish."

A few minutes later she left Siran alone in her room. In a thoughtful mood Siran washed and dressed for dinner. Donning a tan gold mohair sweater that blended with her tweed skirt, she clasped around her throat the twisted gold chain the two aunts had given her when she was sixteen. It was something of home to cling to. A memory of the sea climbing the shingle almost to the door of the cottage. It was strange, but always her security had been tenuous. The little aunts had died, too dear to each other for one to be able to live without the other. Then David had followed them, and the ballet company had dispersed.

Now her stay at Seven Lilacs was curiously threatened...tonight in the alps she sensed strongly that something was going to happen that would again disrupt her life.

Grown afraid of her thoughts, she turned the lamp down low and closed the door of her room behind her. She found her way downstairs to the lounge, where the log fire glowed, a huge cavern of warmth.

"It looks as if we are the first down." Eric emerged from the shadows at the end of the room, where the curtains were half drawn across the windows. Beyond them glimmered the last of the sunset, outlining his lean figure. A brief, grave smile dented the edges of his mouth. "Come and enjoy the alps, Miss Winters. Ah, you hesitate! You are rather afraid of their nearness, eh?"

"I've never been this close to the abode of the storm gods." She smiled and joined him by the window, feeling again that heart turning as her gaze dwelt upon the giant peaks this slender man had climbed many times. Even in the dusk they seemed to shine with an icy radiance. "They are beautiful, but in a cold, rather austere way. I wonder how you can love them?"

"A man's love for the mountains is a mystical thing, *Fräulein*, and perhaps a little hard for a woman to understand. She sees only the dangers and the discomforts...am I right?"

Siran nodded. "Aren't you ever afraid that one day your luck will not hold out...that you might slip on that sheer ice, or be swept away by an avalanche?"

"The danger and unpredictability are all part of the game, Miss Winters. Climbing one of the aloof, gold-peaked mountains of the Himalayas is like taking on the challenge of a lovely woman of uncertain moods. Who knows if she will smile or frown? Who can say whether she will open her arms in welcome, or show her claws? Yes, for the climber there is often great peril, but there is also the excitement at times of being master of what no other man has ever conquered."

"It sounds a little arrogant," she ventured.

His smile was whimsical. "I saw you looking rather seriously at Kurt when he took off on his skis alone. You think him arrogant, don't you?"

"What woman could think otherwise?" She gave a rueful laugh. "We are poles apart, Kurt von Linden and I. We think each other's profession a useless thing. Why, he could have been a doctor—could still be one if only he would apply himself to his studies and shake loose the wanderbug that has such a grip on him. Herr Gerhardt, can't you persuade him to return to his medical studies? You are his best friend, and it would please the baroness so much if Kurt gave up gambling with his life."

"One person can't tell another what he should do with his life, *Fräulein*. The decision has to be personal and spontaneous. If pressure is applied then tension can be the only result."

"But he has such dexterous hands and the concentration that could make of him a first-class surgeon. It seems a waste." She gave a small cold shiver, as if a breath of coldness touched the nape of her neck. "He has made up his mind to repeat the climb that killed

Kristy's sweetheart. What if something happens to him?''

"Yes, *Fräulein*, what if something does happen? Will you be sad?''

Her eyes widened, shocked that he should speak with such coolness. Kurt was his friend. They had shared many dangers together. "Do you blame him...for what happened to Kristy?''

There was an acute little silence, broken only by the crackling of the pine logs with their tang of the forest. "The calamity cycle of three cannot be held back if it is to take place,'' he said quietly. "No, I don't hold Kurt responsible for the accident. Knowing mountains, I know how swiftly death can come. For each of us there are moments of destiny...the sad part is when we are alone and aware that the glow of happiness has been switched off, leaving a darkness. It wasn't that Kristy ever cared for me. She cared for the young man who died...but, you see, I was fond of her. I would have been a father to her child, if she had turned to me after the tragedy. But she ran away, and when Breck found her she refused to return to Seven Lilacs. Kurt went away himself in the hope that she would come home. He knew how she felt about him. How she went on feeling up until the time she....''

He couldn't say it in words, using his hands to express his sense of loss.

"Where did he go?''

"Kurt?''

"Yes...did he go far?''

"He went to Kenya, where there are fanged mountains growing out of the red earth. He explored the Himalayan valleys, filled with wild sheep and the exotic birds. Went high into the hills of Tibet, the strange Shangri-la of silver bells and monks. He returned when Breck sent a cable to say that Kristy had died. He seemed older, less the sportsman and more a man of some deep purpose. Soon we knew that purpose. Not I, or his mother, or anyone who loves him, can stop him from doing what he must. I think in Tibet he learned something profound about himself. He doesn't speak of it, but I believe he has found at last what he has been searching for.''

"Tibet," she murmured. "Land of silver bells, chiming in the peaked pagodas of the monasteries."

Slowly her hand clenched against her heart and she stared into the fawn-colored eyes of his closest friend. "You believe he will return there?"

"I believe there is a chance of it. Kurt learned as a child the hardship of losing his father and being torn from his mother. That lesson has stayed with him. At the various sports arenas, such as St. Moritz, I have seen him enjoy the company of women, but there has always been an aloofness about him that made those friendships no more than the reward of the gladiator. In days gone by, *Fräulein*, the champions took their pick of the prettiest women...for a day or a night."

She smiled, for he looked so serious, as if he thought her too youthful to be told the facts of a man's life. "I can well believe that Kurt von Linden takes the kisses of women without giving his heart. In his hard, tanned, cool way he must be quite spectacular in the sports arena. His face is molded like those faces on old statues or coins. A man of bronze all through."

"You speak like a girl who has made up her mind not to like him. He must find that very challenging."

"He enjoys making me argue with him."

Eric was laughing as the rest of their party entered the lounge, and Breck asked at once to be told the joke.

"That would be unfair to Miss Winters," said Eric. "She was confiding in me."

"Beware, my friend, or you will become yet another victim of our ballerina."

Siran flashed a look at Kurt, which he returned with a suave lift of his brow. Unlike the other two men in their formal dinner jackets he wore a check shirt and cavalry-twill slacks, and he looked much more at home in the rusty glow of the log fire than his brother. How alike their features were; and yet how unalike in their emotions they were. She had thought Breck the deep one, but it was Kurt who had a shading of melancholy around his mouth. She saw it plainly, etched by the firelight, but when he caught her gaze upon him, he turned his head away and seemed to concentrate on the painted tankards that stood along the shelf above the fireplace.

The girl came in and lit the lamps, and she said to Kurt, "*Mein Herr* would like a beer?"

"*Danke schön.*" He gave her the Austrian click of the heels, and she smiled gaily and with a swirl of her dirndl she took the orders for wine or beer. Dinner would be served in the adjoining room in about ten minutes.

"I'm famished," said Marla. "It must be the altitude and so much fresh air. Yes, I'll have a beer, all brown and foamy."

Gaiety took hold of them again and their roast goose dinner at the long wooden table was richly enjoyable. Baked chestnuts were dished up with the goose, and there was a mound of creamed potatoes, a great dish of savory cabbage and a piping hot gravy.

It was like a supper of the gods, enjoyed in a smoky Valhalla far above the rest of the world. The von Linden men with their bold faces and Eric with his lean hawk's face added strongly to the illusion. And the waitress serving them wore an embroidered cap with a starched crest at the back like a dove's tail. She kept casting her eye in Kurt's direction, and Siran thought of the gladiators and the girls who were only too eager to reward them with kisses. Had Kurt kissed so many in the past that he no longer noticed if a girl was pretty? He seemed unaware of the girl in the crested cap, and when she served him with mixed fruit *strudel* he thanked her with an absent politeness that brought a pout to her lips.

"Lots of cream for me," said Marla, and it may have been sheer accident, or because she sat next to Kurt, that the jug tilted and she received a stream of cream in her lap. She leaped to her feet with a cry and shook the cream from her embroidered skirt. "You little fool! Look, you have made a mess of my frock! Just look at what you have done!"

"Be calm, Marla." Trinka rose and took her by the arm. "Come along upstairs and change the dress. You have another to wear, and it was an accident."

"It would be," Marla snapped. "She was so busy looking at the men."

"Come, my dear." Trinka was urging her from the room when the innkeeper came bustling in. He was red-faced with apology. The girl was his niece and new to the work. Would they be good enough to excuse her and allow him to pay for the damage to the dress?

"I don't care for damaged goods," Marla said pettishly. "The dress is now a rag. . .if your niece can clean it, she can have it."

Marla flounced off, and Breck gave a lazy laugh. "The *Fräulein* means it," he said to the innkeeper. He glanced at the culprit. "You might as well have the dress. I daresay it can be cleaned and primped up like new again."

"I would rather not, Herr Baron." The girl began to gather up the empty plates, and now Kurt looked at her, and Siran saw a smile quirk on his lip. He liked spirit and an unbowed head. . .and Siran suspected that he also liked to see his brother opposed now and then, especially when Breck took it for granted that his word was law.

Marla returned for coffee beside the log fire wearing the green suit that made her look a young huntress. Temper had left little flames in her cheeks, and Breck suggested that she sit by his knee on a leather stool and forget the incident at the supper table. She meekly obeyed him, giving him a look that spoke more eloquently than words.

She had created a scene...would Breck forgive her? He was so dignified himself in his dark suit and frilled white shirt. So much a man in command of himself. Too experienced ever to let his temper show more than a fine steely edge.

A musician came in to entertain them, and a boy danced wearing black shiny boots hung with bells. The innkeeper brought in a cake baked in the form of a ring, and they each had a small piece with a glass of wine. They told stories and roasted nuts, and it was like Christmas, with the snow thick and white all around the inn and a frosty moon sailing among the mountain peaks.

"I wonder where each of us will be when this night comes around again, this time next year?" Siran spoke the words as they ran through her mind. Then with a rather shy smile she glanced from one face to another.

"You would really like to know tonight what lies in store for each of us?" Eric peeled a hot chestnut with flinching fingers and shot Siran a thoughtful smile. "I prefer to let the future come as a surprise."

"There must be those among us who have some idea what the future will bring."

Marla glanced up at Breck as he spoke, her eyes like dark gems in her lovely oval face, searching his face hopefully for some sign that he referred to their future.

He gazed straight over her dark head, ignoring her as if she were a pet animal at his knee. Siran felt the brush of his eyes, but with her own eyes she saw every vestige of color leave Marla's face.

"He is cruel!" The thought flashed unbidden and left tiny wounds. She should have seen before that he was man too used to having women at his knee to ever feel a deep, compassionate passion for any one of them. He liked them. He enjoyed their beauty, or their wit, or their warmth. He would never regard them as anything more than sleek, silky pets.

Even as his eyes speared Siran, his hands fondled lightly the shoulder of Marla. At once the color stole back into her cheeks. She was Bavarian. She understood him and would bear whatever he did to her.

Siran gave a start when someone bent over her and a voice said firmly that she was going to see the alps by moonlight. Hands drew her to her feet. "You must not be afraid of them," said Kurt. "Come with me."

"But I don't want to," she protested.

"But I do," he said, and she was swept tyrannously from the warm fireside and bundled into the snow leopard coat that hung with the other coats in the foyer. Kurt belted his shaggy coat of sheepskin and ordered her to put on her boots.

"You are a bully," she said. "Don't you ever say please to a girl?"

"Please will you put on your boots, ballerina, and come for a walk with me."

"Mocking devil!"

She balanced perfectly on one foot as she slid the other into a scarlet knee boot lined for warmth. She met his eyes and for a shattering moment she saw a naked flame in them. The tawny hair was tousled on his forehead, and he swept it back with a hand that concealed his eyes. She stamped her foot down in the other boot.

"Why can't we all go and look at the moonlit alps?" she asked.

"The others have seen them before, and I am one of those who never tire of them. I loved them from boyhood. When I love a thing, I love it from here until eternity."

Then as if he regretted telling her a thing so secret, he took a grip on her elbow and reluctantly she went with him, leaving behind the lights of the inn for the pale radiance of the snowlands surrounding the mountains. The air was crisp and cold and tangy, but after they had been walking briskly for about half an hour, everything silent but for the snow crunching beneath their boots, Siran began to feel a sense of exhilaration.

With a throaty little laugh she bent suddenly and scooped up a handful of snow. She pressed it into a ball and flung it at Kurt. He retaliated, and there beneath the shadow of the alps they pelted one another with snowballs, her breathless laughter mingling with his in the superb silence. . . a silence they shattered as if it were a thing of fine crystal.

Her hair romped free in the wind and her eyes were glowing like beryls. Since the start of the day until now it had been mystery and magic, and she was grateful to the tough, diffident kindness of Kurt for giving her this hour in the high, clear air of the alps. She stood and gazed at them and no longer did she feel as if a giant hand were going to pluck her up and drop her down a fathomless chasm.

She felt Kurt studying her and when she looked at him his eyes were lambent as a night-stalking cat's. "Are you glad you came?" he asked.

"For the weekend, or for the snow fight?" She half smiled, a small fear of him still alive and active, for they were very alone, here in the mountains *au clair de la lune*. The stars were far off, like pointed flowers. Tiny

things like moth wings brushed her cheek, and she
realized that it had started to snow. All around lay the
chain pattern their feet had made in the snow already
fallen. She could hear the wind singing among the crags,
and the snowflakes clung to his tousled hair and his
thick rough eyebrows.

He was elemental, like the peaks. His voice held a
muted thunder; his glance was ice and flame. Sometimes
she had the strangest feeling that she knew him better
than anyone she had ever known. She could say whatever came into her mind. She could hit him, hurt him
and even hate him. She had no need to be always polite
with Kurt. It mattered not a jot that her hair was untidy,
her lipstick smudged by the snowball that had landed in
her face.

He was like his mountains because he was utterly
without falseness.

"Let's go back!" She began to run, following the
trail made by their feet. She heard behind her the lash
and rustle of his boots through the snow...a sound of
pursuit that made her want to beg him not to catch her.
She had known that it would be dangerous to be alone
like this, the chamois pursued by the hunter, but she had
not known the exact nature of the danger. She hadn't
dreamed that if his arms should reach out and catch
her...but they mustn't...they mustn't!

In a panic she sped off the trail, seeking the shadow
beneath a lip of the mountain in an effort to escape him.
She heard him call her name, and as it echoed up the
walls of rock, frosted over by snow and ice, she heard
another sound. An ominous rumble. A slithering clat-
ter. A rushing noise, growing louder by the second, so
that when she looked up in sudden fear she was already
prepared for the curtain of loosened snow that was
tumbling down on her.

"Siran!"

She was covered by Kurt a split second before they were both buried beneath a mound of snow. It kept on falling, rushing down the mountainside, a cascade that took several minutes to subside.

There wasn't a sound...everything fell silent as the snow settled.

CHAPTER NINE

THE STRETCHES OF SNOW were infinitely serene...then suddenly an arm broke through the surface, cleaved a breathing space, through which a moment later a head and a pair of shoulders emerged. Kurt pulled himself to his feet, and with the snow clinging like hoarfrost to his hair and eyebrows he hauled Siran out through the opening and brushed the icy snow from her face.

"Are you all right?" he demanded. He chafed her hands in his and after several shuddering seconds she was able to assure him that she was still alive.

"I—I think I can stand up...oh, my foot!" She collapsed against him, wincing with the pain. "It's the one I hurt before...it feels twisted."

"Let me see." He knelt in the snow and pulled off her boot. She stifled a cry as his fingers played over her ankle. "Yes, it must have happened when you fell beneath the snow. Does it feel very painful?"

He gazed up at her, and she blinked away the glitter of tears in her eyes. The snowfall had frightened her, and more of it was blowing in the wind, accompanied by stinging little pellets of ice. The moon vanished behind a cloud and Kurt was a dark shape, looming tall to his feet.

"If you try to walk on that ankle you will make it worse. I shall have to carry you."

"All that way?" she gasped. They must be at least a mile from the inn, and every second the snow was whirling faster, thickening in the gloom and obscuring the chain of footprints that led back to the warmth and safety of the inn.

Netted in the driving snowflakes, she felt the warm, determined crush of his hands as he lifted her. "*C'est la guerre*," he murmured, with the old return of mockery. "You may trust my muscles if nothing else."

"A blizzard seems to be coming on," she said. "We...we could get lost!"

"We could indeed." And he began to stride through the snow in his hefty boots, holding her in the hard hollow of his shoulder to shield her from the wind. It whipped the snow right at them, big half-blinding flakes and stinging little stones of ice. So sudden was the change in the weather; so treacherous after the display of calm. It was as if they were being punished for breaking the crystal silence with their laughter.

Had they really laughed, but a few minutes ago? Now Kurt was fighting the wind, battling to reach the inn before the snowstorm became even worse.

She wondered what his thoughts were, and she strove to see his face and could see only the forceful thrust of his chin above her head.

"I hope I'm not too heavy for you?" she cried above the tumult of the wind. "It must be hard work, plowing through the storm with a girl in your arms."

"Out in Katmandu I once carried a guide down a mountainside. He had broken his knee in a fall, and that journey was real hard work. You are very slight. The requisite of a ballet dancer, *ja*?"

"*Ja*. And you are built for conflict, aren't you?"

She heard him laugh above her head, and right away the storm gods heard and increased the fury of the snow and hail. It grew really terrifying, because by now they should have come in sight of the inn, whose hurricane lamps would have been lit to guide them home. Instead they seemed hopelessly lost...they might have been in the region of Katmandu, or any other wild and lonely place.

Suddenly Kurt halted and seemed to be peering ahead with some intensity. He shook his head, like a lion shaking its mane, as if the fast, whirling flakes were getting in his eyes.

"I think I see something...yes, it looks like the roof and outline of a chalet."

"But the inn..."

"If it's in the vicinity the people at the chalet will be able to tell us."

He began to make for the place, and Siran felt a strange mingling of relief and apprehension. Not a single light pierced the net of snow, and the nearer they grew to the place, the more apparent it became that they had stumbled upon a small alpine hut tucked beneath the rocky mountains. The log walls and sloping roof were thick with snow, and the windows were utterly obscured. It looked abandoned to the storm, and Siran felt the painful tightening of Kurt's arms around her.

"Now I know where we are," he exclaimed. "We have veered off the path back to the inn and are about a mile and a half off course. This place, *Fräulein*, is a chamois hunter's hut."

"Oh no!" It seemed too much a stroke of fate. "Can't you find the way to the inn?"

"Not in a blizzard," he said dryly. "It looks as if we will have to spend the night alone together. The hunters will have left food and rugs and kerosene for the stove. It will be better than stumbling about in the snow. There are deep drifts into which we could fall, and if I became tired and collapsed...think of all the things more terrible than spending a night alone with me."

"Everyone at the inn will be so worried."

"I have been lost in the mountains before now," he drawled, "but I do take your point. It won't enhance you in the eyes of my brother to be stranded with me for a night. It is my brother you are thinking of?"

"Not entirely...there is your mother. She is bound to be concerned, but you don't take into account the anxiety of those who love you...you regard love as a nuisance. You want to please only yourself."

"It isn't a pleasure right now to stand here with the snow falling down my neck. Now hold on to me while I open this door." There came the sound of a bolt being driven back hard, and the hard-packed snow rained down from the roof as he forced the door to yield to his touch. A darkness yawned, redolent of the smell of skins and oil and damp wood.

"There's a box of matches in my left-hand pocket. Can you reach them and strike a light for us?"

She pushed her hand into his pocket while the snow and hail drove past them through the open door. He stepped forward into the darkness and closed the door behind them, and Siran was aware at once of being carried into a primitive place by a man who had lived primitively all over the world.

Her fingers closed upon several objects in his pocket and they must have pressed the tiny knob of his watch, for suddenly in the dark the tiny, sweet bells of his repeater began to chime.

"I know small girls like playing about in big pockets," he said, "but I'll allow you to do that later. Right now we need those matches."

"I—I'm not playing about," she protested. "The odds and ends you men carry in your pockets...ah, at last!" She struck a match and the tiny flame wavered in her hand and revealed the hut as a rough, one-roomed shelter. She struck four or five matches before they found the lamp and coaxed a smoky light out of it. The wind beat at the log walls and rattled the door, and Kurt stood there holding her and searching the place with his eyes.

"I'd like to be put down," she said. "I'll be all right now."

He looked down at her in the smoky lamplight and there were blue devils in his eyes. "So we are snow-bound in a chamois hunter's hut." His gaze traveled over her, taking in her damp hair that shone like pewter and the snowflakes melting on the fur of the snow leopard coat. "This place is not unlike the houses out in Tibet. I stayed in one where I was offered every hospitality. Tashi, the guide I told you about, wished to share with me his best possessions. One of them was a yak; the other his almond-eyed young sister."

"And which did you accept?" Siran looked him in the eyes and hoped he couldn't feel her trembling. It was partly the cold, the reaction from hurting her ankle and of finding herself so alone with Kurt von Linden.

He laughed, making that deep purring sound in his throat. "The yak came in very useful for toting my bag-gage up the mountain slopes to Kali Gandaki, a fasci-nating gorge I wished to visit."

"Will you return to Tibet?" she asked.

"Yes...all being well I shall go back to see again the friends I made there. The old lama who was so wise and Tashi, who had tears in his eyes when I left. Can you imagine anyone being sad to see me leave?"

"Please, Kurt."

"Come, you think me as hard as rock."

"Rough as rock, but not always hard."

"Really?" His eyes glinted in his brown face. "Don't go soft on me, *Liebchen*, not while we spend this night together in the hut of the chamois hunter. Though I once accepted a yak in place of a sweetheart, I am not immune to the pleasure of looking at a pretty face and holding in my arms a slim shape."

"Kurt."

"You speak my name as if it hurts you."

"I—I'm cold . . . can't we light a fire?"

At once he became practical and lowered her to her feet. "How does the ankle feel now?"

She tried it and winced. "Not too bad."

"Siran," he soft-thundered her name. "You are looking rather as if you felt the earth shaking under your feet. Am I such terrible company, *du bleicher Geselle*?"

"I'm pale because I'm cold."

"Hand me the matches and I promise you a fire in ten minutes. *Danke*."

He set to piling the driest wood into the fireplace and after sprinkling it with a little kerosene he applied a match. There was a spring of flame among the sticks—outside in the night the clamorous wind and inside the sound of Brahms's *Wiegenlied* as Kurt whistled softly to himself. Siran sorted about inside a cupboard above the oil stove, gave a little shiver as a spider dodged her hand and found some cans of soup and beans.

"Well, we can have emergency soup and comfort," she said. "Have you one of those boy-scout knives with the gadgets that take corks out of bottles and stones out of horses' hooves? These cans must be opened and then we can heat it and serve it in these enamel mugs."

He came to her side with a look that was far from boy-scoutish, and dug his knife from one of the capacious pockets of his jacket. He pierced the cans and stood them on the oil stove. "Stand clear while I light this," he said. There was a small explosion and a little tongue of flame that seemed to lick at his hand.

"Kurt . . . be careful!"

He turned and gave her a quizzical look, which changed when he saw how wide and alarmed her eyes were. "You are thinking of that night at the hotel?"

"Yes." She gave a shudder. "Fire is so awful when it gets out of control."

"Like an avalanche, thundering down from out of nowhere and leaving havoc in its wake...but don't let us make ourselves unhappy. The hut is fairly warm and secure, and I spy a can of coffee and a small saucepan. No two people, *Liebchen*, could wish for more when stranded in a blizzard."

"But we have no water, *mein Herr*."

"We are surrounded by snow." His smile held a return of devilry. "I'll pack the saucepan with it and when boiled it will be quite all right for drinking. See if there is also a can of dried milk while I go and brave the cold."

He took the mugs with him so he could clean them in the snow, and left to herself Siran braved the long-legged resident of the cupboard and searched for dried milk. To her delight she found some and also a jar of jam and a china jar filled with flour. She sifted it through her fingers and found it lumpy but otherwise all right. Now if she could find a frying pan...the spider scurried to another corner, but by this time Siran was feeling more sorry for him than scared. She was invading his home and though he looked a bit of a monster he couldn't do her any harm.

Her groping fingers closed on a long handle and with a sense of excitement she withdrew the object and had a vision of hot, sizzling pancakes smothered in jam. A vision that could come true, for the pan had been used as a container for a tin of butter, packets of chocolate and sardines in oil.

"So this was the loot you were guarding, Daddy-long-legs." She carried the small hoard to the table and then realized that Kurt had been gone from the hut for more than ten minutes.

There was a stillness within the hut, a wildness without that tightened her nerves. She could hear the wind battering the walls, seeking a way in, and she remembered with a lurch of her heart what Kurt had said about deep snowdrifts. A person couldn't see them by daylight, and at night they lay in wait for unwary feet.

"Kurt!" She hobbled to the door and grabbed at the latch. The snow and wind drove in at her, clawing at her with cold greedy fingers. Her hair was blown into a wild disorder...she couldn't see a thing beyond the dense cloud of snow.

The night had a demented quality, and Kurt's name was lost in the clamor as again she cried his name. "Kurt...where are you? Oh, please, don't be hurt or lost...."

She clung to the door, striving not to be swept over by the wind. It was raw, driving the snow all in one direction. The log hut seemed as of it would crumble like a house of matches, the bunks creaked and a wicker chair fell on its side.

Did she hear voices in the wind? Those of people who had been lost forever in the mountains. Tears stung her eyes as she felt the slow icy grip of the anguish that must have been Kurt's when before his eyes he had seen his young sister's sweetheart swept to his death...the rope that joined them cutting into him and dragging him to the very edge of doom.

Half out of his mind he had searched and called... the lightning so fierce that it had struck the ice-axe from his hand. In the end there had been nothing to do but leave the crevasse that yielded nothing but strange little sounds...inhuman sounds offering no hope.

Siran, feeling as if a fine-edged cord tightened around her, was drawn beyond the hut into the storm. She fell and the pain of her ankle made her cry out. She stood up and struggled a few steps more, the breath snatched out of her mouth. She was smothered in snow like a small ghost, and though she realized the folly of what she was doing, she couldn't turn back to the safety of the hut. She could feel the pull of something more acute than self-preservation.

"Kurt. . .where are you? Kurt. . .I'll die if you don't come!"

Her weakened ankle twisted once more, and with anguish beyond the physical she screamed his name as she fell. Now there would be nothing, only the cold snow driving over her until she didn't wake again. Now there would be no more dancing. It had ended, the curtain was coming down, and no more would she see the man who dare not love because his love seemed only to hurt those he cared for.

So soft the snow, cold feathers of the softest down.

"Siran!" Hands gripped, pain flared, bringing her fully awake to the wild night once more.

"Kurt?"

"Yes, little fool!" She was lifted and carried swiftly through the torn night to the log hut. The door shook as it was kicked shut and, confused by the light, it took her several seconds to fully focus on the face above hers—a mask of savagery that etched deeply the cleft beside the mouth.

"What were you thinking of?" The voice was as savage as the look. "Don't you realize you could have been lost? Anything could have happened."

"I—I thought you were lost. . .you were gone so long."

"I was packing a handkerchief with snow to make a cold compress for your ankle, and the snow has to be packed tightly in the saucepan or it will melt down to a few mouthfuls." He swept the disordered hair back from her eyes, and he seemed to sink his flamey blue gaze right into hers. "Why did you follow me? Were you afraid to be left alone. . .or were you worried about me?"

"A—a bit of both, I suppose."

"I heard you scream."

"M-my ankle twisted again."

"That ankle seems to have a weakness." He carried her to the lower bunk and laid her down on it. "Wait there and don't move," he ordered.

He went outside and returned almost at once with the saucepan of snow, the mugs and the compress he had made. He drew off her boot and told her to roll down her stocking and apply the compress to her swollen ankle. "It will take out some of the ache. Rest, *Liebchen*. I will see to the meal."

"I—I was going to make pancakes," she said huskily. "I found some dried milk and flour."

"If you fancy pancakes, then you shall have them." He shot her a grin that warmed the recent anger from his face. He was rakish with his windblown hair and the snow drops in the craggy lines of his weather-beaten face. He bent over her and unbuttoned the snow leopard coat and threw it off her shoulders, so close that she could feel his warm breath against her cheek.

"Your eyes seem to plead with me," he said. "Do you wish I could be a gentle man, who would press your head to my shoulder and invite you to weep? Tears would not melt me, or help you. You have had a fright and the best remedy is a hot drink. Attend to your ankle. I will see to the meal."

Deliberately he turned away from her and he shrugged out of the sheepskin coat, the damp wool a mass of shaggy curls, and arranged both coats over a chair near the fire. The hot logs spat and sizzled as snow blew down the chimney, and the kerosene stove smoked and made the air blue. While Siran nursed her ankle, Kurt set the saucepan on the stove and made one more trip outside to wash the frying pan in the snow. He returned hurriedly and closed the door fast.

"It will be a bitterly cold night," he said. "We must thank the saints for putting this place in our way. What would you like? Bean tortillas, or hot jam pancakes?"

"Hot and jammy, please."

"Life is funny," he mused. "Who would have thought that you and I would be thrown together for a night by a caprice of nature, to feast on jam pancakes and coffee made with snow? You will have quite a story to tell your grandchildren in the distant future."

"My offspring will be a row of battered dance shoes," she joked.

He paused in the act of pouring the coffee, having set aside the soup for later on. His gaze flickered the ankle that had been hurt in Vienna, and now in a snowstorm. "You seem the type of girl who would like a family . . . you like young Lorenz, eh? You can't intend to have only love affairs to compensate."

She flushed slightly under his scrutiny. "I think you assume that I want an affair with your brother."

"Is the assumption so far from the mark?" He brought her a steaming mug filled with coffee, so longed for that she could almost forgive him for his arrogant remark.

"Thank you," she said, "for the coffee."

"You would find it impossible to shut affection out of your life," he added, lounging against the bedpost to drink his coffee.

"You don't find it difficult, do you? You can have affairs without your heart being remotely touched, whereas I would have to be lonely or madly in love."

"Most women have to be madly in love before they give themselves.

"Men are less sensitive, *mein Herr*?"

"They have less to lose, *Fräulein*. Take my brother. I admire his business acumen and the care he takes of Trinka, but always he has been a man much liked by women, and he has always been forgiven for being—how shall I put it?—in the tradition of the well-born landowner. He has an eye for a pretty face, but after tonight he may feel less inclined to make a play for you.''

She stared at Kurt and slowly her face went white. "What do you mean...after tonight?"

"Come, do I have to spell it out?"

"You mean people will think that you and I...oh no!"

"I am sorry, *Liebchen*." His smile was infinitely mocking. "I realize I am not the von Linden you would prefer to be stranded with, but others will assume that I am. You see, I know the mountains too well to ever get lost in them. I am too acquainted with high altitude weather not to sense when a storm is brewing."

"You arranged for me to be stranded with you?"

"It was the only way I knew to save you from being foolish and having something always to regret. My brother made up his mind long ago to marry the daughter of his wealthy business partner, and I would hate to see you seduced by him."

"Do you intend to do the seducing yourself?" She gave him a look of infinite scorn. "I realize that with a twisted angle and a snowstorm blowing I couldn't hope to run away from you."

"Be quiet," he ordered. "I intend to give you jam pancakes, not my hateful kisses. You know, *Liebchen*, one day you will remember me with gratitude."

"For abducting me?"

"Yes, for doing that." He strolled to the table and whistled the Lullaby as he beat dried milk and flour together with the water left from their coffee. He put a chunk of butter in the pan and soon the room was filled with the warm sizzling sound of pancakes.

Siran watched him, so big and exasperating, so deft

with those rock-hardened hands. "Now I'll have a questionable reputation," she gasped. "I'll join the list of your gladiatorial conquests, and I imagine it's a mile long."

"Let us say half a mile. I haven't yet won a gold medal for feats in love sports." He nonchalantly tossed a pancake. "It may give me pleasure to know in the years ahead that I helped to give a famous ballerina to the world. I may one day come to London to see you dance. I shall order *edelweiss* and when you receive the flowers on stage you will know who sent them."

"Won't you come backstage to see me?"

"No, I'll let you remember me as the man with whom you liked to fight. If we met again we might be polite strangers only."

"That would be bleak." She smiled and then looked away from him. Her smile wouldn't stay brave and bright. Suddenly she felt more like weeping, for it was bleak already to think of never seeing Kurt again. He was arrogant, infuriating, impossible, but he was also kind in a way no one else had ever been. He had dared censure rather than see her fall a victim to his brother's charm...and all at once she couldn't bear him to think she cared for Breck. All she had felt was friendship and a little flattery.

"It's ridiculous," she said. "You didn't have to kidnap me to keep me from losing my head over your brother. I never intended to. Don't you see, you've created an emotional situation out of very little. You saw me as a foolish young dancer intent on losing her head. It was kind of you to want to save my honor... but I'm in far more danger of losing it with you."

"I said I wouldn't touch you!"

"You touch me each time you look at me."

Did she speak the words aloud, or only in her thoughts? He didn't move, or show any sign of having heard them. He seemed turned to rock, his chin more obdurate than ever, his brows contracted to screen his eyes.

"Eat your pancakes while they're hot," he said.

"Don't treat me like a child," she cried. "Don't look at me the way you do and treat me as if I'm a naïve schoolgirl."

"I dare not treat you as a woman, for you and I could be lovers of only a night. There can be no tomorrow for us. No chapel bells or golden rings...not now, or ever. Do you hear me?"

"Loud and clear, Kurt. As if from the Glass Turret itself, the echo of self-denial, the punishment you mete out to yourself for taking Kristy's young man on that climb. For now and always we love apart, you and I. You in Tibet, and me in London."

"Don't talk of loving me," he said harshly. "I couldn't see you become my brother's mistress, but I can't ask you to become my wife."

"What if I ask you to become my husband?"

"I'll never marry, *Liebe*, but one day I hope you will find another man like David Cassian."

"I think I have found him. He would be crazily gallant enough to kidnap a girl to save her from a bold baron. There is every chance, my crazy Kurt, that when morning comes and we return to the inn your brother will demand that you make an honest woman of me." She smiled slowly and reached out to touch that deep line beside his mouth. "I think I'll blackmail you, *mein Herr*. I'll let everyone believe that you made fierce love to me in the chamois hunter's hut."

"Your eyes would give you away," he mocked. "They are too candid, too innocent, and I don't intend to harm that innocence."

"I don't think you could ever do anything to harm me, Kurt, but if you send me away you will make me

very unhappy. My dear man,'' she traced with a finger-
tip the hard line of his jaw, ''you can't punish yourself
for ever. Whatever happens to any of us is pure destiny.
I thought when Cassian died that never again would I
feel that lift of excitement, that warm thrill to living, but
not even with him did I feel the intense expectation that
came to me each morning at the castle.''

She looked wistfully into Kurt's eyes and found them
guarded against her. ''Cassian taught me how to
dance...you, *mein Liebe* Kurt, taught me how to
love.''

''Don't say it,'' he groaned. ''Don't believe in it, then
like all dreams it will gradually fade away.''

''Do you really believe that?'' she asked.

''I have to believe it.''

''I don't want my love for you to ever fade away,
Kurt. If we have to part, I'll still go on loving you,
tormented by it.'' The tears she had held back slowly
filled her eyes. ''I know I must do whatever you decide,
but just let me say this. You could have been a fine doctor, and I would have given up my dream of being a
really good dancer for you. Won't you at least continue
with your medical studies? You could do so much good
and compensate in that way for what happened to Helmut and to Kristy.''

''You are turning my life upside down!'' Suddenly his
hands gripped her shoulders and his eyes blazed down
into hers. ''Why did you have to come to Seven Lilacs?
All my plans were made; then out of that station tripped
a girl with hair like a misty autumn and eyes equally
dangerous. I wanted to put you on the train back to
Vienna as much as I wanted to tuck you in the sleigh
furs and drive you for miles through the chaste white
snow. Siran, why did we have to meet too late?''

''You are being obstinate,'' she flung back at him.
''You have the chance to make something of your life,

but you prefer to sacrifice it to all to those mountain gods who can be so cruel. It was they who killed Helmut, not you!"

"I thought him weak, shiftless, not good enough for Trinka's golden girl. I challenged him to that climb. If I had cut the rope as Kristy said I could not have been more responsible."

"Will it make up for anything if you sacrifice your own future? I don't think so, Kurt. I think a debt should be repaid with hard work, duty, love."

"We can love, but not always can we make happy those we love."

"We can try, Kurt. We both know there can be no real happiness if we part from each other. The very thought of it makes my heart go cold."

"Come to the fire." He lifted her and carried her to the warmth, and there he looked down into her eyes. "You have brave eyes, Siran, and this is the first time I have seen tears in them. Tears for me?"

"For both of us." Her fingers ruffled the hair at his temples. "You are going silvery just here, Kurt. Think how distinguished you would be, the famous Kurt von Linden, whose hands were made to save lives."

"Stop seducing me," he ordered.

"There is only one way to stop me from saying I love you, need you, will help you with all the heart and strength I have. No, Kurt," she laughed softly, "there are two ways. You can kiss me or kill me."

"*Liebchen, Liebchen*," His lips came down with a ravishing hardness on her soft mouth. "I would die for you."

"I would prefer you to live for me, *mein Herr*." Her arms stole close and loving about his neck. She could feel close to her the vigorous beat of his heart...the strong heart that would go on aching unless he climbed the Glass Turret and said goodbye to his ghosts.

"When do you plan to climb?" she whispered.

"Within a week."

"Will you come back to me, Kurt?"

"I must, my *Liebchen*." That wicked little smile stole back into the vivid blue of his eyes. "To make an honest woman of you."

She smiled as they clung close in the firelight of the chamois hunter's hut...the wind outside had died away, and everything around them was chaste and bridal. The moon shone through the clouds, and beautiful were the wild white glaciers.

Celebrate Harlequin's 30th Anniversary...

...with this special anniversary book!

The first 30 years of the world's best romance fiction

This invaluable guide to your romance reading contains:

- numerical and alphabetical listings of Harlequin titles
- heartwarming glimpses into the lives of many of your favorite authors as they tell their own stories
- photographs of some of these authors
- a fascinating look at the origins of the Harlequin emblem
- 4 pages of beautiful color photographs showing some of your favorite books— old and new
- delightful photographs of book covers through the years

The first 30 years of the world's most popular romance fiction

This exciting 292-page volume contains a complete history of our publishing program—from 1949 to 1979.

Don't miss this beautifully designed anniversary book. A must for every Harlequin reader!

Only $1.25

Complete and mail this coupon today!

Harlequin Reader Service

In U.S.A.:
MPO Box 707
Niagara Falls, NY 14302

In Canada:
649 Ontario Street
Stratford, Ontario N5A 6W2

Please send me the Harlequin 30th Anniversary book. I am enclosing my check or money order for $1.25 for each copy ordered, plus 39¢ to cover postage and handling.

Number of copies _____ @ $1.25 each = $ _____
NY and NJ residents add appropriate sales tax $ _____
Postage and handling $ ___.39___
               TOTAL $ _____

NAME _____
(Please Print)

ADDRESS _____

CITY _____

STATE/PROV. _____ ZIP/POSTAL CODE _____

Offer expires December 31, 1979   OMN 27 (326)

Harlequin Presents...

The beauty of true romance...

The excitement of world travel...

The splendor of first love...

unique love stories for today's woman

Harlequin Presents...
novels of honest,
twentieth-century love,
with characters who
are interesting, vibrant
and alive.

The elegance of love...
The warmth of romance...
The lure of faraway places...

Six new novels, every
month — wherever
paperbacks are sold.